Stories from Lone Moon Creek

Book Four: Splashes

Teresa Millias

Brighton Publishing LLC
435 N. Harris Drive
Mesa, AZ 85203

D0068346

Stories from Lone Moon Creek

Book Four: Splashes

Teresa Millias

Brighton Publishing LLC
435 N. Harris Drive
Mesa, AZ 85203

www.BrightonPublishing.com

ISBN13: 978-1-62183-442-7

ISBN 10: 1-62183-442-5

Copyright © 2017

Printed in the United States of America

First Edition

Cover Design: Tom Rodriguez

Table of Contents

Dedication: i

Prologue: iii

Chapter One: Grow With Me 1

Chapter Two: Back Shirts 38

ChapterThree: The Night of the Double Moon 58

Chapter Four: The Things We Do 69

Chapter Five: Waiting 84

Chapter Six: The Uncovered Cover-Up 101

Chapter Seven: Tomorrow's Another Day 120

Chapter Eight: War Efforts 134

Chapter Nine: The Suds Parlor 154

Chapter Ten: Your Ways Are Not My Ways 166

Chapter Eleven: Cyberspace 184

Chapter Twelve: Gifts 202

CHAPTER THIRTEEN: BUSHEL BASKET LANE...................232

CHAPTER FOURTEEN: THE TRAIN.................................250

CHAPTER FIFTEEN: THE COUNTDOWN..........................285

CHAPTER SIXTEEN: HOWARD'S HOLLOW........................305

CHAPTER SEVENTEEN: THE BARN OWL.........................319

CHAPTER EIGHTEEN: UNDER THE BRIDGE 353

CHAPTER NINETEEN: THE OBIT BOX............................362

CHAPTER TWENTY: A PROMISE NOT KEPT 366

CHAPTER TWENTY-ONE: KNOW THE TEACHER............388

CHAPTER TWENTY-TWO: THE LAST CHORD.................410

ABOUT THE AUTHOR:..425

Dedication

To the Holy Spirit and to you, the reader.

Prologue

How can rural life sustain itself when the ways of the world are continuously "splashing" into its domain? What is there that people can hold onto? Each invasive splash tries to dilute its native sanctuary.

The traditional small farms are disappearing quickly; chain stores are plowing into the countryside, and the media is swamping people's thoughts with suspicion and fear.

There is something about a splash, however. It may dilute and yet it may cleanse. There seems to be something buried deeply in the conservatism of rural life: something intangible, something that can't be washed away. It may be a feeling, a sixth sense, or a pull. From where is this illusiveness coming from? Are people listening to the wind through the trees or the absolute quietness of the falling snow? Do they hear messages in the newness of the flora or the first thaw? Is the fresh air, the creatures in the wild, or the rolling hills somehow responsible for the attachments of the people? Could be.

It could be among the *countryside whisperers* searching for the translucence of dreams. A splash may take one by surprise, and yet it may be just what is needed. How startling it is when suddenly you hear *the rest of the story*! The sequels will give the reader just that experience!

As Agnes and Marjory, the lifelong residents of Lone Moon Creek, continue to introduce each story, they too are splashed many a time by sudden waves of change. In fact, they are the main characters in two of the stories! However, when the waters calm, they transcend with stability and hope, attributes that cannot be captured in a bank account or a corporation's holdings.

So sit back, read, and watch out! I sense a splash coming!

"Why do some people grow their food?"
"All food starts out being 'grown.'"
"Oh no, some come in cans or packages or cartons," Marjory
said, confidently.
"You want to go visit the community garden, don't you?"
"You got it, sista!"
"Marjory Lane, what's gotten into you? Don't be fresh!"
"You mean like food?"

Chapter One

Grow With Me

"**O**h no, does he have to come here every day?" Miranda whispered to herself as she crouched low to peek through her bean-pole plants.

She watched as Fletcher rammed his cart through the pathways, not staying within the limits, but wavering left or right, unconcerned that he was wheeling over someone else's plants. His constant jerking and yanking on the push bar caused enough clamor to cause everyone in the entire community garden to look up, even though they knew it was Fletcher. If he had one, he had ninety-one tools hanging from his cart, which swung and banged against each other in a symphony not conducive to the peaceful aura of the garden.

Those working grit their teeth until they heard the last *ping* fade into the summer morning air. Miranda edged her way along the row of bean poles, looking between each one to determine who was already tending to their little assigned refuge.

Why does she have to sing those stupid songs of hers? Miranda wondered as she did each and every time she heard Lena sing "Oats, peas, beans, and barley grow." She shook her head in disbelief as she heard the nursery rhyme. "With silver bells and cockle shells and pretty maids all in a row." *That woman is definitely off her rocker,* the spy concluded as she turned her gaze to the next gardener.

Hmm, I wonder where old Charlie is this morning. Miranda couldn't remember not seeing him perched on his three-legged stool, pulling weeds or watering plants. She never could quite see, however, what he was concocting as he swirled his gnarled stick around and around inside of the bucket. Once, she nearly fell forward from her spying perch as she craned her neck to see him dump one thing and then another into the pail. *Must be some sort of fertilizer the way his stuff looks so much healthier and bigger than anyone else's.*

Oh, of course, the love birds had to show up. Miranda exhaled as she rolled her eyes. She stepped into another row of tall poled beans to camouflage her existence. *Can't they do anything without hanging all over each other? I don't know how they get any work done. Humpf, I guess they don't; all I can see are those same three tomato plants. All summer with only three plants!* The rest of their plot contained two Adirondack chairs, a small table, a patio umbrella, and a cooler, which they carried in every morning.

It wasn't long before the love birds were nestled in their chairs with their books and their coffee and their adoring eyes lifting ever so often to stare into the eyes of the other.

Miranda gave a sudden 180-egree turn when she heard the Dillon kids come screaming into the garden with their mother far behind. *Oh no, she brought them today? She'll never get any work done with those little monkeys,* Miranda thought as she stepped back into the tall cornstalks. She pushed aside a few of the sprawling green corn leaves and then stopped in a strategic lookout spot. It seemed that the older ones had somewhat of a command over the little ones. Just as the herd veered to the right instead of the left, older hands would tug them back onto the path and just as someone else's gleaming vegetable lured little fingers to pick it, an older and wiser child was alert to the situation and halted the process.

As they somehow managed to get everyone to home base, all became inspectors of their maturing produce. Such glee rose out of the plot that Miranda was sure even people down on the street would look up to find the source of the excitement. *How could they be that happy about a new cucumber or a squash blossom or a tomato that had turned from green to red? Did they know that the carrots were underground along with the radishes and the bulbous part of the onions? Oh yes, they know,* Miranda realized, when she heard, "Sis, don't pull anything up until Mom gets here." The little tyke wiped the dirt from the radish and bit into it.

"Good morning, dearie," came a voice that caused Miranda to pivot in the weedless soil.

"Oh, hello, Edna. What's happening?"

"Happening?" Edna reiterated as she peered over her half glasses. "Don't know if much of anything is happening other than nature doing its thing and making these plants grow!"

"Yeah, plants, plants, plants," Miranda responded drearily.

"You don't sound too excited about being here. Don't you like it here?"

"You know I wouldn't be here if I wasn't forced to."

"Hmm, I just thought by now you would have gotten to like this forced socialization program."

"No way. I never talk to these people."

"But that was the idea of sending you here; you would be forced to socialize."

"Forget it. I have no interest in them."

"Well," said Edna, "maybe one of these days you'll discover that they aren't so bad."

Edna turned and used her hoe as a walking stick as she lumbered along with the utterances of "Yeah, yeah, yeah," resounding in the background.

Miranda watched as Edna stopped to visit with every single gardener along the row. She had work to do; she didn't have time to talk to the others anyway, but she quickly darted behind her second crop of peas clinging to the chicken wire fence when she heard Fletcher's jangling tool cart suddenly departing the area. *Why would he be leaving already?* she wondered, never knowing him to depart before noon. His wrinkled sun-drenched face looked more gnarled than usual, and the quickened tempo of his gait made the tools bang and clash more than ever. Miranda snapped off the tender new green pea that dangled in front of her face and ate it—pod and all.

"Can I have one?" A little voice sailed upward on the breeze.

"What are you doing in my garden? Get out of here, and go back to your mother," the startled gardener squawked with the pea pod stuck somewhere between her tongue and uvula. She listened to the child cry as he responded to the command while she plunged her Styrofoam cup into the watering bucket. Miranda finally gulped enough water to dislodge the pod and ceased her throat clearing. *Kids only cause trouble*, she thought.

"Did you talk with anyone today?" Jane Montgomery asked as Miranda plopped on the couch.

"Yeah, some kid and an old lady," Miranda replied.

"Well, that's better than nothing," the renowned psychiatrist proclaimed as she packed her attaché case for the next day's sessions.

"Don't forget, your socializing coach will be stopping by the garden tomorrow to see how you are doing."

"Oh God, help me," Miranda moaned.

"I pulled a lot of strings to get you into that summer program. In fact, you were the only one your age accepted. That garden wasn't constructed for teenagers who won't be friendly; it was designed for needy folks who will work to grow their own food."

"No wonder they're so weird," Miranda added softly as she walked to the kitchen for a soda.

"Ugh, you are impossible," Dr. Jane Montgomery called out to her daughter.

"Yeah, right, and that's exactly how I want to be," the soda-sipper said under her breath.

"So how goes it?" Michael asked as he poked his head through the cornstalks.

"The damn stuff is growing, isn't it?"

"Yeah, I have to admit you have become an excellent gardener. From where you started, this is like a miracle!" he exalted, seemingly very pleased.

"You know, I kind of like plants. They don't expect me to talk to them," Miranda said in all earnestness.

"Ha!" Michael roared in laughter.

"I thought I heard the good-looking guy over here," Edna interjected as she hurried over to tend to her daily visiting frenzy.

"How are you today, Edna?"

"Better than I ought to be!" she said with a cackle.

"Miranda, do you have something to say to Edna?" Michael asked.

"Nope."

"Try," he commanded with an air of business.

"Um, my corn is almost as high as the bean poles."

"Ah, yes. The better to hide behind?" Edna questioned coyly.

Michael looked at his protégé as she blushed.

"Hey, Fletcher, why did you tear out of here yesterday?" The talkative one asked.

The jangling stopped as Fletch brought his traveling hardware store to a halt. He removed his stained hat as he rubbed the top of his head. "I just wasn't feeling too well yesterday. Figured I better get home before I passed out in the hot sun."

"You OK today?" Edna said.

"Is there anything we can do for you?" Michael asked.

"Naw."

"Miranda, is there something you would like to say to Fletcher?" the socializing coach asked with that serious look in his eye again.

"Um, why do you need all those tools?" she asked as she pointed to his conglomeration.

"Ha, good question, girly," Fletcher said with a laugh. "Let's just say I'm always prepared!" He laughed again as he started his orchestra playing when he began walking again.

"There," Michael said as Edna flitted away to their next neighbor, "was it so hard to have a little conversation?"

Miranda scowled at him.

Miranda and Michael were on their knees picking potato bugs off the leaves of the plants when Miranda said, "Do you hear that singing from the crazy old coot over there in the garden with the blueberry bushes?"

"So? What's the matter with that?"

"Isn't she a little old to be singing kids' songs and nursery rhymes?"

"You come with me, right now," Michael said sternly as he yanked her to her feet and marched with her over to the melodious one.

"Good morning," he said cheerfully. "I'm Michael and this is Miranda. We thought we'd come over and pay you a little visit. Is that all right with you?"

"Oh, yes, yes. I love company," the woman said kindly. "I'm Lena. Are you two married?"

"Oh, no, we are just friends," Michael responded.

"That's nice. I used to have many, many friends, but they are all gone now. We used to babysit all the neighborhood kids until their parents came home from work. We had so much fun with those children. Those were such wonderful days," Lena continued and looked into the sky as if she could see all their faces painted across the horizon.

Michael nudged Miranda's arm as his eyes said, "Speak."

"Um, did you used to sing to them?"

"Honey, I sure did. They loved their little songs and rhymes. I bet you did, too, when you were a little girl."

"Hmm, I wonder if I did?" Miranda asked pensively.

"Well, we better get back to our potato bugs," Michael said with a laugh.

"Thank you for visiting me," Lena said. "Come again."

"Well, you're certainly deep in thought," Michael said as he threw another bug into the jar.

"I'm just wondering if anyone sang to me. I'm going to ask my mother—"

"Yes," whimpered the little boy, "she's the mean one. She told me to go away. I just wanted one of those pea pods."

Miranda looked out of the corner of her eye at Michael. He was glaring at her.

"Come here, little fellow," the coach said kindly. "I think we can spare a whole handful of peas just for you. Right, Miranda?"

"Um, yeah. Right," she said sheepishly.

"See, Joshua," said his big sister, "if you are nice to people, they will be nice to you."

"OK, young man, if you point to the ones you want, Miranda will pick them for you. Why don't you fill up this can so you'll have enough to share with your brothers and sisters?"

"Gee, thanks, mister!" Joshua smiled as if he had been presented with a truckload of toys.

The child's effervescent voice could be heard all through the garden as he ran back to his plot calling, "Mama, Mama, look what I have!"

"Didn't that make you feel good?" Michael asked.

"What? That half of my crop is gone?" Miranda said.

"What's gone?" asked the lady partner of the love birds as they sauntered by with their iced coffees.

"Oh nothing," Miranda snapped at her.

Michael jumped up with a "Good morning, nice to meet you. I'm Michael and this is Miranda."

The men shook hands as the women looked at each other. "You must be the newlyweds!" Michael continued, trying to keep the conversation alive.

"Yes, Victor and Violet."

"What would you like to say, Miranda?" Michael asked.

"Why do you only have three tomato plants?" She could hear Michael sigh.

Victor laughed as he explained how they were waiting for his grandparents to visit and show them how "real gardening was supposed to be."

"His gramps said, 'Don't do a thing until I get there.' So we're not!" Violet laughed. "Well, we're off to do some reading. Nice meeting you."

"And I have another meeting across town," Michael said as he checked his watch. "You have some nice people here, Miranda, and next week, I want to hear about some of your conversations."

"Oh great," she moaned.

"Yes, make them great! See you then."

Miranda was glad that her sunflowers were getting taller.

"How was the session with your coach?" Miranda's mother asked.

"Did you ever sing to me?"

"Sing?"

"Yes, when I was little," Miranda said.

"When did I have time to sing to you? I was getting my doctorate!" Jane noticed the furrow developing in her daughter's forehead and quickly said, "But I'm sure one of your nannies sang to you. Didn't they?"

"I have no recollection of it," Miranda replied slowly.

"What on earth does gardening and socializing have to do with singing? I'm not paying Michael to teach you how to sing!"

"I just thought it would have been nice if someone had sung to me."

"I don't know where you get your strange ideas from," Jane Montgomery replied with noticeable irritation.

"Hi, Lady."

"Don't tell me you want more of my peas," Miranda said.

"No, I brought you something today. Here." Miranda unwrapped the warm napkin. "My mother made them this morning; it's a ciminim bun!" the boy said.

"Oh, a cinnamon bun! It smells wonderful."

"Yeah, it's good too. Taste it."

"Mm, it is really delicious. Your mother made this?" Miranda asked.

"Yeah, she is a good cooker. Once a week, she makes ciminim buns for us."

"Gee, you're a lucky kid."

"I know. Got to go."

Miranda could hear him scampering along the path singing, "She liked it! She liked it!"

What? She stood still to listen. *Now Lena is singing.* "One a penny, two a penny, hot cross buns."

For some reason, Miranda had never heard the song before. She started laughing.

"What's so funny over here?" Edna squawked, seemingly appearing out of nowhere.

"Oh nothing," Miranda mumbled, even though she could distinctly hear Michael say, "This is your chance to converse."

"Well, OK," Edna said, "I guess you don't want to talk about it, but it sure was good to hear some laughter coming out of this somber plot. Guess I'll go see what old Charlie is mixing up today."

"Oh," Miranda was surprised to hear herself speak, "what does he mix up?"

"Lord only knows. He hides his bottles and cans as soon as he sees me coming."

Miranda crouched behind her dill plants as she watched. Sure enough, as soon as Edna approached the chemist's garden, he quickly threw a burlap bag over his elixirs.

"Ha," Miranda chortled.

Charlie held on to his wooden ladle, poised as if he was going to bop Edna if she got any closer.

Something caught Miranda's eye as she noticed an entourage slowly walking onto the pathway. *Oh, they must be the grandparents coming to help the love birds. Well, this should be interesting!*

It was more than interesting. It garnered the attention of everyone around! Luigi and Annamaria called out directions faster than Mussolini ever thought of talking, and Victor and Violet hadn't moved so fast in... ever! There was no sitting in the Adirondack chairs to relax, sip coffee, and read. It was dig this, hoe that, spade over there, fetch the water, take those rocks out of there, mark off the rows with string, put your back into it, and never mind how hot it is! Miranda didn't even try to hide her spying eyes; she stood in the pathway with the others being totally entertained and glad that their gardens were under their own tutelage.

After a long time, Violet looked like she was going to capsize, and Victor wouldn't win any prize for the most coveted gentleman farmer.

Suddenly, Luigi looked up at the sun and yelled, "Now we stop! Mama, the meal!" Annamaria grabbed the basket of bread and cheese and grapes and wine. Out came the glasses and the vino was poured. "Salute," Luigi sang outward as they all raised their glasses. "To the garden," he hailed, and they all drank. "Mama, pass me my squeeze box. Now we sing."

And sing they did! People from other parts of the garden walked over; people down on the street stopped and looked up; Lena and others clapped to the music.

"Now we all rest," Luigi dictated as he pointed to his audience, seemingly thinking that he was the overseer. He collapsed into one of the lawn chairs and immediately went to sleep.

"Well, what did you think of that, girly?" Fletcher asked as he clanked along pushing his cart home for the day.

Without even thinking about it, Miranda entered into a conversation with Fletcher. They stood chatting and laughing about the morning's entertainment until Miranda suddenly stopped and thought about what she was doing.

Sensing that the conversation was over, Fletcher remarked, "Nice talking to you, girly. See you tomorrow," as he doffed his hat and clattered away.

Of all people, why was it Fletcher? Miranda wondered as she gathered her tools to return home for the day. *What made me comfortable enough to converse with him?*

Miranda knelt to reach the end of the hoe. Now, yellow jackets don't necessarily think they have to share their spot with anyone, and if your knee goes down in a place they have claimed, they may be very annoyed.

Such was the case when Miranda let out a scream of terror. Those still left in the hot midday sun ran to her plot.

"Let me through, let me through," old Charlie demanded. "Where did it sting you?"

Miranda pointed to her knee.

"It's OK. You'll be fine in a minute; just sit still."

"But it hurts," Miranda wailed.

Charlie unscrewed the lid of a glass jar, gave his potion a few swirls with a spoon, and slathered the concoction on her knee.

Miranda stopped bawling.

"Wow," she uttered as she dried her eyes on her sleeve. "What is in that stuff?"

"Never you mind. I'm glad I was still here to be of some assistance."

"Oh, Charlie, me too," Miranda spoke with complete sincerity. "I'm going to bring you a present tomorrow!"

"No need for that, but I'll see you tomorrow."

"You look like you are in a daze. Is that gardening wearing you out?" Miranda's mother asked.

"No, I didn't do much gardening today," Miranda answered slowly.

"Why not?"

"How come we never have cinnamon buns for breakfast?"

"Cinnamon buns? I've never made cinnamon buns in my whole life!"

"Why not?"

"Why would I make something that isn't even good for you?" Jane asked.

"I had one today and it was wonderful!"

"Why are we even talking about this?" asked her psychiatrist mother.

"Because I want to feel good one morning a week like Joshua."

Miranda knew why there was no further comment, as she saw her mother reading a report from her briefcase.

Finally, the silence was broken as Jane lifted her eyes from the report and asked, "What are you doing poking around the house like you're on a search. Did you lose something?"

"I'm trying to find something to give to Charlie," Miranda said.

"Charlie who?"

"I don't know. Some old guy who also has a garden and the one who spread his magic lotion on my bee sting."

"You let some stranger touch you?" Dr. Montgomery asked as if she was horrified.

"He's not a stranger. I see him every day."

"Have you ever talked to him?" her mother asked.

"Yes. Today I did when he cured me!"

"You talked to someone?" the doctor paused when she finally realized her daughter had conversed with someone. "Good girl. Here, give him this twenty dollar bill," she said as she grabbed her wallet.

"No, Mother, I want to give him something that he would like. Money doesn't show *care*.

"Since when?"

"Here, can I give him this statue of the bird and the butterfly and the bee?"

"It's fine with me; I never liked it anyway. Your grandfather gave it to me when I got my first degree. I never did understand the meaning behind that."

"Is he still in that home?" Miranda asked.

"Of course."

"Why can't he be here with us?"

"Are you kidding me? You wouldn't be able to stand him ordering you around and being a know it all, and that singing! Ugh, he would drive you crazy."

"I wish I had a grandfather and a grandmother," Miranda said quietly.

"I don't know where you get all your delusional ideas," Jane uttered as she stalked out of the room.

Miranda could see Charlie pour his secret elixir on the base of each of his beet plants as she walked forward with his thank you gift.

"Charlie, No!" she screamed as she saw him lift the liquid to his own lips. "You can't drink that!"

"Why not? I've been drinking it all my life," he answered quizzically as he took a big gulp.

"Isn't that fertilizer?"

"Sure. What's good for my plants is good for me!"

"What's in it?" Miranda asked.

"You promise you won't tell anyone?"

"I promise."

"There's water, molasses, honey, a little vinegar, garlic, parsley, bee balm tea, and chocolate-covered ants."

"Chocolate-covered ants?"

"I was just kidding about that part," Charlie said with a laugh.

Miranda laughed too as she handed him the gift. "This is for you Charlie, for taking away my pain."

The old man slowly took off the wrapping paper and held the statue up to his face. He turned it in every direction and looked at each intricate part. "This is beautiful. Are you sure you want me to have it?"

"Absolutely. I think the man who chose it was very much like you."

Miranda saw a tear leave his eye.

I wonder where the love birds are. Miranda wondered as she approached their garden. *Should I ask Luigi and Annamaria? I don't want to get into a long conversation.*

"Excuse me. Where are Violet and Victor today?" Miranda hesitantly asked.

Annamaria ran over and hugged Miranda with such force, the two of them almost tipped over. "Bambino, bambino!" she squealed as she clapped her hands. "They're at the doctor's to see about the baby!"

"They're going to have a baby?"

"Yes," yelled out Luigi from the bevy of fluttering carrot tops. "We're going to be great bumpas!"

"That's wonderful!" Miranda was able to say, and she was pleased with her comment.

"We'll let you know," sang out Annamaria as they waved to each other.

"Lena," Miranda said as she stopped to tell her the news, "Violet is expecting!"

"Oh, holy day," the old woman exclaimed as she raised her eyes to heaven.

The joy was taken out of the moment, however, when they heard Edna hollering at the top of her lungs, "Help someone, help! Over here at Fletcher's!"

People from all directions ran to Fletcher's garden.

"Call 911," someone yelled.

"Move back," someone else commanded.

"Give him water," came another directive.

Everyone stood and stared as they watched the EMTs lift the gurney into the ambulance. No one wanted to return to their work; they all wanted to just huddle and commiserate with each other. Miranda, for the first time, felt part of a group.

"What's going on over here?" Michael asked.

"Oh, Michael, I'm sorry. I got so caught up in all this, I forgot you were coming today," Miranda apologized.

"Is everything OK?"

"I don't know, Michael. Fletcher had to be taken away by ambulance. I'm so worried about him."

"Do you want me to take you to the hospital?" Michael asked.

"Oh, would you? Yes, let's go."

The socializing coach was astonished that Miranda had met someone she cared about.

"Michael, wait! I think Charlie and Edna would like to go with us. Do you mind if I ask them?"

"Mind?" Michael said, "I would love it. Run and ask them."

By the time they got to the van, the gardening troupe included Lena as well.

No one in their clan looked like they were dressed to go visiting, causing people to turn and look at the closely huddled, soiled workers with the rubber boots and sun hats, work aprons, and gloves hanging out of pockets, Charlie even sported his favorite weed picker, which dangled from his belt.

"No, you can't see him; the doctor is with him. You'll have to wait right in there."

The five of them sat straight as pokers as they watched the people passing by. Each sat with their own thoughts, their own memories, and their own theories about life.

It was Lena who was the most alert as she suddenly called out, "Violet! Victor! Are you really going to have a baby?"

"Yes, we are," Violet answered as she beamed with joy. "But what's the matter that you are all here? What happened?"

"It's Fletcher; he collapsed."

"Oh no! We'll stay with you until we hear that he is OK."

After two hours, Miranda whispered to Michael, "Something must be wrong." Then she looked up and saw Jane. "Mother! What are you doing here?"

"I have a patient to see. The question is, what on earth are you doing here? And who are these people?"

Miranda led her mother into the hallway and whispered, "One of our friends had a heart attack or something; we don't know what. We're waiting to hear."

"Friend? You have a friend?"

"Yes, those people you saw are all my friends. We work together in the community garden."

"I just wanted you to learn how to socialize, I didn't want you to make friends with them; they look like ragamuffins."

"Miranda!" Edna hollered down the hall. "We can go in to see Fletcher."

"Oh good grief," Dr. Montgomery moaned. "I'll talk to you at home."

"Naw, it wasn't anything," Fletcher greeted his visitors with the good news. "The heat just got to me. That's all."

"But," interrupted his doctor, "why are you getting so overheated?"

"I'll tell you why," Edna interrupted brashly. "He pushes around a cart that must weigh two hundred pounds!"

"Is that true, Fletcher?" the doctor asked.

"Well," he drawled out his answer, "yes."

"So what's going to change?"

Fletcher looked at his friends and quickly said, "They're going to push it for me!"

Such a groan went up in the room that it caused three nurses to enter.

Fletcher consented to staying the night. The others returned to the garden to gather their tools and head for home.

"What should we do about Fletcher's cart?" Charlie asked.

"Let's think about it overnight; we're too tired to make any decisions now," Lena volunteered.

Miranda nervously went home to face her mother.

"So how much into being friends are you with those people? I mean, can you get out of it gracefully?" Jane asked.

Miranda couldn't believe she'd pounce on her the minute she opened the door.

"Oh, is that what friendship is?" Miranda asked, coming back with a strong rebuttal (she thought).

"You're just a child; you don't know what friendship is. You don't know that sometimes you have to get out of bad relationships."

"There is no bad relationship here. End of subject." Miranda spoke as boldly as she could while walking to her room.

"You mark my words," was the last thing she heard from her mother as she closed the door.

Edna ran to the entrance of the pathway when she saw Miranda coming. "It's gone! It's gone!" she cried.

"What's gone?"

"Fletcher's cart. It's been stolen!"

"Oh no!"

They met up with their comrades, who looked like the wilted herbs in Miranda's garden.

Lena was weeping into her shamrock handkerchief as she sobbed, "It's my fault. Charlie knew we should have done something with it yesterday, and I told everyone we needed to go home and think about the situation."

Little Joshua pushed forward to hug her legs. "Don't cry, Lena-Lema, we'll find it."

"Aw, thank you, my little Joshie," she uttered as she patted his head.

"All right, let's get our wits about us and come up with a plan," Charlie commanded.

"Victor, you call the police. Edna, you run around and ask everybody you see if they have any clues. Miranda, see if you can get Michael to come here today. Violet, stay with Lena and—"

"Shh!" Joshua hailed as he put his pointer finger in front of his lips. "I hear it."

Within a few seconds, the others began hearing the clanging and banging of the myriad of tools on Fletcher's cart.

"He's back! But he's not supposed to be pushing that monster!" Lena proclaimed worriedly.

"Uh oh," they all groaned.

Then Miranda said, "But that's not him pushing the cart; Fletcher is walking behind it."

Fletcher waved as he shouted, "Good morning! Come and meet my son."

The next day as Miranda watered Fletcher's tomatoes and Charlie picked Fletcher's string beans for Joshua's family and Lena weeded around Fletcher's parsnips, they mulled over their bittersweet thoughts of Fletcher leaving to live with his son. They would miss him; they would miss his clamorous cart, and they would miss his generosity in providing vegetables to the whole town. Miranda was surprised to hear about his custom of leaving produce down on the street for anyone who needed it.

"What are you doing over here?" Michael asked as he stopped to check on Miranda.

"Fletcher has left to live with his son, so the rest of us are tending his garden."

"Well, that's nice of you."

"You can tell my mother that sometimes I do nice things, especially when I have friends."

"Wow! I will tell her that!"

"Why are you so late?" Miranda's mother asked her.

"I'm helping out in Fletcher's garden and working on my own. Plus, we've been putting his produce on the vegetable stand down by the street."

"Oh good grief. Aren't you carrying this thing a little too far?"

"What do you mean?"

"You go from not talking to anyone to being in this club of outcasts," Jane said.

"Outcasts? They are people—from children to the elderly. We have a beautiful young couple who are expecting their first child! If I had had a nice variety of people like them in my life when I was growing up, I might have made some friends. But you only invited the same type of kids to our house. They were snobbish and cruel to others; they never helped other people. I like the people in the garden."

"I wish we had stayed in the city instead of coming to this one-horse-town. I thought it would be good for you to start your senior year in a small school and not be just a number in a huge school. Furthermore, you've gotten your coach to side with you against me. I should just fire him."

"No! Don't fire Michael; he's kind and good to everyone. I'm learning a lot from him," Miranda pleaded.

"Well, I don't like his type!" Dr. Montgomery exploded.

"Oh no! What has happened here?" Miranda said aloud as she surveyed plants pulled out by the roots and scattered everywhere.

"Oh, yours too?" Edna gasped as she flitted along like a crazed bird on a search.

"Who did this?" Miranda managed to squeak out the question before Edna was too far away.

"We don't know," Edna hollered back, just missing a clump of uprooted zucchini vines.

"Please come. Something awful has happened," was the message Miranda left for Michael.

Miranda started to cry as she darted back and forth, bundling as many of her abandoned plants as she could in her arms. She could see her friends doing the same thing: Each gathered their innocent plants after hoodlums had helped themselves to a night of... What? Fun? Excitement? Callousness? Revenge against the world? Payback for life?

No one could escape hearing Luigi's ranting and raving. It was a good thing he alliterated in Italian and not English, thought the ladies, especially the mother of all the Dillon children.

The children! Miranda thought. *What a wonderful help they will be to their mother right now.*

Miranda looked toward Lena. Lena merely sat on her wooden chair, not moving. The girl dropped the cucumber vines and ran to her friend's ramshackle garden.

"Lena! Are you all right?"

Lena looked up into the eyes of the caring girl. She breathed deeply and exhaled just as slowly. "Sometimes," she began, "our plans change….. sometimes easily and sometimes with sorrow. Do you remember that little song everyone would sing to their babies to get the wee ones to sleep? It begins so peacefully with an image of the baby rocking in the treetop, probably the birds are singing and the breeze is stirring just enough to rock the cradle. But then the bough breaks and the cradle falls! How awful to imagine your baby falling to the ground, and yet we sung it as a lullaby. We didn't know why, other than the initial image, the melodious tune, and its ability to sooth the child to sleep." Lena could see the confused look on Miranda's face. "Yes." She smiled. "It's time I got up from this chair and got some work done, and when we're finished, 'Polly will put the kettle on and we'll all have tea!'"

"Do you want me to help you?" Miranda offered.

"No, no child. You have enough of your own work. I'll putter around here and think about how the kids used to laugh when they heard 'And the maid was in the garden hanging up the clothes and along came a black bird and snipped off her nose!' Now, wasn't that an awful thing?"

Miranda turned, not knowing what Lena was referring to, but had confidence that whatever it was, it gave Lena something to think about to get through the present *awful thing*.

"Oh, how awful!" Michael groaned as he surveyed the situation. "I'm so sorry."

"Michael, they're just plants. I have plenty of food at my house. I don't even need any of this food. I'm here to learn how to socialize. Remember?" Miranda said.

Miranda watched Michael's face, which looked as if his very soul had come out of his body to expose itself. His face was filled with shock, despondency, and remorse. She knew that her remark had done that to him. He who had given his sweet soul over to her, a stranger, was now ravaged by her.

She covered her mouth with her dirty hands and cried out, "Michael, I'm sorry, I'm sorry. I don't know why I said that!"

His soul was appeased; his soul forgave.

"Let's get to work," he said.

The gardeners stood back and looked at their replanted "orphans": wilted, pale, and emaciated. Would they ever come back to what they once were? The only sound was that of Luigi, who was still audibly running a mantra that had no commas, say nothing of a period.

"Charlie's elixir!" Miranda said suddenly.

"What?" Michael asked as he put more wooden stakes into the ground to prop up the bedraggled cornstalks.

"Charlie has a magic potion. That's why his plants grow better than anyone else's! Let's go and see if he'll give us some."

They were surprised when they saw a line of other gardeners waiting for a beaker of hope.

"What did you do? Take up residence there?" Miranda's mother grilled her daughter as soon as the girl entered their home.

"No, not really. There's just more work after the vandals went through and caused a lot of devastation."

"What were they looking for? A lettuce and tomato sandwich?" Jane Montgomery quipped in her snide manner.

"No, mother, I don't think so. In fact, I don't believe they were thinking at all. They certainly didn't give any thought to the feelings of the gardeners."

"Feelings? What do you know about feelings? I'm the one with the PhD in that area, not you."

"OK, Mom, whatever you say. I'm going in to make a sandwich and go to bed. I'm exhausted."

"Can't even stay up to visit with me anymore? I don't know what's become of you!"

Things returned to normal at the community garden. Even the shocked, distressed plants felt almost normal again. Michael had been assigned a group of teenagers whom the justice of the peace determined needed something more to do than hang around the streets all day and half the night.

Miranda watched as the teenagers snickered at Edna behind her back, laughed after they had gotten out of earshot of old Charlie, and yawned at Lena's stories. They seemed to like Violet and Victor but immediately became an enemy of Luigi when he told them off for stepping on his onions. They didn't pay much attention to the Dillon kids and probably didn't even realize that they were either helping the mother with her gardening or watching the little ones.

Oh no, they're coming to me next. She could feel a trickle of sweat run down the back of her neck.

"Everyone, this is Miranda."

They mumbled and she mumbled.

"Miranda has become a wonderful gardener! Just look at her neat and tidy garden!" Michael pronounced energetically, trying to illicit a common reaction from them. "Do you have any questions for Miranda?"

"Yeah! Was it this or jail?" a tall, gangly fellow asked. The group laughed.

Miranda waited for Michael to answer for her, but he gave her the go-ahead signal, and she knew she had to speak. She cleared her throat. Had she regressed so much that she couldn't speak? What was the matter with her? She looked pleadingly at Michael as she pointed to her throat.

"Oh, that's right, sorry, Miranda." He turned to the group and said, "Miranda has just gotten over a serious throat problem, so I can speak for her. And, no, Jessup to your question. This was an elective class that Miranda's mother wanted her to take. Are you glad you enrolled, Miranda?"

Miranda gave a thumbs-up sign and sported a big grin.

"This really is a cool garden," commented one of the girls.

"Would you like to learn?" spoke Miranda before she remembered her throat problem. She quickly reached for her bottled water and took a long drink to rescue herself.

"Maybe I would," the girl answered.

"Well, gang, let's board the van and go back to our meeting room. We can talk about the possibility of some of you coming to work under the tutelage of these folks you met today."

"Just stay away from Luigi," Jessup snarled.

Sure enough, Michael brought back five students.

Oh, I hope I get someone nice, Miranda thought as she suddenly had a sinking feeling when she remembered how she was never nice to her teachers. *What was the matter with me? Why was I so ornery? Oh nuts. Lena is getting that nice girl who thought my garden was cool. They are already hugging!*

Luigi and Annamaria didn't want anyone, and they didn't ask Violet and Victor what they wanted. Edna was promenading with a girl, giving her the scoop on everyone. Charlie had a young man loaded with tattoos, and Mrs. Dillon said, "Yes," to a girl who said she loved children.

Oh no, here comes Michael with Jessup.

"Don't look so worried, Miranda; you and I both have Jessup," Michael said.

"Oh great. Thrill me!" Jessup snarled as he kicked at the dirt.

While Miranda worked, she analyzed Jessup. Everything he did reminded her of herself; it became quite the rude awakening for her. As Michael worked, he thought of ways to change Jessup's attitude, and as Jessup worked, he wished he hadn't consented to being there.

Jessup only came on the days that Michael was there. Miranda was relieved about that. He was a big help on the day he hauled hundreds of pails of water for the dry plants. As each day passed, everyone looked at the hot sky and uttered one statement or another about the need for rain. The watering was the main activity of the morning and of the evening. They were ahead of nature's game until the water pump broke.

"What?" everyone gasped. "How can that be?"

No water came out of the pipe. They had to have water or their plants would die. All of their gardening would have been for naught. The water commissioner shook his head and said it might be a week before the system could be replaced and that they would have to walk down to the street level and ask the business owners and residents if they could use their water source.

"Michael, our older friends can't do that. We have to do something," Miranda said.

"I'll start a water bucket brigade," Jessup volunteered. "I know lots of kids who do nothing all day long. They'll think this is fun."

Lone Moon Creek went viral after the newspapers and TV stations ran their stories of the youth saving their town's community garden. And save it they did, until the fifth day when it finally rained.

"You did it Jessup! You saved our gardens!" Miranda and the others applauded.

"I'm feeling pretty good about myself right now," Jessup replied.

"You should, Jessup, you should."

"Well, well, well," drawled Dr. Jane Montgomery as she stood perched ready to jump at the national figure. "You have finally done it."

Miranda could tell she wasn't going to get any accolades.

"You managed to have your name and face spread all over the country. You tried to embarrass me, didn't you?"

"What do you mean?" Miranda asked in exasperation.

"I saw that display of yours. It's now viral with everyone watching! I've had several communications from my peers! Tomorrow I have to be in Chicago at a conference, and I have to defend myself against your antics. Would you like to see what you and your street urchin friends look like, passing buckets of water up that hill like common laborers? Here, I can turn on the news. I'm sure it'll be on there!"

"No, I don't want to see it. I just want to get in the tub and soak; my body is aching; my hands are bleeding again; my hair is matted with sweat."

"Well, clean yourself up good. When I return from the conference, we're moving back to the city where you can become incognito again."

Miranda wondered if she could cry underwater.

"Bella, bella!" Miranda could hear Annamaria singing to her plants.

Ah, they are beautiful, Miranda thought as she looked at everyone's garden. The rain had rejuvenated every inch of soil and brought out a scent of newness and life. She stood just to inhale something that she had not experienced since springtime. Her friends, too, were not hunched over their gardens in labor; they were upright looking from the sky to the ground and looking from side to side at the miracle of water— the miracle of being alive.

Neighbor after neighbor passed along a wave of hello and good morning. They had survived a near disaster. If the young men and women hadn't watered their crops, even the rain would not have done them any good.

"Good morning!"

"Jessup! What are you doing here so early?" Miranda asked.

"My mother and father are so proud of me; they want to take me out for supper. They have never taken me out for supper before. I am psyched! Do you think I can leave an hour earlier today?"

"Of course you can. And Jessup, you did good!" Miranda quickly turned so he wouldn't see her tears.

"Hey! What's the matter?" Apparently, she hadn't turned fast enough.

"I'm just feeling a little sad because we have to move back to the city," she answered wiping her arm across her tears.

"Oh, that's too bad. Me and a lot of my friends were looking forward to having you in our school."

"You were?" she asked in complete surprise.

"Yeah, we think you are pretty cool the way you worked right alongside of us all. And they thought your garden here was pretty cool. They were surprised that you could make things grow like this."

"Believe me, I'm pretty surprised myself!" That comment brought about a youthful laugh between the two.

"What are you laughing about this morning?" Michael asked, happy to see some camaraderie between them.

"She's gotta go back... oops! I guess I better let you tell it," Jessup pulled himself up short.

Michael looked inquisitively at Miranda.

"My mother says we have to move back to the city," she mumbled the words to avoid letting her sobs out.

"Why?"

"She says I've made a fool of myself and of her." Miranda hung her head much like the plants had done last week.

"I'll talk with her," the coach volunteered as he saw her spirits plummet below the earth.

"She's in Chicago right now, but when she comes back, we have to start packing."

"Don't give up hope, Miranda. I'll get Grannie Fern to pray for you."

"Who?"

"She has a garden on the other side of town, and when she prays, God listens!"

"My Grannie Fern?" Jessup interrupted.

"Is it?"

"Yes! I know because she has been praying for me for seventeen years and, look, I finally did something that my parents are proud of! Yahoo!" he yelled and jumped straight up in the air. "You've got a real chance now, Miranda!"

"You think so?"

"I do!"

"I do too!" Michael added

Miranda tended her garden that day with a ray of hope nestled on her shoulder.

"Edna," Lena called out across the pathway the next day, "Fern phoned and said we've got someone over here who needs a miracle."

"Really? Who is it?' Edna wriggled with excitement. "Is it old Charlie? Is it Violet? Is it Mrs. Dillon? Is it—?"

"Edna, stop and listen. She said it was a young girl who has to move away."

Immediately, Edna turned west toward Miranda's garden.

"Now, don't go over there and proclaim you know everything. Just spread the word that everyone has to pray. Can you do that?" Lena asked.

"Can I do it?"

Lena knew she could as she watched the social butterfly walk over to talk to Annamaria.

"Who's going to take care of my garden when I move?" Miranda asked as she looked up from the frothy carrot tops.

"Don't worry about something that may never happen," Michael lectured as he pulled the ears of corn from the stalk.

"Yeah, give my Grannie Fern a chance; these things take time you know," Jessup added.

35

"Well, I know my mother, and when she makes up her mind about something, that is it. She'll never change her thoughts."

It seemed that all the gardeners on the hill had their thoughts on Miranda. Edna recalled the strange girl who once hid from everyone and everything, and how she used her plants as her safety shield. Charlie laughed to himself when he thought about the shy girl who lunged forward to save him from his own elixir. Lena wondered why the young girl had never heard the basic nursery rhymes that all children grow up with. Mrs. Dillon grew to love Miranda when she saw how much Joshua and his siblings enjoyed the teenager. Violet felt more at ease in the garden knowing there was someone younger than she in attendance. She often walked to Miranda's garden for some girl talk.

"She'll be back tonight," Miranda said matter-of-factly as she tenderly looked at her prized pumpkins. They would be fully orange in October, but she wouldn't be around to see them. Someone else would be digging out the potatoes, and the heads of cabbage would also be offered to anyone who wanted them. She was happy that her produce was available to others. Miranda had provided food all summer and it had brought her happiness. She lovingly filled one bushel basket with squash, corn, peppers, and tomatoes.

"I'll stop by tomorrow to say good-bye to everyone," Miranda said meekly as she carried her produce off the hill.

"I might as well get started," Miranda said aloud to an empty house. Into the suitcase she threw her work clothes. *Wait! Why would I pack those? I'm never going to need them again.* She grabbed her clean, folded flannel shirts and buried her face in their softness as she cried.

"What's the matter with you? Why are you crying?" Jane asked.

"Because I don't want to leave this town."

"Well, guess what? We're not going to move! We're staying here!"

"What? What happened?"

"I walked into the conference room in Chicago and got a standing ovation from all my peers and the bigwigs of the profession! I was totally in awe of their respect and admiration of a great psychiatrist. Me!"

"What are you talking about?" Miranda asked.

"They were well aware of your escapade here in Lone Moon Creek, and they attributed your compassion, empathy, perseverance, and all that other stuff to me! They said a teenager would never have those qualities without the influence from her mother, and of course that was me! So what do you think?"

"Granny Fern did it. It's a miracle!"

"Where are you going?"

"Out to the front porch to call Michael," Miranda said.

"Well, you could have at least thanked me," Dr. Jane Montgomery, PhD hollered at her daughter, who didn't hear her at all.

THE END

"Why don't Taylor's kids have any father?"
"I don't know, Marjory."
"Why is this world so goofy?"

⊂✒Chapter Two✑⊃

Back Shirts

Win $1,000 for your most creative and original product.

"Wow," Taylor emoted as she stood with the words jangling from the newspaper to her mind. "I should be able to think of something!"

She began walking around the kitchen table to the dining room, around that table to the living room, around the coffee table to the bathroom, which had nothing to walk around, to each bedroom where she could navigate three-quarters around the bed before she had to turn and retrace her steps.

"Mm, something creative, creative…" Taylor continued to repeat the word as she looked at every item in her apartment. She needed inspiration from something—something that was invariably in plain sight. Something that could be turned into a debutant—a star!

"What might it be?"

Maybe it wasn't in plain sight; maybe it was something covertly cowering in a corner or on a shelf just begging to be rejuvenated with a new function or a new lilt on life!

"Oh! That's what I need. A new lilt on life," Taylor said with a sigh as she slumped to the couch.

She put her head back on the faded green pillow and thought of the $1,000 she could win. "I've got to think!" she shouted as her body rose to attention. "I will! I will think!"

Taylor looked at her watch to see that she had a half hour before the kids would be home from school. She quickly sat at the dining room table to resume stuffing the hundreds and hundreds of envelopes from the Ever in Touch Company. The less than minimum wage job plus her part-time job at the deli were the only means of income for the young mother and her children.

Fold, fold, stuff, seal. Over and over, Taylor performed the manipulation while thinking of what she could invent.

Maybe something that would fold these papers for me, she thought, but was sure the big companies had such machines; it would be nothing new.

"Mom, Mom, Mom, we're home!"

"Yes, I hear you are home! How was school?" Taylor asked.

"Good, good, good," they answered in a row.

Most things they did were in a row. They were aged five, six, and seven in grades kindergarten, first, and second. Their heights were like steps, with no missing teeth, one missing tooth, and two missing teeth. Their book bags held three books, two books and one book.

"Do you want us to help you fold and stuff the envelopes?" Trey asked.

"Oh that would be great," Taylor replied. "But first, get your brother and sister a snack, would you?"

"Mom, is there only crackers?"

"Yes, that's it, but I'll get paid tomorrow, and then I'll buy something a little more creative. How's that?" She paused as she said the word "creative."

"Great."

"OK, can everybody reach their pile of papers?" Taylor smiled as she scanned her little workers. Then she did a double take at Wyatt.

"Wyatt Joseph, did you wear that T-shirt backward all day?"

The first grader looked down. "Is it backward?" he asked.

"Yes."

"I had my good shirt over top until I got on the bus to come home."

"Hey, Mom, you should write 'back' on the back so he'll know," Trey contributed.

"That's funny," little Marina said with a giggle.

"Well, we're not going to write on our shirts, so don't worry."

"But, Mom, you could write front on the front and back on the back!" Trey proclaimed, trying to get his little sister to laugh.

They all laughed until Taylor stopped and looked pensively at Wyatt's T-shirt.

"Mommy, are you mad?" Marina asked with her red ringlets swaying.

"No, honey, no. I was thinking about something."

Taylor thought all through supper, clean up, baths, and homework. After the good nights, she dashed to her sketchpad.

This might be it! she thought. *This might be the unique product.*

Taylor sketched two T-shirts, representing front and back. On one, she printed *Where's the tag?* On the other, she printed *In the BACK.*

If a little kid saw the word "back," he or she would know which way the shirt went!

She sketched two more shirts. *Were Trey's words that farfetched?* she contemplated.

She printed *I'm the front.* On the other, she wrote *I'm the BACK.*

"This is cute and it's funny," Taylor laughed, "and the word 'back' is on the back!"

"Mommy, what are you doing?"

"Shh, go back to sleep. I'm just getting some shirts from your dresser."

"OK."

Taylor dragged a kitchen chair to the cupboard and reached up to the top shelf. She pulled forward her box of art supplies, which at one time her life represented her dreams—her future. The box contained her tools for creativity. Every professor had told her that. But life happened, and she was blessed with three of the most creative products of her lifetime. She reached for her inks and pens.

Her own nervousness startled her. It even made her chuckle. Very carefully, Taylor inscribed the words on the T-shirt: *I'm the front. I'm the BACK.*

"Mm," she murmured, "the word 'back' is important; I need to make those letters unique." Which she did with her artistic talent, as latent as it might be.

I can't start the other one tonight, she thought as she stretched her legs out from under the table and shook the stiffness from her arms.

"Mommy! Is this for me to wear to school today?"

"Well, yes, Wyatt, if you want to."

"This is perfect! My teacher told us to bring something to school today that everybody could read."

"Now you're telling me?" Taylor said.

"Sorry. I forgot to tell you last night."

"Well, you lucked out today. I hope the teacher likes it."

"Mommy," Marina whined, "I want a reading shirt too."

"Here's a note from the teacher, Mom," Wyatt said nervously.

"Uh, oh," Taylor uttered.

Dear Mrs. Vandermark,

We loved Wyatt's shirt! What a clever idea.

Do it anytime!

"She loved your shirt, kiddo!"

"Yeah!" Wyatt clapped.

"And I got another one done today for Miss Marina!" Taylor held it up. "Now, boys, give her a chance to read it by herself. If you don't know one of the words, Marina, point to one of us for help."

Marina puckered her lips for the "w" sound but then pointed to her mother who helped her with the word "where."

"Where is the dog?" she read.

Taylor flipped the shirt and Marina laughed, *"Out BACK."* Her mother had embellished the word "back" and painted a little dog under the words.

"Can I wear it tomorrow?" the kindergartener pleaded unnecessarily.

Was it another glowing teacher's report and Trey's begging for a shirt that kept Taylor's enthusiasm climbing to try for the entrepreneurs' $1,000 prize?

It could have been, or it could have been plain financial hardship that kept the young mother creating.

After supper, Trey whispered to his mother, "Could you make mine a little more grown-up?"

Taylor nodded and smiled at her "big" son. It wasn't until later that she stopped working to wipe a few tears away from Trey's request: *Go forward. Don't go BACK.*

"They thought it was pretty cool, Mom," Trey reported as she swore he was walking with a bit of a swagger.

"OK, kids, this is the evening I work at the deli. KT will be here shortly to be with you. Remember our rules. Be good."

"How was work, Mrs. V?"

"It was all right. I got some salads and cold cuts before they threw them out. Do you want some?"

"I wouldn't mind a little of that potato salad," KT responded.

"Was everyone well behaved tonight?"

"They were, and they showed me their shirts. You know, I would love having one. And I bet my friends would too!"

"Really? But I don't have any T-shirts for teenagers."

"No prob. We can supply you with tons of them."

That is exactly what they did.

"My goodness, KT. How will I ever do all of these?"

"Some of my friends and I can help you, Mrs. V."

"Oh, that would be great! But would you mind if we kept the finished shirts here until after the show?"

Taylor told KT about the chance to win $1,000 at the new product trade show and that the BACK shirts would be her entry.

"Ooo, now this is getting really exciting!" KT exclaimed. "Yes, we definitely want to keep this a secret until the big coming out party."

The teenagers bounced back and forth from helping with the printing to helping with the stuffing of the envelopes. Christopher became the snack man and supplied lots of munchies; Jennifer was the clean-hands lady and was vigilant about being sure that there were no greasy or salty fingers touching any of the products; KT was the music girl and through her wonky taste in tunes, brought about Taylor's release of "That's it! That's it!"

All eyes widened as Taylor jumped out of her chair, donned a finished shirt, and began dancing to the music. The pronounced beat lent itself to the basic steps that she was doing; in fact, in ten seconds, Marina was able to follow her mother's exact motions. The song ended with drums booming and cymbals crashing while the two dancers turned, showing the back of the shirt.

Taylor looked from face to face, waiting for her ah-ha moment to kick in. "This will be part of our show!" she said.

"Show?" the teenagers asked.

Taylor realized that all of her planning and ideas were still in her head. She hadn't released her thoughts to her crew!

"Oh, forgive me! I was thinking about how to make our product fun, eye catching, and alluring to the crowd and the judges! What would you say if we had maybe twenty of us wearing the shirts, going into our dance when we are introduced, and all turning on the last slam of the music?"

Christopher sailed a piece of popcorn high into the air and yelled, "It's a winner!" Then he caught the dive bomber directly in his mouth. Everyone cheered.

It wasn't until Taylor was at the deli that she thought about including adults and the various sizes for them.

"Good evening, Mrs. Quinto. That looks like a new sweatshirt. What does it say?" Taylor asked.

Mrs. Quinto pulled the bottom outward so she could read it upside down.

They went to Kallon Beach

and all they brought back for me

was this crummy sweatshirt.

"That's a lot of words. Is there anything on the back?" Taylor had noticed the word "back" on the front.

"Huh, I don't know. Is there?"

"Nope."

"How are you tonight, Mr. Winstock?"

"Good. Give me the usual."

"Do you like that kind of ketchup?" Taylor asked.

"Ketchup? What ketchup?"

"On your shirt."

"I slopped ketchup on my shirt?" he sounded horrified as he quickly pulled his shirt forward to find the mess.

"Oh, no, I'm sorry," Taylor said sincerely. "I meant that advertisement—the words and the picture."

"This ketchup? No way. I would never buy it. My wife brought this shirt home from the rummage sale—fifty cents. Beggars can't be choosers, you know."

"Oh yes, I know," Taylor replied as she sliced off a quarter-pound of bologna.

Taylor motioned for Mrs. Quinto to return to the meat counter and quietly asked both customers if they would participate in her plan.

They said, "Yes!"

Taylor nearly skipped home with the delight of her entrepreneurial skills! She was going to ask more adults next week.

"KT, how was everything?"

"Great. We even practiced the dance!"

"Do you know where we could get some larger-sized shirts for adults?"

"Oh, I see where you are going with this. Good idea! How about going to Charities Aglow?"

Charities Aglow was "aglow" with just what she needed.

"Mr. Sedforth, would you mind wearing a shirt like this?" Taylor held up an XL shirt for him to survey: *My trip means... I'm BACK!*

"Why would I wear that?"

Taylor told him the story while she dipped out five pickled eggs and a pound of pig's feet.

"Sure, why not? I'll help you out. Plus, my bowling buddies will get a kick out of that shirt. I can keep it after the show, right?"

"Right."

"Hi, AJ, what'll it be?" Taylor asked.

"The hottest sausage you've got and three sticks of pepperoni," the black-leathered biker ordered.

Taylor took a deep breath; she needed to ask the question again.

"What are you worried about?" AJ asked. "Don't tell me you don't have any pepperoni!"

She laughed, told her story, and held up the shirt: *You're Blocking me... BACK up!*

"Cool! Yeah, I'll do it!"

"How was Bingo this afternoon, Mrs. Soloman?"

"Oh, I creamed them. I won the challenge and seven of the games. They're all mad at me."

"You know..." Taylor began as she whipped out a shirt.

"What a riot. Wait till they see this!" Mrs. Solomon laughed as she looked at the T-shirt, which read, *"You're forgiven... Forgive my BACK!"*

"Taylor, what's going on back here?" Sissy asked as she left the cash register. "My customers are all chattering about something."

Taylor pulled out a shirt. "Would you wear this?" The shirt read, *"Lunch is over... BACK to work!"*

"Sure! Are they for sale?"

Again, Taylor touted her idea.

"Oh, I can have it after the dance? Sweet!"

"How was school today?"

"Good. Good. Good," came the answer from the three parrots.

"Anything else?"

Trey handed his mother a note.

Dear Mrs. Vandermark,

Your children have all told us about your venture.

If there is anything we can do to help, let us know.

It was signed by all three of her children's teachers.

"Wow! Do you think your teachers would wear one of our shirts and join us on our big day?"

"But, Mommy," Marina said, looking like she was going to cry, "my teacher doesn't wear clothes."

"Oh my God," Trey exploded as he slapped his hand against his forehead and shook his head. Immediately, Wyatt copied his brother.

"Stop it, you two, and don't say God, say gosh," Taylor said.

"But, Mom, I really was praying."

"Now, Marina, honey, do you mean because they wear their nuns' habits they can't wear the shirts?"

"Yes," came the quivering little voice.

"Doesn't your gym teacher wear a shirt over her dress when she is coaching a game? And doesn't the art teacher wear a big smock over her dress?"

Marina brightened and broke in with, "Sister Rita wore a big old shirt when we planted those tulip bulbs, and on cold days she puts on a coat!"

"There! Would you kids like to invite them? We'll give Sister Rita the shirt that says *Bring laughter... BACK!* because she is always laughing, and how about *Bring good books... BACK!* for your teacher, Wyatt?

"Yeah, she'll love that."

"Mom, we better give Sister Francesca something really serious," Trey, Taylor's second grader, implored.

"Hmm, how about *Your words... BACK them up!*"

Trey jumped with delight. "Perfect! She'll love that!"

"Mommy, can I invite my best friend? We can give her this one because she loves cats: *The kitten... is on his BACK!*"

They had five more days to get everything organized. Taylor was on top of it all; she was becoming a businesswoman. She laughed at the thought as she walked to work. This was exactly what Bernard wanted. He talked about them being CEOs of their own companies. He would introduce them as the "dynamic duo." Taylor stubbed her toe as she thought about the departure of half of that duo.

"I'm going out to make something of myself. Obviously you're not." Those were Bernard's parting words as he took off to build his fame and fortune.

Oh well, she thought, *I have the three gold mines and he doesn't.*

"Hi, Taylor," Sissy called out as she motioned behind her hand that the boss was in the building.

"Hello, Mr. Drone. How have you been?"

"Maybe better than you," he replied icily.

Taylor put on her work apron.

"You don't need that any longer; I'm letting you go."

"What? Why?"

"I heard that you're running a little business in my store, and I don't appreciate it! You're done."

"But, Mr. Drone…"

"Mommy, you're home!"

"I'm home all right."

"What's the matter, Mrs. V?" KT asked.

"I just lost my job because I asked some of the customers to be in our show."

"Here, you should give him this shirt: *You're on a slippery slope... BACK it down!*"

"No, we've just got to be sure to win that thousand dollars while I look for a new job."

"OK, gang, everybody circulate throughout the crowd. All kids, stay with your assigned partners. Partners, don't lose those kids. Meet back at two o'clock by the stage. If people ask you about your shirts, tell them they are part of the competition. There will be a viewer's choice category as well, so smile! And turn so they can see the... what?"

"BACK," they all yelled together.

"Go get 'em!" Taylor hoped against hope that her potential as a businesswoman would surface.

Taylor slowly walked from table to table, knowing that the BACK table was covered for every hour beginning with Sister Rita and Marina on duty.

Taylor was amazed at the other new products. Some were food related, some guaranteed weight loss, weight gain, muscle enhancement, better mileage, fatter checkbooks, no checkbooks, animal longevity, spam control, secret investigating, jewelry polish, no-polish jewelry, foot supports, robotic toys, and so on.

"Excuse me, ma'am. Where'd you get that shirt?"

"Oh hello! We make them!" Taylor swirled to display the words *I've got your... BACK!*

"I have been noticing them all over the place. They are so clever."

"Thank you. I appreciate your comment!"

Taylor took a quick little elf-like step as her load seemed to be lightened a bit.

"Oh my! Look at that," she said to no one in particular. A large crowd had gathered in front of a robot. The inventor proudly worked the remote. The people laughed hysterically as the robot approached various people and made several comments: Will you marry me? How much money do you make? Is your mother going to live with us?

Taylor looked over to see two of her team members twirling and talking to a small group of people. They seemed to like *Where's the tag?... In the BACK!* And *Put it... BACK!*

Her slow stroll continued as Taylor came across more and more of her competition. Her jaw dropped as she saw an absolutely fascinating product. A woman was demonstrating a scarf that could completely be tucked into its fabric enclosure and magnetized to the back of the coat collar. You would never lose your scarf! With two hands, the scarf could be pulled out of its envelope and then the no-wrinkle scarf could easily be tucked in to never show.

"Hmm, clever!" Taylor said.

She was proud of her shirts; they were everywhere. The sisters were a big hit wherever they went with Taylor's children. She was proud of them all.

As she looked up from her wristwatch, Taylor caught sight of someone and said, "No, it couldn't be! No." Then "the ghost" was lost in the crowd. *It's just my nerves*, she thought, consoling herself.

Her crew gathered next to the stage and just like a football team huddled together, they listened to the plays. They waited for the introduction and then stormed the stage with the music pounding. All eyes turned toward the stage. Every shirt person did the motions in unison. They turned enough times so the audience could read the shirts. Taylor watched the crowd, some clapping to the music, some doing the steps themselves, and some nudging another person while pointing to one shirt or another. As the last chord resounded, the troupe gave one last jump to the BACK, while the crowd whistled and hooted. AJ and Christopher took a few extra bows.

Other debuting products were done in a demonstration mode, but they couldn't be called an entertaining presentation. Still the uniqueness and interest generated by each product was captivating to Taylor.

"Mommy, are we going to win?"

"I don't know, sweetheart. There are a lot of great things here." All day, Taylor had noticed several people roaming through taking notes and asking questions. Many were wearing business suits. They were entrepreneurs, she concluded.

"Attention, ladies and gentlemen, attention!" the emcee shouted through his microphone. "We have had a chance to tally your viewer's choice cards and the winner is... the BACK shirts!"

Applause showered down upon the hugging and jumping shirt people.

"Mom, do we get the money?" Wyatt asked as he bounded up and down.

"No, that'll be determined by the judges. Now listen, that's going to be announced next."

"Ladies and gentlemen, thank you all for sharing your wonderful new products. You are all winners, but, unfortunately, only one product can receive the thousand dollars. The judges had a difficult time deciding."

Taylor closed her eyes, and sixty-two others closed their eyes. They all wanted to win; they all had reasons why they wanted to win.

"Now without further delay," the emcee continued, "the winner is the Hideaway Scarf for Your Coat!"

The woman who created the hidcaway scarf was screaming, but no one else was displaying much emotion.

"Sorry, Taylor," her team said as they surrounded her with looks filled with compassion.

"We tried. That's all we could do. You guys were great. Keep your shirts to remember this fun day," Taylor said with all the enthusiasm she could muster.

The arena emptied quickly as the want-to-be businesspeople packed their wares. Taylor only had a few shirts to drape over her arm. "I'll take the kids home for you, Mrs. V."

"Thanks, KT."

Oh well, I'll start looking for a job tomorrow, Taylor thought as she started for the door.

"Excuse me, shirt lady, can I speak to you?"

Taylor twirled around to see a man running toward her. "Oh, I'm so glad I caught up with you; the hideaway scarf lady nearly talked my ear off. I'm Ron Yardley, and I love your product."

"The BACK shirts?"

"Yes, the BACK shirts! They are so creative, so different. And it was obvious that the people liked them too. Is BACK the trademark? Have you patented the name? What kind of production do you have? Have you sold any?"

"Mr. Yardley, whoa." Taylor laughed. "This is all brand new. I have little kids and teenagers helping me. This is a mom-and-pop operation without the pop. Those weren't even new shirts, and I lost my job trying to round up models."

"Well," Ron Yardley said as he scratched his chin, "I think I can run with this; I think I can make it successful. Would you consider going into business with me? I'll put in a half-million dollars."

Taylor went blank. She didn't even see the robot spring out of control and knock her to the floor. She laid on the floor, looking up at flashing lights as the robot asked her if her mother was going to live with them.

With a great deal of consternation, the robot was pushed away as it emitted strange noises, and Taylor was raised to her feet while trying to recall what Mr. Yardley had asked her.

"Maybe the robot ordeal was an omen that you should take the deal," Mr. Yardley said with a laugh.

"You want to go into the BACK shirt business with me, and you'll put in a half-million dollars?" she said.

"That's it. What do you say?"

"I'll put in a million," interjected someone who stepped forward from behind a rack of chef's aprons.

Taylor gasped. *The ghost. It was him!*

"Bernard! What are you doing here?"

"You two know each other?" Mr. Yardley asked icily.

"We used to," Taylor answered disgustedly.

"I see you've finally turned into a businesswoman," Bernard offered the unwanted evaluation. "At last, you've decided to use your potential, after wasting eight years of your life doing nothing."

"Good-bye, Bernard. Come on, Mr. Yardley, we've got business to discuss."

THE END

"Grandma, are you afraid of "weird things?""
"What on earth are you talking about?"
"Well, if a star shoots by, will something bad happen?"
"They say it brings you good luck!"
"Oh, yay! I'm going upstairs to look at the stars."

Chapter Three

The Night of the Double Moon

I t started with the train chugging through the town with nary a sound. Old Clinton Hodges noticed it first; he noticed it by sight but not the silence, seeing how Clinton was deaf. Yet it was strange how he knew that the train was making no sound.

The tattered Clinton shuddered every time he recalled those dreaded "fifty-ninth" years.

Now, it was another night of the double moon. Hear tell, it was to be every succession of that many years that the full moon would be double before the very eyes of the town's people.

He remembered when the three young people were killed on the railroad tracks as they staggered on the well-placed ties and probably couldn't balance on the steel rails as they swigged their moonshine from the blue bottles. No one even knew of the slaughter until the next day when John Groden heralded his sheep across the tracks to their other pasture.

Stories were kept of the years past; some were embellished, and some were never spoken of again. As the current fifty-ninth year approached, the natives hoped against hope that the night of horrors would sail past them, never to be repeated.

However, when old Clinton's grandson ran to the town square with the look of terror in his eyes, the people knew they were not to escape the calamities.

"A tour bus is on its side over at Skettle's place," he hollered, causing everyone to begin running for the accident.

Sure enough, bodies were being dragged from the bus and placed on the ground as they stared upward at the two moons. Most thought that the jolt they had received had caused double vision. No one told them that they truly were seeing two moons; the battered and bruised had enough to contend with without being burdened with that oddity.

After the melee was sorted through, the volunteers walked silently through the white snow illuminated by the uncanny illustrious sheen to return to their homes, where they would be safe.

Children hung onto their parents' arms, begging for answers as to why there were two full moons. Some were given a tepid answer: "It's just one of those things that happen every fifty-ninth year, just like leap year in every four."

Other answers were accompanied with rude replies: "Stop with your questions; I'm sick and tired of your questions all the time. Now button it."

Others simply had no idea, having moved to the area only recently.

The old-timers harbored the memories as they lifted their boots in and out of the thick snow. Mary Carlson remembered the three babies born on one of those nights and the delight of all, until around their first birthdays, when they were finally diagnosed. One was totally deaf, one would never utter a sound, and the other was blind. She glared at the sky and shook her finger at the two orbs.

Lars Lindstrom grated what was left of his failing teeth as the coldness sailed through his mouth while he recalled the fire that destroyed all of Lon Swanson's horses, all forty of them. He, too, looked to the two moons and growled in disgust.

Mae pushed the wooden door closed against the wind, which wanted to enter with her. "No you don't," she hollered, "you stay out there." As she put wood on the fading embers, she noticed the two moons staring through her window. "Go!" she screeched as she hurried to close the burlap curtains to their intruding eyes.

Mae collapsed into her sagging overstuffed chair as she thought of the night long ago when the wind took five lives, all from the immigrant family that had been in town for only a short time. They had no money and no burial spots. The town had donated plots for the dead.

What would the night bring this time, thought the old-timers, the generation who had heard many of the stories, and the youngsters who nervously wanted something horrific to happen, but not happen—but yes, maybe to happen.

Last time in the wee hours of the morning, the siren had pierced through the pores of every person who was transfixed on the tales of the double moons.

Last time, a fire had begun to spread through the business district of their town! The volunteer firefighters had jumped into their vehicles: trucks roared, lights flashed, and sirens blew. Other volunteers secured the area, directed traffic, and started the huge coffee urns and made sandwiches. All the while, the two moons looked down upon the conundrum of the fire and watched the people in their concentrated effort to save their town.

In the meantime, hungry wolves had managed to make short order of Bern Fielder's chickens, even after Bern had laboriously constructed the best wolf-proof coop he had ever constructed. The ambulance from the next town couldn't make it up the hill to the Lambert's place and had to back down and take the long way around while a child lay screaming with no one knowing why. It was the night Roy Henderson's prized hunting dog was stolen, and Leon's boy ran away with Ellie to elope.

Who could explain it? Were they cursed, or were they blessed? Everyone had his or her own theory. But as always, the night came to an end; the moons disappeared, and the people knew the pair would not return for another fifty-nine years. Many knew they wouldn't have to worry about it; their lives would be over by then. Some figured they'd see them one more time, and the youngsters looked forward to it already. The stories immediately began to be solidified and embellished and changed. Within the next five decades, who would know what tales would be told?

One day, someone came to town who was extremely interested in the double moons and the happenings during their time in the sky. He claimed he had been studying the phenomenon for years, going around the world wherever the occurrence was reported to happen. Charles Daniel Effins III was his name.

He came along during the fifty-third year, leaving the next six years to write another book or a series of articles or maybe even a TV documentary. He immediately canvassed the town, searching for stories and people who remembered the last occurrence.

"Go talk with Chadwick's son. His brother was one of those killed on the railroad tracks. Let's see, it's just past four o'clock, he'll be in Billaby's Bar on the third stool."

Charles Daniel Effins III walked into the dimly lit bar and saw a man hunched over his drink. He was sitting on the third stool.

"Excuse me, sir. May I join you?"

Chadwick looked sideways, nodded, and returned to his straight-up drink.

"I'm doing research on the double moons, and I understand you had a terrible experience because of that night."

Everything visible and invisible stiffened outside and inside of the old man. Charles could see the hollows of his face recede further into his profile; he saw the gnarled hands tighten around the glass and hoped it wouldn't break; the hairs on the back of his neck looked like a row of pokers with the Utica Club neon beer sign shining behind him in the distance.

Charles waited, not thinking that the man would give him a response. They drank their drinks in silence, and the interviewer was preparing to leave when Chadwick cleared his throat.

"Probably for the best," he mumbled.

"Excuse me?"

"He died having fun, goofing around with his buddies. I can't deny him that."

"Have you always thought that?" Charles asked.

"Hell no," Chadwick answered as he slammed his glass on the bar for another drink. "I've been mad for fifty years and for what? It finally came to me, if Randy hadn't died way back then, what kind of life would he have had? He'd been a drunk just like me and my father and his father before him. He would have messed up his life just like we did and lived with remorse and misery. For what?"

Charles didn't know if he was supposed to answer or even if he could. He stared into the bar mirror and watched the old man's tears reflect the light from the Pabst Blue Ribbon sign.

"No, those three children don't live around here. Their folks moved to Chicago where they had family to help them," answered the editor of the weekly newspaper.

"Do you know if they blamed the *double moons*?" Charles asked.

"I think they did at first, but look at this article. My wife discovered it and realized that they were the triplets who were born here almost fifty-nine years ago."

Charles sat in the antiquated brown swivel chair as he perused the article titles "Triplets Use Handicaps to Help Others."

"So how about that?" the editor asked the researcher as he looked up.

"Do you think they are glad for their handicaps?"

"Not glad, but as they say in the article, they feel blessed. They never would have established those schools if they didn't have firsthand experience."

"Hmm," Charles uttered as he scribbled some notes underneath those concerning Chadwick. "You wouldn't happen to know if there is a Lon Swanson around here, would you?"

"I sure do! He lives up Buttermilk Road about three miles from here. He just returned from another trip."

"Afternoon, Mr. Swanson. Could I ask you a few questions about your reaction to losing all your horses in the fire of the double moons?

"Lord o' Moses," the man howled as he slapped his knee with his huge ten-gallon hat. "Nobody has asked me that in a coon's age," he continued, still laughing.

"You surprise me. I never thought you'd be laughing about it!" Charles spoke arrogantly.

"Believe me, I cried long and hard for years, until I woke up one day and said, '*Enough.*' I took what little money I had from the insurance, and I went out and bought one horse—one spectacular, terrific horse—and I learned how to train and raise a winner. That was the beginning. From then on, it was Double Moon all the way!"

"The famous Double Moon was your horse?" Charles gasped.

"He sure was, and he has sons and grandsons and great grandsons who are as good as he was. So, as you might know, I'm livin' on easy street these days because of those two moons."

Back at the editor's office, Charles scribbled more notes in his notebook.

"Do you have any information on an immigrant family who lost five members in a storm or a fire or... I'm not sure."

"Well, I've got a paper to get out, but you can sit and go through old newspapers if you'd like," the editor replied.

"Thanks."

Charles read far into the night. *Was this sensationalism or truth or conjecture or embellishment or what?* He read about dead animals and uprooted trees, cars being flipped on their tops, and tire swing ropes being braided. He also read about reunions of long-lost relatives and Hazel Lampeer getting word that her paintings had been accepted in the art gallery.

"Ah, here it is."

"House Collapses on Bernstein Family, Killing Five"

Only in this country for two months, the Bernstein family suffered a terrible loss when the wind of the century ripped their meager abode into shreds, causing five of its members to succumb to the violence. Some of the townspeople were heard to say that the double moon was the cause of the tragedy.

Immediately, neighbors and folks from great distances rushed to help the family. Even though most were strangers, assistance of all types including lodging, food, clothes, money, and prayers were given freely to the Bernstein's.

Are they sorry they came to this country? In broken English, both Julius and Sarah cried as they remarked about the terror they had fled from—terror caused by humans and not the wind. They could not be angry with the wind. "The wind was just part of nature," they said.

"Someday, we will repay the wonderful people who came forth to aid and shelter us and give us land to bury our people," Mr. Bernstein added.

"Are you still here?" the editor said with a laugh as he walked into the office.

"I guess I am." Charles laughed in response as he yawned and stretched. "Do you know who the Bernstein's were?" he asked.

"You mean *are*; they're all over this town."

"Where?"

"Well, there's Bernstein's Jewelry Store down the street, and there's Bernstein's Pastry Shoppe across from the park. Some of the children and grandchildren work at the plant, and one of the sons has a big organic farm just west of the town. Others come back from college each summer to help with the recreation program. They're all over the place."

"So they've done well in this country?"

"They really have. They never gave up hope, and they worked hard for their accomplishments. Old Julius kept his word: he and his family repaid this town a hundredfold."

"Hmm." Charles leaned back in the swivel chair, giving it just a tad of a rocking motion and again muttered, "Hmm."

"Whatcha thinking?"

"This double moon thing, is it a blessing or a curse?"

"Being a man of the media, I'd say it can go either way, whichever way the reporter wants it to sway."

"Yeah, I see what you mean," drawled the tired but anxious-for-a-theory investigator. "Who was the first editor to report on this phenomenon?"

"That would have been old Jethro Rothbone."

"And?"

"Ah, I see what you're getting at. Yes, old Jethro was known for his sensationalizing. The word was that he published more of a gossip rag than anything else. They say more than one irate patron came through those doors scorching mad, demanding to know why he'd published this or that."

After some much-needed sleep, Charles continued interviewing people about their views on the double moon.

"At first, I was scared to death of the saga. I wanted my husband to turn around and relocate somewhere else. I did not want to be here in fifteen years when the next fifty-ninth-year episode would be upon us."

"Why did you stay?"

"The more I talked with people, the more I realized that there was more good that came out of the disasters than bad."

"Do you realize that in six years, it's going to be the time of the next double moon?"

"Oh, that! Yes, I'm looking forward to it in a way!"

"What? Aren't you scared?"

"You know, when fear and terror get into people's minds, it's as dangerous as a weapon. As far as I know, those affected came out better for it on the other end."

"How so?"

"That fellow who lost all his chickens to the wolves later developed and patented a lock that's used all over the world. He was able to leave his family a healthy inheritance. And isn't it rather normal for two young people to run off and get married? I sure wouldn't call it a phenomenon; in fact, after seventy years, I'm still married to my young filly."

Charles Daniel Effins III managed to get his book published just prior to the big happenings. In fact, the publicity was so good, scores of news people were assigned to the little town on the night of the double moons.

The town overflowed with spectators. People wore T-shirts with the words "I Survived the Double Moons" written on them. Kiosks were stocked with memorabilia galore. Music blared and food tantalized. It wasn't until darkness finally made its appearance that the crowd huddled more closely and the din subsided. The rising of the two gleaming orbs actually did force muscles to tighten and nerves to twinge. Infants were held tighter and many returned to their cars and locked the doors.

The town siren blasted through the cold moonlit night as if on schedule. The wind suddenly released its fury. People could hear the sap in the frozen trees snapping inside of the tree trunks. No flashes in any cameras worked. Birds flew in circles in front of the two moons. All the lights in the bank suddenly shone out into the street.

Would the reporters have a story? It would be all in what one thought.

THE END

"YES, YOUR MOTHER AND FATHER USED TO GO IN THERE AND DANCE
TO THE JUKEBOX AND HAVE ROOT BEER FLOATS.
NO, I CAN'T TEACH YOU HOW TO DO THE JITTERBUG.
BECAUSE I DON'T KNOW HOW TO DO THE JITTERBUG.
NOW, STOP LOOKING IN THAT WINDOW AND COME ALONG."

Chapter Four

THE THINGS WE DO

"**H**ey, doll face. How are you tonight?"

Oh no, it's Sullivan, Nikki thought to herself.

"Better than I was yesterday and not as good as I'll be tomorrow." The waitress sprinkled her words in her usual "I-have-to-make-some-tips-tonight" enthusiasm.

Sully let out a howl, "You never disappoint me, sugar."

"How about a little sugar with that coffee?" She slid the bowl over to Sullivan.

"Just stick your finger in it; that'll sweeten it."

"Not tonight, cowboy. I'll need these fingers for bowling my perfect three."

Another howl ascended as the tattered menu descended in front of Sully. "Pick your poison."

"Poison all right. I left here last night with indigestion so bad, thought it was going to kill me."

"But you came back," Nikki said facetiously, being careful not to cross the line of humor and arrogance. She managed a quick little wink at Sully to let him know his tip was going to be worth it.

"What's this new thing penciled in on the side? 'Take a stab at beef still bellowing from the knife on a bun with sauerkraut.'"

"It's something the cook came up with. Do you want to try it?"

"Gosh all Friday. I don't know if I dare," Sully nearly whispered as he tipped his baseball cap to scratch his head. "If I have another night with that gut ache I... I... well, I don't know what I'll do."

"How long have you been bothered with that, Sully?" Nikki asked.

"What are you, a doctor now?"

"Excuse me for asking. I was just trying to be kind."

"I don't want your kindness. I want your... well, you know."

"No, I don't know, you crazy old fool."

"There! That's it! I want you just like that: fire and brimstone and full of fun! If I wanted kind and nice, I'd stay home with my mother."

"I suggest you order that beef-bellowing thing with sauerkraut! And I'm writing down that you want it smothered in onions!"

"Lord have mercy! This girl is trying to kill me!" Sully howled as he slapped his knee.

"Who's trying to kill you?" Clyde asked as he slid onto a stool.

"This young filly here with the long eyelashes," Sully replied.

"I think she knows what she's doing; you need to be put to rest."

"All right, Clyde. Clyde Double-Wide. Just 'cause she favors me, you don't need to get hostile."

"No hostility here. I merely stopped for a cup of java and some pecan pie."

"Did I hear you say pecan, Clyde?" Nikki called out from the kitchen. "Sorry, we're out. Can I interest you in peach?"

"I will take anything you suggest," Clyde said.

"Ha! What if she said liver pie? Would you take that?" Sully asked smugly as he stirred in another spoonful of sugar.

"If Nikki said liver pie, I would take it, you old bullfrog."

"Here you go, men: dinner for Sullivan and pie for Clyde."

Nikki began cleaning the counter while the two men ate in silence.

Six more months of this and I'll have my degree and then I can get a real job with normal people. "Yippee," Nikki exclaimed not realizing she had said it aloud.

"There! Our girl is alive!" Sully regaled as he gulped a large swallow of water.

"How's that beef dish?" Nikki asked.

"Wow! It just might knock me right off the stool. Then you'll have to be my Betsy Ross, no, not Betsy Ross, Clara Barton, yeah Clara Barton. She was the nurse, right?"

"I believe you're right, Sully, and do you really think I could resuscitate you?" Nikki asked, knowing that the question might bring on a five-dollar tip.

"She's too high class for you, fire breath," Clyde interjected between a large bite of his peach pie.

Nikki knew the coffee and pie wouldn't warrant much of a tip, so she sided with fire breath. "I'm here for you, Sully. Now slow down, and I'll get you more ice water. Keep your eye on him, Clyde, while I fill this pitcher."

"What's he rubbing his chest for?" Casper asked as he sat on the squeaky stool.

"Oh, he's such a baby, Can't handle the hot sauce I guess."

"Well, by golly, I'll try it. I'm starving. Evening, Nikki. Dish me up some of that beef that Sully's crying about. Load on the onions too. We'll see who the real man is around here." Casper looked into the kitchen to see who was cooking, not even hearing his 1950s chrome stool screech as he rotated his large belly around.

"Good God Almighty," Clyde screamed as he covered his ears with his hands.

"Clyde, what's the matter?" Nikki gasped as she rushed to him.

"That screech nearly punctured my eardrums!" he said.

"Now who's a baby?" Sully laughed as he finished off another glass of water.

"How long have you had this problem, Clyde?" Sully's Clara Barton asked.

"Oh, I don't know. I'm supposed to be making an appointment with a specialist but I think this thing will go away."

"You better do it, Clyde. Ears are nothing to take for granted. And Casper, please move over to the next stool so Clyde won't hear that squeak again," Nikki implored, knowing she'd have to work some magic to get back into Casper's good graces and his big tip pocket.

"That's a nice shirt, Casper. Is it new?" she asked.

It didn't take much schmoozing to get Casper back. "Why, yes, Nikki it is. Thank you for noticing," Casper said as he brought in his big belly and sat a little taller. He didn't fail to look over at the two men with his eyebrows raised and a smirk on his face.

"Golly darn, Sullivan, this is like eating baby food; what were you complaining about?" Casper bragged as he shoveled in another mound of dripping explosives.

"Yeah, yeah, eat all you want. Nikki, dish me up a bowl of vanilla ice cream, would ya? And put some of those peanuts on top with a touch of caramel sauce. That'll put this fire out."

"Are you sure you want that on top of onions and hot sauce?" Nikki asked.

"Sure do. I'll show this indigestion who's boss."

"Humph, it won't be you at three o'clock in the morning." Clyde smirked as he pushed his pie plate forward.

"Another piece, Clyde?" Nikki asked, hoping to get his tab up a bit.

"No, madam, but I'll take more coffee."

Right, Nikki thought to herself, *always more free coffee, but nothing to guarantee an increase in her gratuity.* "How about you guys? Do you want more coffee while I'm pouring?"

"Sure."

"Well, well, well, if it ain't the three stooges," Jake proclaimed as he prepared to board the squeaky stool.

"Don't sit there!" chorused four people while Jake stood like a statue.

Nikki jumped on the opportunity. "Here, dear heart, come over here closer to me. That stool makes such an awful screech."

Jake strutted past the other men as he saw their ire rise up out of their collars.

"Well, this is much better," Jake remarked as he looked from one deflated Romeo to the next.

"Having a big dinner tonight, Jake?" the waitress asked hopefully.

"I'm not really certain if I want just soup and sandwich or if I want the whole nine yards."

"Got some good bellowing beef in there," Sully called out as he quickly threw his napkin over his uneaten portion.

"We also have a lovely turkey dinner with mashed potatoes and gravy and all the fixings," Nikki suggested graciously and coyly.

"What! Why didn't you tell me that?" Sully whined as he rubbed his chest.

"Oh, I'm sorry, Sully. I guess I was looking at you with cowgirl eyes tonight."

"Yeah," droned Sully, "cowgirl eyes!"

"Oh, knock it off, you big galoot," Clyde pitched in as Casper grabbed for the water pitcher.

"Mm, does this ever look good," Jake sang as the three stooges wished they had placed that same order. Nikki knew she would have to do something to get the spirits up or the tips would be next to nil.

"I'll flip you for the jukebox, gentlemen. Who wants to go first?"

"Me," Sully responded quicker than greased lightning.

"OK, got my coin here," Nikki said as she pulled her "you-lost" coin out of her apron pocket. "Oh darn, you win, Sully, you get to pick the tunes."

The strut now belonged to Sully. Walking to the jukebox was a man's claim to a diamond mine, his signature at the car dealership for a new vehicle that he would never own—his handing of the house keys to his new girlfriend, whom he would never have either. Hearing the coins drop into the slot and pushing the buttons brought forth a kinship with the singer. Sully had directed the star to perform because he had commanded it. Sully returned to his perch much as a crowned speckled rooster would.

"What did you choose that one for? I hate that song!" Casper snapped irately while digging into his pocket for his antacids.

"Nikki, you like it don't you?" Sully asked, much like a nine-year-old.

"Sure do, Sully. Casper, you can make the next three picks—if I don't win."

"You're on, sister."

"Hey, Jake, show the guys that thing you do with the deck of cards." Nikki laughed, hoping to get some free time for herself. "Here, take this table so you can spread out the cards."

It worked! Nikki was able to finish her reading assignment for school, plus do her pages in the physics workbook.

"So how's it going, men? Did you figure it out yet?"

"Almost, almost. I think I know what he's doing," Clyde said pensively as he worked a toothpick in and around his teeth.

"Oh, you do not," Sully remarked, not wanting Clyde to get the best of him.

"How about we top off the night with some dessert and coffee? Everybody up for that?" the college student chirped hopefully.

"Only if you join us," Casper interjected as he made sure to make eye contact with the other three.

"Of course, I will," came the desired answer. Nikki knew one of them would treat her to pie and coffee. "Hey, when did the jukebox stop?"

Nikki spread her tip money on top of the dresser, much like she did after her birthday dinners with the relatives. This time, however, she had to work for the money, not just step up like the revered princess.

Mm, not too bad tonight. Nikki theatrically gave herself a pat on the back. She was getting the hang of cajoling and actually trying to be nice. Her conscience suddenly had a pang as she thought about having to work at being nice. She was nice, just not so much to people out of her league like Sully and Jake and Casper and Clyde. But she was smart, wasn't she? She used her brain to figure how to get the biggest tips out of them. Now that was work. That was her intelligence. It wouldn't be long before she could say good-bye to that ratty diner and get to the city where the big jobs and the big money thrived.

Nikki hid her books under her coat as she hurried into the diner.

"I had a super-duper tip day!" Tammy cried as she hurried to the door, waving her wallet in the air. I'm heading for the mall."

"Great," Nikki said to the back of the door. "Oh well, someday soon I'll be able to fritter my money away, too!"

"Who are you talking to?" the cook asked as he poked his head through the pickup window.

"Just myself," Nikki said. "Just myself."

"Evening, Clyde." Nikki exhaled, knowing her work had begun.

"No pie and coffee tonight. I'm having that turkey dinner!"

"Yahoo! You're my man!" Nikki felt her cheerleading days coming back to life.

"Who's your man?" Sully whined as he walked in and shot a ferocious look at Clyde.

"Hey, hey, hey. I'm woman enough for all of you, boys!"

"That's my girl!" Sully seemed comforted as he slapped his knee.

"Are you having the turkey dinner tonight, Sully?"

"I sure am if that's what you're recommending."

"I am. I am," Nikki said sweetly. "I think this won't bring on so much indigestion for you, Sully."

"Gosh dang, it sounds like you care," Sully said without a howl.

"Of course, I care," Nikki replied, surprising herself.

"I've got my antacids right here," Casper hollered as he barreled through the door. "I'm having two of those bellowing cows tonight; I guess I'm the real man around here!"

"You know what, Casper? Bill has made a wonderful meatloaf, which might be a little more a... a... digestible, if you'd like."

"Oh, I love meatloaf. You know, my mother used to make the best meatloaf in the world."

"So did my mom!" Nikki squealed.

"Well, we have something in common, dear lady," Casper gloated.

"Clyde, did you make your appointment with the ear doctor?"

"I did, Nikki. I did. I guess your little lecture last night got me movin'."

"Good. I'm so glad, and I'll be sure no one sits on that squeaky stool. Hey, where's Jake tonight?"

"Well, speak of the devil and he shall appear."

"Hi, all. Did anyone figure out the card trick?" Jake asked.

"I did."

"Yup, me too."

"Sure as shootin'."

"Yeah, I bet you did," Jake growled as he gave them his disgusted you're-a-liar look.

"OK, boys, let's rev up our appetites and even think toward dessert, which is strawberry shortcake tonight," Nikki announced.

Four old coots, aka *four little boys*, all yelled together, "Strawberry shortcake!"

Without even thinking, Nikki went into her cheerleading routine:

Strawberry shortcake

Huckleberry pie

V-I-C-T-O-R-Y

Are we in it?

Well, I guess.

Lone Moon Central

Yes, yes, yes!

She ended with a jump and a twirl that brought the men to their feet, clapping like their team had just won the game.

"Oh my goodness. I'm sorry. I don't know what got into me." Nikki gasped as she blushed.

"Sorry? Don't be sorry. That was more fun than we've seen in a long time," Sully expounded.

"Yeah, that's why we come in; you give us a little excitement in our old boring lives," Clyde continued.

"I do?" the surprised waitress asked.

"OK, Miss Varsity Sweater Letter Girl, let's get the orders in," commanded the cook.

As Nikki put her tip money on top of the dresser, she thought about the fun she and the "old coots" had enjoyed at the diner that evening. It wasn't drudgery; it wasn't a process of conning them; it wasn't a chore to be nice to them. *Huh, weird,* she thought.

"What are you doing in there to create so much business?" Tammy asked as the shift changed.

"What do you mean?" Nikki said.

"I hear this place has a lot more evening business."

"Whew, that's for sure. I can hardly keep up with it."

"Thanks for filling the water glasses, Sully," Nikki called from the kitchen as she hung up her coat.

"My pleasure, my pleasure."

"Brought in those fresh flowers from my garden. They're in the little bud vases. Do you want them on the tables now?" Jake asked.

"Terrific, Jake. Thanks so much."

"The silverware is all bundled in those napkins. Should I put them out on the tables?"

"Super, Casper," Nikki said.

"Where's Clyde tonight?"

"Oh, he called and made reservations."

"What?"

"Yeah, he's got relatives visiting; eight of them are coming in for dinner."

"Wow-ee-dow-ee-do!" Nikki laughed.

"Oh, you kill me," Sully howled as he slapped his knees.

"Well, men, we did it! I can never thank you enough for helping me out tonight. Here, let's sit for a minute. Coffee and cake on me. There's something I want to talk to you all about," Nikki said. "I don't know if you heard, but I got my degree. I graduated!"

"Huh?" Graduated from what?"

"From college."

"When did you go to college?"

"During the daytime. Didn't you know?"

"Well, heck no. You mean you drove there every day?"

"I did."

"And you worked here until eleven?"

"But that's not the real exciting part," Nikki added. "I got a job in the city!"

Suddenly, eyeballs became larger than the rims of the coffee mugs; mouths drooped somewhat like the old paint-peeled sign outside the door, and the old bodies became cemented to the chairs.

"Hey, guys, aren't you happy for me?"

"When are you leaving?"

"I have two more nights."

The next night, Nikki had plenty of customers; she was busy from the minute she walked in until closing time, but there was no Sully, no Clyde, no Casper, and no Jake. Each time the door opened and jingled, her eyes darted to that direction, but the look did not make them enter.

On the last night, the boss hosted a farewell party for Nikki, but once again, the four old-timers did not appear.

Nikki left Lone Moon Creek, and as she wanted, she worked at a real job, with real money, and normal people. Well, maybe not so normal.

The End

"I can't believe Katie is going to move from her house."
"Are we going to move too?"
"No, Marjory, we're here to stay."
"Yay!"

ᑸᔆ᠊Chapter Five᠊ᔆᑸ

Waiting

"Hi, Ma, how's the packing coming along?"

"Pretty good, pretty good."

"That's good, that's good," Bren answered, wondering if doubling every answer was a hereditary thing or would it cease and desist with Ma. "How much more do you have to do?"

"Just the steamer trunk in the storeroom."

"That's good, that's good... darn, I did it again," Bren mumbled.

"What did you say, hon?"

"Oh, nothing, noth—Ma, why don't you just move out here to California with us? We've got lots of room for you."

"Thanks bunches, but I couldn't handle that fast pace you've got out there!"

"Ma, in one month, you'd be cruising along with the rest of us!"

"Oh sure, sure, I'd be cruising all right." Katie laughed. "I'd be sitting in the Lost and Found with the puppy dogs."

"Oh, Ma, you're too funny!" Bren said.

"Well, funny or not, I have a nice little apartment to go into on the first of the month. It's only two blocks from our house."

"You've got to stop calling it 'our house,' Ma. In a few weeks, the new owners will take over."

"I know; I know." Katie paused, and Bren was sure he could feel his mother's heart weeping.

"Listen, why don't I fly out and help you get situated in your new place? Would you like that?"

"No, no, dear, I've got the Livingston brothers lined up to help me. Plus, I really don't have that much. I've gotten rid of so much—a whole lifetime of things."

"Well, forty years in one house is pretty phenomenal," Bren offered

"It is; it is. By the way, do you have any memories of our house?" Katie asked.

"Ma! Of course I do! That'll always be *our house*."

"There! Now you said it."

"I did; I did. You got me, Ma."

"Wasn't hard!"

"Listen, I've got to run, and if you need anything, you call me, do you hear?"

"I hear, I hear. I love you."

"Love you too."

"Well, into the steamer trunk I dive." Katie chuckled to herself. "How could people have traveled with these heavy things?" she wondered just as the phone rang.

"Hi, Ma, how's it going?"

"I'm on the last leg of this journey and all set to get right into the trunk."

"You're doing what?"

"Oh, don't mind me, Elizabeth. I'm just crazy with the heat."

"What do you mean, Ma? You're not feeling well?"

"Elizabeth, stop! I'm just trying to lighten the day!"

"I know this is hard on you, Ma. Why don't you just come to New York and live with us?"

"Me in the Big Apple? You must be out of your mind!"

"Thanks a lot, Ma," Elizabeth replied.

"Oh, you know what I mean; I love visiting you, but I could never take it forever. I'm just a Lone Moon Creek type of girl."

"My friends love to hear me tell stories about growing up in Lone Moon Creek and me being a Lone Moon Creek type of girl too!"

"See, we have something in common."

"How about I fly up and help you out?"

"I've really got everything under control, hon, but thanks."

"That was a lot for you to do all by yourself. How did you do it?" Elizabeth asked.

"Well, I had all winter, and there were lots of people right here in this little berg who helped. The service organizations were thrilled to get the things I offered."

"Yeah, I can see that happening. Folks are that way at home aren't they?"

"I'm glad you have a few good memories of home," Katie said.

"Don't be silly, of course I do."

"Well, sometimes I wonder."

"Bren said you have an apartment to go into only two blocks from *our house*."

"*Our house?*"

"Mm, that's going to be a hard habit to break," Elizabeth said sadly. "Well, Ma, I've got to run. If you need anything, you just let me know, OK?"

"OK, I love you."

"Love you too."

"Oh my gosh!" Katie whispered to the aroma of old paper that slowly wafted upward from the trunk. "I had completely forgotten about Aunt Katy's scrapbook!" she exhaled and spoke to the absolute "no one" who seemed to be in the room. The same no one whom she'd embarrassingly explained away as, "Oh, no one. I was just talking to myself."

Katie lifted the abundantly full scrapbook of her mother's sister Katherine, Katy, Kay, into her lap and read the titles: "1940–1941 Waiting." Another title read, "Time Marches On." The niece and namesake gently touched the tattered paper cover with one rip jagging in about three inches and the others smaller but prominent. There, without a mar or a fray was the picture of a cocker spaniel and a little white Boston terrier.

"You're good at waiting, aren't you doggies?" Katie laughed.

What was her Aunt Kay waiting for? Ah, yes, those years in history; her first three pictures were like miniature baseball cards: an American Airlines "flagship," a US Navy Transport, and a US Navy Scout Bomber. But that was it for thoughts of war on that double page, for an inch away were the beautiful faces of two movie stars and six clippings of birds (in color) and three clippings of roses.

Kay had left the farm. Kay was a beauty. Kay wanted a life of glamour and romance, but Aunt Kay couldn't forget her roots, at least that's what Mom always said about her sister. The birds were those she would have seen as a child on the farm. Two of her brothers were soldiers in the war. Flowers intermingled with movie stars.

There! On the next two pages, the letters for "Hollywood" were carefully clipped from a magazine and pasted. Underneath the bold red letters was a gorgeous Olivia De Havilland. Above was a painting by Ralston Crawford of a 170-mile Florida Key West highway. An August 17, 1940, cover of *Liberty* depicted a beautiful, but sad, glamour girl looking from her rain-spattered window. Kenneth W. Thompson's signature could be seen under the windowpane with the word "secrets" carefully included.

Yes, the "roots": a black and white clipping of "Missouri Winter" by James B. Turnbull. Did the ominous winter day with the horses and wagon and milk cans remind her of her pa?

More red roses. Her sister Rose would never leave the farm. Kay had dreams—ah! So did those three movie stars: Hedy Lamarr, with the caption "An ex-script girl"; Dorothy Lamour, "Ex-elevator girl"; and Kay Frances, "Formerly a

88

secretary." Did Aunt Kay dream of her picture labeled, "Ex-farm girl?"

Oh! Loretta Young! How gorgeous with her auburn hair, red lips, and cobalt blue sweater with an applique of two hearts being pierced by an arrow.

Hollywood meant romance.

Again, in black and white, there was one painting of horses in the snow and the other of two people in the field, with the man plowing behind the horse and the woman dropping seeds from her basket. Were they her pa and ma? *My Grandparents?*

On the next page it said, "A skirt eight yards wide of red-and-white checkered surah and a blouse of organdy with hand-cut ruffled embroidery costs $39.95. The desired little-girl effect can also be attained with separate skirts costing from $5 to $25 and blouses costing $3 to $50."

"Gee! Fifty dollars way back then?" Katie spoke to the "no one" who listens so well.

"Oh, dear, here's a young woman crying with her little dachshund. More roses with exact cutting around the petals. Judy Garland, Mickey Rooney, and five of Laughton's movies with him in character. James Stewart and Robert Young in uniform featured in *The Mortal Storm.*"

War in life. War in the movies. There was an eye-catching illustration depicting Kentucky Tavern—"A Straight Bourbon Whiskey"—with stemmed cocktail glasses each holding a red cherry on a floral painted tray. Nestled in the grouping was a small-handled basket of cigarettes. Those were the markings of glamour that all of Hollywood knew, especially when surrounded in a scrapbook with Carole Lombard and Cary Grant. Of course, there was another war plane card, Monocoupe "Zephyr," next to a photo of a hen "mothering the puppies."

A synopsis of Samuel Goldwyn's *Dead End* reads, "A grim drama of mean city streets and of unrelentingly bitter struggle for existence among those to whom hunger is a constant threat and danger a faithful companion." Did Aunt Kate know that they weren't starving on the farm? They didn't have much money, but there was always food and... danger? No, not really, but no one posed like Joan Crawford or wore the latest styles like Jean Harlow or drank martinis like William Powell.

Across the page was a sad little girl hugging her doll with devastation in the background. The Red Cross emblem said it all. There was no caption.

I wonder if Aunt Kay...

"Oh, hi, Megan."

"Ma, why are you out of breath? Are you OK?"

"Yes, yes, I was on the floor looking through stuff, and I ran down the hallway to get to the phone. What's up?"

"I just got e-mails from Bren and Elizabeth. They seem worried because you are managing so well. Is that true?"

"No, they're big fat liars." Katie laughed.

"Ma, stop it! Really, are you getting forty years of accumulation removed all by yourself?"

"Accumulation? Is that what your home was? An accumulation?"

"Oh, Ma, you know what I mean. It must be so hard on you, getting rid of all of your and daddy's things. I know you loved your home, and I did too."

"You know, Megan, I have already been doing it for years," Katie said.

"What do you mean?"

"Well, I've already given away my best *accumulations*."

"What?" Megan said.

"Your dad, when he passed away, and now all you children are gone. This last stuff is nothing compared to that."

"Oh my gosh, I never thought of that."

"Well, you wouldn't, you're young."

"Ma, I can take off a couple of weeks from work. Let me come and help you."

"Oh my heavens no. I'm at the end of the trail; all I have left is the steamer trunk in the storeroom. But thanks anyway. Megan, are you crying?"

"Yes, I'm crying and I love you."

"I love you too. Now settle down and be happy that I'm happy. Talk to you in a few days."

Now where was I? Of course, the basket of strawberries! I wonder if Kay thought about the sun-drenched, mouth-watering wild strawberries she picked as a child as she pasted in these cascading berries. Did she think of one of her brothers as the Grumman Model G-21 landing on the water? They used to play in the creek with twigs and sticks as their crafts, Ma said.

Who was this Katherine, Katy, Kay?

The breathtaking Carmen Miranda shared a page with Alaskan Huskies and a calendar page of a little welcoming farmhouse next to a wintry silver creek, still unfrozen, made for a thought-provoking display.

The last paragraph of *Portrait of the Man Who Came Back* by Joseph Henry Steele says, "Lew Ayres does not believe in Matrimonial vacations."

Kay, too, had gone the way of many of the stars: divorced, one son, and a new debonair gentleman as her escort.

There were more war planes, roses, and a clipping from the *New York Times* magazine, January 12, 1941: *a wintery scene of a horse standing in the snow by a country farm* by F.B.A. and Ewing Galloway with the caption: "Winter Will Be Winter, Neatly Adorned with Winter Weather."

The first three children in her aunt's family were girls. Did Kay and her sisters have to work as hard as would boys? *Probably*, thought Katie.

"America now faces calmly the dark abyss and has girded spirit and arm beyond what seemed possible to the sleeping democracy of 1939," read the caption under a news photo of the Statue of Liberty of Fairchild Aerial Surveys.

Could a full-page portrait of Edward Arnold with his slicked-down hair and diamond pinky ring be smiling at the Beechcraft Model 18 or at Miss M. L. Constable's acacia garden, which won a trophy or at the lonely sheepherder's wagon on the plateau? Katie wondered how her aunt Kate learned how to do these collages.

Was Kay old enough to remember the winters in South Dakota or the covered wagon trip to their new homestead?

Would the beautiful Ginger Rogers…

"Hi, Ma."

"Well, surprise, surprise!"

"I know. I know, but I've been so busy."

"It's OK, I know you have. So what's up?"

"Our little drama queen, Megan just called, and she was crying. I couldn't tell if she was having a problem or were you?"

"Wasn't me," Katie said.

"I figured that, but I just wanted to check. So you're almost out of there! Good for you, Ma," Reagan said.

"Yeah, it's a next step all right."

"That's what you used to tell us! You've got to take that next step."

"I did?" Katie said.

"Oh, Ma, you're so funny, but seriously, you're doing the smart thing; there's no sense in keeping that great big house."

"I like those words: 'no sense.' I don't know if I've made any sense to my life, just like Aunt Kay."

"Who?"

"Oh, never mind, you never knew her. She was an aunt of mine who died of a massive heart attack way back in 1950."

"Why didn't you ever tell us about her?"

"What was there to tell? She had her life just as you kids had yours. Sometimes we don't get into someone else's life until years later."

"Yeah, I suppose. But, anyway, are you doing OK? I could drive up this weekend if you need help."

"No, no I'm fine. In fact, I'm having a leisurely day going through the old trunk in the storeroom."

"That's great, Ma. You just take it easy."

"I will, and it's good hearing from you, Reagan. Love you."

"Love you too."

"Why does that phone have to be down the hallway?" Katie asked herself as she settled back with Ginger Rogers. *Would the beautiful Ginger have any worries? Wasn't she just too pretty to worry? Of course.*

Mm, look at this! It says it's the southern shore of Sanibel. Did Kay and her son and new beau go there?

There was another Dole Pineapple ad painted by Georgia O'Keeffe followed by a farm boy with his dog.

"This is the second time I've seen this picture," Katie said aloud. "Yes! The same four roses frozen in a block of ice. Oh, wait a minute. I remember mom saying her sister used to drink something called 'Four Roses.' Here's a style she would like: a slacks suit. All the movie stars were wearing them, so Kay would have too."

"Down She Goes... And Another Sub Joins Our Navy" from the Sunday paper of January 26, 1941, with an Associated Press wire photo. "Completed in record time, the new $6,000,000 submarine Grudgeon slides down the ways of the navy yard at Mare Island, Cal."

"So You'll Know Them When You See Them" was the title of the article in the *Daily News* on Monday, January 20, 1941. It showed a complete illustration of military insignia.

What did Aunt Kate see in the eyes of Joan Bennett and Spencer Tracy? Did the title "Your Hollywood and Mine" draw her into that world to escape reality? Could George Raft saying, "Come with us, Katy, farm girl, we'll change you!" have been the lure? Would the captivating allure of Gene Tierney coax Kay away from her roots in Lone Moon Creek? *I don't think it would take much more coaxing, but the clippings of rural life, animals, and flowers? She couldn't let go.*

"Germany Strikes at Britain through the 'Low Countries,' Total War Starts" was pasted in the scrapbook dated May 20, 1940, vol. 8, no. 21. The title *Sky Murder* was attached to the top. Was this reality or a movie? The caption read, "Oh, glory be to St. Peter."

Katie mumbled as she hoisted herself up to run for the phone.

"Mom! Are you all right?"

"I will be in a minute. I've got to rub out this crick I have in my back."

"Why do you have a crick in your back?"

"I was sitting on the floor in the storeroom going through papers."

"Oh, I thought you got it from all those years of living in Lone Moon Crick."

"Ha, ha, miss smarty-pants." Katie laughed. "Tell me, Julianna, how do you like island life?"

"We absolutely adore it; this has been the best decision we ever made!"

"I'm glad you're happy."

"Mom, I've been getting lots of messages from my brothers and sisters. Is everything OK? Do you need some help?"

"I'm fine, Julianna. Really!"

"You know, with the money you get from the house, you could afford to spend at least six months here on the island with Park and me," Julianna said.

"Oh, now, wouldn't that be something?!"

"Well, I don't want to be the only one in the family who loves islands."

"I think there was someone else who loved islands," Katie said.

"Who?"

"My aunt Kate."

"Oh, the one you were named after? How do you know she loved islands?"

"I know a lot about her now. Someday, I'll tell you about her."

"Yeah, while we're sitting on the beach!"

"Sounds good to me."

"OK, as long as everything is good, I'll say bye and talk to you soon. Love ya."

"Love ya too."

"Now, where was I? Oh yes": "Germany's Henkel bombers issue at dawn May tenth from the great underground hangar at Wertheim, thirty-six strong, to launch blitzkrieg. The farmhouse on hill houses staff; the barn is for weather and radio crew; the windmill is a beacon, and poplars hide radio. Sides of hill move on rails. The hangar holds two groups, totaling seventy-five planes, twenty-five in reserve, and more in storage."

Did she think that could have been her farm? Could this be her Creek?

Today I'd rather have a brook.

Than the most fascinating book.

For books are apt to make one hot

And bothered, whether good or not!

But brooks are just the other way—

Call, brook, and I will come today!

-Anonymous

"F.D.R. Greets Halifax at Sea" was pasted across the page from Jack Benny, his wife Mary Livingston, and their adopted daughter, Joan.

Joan had a chance to sail into wealth and notoriety and fame. How easy it was for her. Probably not so much for Aunt Kate, Katie thought.

Helpful hints on the care of animals, how to grow flower gardens, beautiful living quarters, and gorgeous fashions next to "American Eagles of War—Army Bombers over Mount Rainier" from the *New York Times* magazine, February 23, 1941, Section 7.

Katie read the words, "Are the Robert Taylor's Divorcing?" with an illustration by Jack Murray. Those sleek white wolves and green eyes that could pierce your very soul almost jumped off the page.

There! She didn't give up on God! As my mother thought she might have, so she prayed constantly for her sister's soul. In her own handwriting, Aunt Kate wrote, "God Bless America" under a full-page color photo of a woman and a girl raising the flag.

Oh my goodness! I thought this was her standing on a huge boulder with the sky as her background, but I can see that it has been cut from a magazine.

The caption underneath reads, "There Is a Vision in America."

Today, the women of America are lifting their eyes from the small, warm ways

of home to watch a young country awake and stretch itself. Their hearts quicken

to the tempo of steel and steam—the thrust of great machines newly forged. On

farms and city streets, in homes and shops and mills, their will is firm: to keep

the freedom for their children that their mothers won for them.

-The Editors

Ah, beautiful apple blossoms...

"Oh, my good glory be! What's the matter with those kids?" Katie groaned as she rose again. "I'm coming if the good Lord's willing and the creek don't rise." She laughed.

"What? The creek is rising?" asked a startled Timothy.

"No, no," laughed Katie. "The creek is fine. What's up, Doc? Oh, don't tell me, your sibs have been calling you and telling you there is something wrong, but they don't know what it is. Right?"

"Yeah, something like that! How are you, Ma?"

"I'm beginning to wonder? Six kids call in one day! I might as well lay right down and die!"

"Ma, stop it! I didn't think anything was wrong. I just wondered if you still had my old jersey from baseball days?"

"You've got to be kidding me! I told you kids to get all your crap—I mean stuff—out of here five years ago and that anything left was going to be thrown out."

"Just wondered, just wondered," Timothy mumbled. "How about that little statue of the Collie dog?"

"Gone."

"The birdcage?"

"Gone."

"Well, I guess that's all I wanted from the house."

"Doesn't sound like you were very attached to anything," Katie said.

"Just you, Ma."

Katie couldn't speak. She grabbed for a tissue to not only catch her tears but also stifle her sobs.

"Ma. Ma, you all right?"

"Oh, I don't know what came over me; I had a little bit of a breakdown, I guess. I wonder if it came all the way from Aunt Kay."

"Who?" Timothy asked.

"I'll tell you some day, Tim. I'm sorry that I don't have your jersey and the statue and the birdcage to give you."

"No problem, no problem."

"Do you always repeat your words like Bren?" Katie asked.

"And you! Gotta go, Ma. Love ya."

"Love you, too, and you be sure you get yourself to church."

A few more tears fell appropriately on the apple blossoms: some for her, some for Aunt Kay, and some for the whole world.

"A Ring of Steel around a Mighty Nation! Let's Make It Tough!"

Two pen-and-ink drawings, *Bringing in the Sap* by Philip Cheney and *Opening the Road* by Eloise Howard, bring the scrapbook "Waiting" to an end with Fredric March and Margaret Sullivan holding hands in a movie setting across from a still life of wild flowers that could have been seen growing on the farm.

THE END

"GRANDMA, WHERE DO THE OLD FOSTER KIDS GO?"
"THE 'OLD' KIDS?"
"YEAH, LIKE WHEN THEY GET BIG AND DON'T LIVE IN THE FOSTER
HOUSE ANYMORE?"
"WELL, THEY GO OUT AND MAKE LIVES FOR THEMSELVES."
"HOW COME I DON'T MOVE OUT AND MAKE A LIFE FOR MYSELF?"
"DO YOU WANT TO?"
"YES... NO... YES... WAIT. MAYBE SOMEDAY."
"YES, MAYBE SOMEDAY."

 Chapter Six

THE UNCOVERED COVER-UP

A SEQUEL TO "THE COVER-UP" FROM BOOK TWO

McKenna fixed her makeup before she proceeded to the boardroom.

"All right, team, let's go around the table and each of you cite your conclusions on this case," Bob Wilkashire commanded.

"As far as I see it," Edmund superseded the others who were posed to respond, "Mr. Jones embezzled the money from his wife's company."

"Nonsense," Millicent scoffed, "I extensively researched his work record, and Mr. Jones didn't have the smarts to pull off something like this."

"That's true, Millicent, but Mrs. Jones's secretary not only had the intelligence but was in a prime position to wangle her way into all the private business," Dexter proclaimed with all assertiveness and confidence.

"Hmm, interesting," the boss nodded his head. "Any other conjectures?"

"I go along with Edmund; I think Mr. Jones had a lot more on the ball than he let on," Willard interjected.

McKenna cleared her throat as they all turned to look at her. "It was Mrs. Jones, herself," she proclaimed without batting an eyelash.

She sat through a barrage of comments. "No way!" "You must be kidding." "That doesn't make sense." "Where did you get your facts?" "Be serious."

When the onslaught faded, McKenna continued, "Here are my findings. I hope you will take the time to read through the report and comment."

"Well," responded Bob Wilkashire, "I am impressed with this report."

The others looked up and then back at their papers. *Were they that slow in reading or did they not wish to comment?* McKenna wondered.

With no comments coming forth, Mr. Wilkashire went ahead to utter, "I'm passing this report on to Jim Field. You're excused, everyone. Keep up the good work, and keep your noses to the grindstone."

Four of the five inaudibly mumbled, *"With your nose to the grindstone,"* in unison with the boss as they turned and left the boardroom.

"Wait a minute, McKenna. Can I talk to you? Tell me, how did you come up with your conclusion?"

"I… a… I just have a sixth sense about these things, I guess," she answered.

"Well, I never would have thought it would be Mrs. Jones. Good investigative work, McKenna, and always *keep your nose to the grindstone!*"

This time, she chanted the little ditty silently as he spoke it aloud.

"Of course it was that Braggfield character; he was the one who tried to pawn the rings!" Millicent exclaimed with conviction as she slammed her folder closed.

"I'm not so sure," Willard dragged the words from his thoughts. "Braggfield could have found the jewelry on the street or in a trash can. It doesn't mean he stole it from the Potter household."

"Absolutely!" Dexter chimed in, "Braggfield may live on the street, but he has no history of robbery or breaking and entering. Why at eighty years old would he smash out a window, climb through, and try to ascend that long staircase. You know how he can barely breathe without coughing."

"You'd be surprised what people can do when they have a motive," Millicent said, defending her case.

"Edmund, we haven't heard from you," Bob Wilkashire contended as he and the others looked at Edmund.

"I'm waiting for the lab to send back information on the fingerprints and a mold of the footprint found in the flower garden under the window. What bothers me is that there were no particles of dirt on the floor or on the staircase."

"Hmm," uttered the boss. "McKenna?"

"I have no conclusions yet, Mr. Wilkashire."

Three out of the four investigators around the table thought, *There! She's not so smart.*

The next day, Edmund was ready to evaluate his findings. "The only fingerprints found in the house were the Potters' and their staff. The footprint was matched to the gardener's work shoe. Therefore, this must be an inside job. It might even be Mrs. Potter, herself!" Edmund expounded, making everyone think of the last case, when the culprit was *Mrs. Jones, herself!*

"What did she do, throw a couple of the rings out of the window so Braggfield would find them?" Millicent laughed.

"I really don't want to turn this report over to Jim until we all have our evidence included," Bob spoke sternly as he stared directly at McKenna.

"I'm keeping my nose to the grindstone, sir," McKenna said apologetically.

Bob Wilkashire seemed to like her reply, as he half smiled upon exiting the room.

McKenna grabbed her folder and dashed to the door. "See you later, guys. I have to follow up on something, and fast!"

"I don't see what she is going to uncover. We found everything there was to be found," Dexter mumbled dismally.

"I've got it!" McKenna pronounced as she sailed into the boardroom. No one smiled except for the boss.

"What is it?" Mr. Wilkashire asked as he leaned forward, knowing he had to submit his report to Jim Field in two hours.

Arms were being folded across the chests of the others; jaws sporadically jutted to one side or the other; eyebrows were either being raised or furrowed. Would the newest member to the team have the conclusion again?

"I have indisputable evidence that Mrs. Potter is addicted to gambling, and with years of mostly failures, she has taken to selling many of the family's valuables. I believe she staged this robbery herself for the insurance."

The investigators could find a needle in a haystack, but they couldn't hear a pin drop in the room—their heads were thundering with disbelief over what they'd just heard.

"No way! Not the distinguished Mrs. Potter!" Millicent's comment torpedoed across the shiny table.

"Yeah," Willard corroborated, "that's ridiculous!"

"Let me see your evidence," Bob Wilkashire remarked as she passed the papers forward.

There was silence again as McKenna didn't know what to do with her eyes except to keep them lowered.

"Well, well, well," the boss said slower than the nightly drip of the faucet McKenna was forced to hear each night. "You've cracked it! You've nailed it!"

The others watched as he ran off to the next office.

No one offered "Congratulations" or "Good Job." It wasn't until Edmund reached the doorway at the same time as the "solver," was there a comment.

"How is it that you can come up with those bazaar conclusions, which, ironically, are true?"

"Um… I don't know, Edmund. Just lucky, I guess." McKenna spoke sheepishly, never wanting anyone to know about her past.

"Mc Kenna, Jim Field wants to talk with you."

"Great job on our last two cases. But, you've only worked here during that time, right?"

"Yes, sir."

"How would you like to be transferred to our cold cases?" Jim asked.

McKenna could feel the color drain from her face and her shoulders slump. "Thank you, sir, but I never have liked cases from the past; I like working on the future," she answered weakly.

"Well, all right, but if you ever change your mind, let me know. Keep up the good work and no, I won't say keep your nose to the grindstone." Jim laughed.

McKenna laughed in return as she felt her composure resurfacing.

"OK, when we get the next case, are we all agreed that the criminal will undoubtedly be the most innocent acting?" Millicent whispered to everyone except McKenna.

"Right!" the three men concurred.

McKenna entered and took a seat. The boss followed.

"What we've got here is pretty much an open-and-shut case. There are missing funds from the Little Kids Foundation, and the parents are up in arms. The treasurer claims she is innocent. All the details are there in your folders. Go get 'em. See you in two weeks."

"OK, gang, what's the verdict?"

"It's definitely Mrs. Allison," Dexter began.

"I agree, the treasurer had her hands in the till," continued Willard.

"She certainly had opportunity. Yes, Mrs. Allison was the culprit," Edmund concurred.

"I'm not so sure about that," Millicent added, causing the three men to tilt their heads in wonderment of her switching allegiance. "Let's let McKenna speak next while I do a little more thinking," she said coyly.

"It would seem that it would be Mrs. Allison," McKenna began, "but upon investigation, I can tell you without a doubt that she is as honest as the day is long."

Bob Wilkashire turned his head to look at the three males. They shuffled their eyes.

"But how about Mrs. Jenio? Or Mrs. Falstaff? Or Mrs. Raylium? Millicent, what do you think about them?"

"Who?"

"The three women who sold concessions every week."

"Oh, I never talked with them. Should I have?"

"I do believe so! Here's their confession given to the police."

"What?" Millicent retorted as she grabbed the paper.

"All right folks, that's it for today, but I think some of you better get your noses to the grindstone and produce some real results."

"Ah, good! A murder! I love murder cases!" Dexter proclaimed as he wrung his hands joyously, almost salivating.

"Don't get too excited over there, Dexter. You're track record hasn't been that good lately; you might be transferred to another department."

"Don't worry about me, boss; this is where I excel."

McKenna had no idea what cases Dexter had ever solved, but in all fairness, she hadn't been around for very long. The team apparently had done some excellent work to be employed for years and years.

"OK, what have we got here?" Willard asked, also rising to the special occasion of having a murder.

Edmund and Millicent were not as jubilant. Millicent released her feelings with, "Ugh, messy murders," while Edmund remained silent.

Hmm, I wonder why? McKenna thought as she looked at Edmund.

Wilkashire distributed their folders. "Go over this and meet back here in two hours."

Over the top of their cubicles could be heard: "What the hell?" "I don't get this?" "Oo, nasty!" "Damn, I'd rather have ten embezzlement cases than this." "Hmm, interesting."

"So do you have your work cut out for you or what?" Bob Wilkashire asked with a half grin on his face.

No one commented, and they refused to allow the little ditty to enter their ears as they exited.

McKenna lay in bed listening to the drips of the bathroom faucet.

Why hasn't the super been here to fix it yet? How long do the tenants have to wait for any kind of service around here?

She began to wonder how many drops of blood escaped the homeless man's head before he died. If it was a robbery, what was there to steal? That man had nothing. Who was he before he became homeless? Did he have a family? Would his fingerprints show up on the computer search? What was he running from? Did he try to hide from the world, his memories, his conscience, his family, or maybe even his successes?

McKenna thought maybe the drips from the faucet were coming faster as the nights went by. Would they eventually escape so quickly that they turned into a stream? She thought of her stream back home. In the summertime, the water barely had enough gumption to creep overtop of the round, smooth stones, but in the spring, Lone Moon Creek gushed ferociously, completely covering the stones and escaping its banks to devour what? The fields, the roads, the people?

McKenna shuddered as she pulled another blanket over herself. She remembered being in a foster home when the news of someone drowning ran rampant through the town. She remembered praying that it wasn't her mother. Her mother. She hadn't been to the jail lately to visit her mother.

In the morning, McKenna went to the alley where the man had been bludgeoned. It wasn't a crime scene anymore; the man's blood had soaked into the dirt with the evening's rain; his last thoughts were nowhere to be found. And his soul? Gone.

McKenna poked around anyway, looking for clues, looking for some sort of tie to the man—the man who now had a name: Fernando Augustine Domingo. From the police report, the investigator knew he was sixty-two. *Only sixty-two?* she thought. He came from Olympus three years ago. He had been a college professor.

"He probably got whacked for his wine," Edmund reported. "They said there was a broken wine bottle in the alley."

"Or his drugs. There were hypodermic needles all over the place," Willard added.

"It wasn't for his money," Dexter imploded. "His wallet was found in the dumpster with fifty dollars in it!"

"Hey! Where's McKenna?" Millicent asked.

"She flew to Olympus," the boss responded.

"Why didn't we go?"

"You never asked," he answered glumly. "And your report?"

"I think it was a lover's quarrel. They found a lipstick, a scarf, and a hairbrush in the alley," Millicent answered importantly.

"We'll see what McKenna turns up," he disgustedly interjected as he left the room.

"What's the matter with him?" Millicent whispered to the others.

"He's probably mad because with the draining budget, he had to purchase plane tickets for you know who."

"Yeah, I bet that's it."

McKenna tossed and turned in the hotel room. *I don't know if I can sleep without hearing the water drip.* She chuckled, almost startling herself; she couldn't remember the last time she had laughed. She knew she had laughed as a kid. She and her mother used to have some fun times. But why did her mother set her up to go out to those foster homes and steal? *What an awful thing to do to a child.* McKenna pounded the pillow, trying to disclose a comfortable valley. She wondered about the pounding that Mr. Domingo had received. Tomorrow, she would find out if he had a daughter or a son.

"He said he had to go and find himself," Annieann cried. "I think I was the only one who understood. Mom was livid, and Devon really went into himself with anger and depression."

"Hmm," McKenna responded. "Was your father distraught at work or home?"

"It was everything, I guess. He said he was sorry, but needed to get away to think."

"Why did he live as a homeless man?"

"I didn't know that," Annieann cried into her hands.

"Was there any contact with your dad?"

"He'd call once in a while. Mom would end up screaming at him, and Devon refused to talk to him. If I was lucky enough to take the call, he sounded sad, but he told me he was getting through it, and he would be home one of these days. I can't believe he's dead," she wailed.

"Would I be able to speak to your mother?"

"I'll try to set it up."

"I'm glad he's dead," said the emotionless Mrs. Domingo.

"Do you know where your husband was living?"

"No, and I don't care! The day he walked out of this house was the day I disowned him. He meant nothing to me after that."

Devon had the same attitude as his mother and he had even less to say. McKenna also verified their alibi's and they definitely weren't anywhere near the bludgeoned husband and father.

"Good, you're back! Do you have some breaking news for us?" the boss asked.

"I'm afraid not, but at least we know that his family didn't do it. We just have to concentrate on who *did* do it."

Wilkashire turned abruptly on his heel and stalked into his office.

"Ah, here it is," McKenna chuckled, "my drip, drip, drip." She recounted the events of her investigation. *How did things go so wrong? What's the matter with parents anyway? Oh, no, I must go and visit my mother soon. I wonder if she sits in jail and contemplates how bad it was to put me in those situations of stealing for her. Is that how she wanted me to grow up? What happened to teaching kids right from wrong? How come the foster parents seemed to know how to bring up kids but my own mother didn't?*

"Stop!" she told herself. With that command, the drip faded into her subconscious, and her dreams became the flooding waters of Lone Moon Creek trying to devour her mother while she was desperately trying to save her.

"Hello, Mother."

"Hey, baby girl. How's my precious one?"

"Your 'precious one' is OK."

"Just OK?"

"I'm working a hard case right now—a murder."

"A murder? Now those people are really bad. I never did anything that bad," whined Meredith.

McKenna stared into her mother's face, the luster was gone; the wrinkles were starting to show; years of being incarcerated weren't adding any beauty to her once youthful face.

"Mother, do you think you actually did anything wrong?" McKenna asked.

"No, I don't!" she said emphatically. "You were always in good hands. I never would have put you in any danger. When we had a bundle of money, didn't you and I always go on the greatest vacations?"

McKenna sighed. Her mother would never realize that she did anything wrong.

Meredith could see that her daughter was going into one of her contemplative moods; she didn't want that.

"You knew I loved you, right?"

"Yes, I did know that," McKenna replied.

"Well, then there you are! Let's talk about something else; let's talk about that awful murder!"

McKenna couldn't help but laugh.

"There, now you're getting into a better mood. That's my girl!"

McKenna sketched out the basic details of the case while her mother listened intently.

"Mm," Meredith uttered, scrunching her face like she always did when she was scheming. "I would say," she began slowly, "that you need to look at someone who is totally out of the realm of suspicion; someone close to the case, but in everyone else's eyes, a million miles away from being the culprit."

McKenna was used to getting these riddles from her mother. Her mother thought differently than most people.

"Well, I have no idea what you are talking about, but it sounded good. By the way, do you ever see Mrs. Calderon in here?"

"Hell no! She's over in that unit with the stupid people."

"Mother, that's not nice."

"She was the one who turned on me, wasn't she?"

"Well, I've got to go. I'll see you next time."

"I think we better shove this case into the cold case cellar," Mr. Wilkashire pronounced at the next meeting.

"But, boss," McKenna interrupted, "we can solve it; we just need more time."

"I don't think so, McKenna. We've followed every lead we could think of," Edmund said.

"Yeah, right," concurred Dexter, "these homeless cases are the worst to try and get any leads. It's like two ships passing in the night; there are no clues."

"But, but—"

"McKenna, get real," Millicent almost snarled. "When there are no survivors who care, then we don't care that much either."

"That's terrible," the newest investigator quipped.

"But you have to understand, McKenna, they're out there on the street; they're asking for it. They're probably expecting to get robbed or beaten or killed every time they bed down on public property," Willard added unemotionally.

"But we can't let such things go on! Criminals have to pay for their misdeeds," McKenna shouted as she quickly wiped the sweat from her forehead with the back of her hand. She thought of her mother and herself.

"Are you all right, over there?" Bob Wilkashire asked.

McKenna motioned him to go on with the meeting as she reached for the water pitcher.

He continued, "I don't think Jim Field is going to give us any more time. He said to wind it up and go on to another case. Check with me tomorrow, and I'll clue you in on what's next on the docket. Sorry, McKenna. We can't solve them all."

"Excuse me, Mr. Field, may I ask you something?"

"Certainly, McKenna."

"I think if you gave us more time, we could solve the homicide case."

"Of course you can have more time, those things are never easy. That case won't be closed for a long, long time."

Where is it? Where's my rhythmic drip, drip, drip? Don't tell me, it finally got fixed! Miracle of miracles.

McKenna giggled to herself. She covered her mouth, not wanting the quiet room to hear her giggling. The thought of that made her laugh harder. It wasn't long before her shoulders heaved with the silent, mouth-covered laugh. Tears streamed from her eyes before she could get herself under control.

Ooo, I guess I needed that. Now she could sleep.

But no, thoughts of Daisy and Wilson and Jacqui and the Abernathy's and Scott and Janine floated through her mind.

I got to meet a lot of good people in my lifetime. I wonder what they are all doing now. I wonder if they remember me. Oh yeah, they would remember me.

I guess I'll have to break the news to the team that, yes, we are going to keep working on…

"Oh my dear God," McKenna said as she sat upright in her bed. The words her mother said resonated in her mind. *That riddle. It was more than a riddle.* Now she thought she understood it.

"I don't know what she's doing; she's been in Jim Field's office for two hours," Millicent said, steaming.

"She's barely been any help to us on our new case. She claims she's always too busy on something. On what? That's what I want to know!" Dexter growled as he slammed his coffee cup, making it slop over the top.

"I surely don't like it either," Bob Wilkashire added. "I keep asking Jim what's going on, and he says he's got her working on something special. It's giving me the creeps. Do you suppose he's prepping her to take over my job?"

"Naw, she's no boss; she thinks she knows it all."

"We might have to get rid of her," Wilkashire whispered to the others.

"Rid?" They all said in unison.

"I've got it!" The boss motioned for the investigators, minus one, to huddle close. "I've got the goods on her," he beamed as he held a folder close to his chest. "Listen to this!"

Eyes rolled and eyes widened while eyebrows raised; jaws dropped while mouths opened; arms crossed while weight shifted from one leg to the other.

"Yes! We've got her!" Millicent squealed.

"I'll set up a meeting with Jim Field and ask that McKenna be there too. Her goose is going to be cooked when he finds out about her background."

"We're here for the meeting, Bob. Do you have something that's bothering you?" Jim asked.

"Yes, as a matter of fact we all think you should be aware of something."

"Great, what is it, Bob?"

Bob straightened his shoulders, readying himself for the proclamation of a lifetime. He was radiant. "We think you should know about McKenna's criminal history."

"I already know about her life as a child. She was not the criminal. She was a minor," Jim replied.

"But... but..."

"In fact, Mr. Wilkashire, there are two policemen in the hallway who are coming in while I tell you about McKenna's findings."

"McKenna's findings?"

"Arrest him, officer. Good job, McKenna," Mr. Field said as he shook her hand.

"What's happening? Why was Bob arrested? What did he do? Where is he going?" Millicent's staccato questions filled the room.

"Come to find out, Bob Wilkashire and the murder victim were half-brothers. There had been a long-standing war between the two for decades. Mr. Domingo's family never even knew about this half-brother."

The four team members gasped, and McKenna was promoted to the new headquarters in Monroe, where she knew she would be keeping her nose to the grindstone.

The End

"Isn't it exciting to have a radio station in Lone Moon
Creek, Marjory?"
"It's not fair."
"What's not fair?"
"That you won't let me listen to that 'telephone show.'"

ᴄ◈Chapter Seven◈ᴐ

Tomorrow's Another Day

"**G**o ahead. You're on the air."

"Hello, Janice? Thank you for taking my call."

"Yes. What's your question?"

"It's about infidelity. Shall I just throw him out of the house?"

"Absolutely! Get rid of the bum!" Janice looked over at her coworker. "What do you think, Carletta?"

"Um, well, a... maybe."

"And there you have it, listeners. We both agree. *Can* him."

Carletta looked sheepishly at her boss, wishing she had spoken out.

"You're on the air, go ahead."

"Janice?"

"That's me!"

"Janice, I have a problem. My husband confided in me that he has been using a scheme to embezzle money from his company. I wondered how we could afford so many nice things for the past two years. Should I insist that he stop?"

"No way! If he's smart enough to pull it off, it must mean that the others are too dumb to catch on. You like all the nice things he can buy now, don't you?

"Well yes, but—"

"Mums the word, sugar. Don't you agree, Carletta?"

"Well, actually she ought to—"

"Great! It's settled, and, sugar, buy him something nice too!"

"Janice," Carletta said pleadingly, "I'm not—"

"Hell-o-o-o, listener! We are on a roll tonight. What's your question?"

"My son is twenty-eight and still lives at home. He stays in his room all the time except when a car pulls up out front and beeps the horn. He never talks to us. What should we do?"

"Do? You've got a dream kid there, lady! He never bugs you; what more could you want? Let sleeping dogs lie. Don't fix what's not broken. Do you need any more clichés? That kid is the best. Right, Carletta?"

"I was thinking that perhaps—"

"You're the best, Carletta. I think you're going to last longer than the last three did."

Carletta averted Janice's eyes as she thought about the necessity of the job in paying for her college courses.

"We're here for you! What's your problem?"

"My sister is only four, and she steals my things all the time. Every day when I get home from school, something is missing. Sometimes I spend hours searching the house or the yard, and sometimes I never find it. My parents think it's funny. What do you think?"

"She's four; she's still a baby. Lighten up, girlfriend. Is she really doing any harm? How important is your stuff in the grand scheme of things? Right, Carletta?"

"I don't think—"

"That's right, and we are out of time. We'll be here tomorrow night, same time, same station. So long! Great show, Carletta. You like working here don't you?"

"Well—"

"I'm glad. Gotta run!"

"Hi, Grandpa. You're still up!"

"Thought you might want some hot chocolate."

"Ooo would I ever. I don't think those buses have heat anymore," Carletta said.

"Someday, you'll have a car with all the heat you want, honey."

"I know, Grandpa. I'm not complaining."

"You never do," replied Gramps as he touched her shoulder.

"Well, did you listen to the show tonight?"

"I did. I did."

"And?"

"Well," Gramps began diplomatically, "that Janice lady sure fires off her answers pretty quick. I mean without much thought. How about you puttin' in some of your thoughts?"

"I try, Grandpa, but she doesn't give me time to say much, plus I don't know about my answers."

"You mean they'd be about as opposite to Janice's as day is to night?"

"Right, and I don't want to get fired. I need that job."

Gramps cast his eyes downward. "I'm sorry, Carletta, that there was nothing much to give you for your education."

"Oh, Grandpa, you've done so much for me, for all of us. You held us together and taught us right from wrong."

"Well, I know I would not have let you steal your sister's things when you were four years old." He laughed.

"Could you believe Janice's answer?"

"Yeah, she had some beauts tonight. Can you just picture me letting Danny or John lie around their rooms at twenty-eight?"

That bought about a much-needed laugh for Carletta. She was the youngest of seven—the one who lost her mother at childbirth and her dad five years ago to cancer. Her grandma was buried last year, so now there was just her and her Grandpa in the house. Six siblings were out on their own: some with families, some building their careers.

"There you go, sweet potato," Grandpa interjected as he placed the mug of hot chocolate under her nose.

"Grandpa, how would you have answered that question about the husband who was unfaithful to his wife? Do you think he should be thrown out?"

"Oh, Carletta," Gramps answered thoughtfully. "That Janice character had none of the facts. No one can make such judgments like she did. When a man and a woman have such serious problems, there is always forgiveness, always hope, and always prayer."

"You mean the way you and Grandma prayed for Emily and her husband?"

"That's right, honey. We prayed our heads off."

The two drank in silence, as if the generation gap was not a gap at all.

"Well, tomorrow's another day," Gramps offered the same good-night salute that he always proclaimed.

"Good night, Gramps. I'll be here studying for a while, and thanks for waiting up for me."

"You're on. How can we help you?"

"Oh, Janice, I'm so glad I got through; I'm at my wit's end. You see, my husband treats his children better than he treats mine. It's not fair. After all, we live in the same house. What should I do?"

"Throw him and his kids out! You don't need that aggravation. Right, Carletta?"

"Wait a minute. Don't be as rash as to—"

"There! You've heard from the experts! Hello, you're on."

"I've never called before. I'm very embarrassed."

"Now, sir, don't be embarrassed. We've heard it all. Right, Carletta? Tell us sir."

"Well, every Saturday night my wife goes out with her girlfriends and stays out half the night and then is useless for all of the next day. What should I do?"

"Let her have some fun. Let Saturday night be her night out. Sunday isn't important anymore; it's not a family day like it used to be. You know that's right, don't you, Carletta?"

"Janice, wait, I want to—"

"There you go, sir. Get with these modern times."

"Janice, can we talk?" Carletta implored.

"Sure, oops, call coming in! Hello? Hello? Ma'am, you'll have to speak up. Are you crying? Stop crying, ma'am. Are you saying your children are forcing you to go into a nursing home? But it's your house? Now listen, ma'am, it sounds like you'd be better off in a nursing home. Your kids can't take on the responsibility of caring for you; they have lives of their own. Oh my, that's a wrap good people out in radio land. Tune in tomorrow. Carletta and I will be waiting for you!"

"Excuse me, Janice, can we talk?" Carletta said.

"Not tonight, hon. I have a late dinner date with Stewart. Bye."

"Grandpa, you've been dozing in the chair!"

"I guess I have." The old man laughed as he pulled the lever of the recliner upward. "They always play that classical music after your program. Puts me to sleep sometimes."

"I think people need something relaxing after Janice gets through with her fire crackers."

"They're *fire crackers* all right," Grandpa agreed as he shuffled to the kitchen in his worn oversized slippers.

"Hot chocolate?"

"Hot chocolate," Carletta said.

"I heard you trying to break in with your comments to Janice. Your voice is getting more and more assertive."

"I try, Gramps, but as you can probably tell, she doesn't want my opinion."

"Very true, very true. You know, your sister Athena was a little like that."

"Athena had opinions like Janice?" Carletta gasped as her spoon swirled so quickly, a splash of chocolate flew to the table.

"No not that bad," Gramps said with a laugh. "But when your dad tried to insert his opinion, she would talk faster and faster. She knew what he was going to say, and she didn't want to hear it."

"I never knew that."

"You were little."

"And I knew better than to steal her stuff," teased Carletta.

"That's for sure! And sweet tater, tomorrow is another day. Good night."

Carletta opened her book, but her mind was on the past. She probably had missed a lot of what was going on with her older brothers and sisters. The household always seemed so busy, and it took Dad and Gramps and Gram to "corral" the kids and keep things running—not always smoothly, but running. She knew her dad struggled, but his parents had a kind, soft approach to things that gained the respect of her siblings and herself. Somehow they made it work. Why couldn't Janice ever give advice other than kick 'em, stomp 'em, and throw 'em out, and steal on the way?

"No, Janice, I don't think that's the thing to do," Carletta spoke assertively after the host of the show advised a young woman to return the clothes that she had already worn.

"Well, she speaks!" Janice proclaimed, trying to make her audience think she was welcoming Carletta's opinion. Only Carletta could see Janice's face. Carletta lowered her eyes and felt the redness creep up her neck.

Carletta didn't make any more proclamations that evening, even though she sat and listened to advice that curdled her blood.

"I need to get out of there, Grandpa; that job is not for me."

"Maybe you're right, honey. It seems to be a no-win situation with that Janice. I wouldn't even tune in to that garbage if you weren't on the show. Well, tomorrow's another day. Off to bed with me."

"Thanks for waiting up, Grandpa. Tomorrow night might be the last night that you have to listen to all that nonsense."

The old man gave a wave as he went up the stairs.

Carletta was met at the radio station by her panic-stricken producer. "Carletta, you've got to do the show! Janice has been in an accident!"

"What?"

"Yes, you. Get in there. Hurry!"

Carletta forgot to breathe; she forgot who she was; she forgot to put on her headphones until the producer ran in and plunked them on her head.

"Hello, Janice?"

"No, this is Carletta," she answered sheepishly.

"Well, whoever, I'm in a real pickle. Did you hear me? A real pickle."

"Yes, I'm listening," Carletta answered timidly.

"Well, this is it. I want to un-invite my father to my wedding because he won't give me everything I want. I want a $50,000 wedding, and he says he'll only give me $10,000. Can you believe it? My mother says he can afford it. I hate him, the old tightwad. Should I tell him to hit the road?"

Carletta sat with her eyebrows raised and her month poised to say something, but nothing came out until the producer banged on the glass partition.

"Well, ma'am," she started, her mind flashed to how Janice would respond, "I think you need to seriously think about this. It sounds like you're ready to make a very hasty decision that you may regret for the rest of your life. Let me ask you something. Would you be more married if you spent $50,000 instead of $10,000?"

"Well, of course I would," the woman snapped at her. "I'd have more guests, more flowers, a bigger cake, a bigger dress. You know, all that stuff."

"Yes," replied Carletta as she sat up a little straighter, "all that stuff. And when you and the groom make the covenant before God, won't it be the words, the promise, and the love in your hearts that makes it a marriage?"

"Huh?"

"I just wanted you to consider what a marriage really is. It's not all the extras, the trimmings, the expensive things, and maybe your father knows that!"

Carletta couldn't believe she spoke that strongly. She forgot to breathe again, waiting for the response.

"Well, you are worthless! I wish Janice had answered the phone; she would have agreed with me."

As the line clicked, Carletta knew that Janice would have told the bride-to-be to get rid of her father or to make his life miserable until he gave in. The novice knew that she had given her best response and felt an aura of confidence creep into her microphone.

"Hello, Janice?"

"No, it's Carletta tonight."

"I am livid, Carletta, just livid."

"What's the problem?" she asked, breathing this time.

"My grandfather passed away recently and..."

Carletta gasped!

"Hello, hello, are you still there?"

"Oh, I'm sorry. We had a… a little technical problem. Please go on."

"As I said, Grandpa passed away and in his will, he split up the money equally between us three grandsons. Now here's the rub: Tim doesn't need the money. He's a priest, and they're supposed to be poor. Teddy is still unmarried, a real playboy; he's already got everything—"

"And you?" Carletta asked quickly.

"I'm the one who needs it—all of it. I have five children and times aren't easy you know! How can I go to court to fight the will?"

"Why do you think your grandfather set up his will like he did?" Carletta asked.

"He was always like that; if one of us got something, we all got something. No one got more; no one got less. But that's when we were kids; we're adults now."

"Did he love you all the same?"

"Yeah, sure he did."

"Do you love all your five kids the same?"

"Of course I do."

"You know, even if Tim and Teddy don't want or need the money, they can decide what they want to do with it. Maybe they'll donate it to the needy or set up a trust for your kids or just blow it. Your grandfather wanted them to have something that he probably saved a lifetime for. It's theirs. Are you starting to understand?"

"Yeah, I understand all right. I understand you don't know sh…"

Carletta sighed as she went to the commercials. She didn't dare look through the glass at her producer when suddenly the intercom snapped on and Carletta jumped as she swung her chair toward the glass.

"I want to see you after the show," Mr. Gordon said sternly.

"Yes, sir," Carletta said respectfully. *Oh well,* she thought, *even if he fires me, I'll give it my best on my last night here.*

"Good evening, you're on the radio."

"What's the matter with this show tonight?"

"Oh, I'm sorry, ma'am. The regular hostess isn't here and I'm filling in."

Click.

"Hello, I'm here. Hello?"

"I'm scared," said a tiny little voice.

"What's the matter, honey?"

"My mother has been sleeping all day, and now it's night, and she's still sleeping and I can't wake her up."

"Do you know who to call when you need help?" Carletta asked.

"Ah-huh, we learned it at preschool. We 'pose to call 119."

"No honey, it's 911. You put the big number first."

"Oh! I been calling the wrong number for a long time."

"You call 911, OK? And if you have trouble, you call me right back, OK?"

"OK."

"Mr. Gordon," Carletta used the intercom on him this time, "if this number comes up again, break through to me right away."

"Will do."

She was glad that he had been keeping abreast of the calls.

Carletta carried on with the show for the last hour. "You wanted to see me, Mr. Gordon?"

"Yes, Carletta, sit down. I've heard that Janice won't be coming back; her injuries are pretty serious. Would you consider hosting the show until you get your college degree?"

"Me?"

"Yes, you! I've listened to the whole two hours tonight, and you were fantastic!"

"I was?"

"I've been trying to turn Janice's opinions around for over a year to no avail. Some people like her approach, but we've been losing our advertisers, and I'm tired of making excuses to the mayor and the clergy and teachers and parents."

"I really need this job, Mr. Gordon. I will certainly try to give the people the best advice I can," Carletta said.

"Welcome aboard, Carletta."

"Thank you, Mr. Gordon."

Carletta ran from the bus stop to her house. She couldn't wait to see her Grandpa. *Oh nuts*, she thought, *he didn't wait up tonight.*

Carletta walked into the dark house. Before her fingers could grasp the knob of the lamp, the ceiling light flashed on, and she was welcomed by the feeble fluttering of crepe paper strung from wall to wall and a big sign that read, GOOD JOB CARLETTA.

"Grandpa! Did you do this?"

"I sure did. You deserve a celebration after that show!"

"Grandpa, I got Janice's job. They want me!"

"I bet they do; you were terrific! Now let's toast with our hot chocolate. Here's to you, honey."

"And here's to you, Grandpa."

They discussed the whole show before Gramps said, "Well, tomorrow's another day."

THE END

"MARJORY, DO YOU WANT TO RIDE OUT TO THE OLD COUNTRY
CEMETERY AND HELP ME PUT FLOWERS ON THE GRAVES?"
"No!"
"WHY NOT?"
"BECAUSE I WANT TO KNOW WHERE MY MOTHER AND FATHER ARE,
AND THEY'RE NOT IN THE CEMETERY. THEY'RE NOWHERE,
NOWHERE, NOWHERE, NOWHERE!"
"MARJORY, HUSH."

Chapter Eight
WAR EFFORTS

"Here you go, Mrs. Lin, fresh strawberries, tea, and writing paper."

"Thank you, Cathy, you're an angel."

"Anytime, Mrs. Lin. It's no trouble whatsoever."

"I just don't feel confident driving anymore. What a pain it is to get old."

"It happens to everyone, Mrs. Lin. Someday, I'll be saying the same thing."

"I suppose you will. I suppose you will," Mrs. Lin reflected.

Cathy opened the box of writing paper. "I hope you like this. I thought it was the prettiest they had at the store."

"Oh, Cathy, it's beautiful. I love the little purple violets!"

"I see you have the list of local armed services people that was published in the newspaper. I like the way they included the photographs too."

"Yes. That damnable war! The least I can do is write to our boys and girls who are over there."

"It seems like everyone in town is sending cards and notes; we all feel so helpless," Cathy said.

"I know," Mrs. Lin said quietly as she gently touched a violet on her new writing paper before beginning her first letter of the day:

Dear Brad,

Greetings from Lone Moon Creek!

I just wanted to tell you how proud I am of you.

I'm not sure if you know me. I live out on County Route 48 between the Taylor's farm and Edwin's Veterinary Service. I was your dad's fifth grade teacher years ago! I'm sure he's proud to have such a brave marine for a son.

I remember when my five brothers all went into the service during World War II. My mother and father and we girls kept them in our thoughts and prayers every minute. You boys and girls are no different. Stay strong. War is never a good thing. I'm sorry we adults didn't get things straightened out in the world by now. It's so unfortunate that you young people have to go in and try to bring justice where we couldn't. Also, it just amazes me how you stepped forward and vowed to defend goodness and liberty—not only for our own country but also for the sake of other people. Where would we be without our soldiers?

You wouldn't think an old lady would get so riled up, would you? Well, I merely wanted to wish you well and tell you that we are all thinking about you.

      Stay well, Brad. We're all praying for a quick solution to peace.

Love,

Mrs. Sarah Lin

Dear Christine,

Hello! Greetings from Lone Moon Creek!

      I saw your name in the paper and your picture, too! As soon as I saw your photo, I said to myself, I know that girl! It took me awhile to go through my school handbook but I figured it out! I went to your mom and dad's wedding. I was teaching seventh grade Latin when they were in my class. You look exactly like your mother!

      I had no idea you had gone into the service! You girls today are so brave! We never would have thought of such a thing. I remember we stayed home during World War II and milked the cows, shoveled out the barn, fixed fences, but we never thought about going off to war! I know now that there were lots of women who joined up. You know? I think we could have done it; we were as strong as men, and we worked as hard as men. I guess the mind-set of the world changes; people can do what's expected of them.

      I heard on the news that your ship is in the war zone now. How very courageous you must be. I've only seen those ships in the movies. After the Second World War, my brother would sit for hours and tell us about his experiences on the ship. That's as close as I ever got to a real war!

I wish this war could have been averted; I'm sorry that evil has been allowed to consume pockets of our world. Bless you all for trying to squelch the evil and replace it with hope for all people. Everyone needs hope.

Oh my, Christine, I didn't mean to go on and on! I do want you to know, however, that we're all thinking of you, and may God watch over you.

Love,

Mrs. Sarah Lin

Dear Bryan,

I can't believe it! I just got off the phone with your dad, and he said, yes, you are his "Air Boy" son! I wasn't surprised that you would be in the air force.

You probably don't know this, but when I was teaching the combination third and fourth grade, your dad just about drove me up the wall with his paper airplanes! It seemed that making paper planes was all he thought about. I was just about at my wit's end when the principal suggested I make a "field day" out of your dad's passion for airplanes. So to make a long story short, I incorporated airplanes into reading, arithmetic, spelling, art, writing, music, history, science—everything! We even had a K–6 paper airplane flying contest. I think it was the highlight of our year! I know it was for your dad.

He told me you're an officer already. He's so very proud of you, Bryan. He also said you plan on making a career of the service. I had one brother who stayed in after the war (WWII). He made a good life for himself and his family.

I've been invited to your parent's home to see your collection of model airplanes. (Actually, I think your dad implied that he had about as many as you do! I wouldn't doubt it!)

I'm sorry you have to use your skills on something as awful as war, but I think I speak for everyone when I thank you for protecting our country's freedoms and establishing freedoms for people around the world.

I remember volunteering after the war in our town's "Observational Tower." I recall being up there and praying I wouldn't spot a foreign plane. (See how brave I was!) I vividly remember, also, the drills we had in school where the students had to sit under their desks or along the walls of the hallways during the Cold War. It really gave me the willies, even though I wouldn't show my fear in front of the pupils, of course.

Well, my goodness, how I do go on and on! My thoughts and prayers are with you.

Love,

Mrs. Sarah Lin

Dear Jonathan,

Your grandmother said you love to get mail, so here goes! She also said that all the young girls are writing to you but "maybe someone (me) with more maturity" would make for a nice balance! Can you believe it? Thank goodness she's my lifetime friend!

All kidding aside, I know how proud she is of you and how scared too. It's not easy to get to where we are in life and watch our dear ones sent one by one into war. It makes us realize what our folks went through. Wars never stop coming, it seems. What a shame. With all our intelligence, with all our ... well ... with nothing does man have the capability of controlling others' thoughts. My father used to say that WWII would be the war that ended all wars. Look how many we've had since.

If we truly can go in and alleviate servitude, I suppose it is justified. But sometimes I wonder what's going on? Your grandma and I, we kind of sit back and put our trust in the younger generation. All we can do is pray for your judgment and your inheritance of knowing how to discern good from evil. If nothing else, we as parents and grandparents hope you know how to sift out the evil and keep the goodness.

Be sure to write to her; she worries so. And I know all the young girls think you're a hero, but we old girls do too! There. How's that for balance?

Love,

Mrs. Sarah Lin

"Good morning, Mrs. Lin. Do you need anything from town today?"

"Good morning, Cathy. How sweet of you to stop. Actually, I do need stamps. I thought I had five or six more, but I can't find them. It seems I spend half my day looking for things. Would you mind stopping at the post office? Then I don't have to wait until this afternoon for the mailman."

"Oh, I'm going there anyway! My scout troop prepared a care package for the servicemen and women."

"Oh, how nice! That was a wonderful project for them; they need to know compassion. Could you put stamps on these letters and mail them out this morning?"

"Sure. My goodness, you've been busy!" Cathy exclaimed as she saw the four envelopes.

"Well, I figured out who four of the people are," Mrs. Lin said as she handed Cathy the newspaper. "The ones I have checked off are the ones I know. Is there anyone else I should know?"

"Well, yes! This is Dan from up the road." When Mrs. Lin had no reaction, Cathy went on. "You know those three kids and the mother who are always out riding their bikes? This is the father; Jenny's husband."

"Oh, my goodness! I had no idea he was in the service!"

"Yes, that's why they moved here three months ago; they knew Dan was going to be on military duty for an extended amount of time, and they wanted the kids in a safer environment."

"I will definitely write to him. And poor Jenny. I'm going to give her a call, too. Women need other women during these trying times."

"You're a good soul, Mrs. Lin." Cathy's kind smile accentuated the bluest eyes the teacher had seen since little Cecilia Johannsen of third grade.

"I don't know about that, dear. I didn't even know my neighbors from up the road!"

"Do you need anything else from town, Mrs. Lin?"

"No, just the stamps. Thank you. Oh wait! I only have two aspirin left. Could you pick up a bottle for me?"

"Sure. Have you been bothered with your aches and pains again?" Cathy asked.

"Oh, yes, a new ache or a pain comes every day; it's the earned privilege of living this long, you know!" Mrs. Lin said with a smile.

"I'll be back in a little while," Cathy called out as she and her blue eyes sailed past the abundantly full perennial garden.

Dear Dan,

I received a nice surprise this morning. You and I are almost neighbors! I live in the white house between the Vets and Taylor's big farm (which used to be my family's farm years ago). I understand those are your children and wife who ride their bikes past here. I'm going to call your wife and invite her to visit. The war must be terribly hard on you all. I'm sorry there has to be such a thing as war. I know everyone in Lone Moon Creek will keep you and your family in their thoughts and prayers. They'll be good to your family too. There are a lot of caring people here. I'm sure you won't be sorry about moving to our neck of the woods.

I was a teacher at the local school for years and years. I think I taught every grade at one time or another! Of course, years ago, there were no teachers for gym, music, computer, art, and so forth. We did it all. Well, not computers! What a hoot when I think about it now! I imagine your kids have told you many things about the school already. It's a great environment and the teachers are super, if I must say so myself!

Cathy Betts from up the road (another neighbor of ours) says she has met you and your family. She will be a wonderful help to your wife. Cathy is so kind and thoughtful. In fact, she has a wonderful scout group and knows all the connections for other groups too!

Well, Dan, I'm glad we got to meet (in a roundabout way), and I'll write again after I've met your family.

Be careful over there. We know America has the very best, and we're proud of you.

Love,

Mrs. Sarah Lin

"Welcome, Jenny! I'm so glad you could come! And who is this little darling?"

"This is our Angela; she's two years old."

"Oh, this is the little one who rides on the back of your bicycle!"

"Yes, we ride double." Jenny laughed as she swooped a blond curl off to the side of Angela's forehead.

"I have a basket of toys just perfect for little ones. Would you like to see the toys, Angela?" Mrs. Lin asked gently.

Angela buried her face in her mother's shoulder, and Jenny said in a whisper, "It'll take her a few minutes, but then she'll venture over to the basket."

"I'm sure she will," the veteran teacher spoke confidently. "We'll have our tea right here by the toys."

"Tell me about your boys," Mrs. Lin said as she stirred her tea.

"Dan Jr. is nine and Tommy is seven."

"Second and fourth grades?"

"That's right! And so far, they have adjusted beautifully to their new school. I cried the entire morning of their first day, however."

"I know what you mean, dear. I used to have mothers standing out by my classroom door crying their eyes out!"

"I am just so stressed over Dan being in the war," Jenny said.

"Of course you are, Jenny; it's an awful thing for you and your family to go through. We can only hope that after this is finished, the families over there will be able to have peaceful and good lives too."

"I know," Jenny uttered. "Just what I've seen on TV about the conditions. It is horrendous. Dan says the troops have to go in to bring change and restore the country to its people. Such evil. Such evil." Jenny started to cry.

Mrs. Lin and Angela hurried to her side, the young one and the old one both hugging the young mother, trying to take her sorrow away.

"Mommy is OK, Angie; see Mommy is smiling. Here's a cookie for you, honey."

The young one was easily convinced, but the old one knew better.

"Sorry, Mrs. Lin. I go into these little crying spells at the drop of a hat, it seems."

"Don't be sorry, dear. I know how you're feeling; in fact, I want you to promise me that you will come to my house whenever you're feeling blue. The children too."

"Thank you, Mrs. Lin. I appreciate that. I tell you, there are days when—"

"I know, dear, I know."

Mrs. Lin watched from the front steps as little blond curls bounced out from under a tiny helmet and in front, she admired the larger helmet, which held a pretty head filled with the agonies of war.

"Dear God," Mrs. Lin prayed, "have mercy on them."

Dear Mrs. Lin,

Can't write much. Just wanted to thank you for your letter. I can't believe you were my father's teacher! Boy! You must have some memories. He always told me he was a cutup in school and didn't want me to be that way. How bad was he?

That must have been something to have five brothers go to war. Your mother must have been a basket case; I know mine is, and it's just me!

Thank you for all your good wishes; things like that mean a lot to us guys.

Write again if you can.

From Brad

Dear Mrs. Lin,

What a delight it was to read your letter! I know I look a lot like my mom when she was younger—for you to detect that was really rad! You've got a good memory. But Latin? What did they take that for?

Anyway, isn't it something how they liked each other all through school, got married, and are as happy, still, as two clams? My friends can't believe it. You know? I miss them. It's pretty miserable over here, waiting and waiting on the ship, not knowing what's going to happen. But we're helping each other keep our morale up. We have a strong belief that we're going to bring some relief to these people. I certainly hope so. I don't want to be here in vain.

You're right about women's roles. I guess you have really seen big changes in your lifetime. Sometimes I wonder if they were all for the best.

Well, its lights out, and I don't want to miss the chaplain's good-night prayer. I would consider it bad luck if I did, and that's one thing we don't need.

Write again if you can.

Bye now,

Christine

"Yoo-hoo, Mrs. Lin. It's Cathy."

"Hi, dear. Come in, come in. How are you today?"

"I'm fine, but how are you?"

"I'm actually feeling better now that I'm on this new medication."

"Thank goodness. You had me worried!"

"If I could just get my lungs cleared out, I know I'd feel fine again."

"How are your aches and pains?" Cathy asked.

"Oh, they're just a part of me, like an arm or a leg. My old bones are wearing down, that's all. I'm just a soul pulling along a body."

"Well, that's a different way of looking at it!"

"Yes, when you're old, you have a license to come up with different thoughts." Mrs. Lin laughed as she waved her letters in her hand. "Do you have time to read these?"

"Sure. Gosh, sounds like they really enjoyed hearing from you."

"I thought so too! I'm so glad; I don't know what else I can do for them."

"Do you need anything from the store today?"

"I hate to bother you, but I am all out of flour and raisins. I've been trying to have fresh cookies for the kids when they go biking past here. It's gotten so they stop to visit almost every day now that it's summer. I just love it!"

"I can do that. Anything else?" Cathy asked.

"Maybe some aspirin. The doctor said I should take it when the pain gets bad."

"Can't he prescribe something stronger?"

"Sure he could, but as I told him, I'm a tough old bird; I don't want to rely on that strong stuff."

"OK, see you shortly."

Dear Brad,

Thank you for your letter. I heard on the TV that mail was not going in or out for quite a while, so I was so pleased that you received mine and even more thrilled that I received yours!

Your dad and I have communicated on the phone a few times. He always says, "Now don't tell Brad all the mischief I used to get into in fifth grade." Of course, I really can't remember any of it, so I always said innocently, "Now, Joe, what might that have been?" He laughs and tells me all sorts of things! I duped him, Brad! Can you believe it? I laugh every time I get off the phone. For starters, he put Limburger cheese in the radiator. Then he brought two rabbits to school in his satchel, also a snake, a frog, and a lizard, which, of course, all escaped; he would leave notes from the "principal" on classmates desks. One girl became hysterical when she read she had been expelled. He used to put sardines into lunch boxes! Oh, he was a character all right! I couldn't help but love him though; he never did it in a mean-spirited way. I think he just liked to get a reaction out of people.

Now don't snitch on me to your dad!

As always, Lone Moon and the nation are holding you in their hearts. Semper Fi.

Love,

Mrs. Sarah Lin

"I'm back, Mrs. Lin."

"Oh, good. I just finished this letter to Brad."

"I heard some sad news at the store," Cathy said slowly as she sank into a chair with her blue eyes flooded.

"My dear, what happened?"

"Trina Armer's son was killed in the war," she cried.

"Oh, no, no. The woman who works at the insurance agency?"

"Yes," Cathy sobbed. "I just saw her last night at our Den Leader's meeting."

"Oh, Cathy, I'm so sorry. What can we do?"

"I don't know. I don't know."

Dear Mrs. Lin,

Thank you for your letter. I've had it for quite some time but we couldn't send anything out, as you might well suspect.

You've probably gotten to my parent's house by now to see the model airplanes. Quite a display, right?

I loved your story of my dad in school and his paper airplanes! To this day, we'll sit and fold paper for competitions. My mom just throws her hands up in the air and leaves the room. You know, I sure hope there will be a tomorrow so I can do that with him again.

We've been on many flying maneuvers, which include dropping bombs; I hate that part, Mrs. Lin. I really hate it.

Thank you for your prayers and concern. I think that's what keeps us going.

Take care and let me know what you think of the model planes!

Sincerely,

Bryan

"Hi, Mrs. Lin," came a voice sailing across the gladiolas to the lawn chair.

"Hello, children. Hi, Jenny! How is everybody today?"

"Great!" said Dan Jr.

"Great!" said Tommy.

"Great!" said little Angela.

"Well, that's good. How about a *great* cookie?"

The troop went into the house and directly to the cookie jar.

"Why don't you kids sit out on the steps while Mrs. Lin and I visit for a minute," Jenny said. "Boys, watch Angela."

"How are things going, dear?" Mrs. Lin asked as she touched Jenny's arm.

"Oh, I don't know, they're going. That's about all I can say."

"It's so hard on wives and children, isn't it?"

"Yeah," Jenny said.

"I wish I knew how to tell you to be strong, but I'm no example to follow," Mrs. Lin said sadly.

"What do you mean?"

"Well, I was no shining example when my brothers were in the war, or when my husband was in the Korean War, or when my son was sent to Vietnam."

"Oh, Mrs. Lin, you've really had your share of experiences. I'm sorry for being such a complainer."

"Don't be sorry. We'll get through this somehow."

The two women hugged as women have since the first war in time.

Dear Mrs. Lin,

Thank you for your letter. You're pretty funny! No wonder my grandma likes you so much. I'd have liked to have seen you two in your heyday. See, I know some of those old-time expressions!

Grandma has written to me every single day! Can you believe it? The day they began distributing the mail, I had forty-two letters just from her! My buddies had a big laugh over that until I also showed them all the letters from my girlfriends! They shut up in a big hurry.

Thanks for telling me how great we are, but we're not doing anything that great, just following orders. I hope it's all going to be good for something. It's hard to tell from here.

I hope you keep phoning grandma and visiting with her. She worries too much. Tell her jokes. Keep her laughing and get her mind off the war the best you can. I worry about her.

Jonathan

There goes the school bus, Mrs. Lin thought, as she sat by the kitchen window having her breakfast. Dan Jr. and Tommy would be on it. Angela would be wondering why she couldn't go on the big yellow bus, and Jenny would have tears in her eyes. *Oh dear God, help the children, help the parents, and help the teachers. It's not going to be easy starting the new school year with students who are scared, worried, confused, and some even in mourning.*

"Good morning! My goodness, Mrs. Lin, that cough sounds terrible!" Cathy exclaimed as she hurried over to her friend. The coughing continued; in fact, Mrs. Lin couldn't stop coughing.

"Oh my gosh!" Cathy uttered. "You're coughing up blood! Come on, I'm taking you right to the doctor's."

Mrs. Sarah Lin spent the next three days in the hospital.

"I won't need any health-care nurses coming in. I'll be fine," Cathy heard Mrs. Lin say to the doctor as she went into the hospital room to collect her things.

"Now, Sarah, don't be so stubborn. You're going to need a little help."

"Oh look, Mrs. Lin, you've got a letter from Dan Sr.," chirped Cathy as she brought Mrs. Lin's mail in from the ivy-covered mailbox.

"Oh? Would you read it to me, dear? I need to lie down for a few minutes."

Dear Mrs. Lin,

I love the letters you send me! You have such a special way of describing my children and my darling wife. Your words are the next best thing to being home. I don't know how many times you've brought me to tears or to complete laughter! I like the way you can take a minuscule detail and create a whole scenario around it.

If God is counting the prayers that are ascending from this place and those that are ascending from all around the world, I bet he must be... be... I don't really know what, maybe you've got a good word for it, Mrs. Lin.

I miss my family so much. Keep praying that this will be over soon, and thank you for being such a good neighbor to my family.

Love,

Dan

"How sweet," Mrs. Lin remarked weakly as she looked at the photographs on her dresser.

"Are those family?" Cathy asked.

"Yes, all my men who were in the armed services."

"Is there anything I can do for you before I go, Mrs. Lin?"

"No, dear. I'm just going to rest. I understand the county will be sending someone around every afternoon at one o'clock," Mrs. Lin replied.

"Yes, the schedule is on the kitchen table. I'll see you in the morning."

The autumn metamorphosed into winter; the war continued. Cathy wrote letters, which Mrs. Lin dictated. The nurses, Cathy or Jenny, read the letters to Mrs. Lin. Angela, Tommy, and Dan Jr. brought homemade cookies to their friend, and the winter loomed.

Mrs. Lin wanted to hang on to life until *her boys and girls* came home from the war.

Mrs. Sarah Lin died in the spring and was laid to rest on the apple-blossomed hillside with the four flags fluttering outward as far as possible.

Mrs. Lin was buried in the family plot alongside her two brothers, killed in WW II; her husband, killed in Korea; and her son, killed in Vietnam.

THE END

"Why do people go to a laundromat, Grandma?"
"For all sorts of reasons, Marjory, but most of all to wash
and dry their clothes."
"Can we go to that big one in the city someday?"

Chapter Nine

The Suds Parlor

"Let's go in and bug Stella for a while," Jason, aka Freak, said to his buddies as they neared the Suds Parlor.

"Forget it, Freak. We got chicks waitin' for us at the Shack," Bruno reminded him.

"I thought we could do both; apparently you can't!" Freak laughed as he jumped sideways to slap Bruno on the top of the head.

"Cut it out you two; you're both morons," the tattoo king, Jigger, proclaimed haughtily.

"Oh yeah, Jig-Pig, we'll take you right to the sidewalk and give you a tattoo you'll never forget!"

Jigger spat on the sidewalk and ground it into the concrete with his heavy shoe. "There. That's what I would do to you."

"Knock it off; we're almost there," Antony, aka Sweet Stuff, exclaimed.

"Well, well, well, look what the rats dragged out from the sewer," Carla announced when she saw the gang of troublemakers walking toward her.

"Good things come up from the lower world, sugar face," Freak said defensively. "Now shove over."

"Not in a green moon, ugly."

"Blue, dopey, don't you know anything?"

"Come on," said Bruno, "let's get out of here; these chicks don't deserve us."

"Sweet Stuff can stay," Andrea interjected quietly. "He's nice."

"Ooo," howled the gang. "Sweet Stuff is nice."

"I am not. I'm just as rotten as you are!" Antony Sweet Stuff remarked lamely.

"All right, now what?" Jigger questioned their next stop.

"Let's stop by the Suds Parlor and see old Stella."

"What are you, in love with the old hag, or what?" Bruno teased.

Freak jumped on Bruno's back and tried to chock him as Jigger cheered.

"Stop it or Old Man Garretty will be out here with his broom," Antony warned.

"Yeah, yeah. I guess Sweet Stuff saved your hide."

"No I didn't; I didn't save anybody," Antony retorted in a lower voice than normal.

"Now don't say a word; just sit still and stare. It'll drive her crazy."

The hoodlums entered the laundromat and sat in a row of chrome chairs with seats and backs covered in turquoise plastic.

"Stella, can you please hold the baby just until I transfer the wash into the dryers?" a young lady asked. "She is just so fussy today."

Stella sat in her normal overstuffed chair and held the little baby.

"What's the trouble today? Don't you feel good?" she softly asked. "Here, let's get you up over this shoulder and let me rub your back. You probably have a little bubble. Let's see. Well, that was it!" she chuckled. "You got any more at home like that?"

By the time the mother came back, the baby was content in Stella's arms. "I'll hold her for a while longer if you'd like? She reminds me of my little girl from a long time ago."

"Oh, that would be great; then I can look at my magazine in peace."

"Yes, peace," Stella replied as she looked into the baby's face.

"Stella," a small voice said, "I don't mean to disturb you, but, well, it has happened again. He left me no money to do the wash. I am so sorry, but if you could... I mean... I'll pay you back."

Stella limped over to the baby's mother to deposit her sweet bundle and walked into the backroom. In a few minutes, she handed the lady something, not letting anyone see what it was.

The younger woman hugged Stella.

Freak handed Bruno his jackknife. "What am I supposed to do with this?"

Freak pointed to the slit he had just made in the turquoise plastic.

"Do it. Leave your mark."

Bruno followed suit, handing the knife to Jigger, who handed if off to Sweet Stuff.

Sweet Stuff's hand shook as he punctured the seat.

The four sat and stared at Stella as she rolled the mop pail to a soda spill.

"Here, Stella, let me do that for you," a middle-aged man said as he jumped up. "You shouldn't be doing all this hard work."

"I'm not afraid of hard work; this is nothing compared to the job I used to have."

"What was that?"

"Well, in my country, the women went into the mines right along with the men," Stella said.

"Good grief! But this country has been good to you, right?"

"Oh yes, my husband had three businesses, and we worked day and night, but it was work that had hope attached to it. Now he is gone and I am alone, so I stay here every day just to be with the nice people."

"Your son helps you out, doesn't he?"

"Oh, yes. He fixes the machines if they break down."

"Do you have any other children?"

"I had a beautiful little girl, but she died in the old country."

"Hi, Stella! Kids, listen, if you're good, I bet Stella will tell you some great stories. Now you go over and ask her nicely."

"Of course, of course, come over by me."

"Let's bug this joint," Jigger said to the others.

They sauntered to the door and Freak leaned low to tip over the mop bucket.

"Don't look now, but do you see who's coming out of the Shack?"

"Yeah, with Carla and her friends. This is making me mad!"

"We're going over."

"Plug your noses, girls, here come the stink-o boys."

"Stink-o? What would you call those losers you're with?"

"They are not stink-o; they have class."

"Yeah, the loser class."

The pushing and shoving started. Punches were thrown. Mr. Garretty ran out of his store with a broom, except it wasn't a broom, it was the broom handle, and he was holding it like a baseball bat.

Andrea ran forward and grabbed Sweet Stuff's arm. "Come on, run!"

"No! I'm staying; I'm not afraid."

A squad car pulled to the curb. They were all taken downtown.

"A warning! Big deal. We'll go back and catch them off guard; we'll show them who rules around here."

"Yeah, we'll show them!"

"We've walked all day; those *chickens* are hiding. Let's go into the Suds and see what ugly Stella is doing."

"Look at the stupid gray tape she put over the cuts. Sit."

"OK, Ma," said Stella's son, "the vending machines are all full, and washer number three has been fixed."

"Thank you, son. I don't know what I'd do without you."

"Call me if you need anything."

Stella sat in her chair and reached for her crocheting. Many an hour had passed as she made the crochet hook maneuver faster than lightening. Antony could see the baby blanket lying across her legs as she manipulated the stitches.

"Oh, thank you Stella. I'm not used to these crutches. I thought I could get through the door with no problem, but somehow I dropped the laundry basket and then I lost my balance and, as you can see, here I am!"

"We'll get you up, don't worry. Ah, our angel! Salvatore, can you give us a hand?"

"Thanks again."

Stella halted at her chair. There was no baby blanket, only a huge pile of yarn—the same yarn that five minutes ago was a baby blanket. The whole thing had been unraveled. She looked over at the boys in the four taped chairs; then she turned away and wiped her eyes.

"Stella! Can you show us those tricks again?" came the voices of the twins who scurried in every Tuesday with their father.

"Sure, I need to get my mind on something fun," she said.

"Do it again, Stella."

"Where did you learn all those?" the dad asked.

"This used to be our entertainment in the evening."

"What do you mean?"

"We had no TV," Stella said.

"No TV?" chimed in the twins.

"Just our imagination, our music, and a few books."

"Wow!" responded her captive audience.

"Hey, Stella. I brought you in some new magazines!"

"Oh, thank you, Madeline. Lots of people read through them while they wait, but, Madeline, excuse me, I can't put out something like that. I have lots of children who come in here."

"Oh my gosh! I didn't know those were in there. My husband must have put them in the pile. I'm sorry."

"Don't worry; just take them with you," Stella said.

"Lady, could you tell me how to wash these?"

"Sure, honey. How old are you?"

"Eight."

"Isn't there any school today?"

"It's summer vacation."

"Oh," Stella said with a laugh, "you're right. Where's your mom?"

"She had to go to work, but she said I could go to the laundromat, because I'm big now."

"And that you are. I'll help you."

"My mommy said you would."

"I'm bored," Freak whispered to the others. "Let's have some fun."

"OK, got it." Jig-Pig laughed.

"Got it. Yes, I know what to do."

"Cool, really cool," Antony Sweet Stuff replied as he felt his heart palpitate and beads of sweat rise on his forehead.

"Stella, help! Come quickly!"

Long before she reached the distraught customer, Stella could see mounds and mounds of soap bubbles rise from five of the washers.

She turned to face the four but their chairs were empty. Through the front window she could see them rollicking and laughing on the sidewalk.

"There they are. Those chicken livers! Quick, get behind the fence! Now this is the plan: We're going to follow their every move. They're probably like animals, navigating from place to place in a regular pattern. And when they least expect it, we'll strike."

"What are we going to do when we strike?" Antony asked nervously.

"Are you getting afraid, little man?"

"Not me. I'm with you a hundred percent."

"Good, together we succeed."

"Yeah, you're right, every day at two o'clock they walk past here on their way to the Shack."

"Can you sneak it out of your uncle's warehouse? Great."

"OK, we've got to come up with some kind of platform; we need to be up high."

"All right, this is the day! Does everyone know the plan? Don't make a sound; here they come."

"Now!" Freak yelled.

The deluge of black ink soaked the archenemies, but that was only on the surface. Leaving an indelible mark would be the retaliation.

The rumblings in the neighborhood were strong. The girls didn't go to the Shack anymore. Mr. Garretty kept more than a broom and a broom handle by the front door. Stella's son stopped by every day. The police had no proof of the culprits. Andrea worried about Sweet Stuff.

Stella had no customers when the four walked in. Stella didn't get out of her chair; she kept crocheting. The four sat and stared. There was no sound: no dryers whirring, no washers agitating in a monotonous drone, and no kids intermingling with Stella. Nothing, until *bam!* The ceiling collapsed and a smoke bomb went off and there was chocking and moaning.

Stella was face down on the floor, crawling to get the ceiling tiles and beam off her back. Antony Sweet Stuff was screaming with pain as a piece of glass jutted from his leg. Jigger's face was a mass of blood. Bruno was holding his stomach and vomiting. Jason, the Freak, didn't move.

Stella snaked her way over to the boys.

"Sh, calm yourself. No, don't pull that glass out; we'll never stop the bleeding. Wait for the ambulance people. I know it hurts. Be brave. OK, you, turn on your side. Take my handkerchief and press it on that wound. Give it pressure. Sit up if you can, or you'll choke on your own vomit. Lean against that dryer. He's not breathing." Stella pushed on his chest. "What's his name?

"Freak. Come on Freak. Take a breath. Breathe, Freak. Breathe. That's it, come on. Take another breath," Stella pleaded.

Sirens blared. Ambulances lined in front of the Suds Parlor. Police came in droves, and the old woman who had lived through a mine collapse in her old country, the same collapse that had killed her little daughter, reached out to help the four who had tormented her.

THE END

"WHY DOESN'T EVERYBODY LOOK THE SAME?"
"OH MY STARS IN HEAVEN. WHAT ARE YOU THINKING ABOUT NOW,
MARJORY?"
"I'M WONDERING WHERE THE PUZZLE PIECE IS."

Chapter Ten
YOUR WAYS ARE NOT MY WAYS

The school bus stopped in front of Zeb's house.
"Morning, Zeb."
"Uh," Zeb grunted as he did every morning.

Charlie pulled away from the carless, quasi-kempt house wondering why he never saw any other human at the first and last stop on his route. He peered into the rearview mirror and saw the tall, gangly student already sprawled sideways in the seat with his black motorcycle boots nearly touching the seat across the aisle. His head was flipped back with the window as a pillow; his eyes were closed.

Charlie sighed. After thirty-two years of driving a school bus, he still didn't understand teenagers, especially the really *odd* ones. To Charlie, Zeb was odd. Who would wear a black leather jacket with embroidered blood dripping from his name, which was stitched across the back? Why did he think he needed all those chains and bracelets and rings? And that hair? All spiked up like some kind of rooster.

Charlie jerked the steering wheel as Bob Fester's chickens suddenly decided to scurry across to the corncrib. Had Zeb noticed the zag in Charlie's driving? With eyes just high enough to look at the "oddity," Charlie uttered "Damn" to himself as he saw the gawking, dark eyes open wide to the obvious irregularity of the morning trek. Charlie frowned, not wanting the *weirdo* to think there was anything wrong with *him*. He, who could decorate one wall with all the framed accommodations he had been given for safe driving.

Charlie dug into his duties, determined not to let anything else cause a variance in his smooth maneuvering in which he prided himself. Zeb returned to his eye-closed position, and thought about what? No one ever knew.

Oh great, they're all going to school today, Charlie mumbled as he saw all five Lansings run from the house. Usually, there was one or two who missed school every day. He always asked and got the same answer: "Someone's sick." He didn't know how there could be so much sickness in one family. Charlie didn't recall missing a day of school when he was a boy for sickness.

They all rushed to the back of the bus screaming, "Zeb! Zeb!"

Charlie waited until they were all seated before pulling out. *Why do they like him? What is their fascination with him?*

"Hey, you little hamstrings, quiet down your yakking. Can't you see I'm trying to sleep?"

The little girls giggled and the boys started begging to try on Zeb's bracelets and rings."

Zeb took his sunglasses from an inner jacket pocket and slowly placed them over his dark eyes. "I can't stand looking at you guys. Go away," he said.

More giggling and more pleading came from the Lansings as the bus stopped for the Bulldin twins. Fallen led the way to the rear of the bus as his brother jostled for the lead.

"Zeb! Let us see the blood dripping out of your name, will ya?"

"Sit down, you polecats, before you see blood dripping out of your lunch pails!"

Fallen and Finnegan went into peals of laughter as they clinched their lunch pails to their chests.

"Settle down back there, or I'll move you to the front of the bus!" Charlie let his authority peal through the ears of the young ones. He was sure Zeb had no respect for his commandeering.

The noise immediately ceased as Charlie's chest puffed slightly with pride. No way would the kids want to be relocated.

Fallen and Finnegan, both peeked around their seat to look at the huge leathered enigma while the Lansings looked across the aisle. No one said a word. They listened to the slow breathing of Zeb; they watched the chains on his chest rise and fall; they covered their mouths with their hands when he snorted. It must have been the snort that caused the huge mountain to suddenly rise, swing his legs, and let his heavy boots thump to the floor. The seven of them let out a yelp that caused Charlie to yank his eyes to their direction.

Fortunately, it happened just when he opened the door for Mrs. Oliver. Several times a week, Mrs. Oliver would have directions for Charlie, and she would go on and on about the matters as her three kids waited for her to unblock the stairway. They, too, looked in Zeb's direction as the oldest boy immediately took his comb and furiously tried to make his hair stand straight like Zeb's. The two girls asked if they could trade seats with two of the Lansing girls. No they couldn't, and they immediately went into their customary snit.

Jake, the rich kid, had better success. Zeroing in on Finnegan, he dangled his new video game high in the air as he fluttered his eyebrows, everyone knowing that that was one of Jake's signals for a bribe.

"Hey, Zeb, it's me," he said as he slid onto Finnegan's seat and tried to high-five the giant.

"Go away, you little weasel!" Zeb replied as he reached forward to tussle Jake's hair.

How can those kids put up with that guy? He is miserable to them. He's never nice. Ornery and cantankerous. I guess those are the words.

Just before the big curve, the children knew that Zeb was going to act differently. He was going to sit straighter; his comb would go through his hair one more time, and he would neaten his gold chain necklaces.

There she was! All eyes went from Danielle to Zeb and to Zeb to Danielle. Of course, she never looked at him, only slid effortlessly into her seat. Even before they reached the big farm, and the farmer boys, notes were already starting to be passed between the beautiful Danielle and the mysterious Zeb. All the kids not in the line of hand passing wished they were, and all the kids who hand delivered the notes held each one as if it was etched in gold.

No one dared to peek inside the note, even though he or she easily could have; it was only folded once. And no one dared to gawk at Zeb as he used his pencil stub to scrawl a message.

Charlie knew what was going on, but he allowed it. At least they were quiet.

It wasn't long before the orange bus snaked around the infamous curve, making all the children proclaim their daily,

"Ooo." Charlie chuckled, for all the years on that particular bus route, it was customary to have them react in that manner.

The farmer boys were another sight to behold. There were five of them, all huge compared to the little tykes. One set of twins who captivated Fallen and Finnegan, and the other three who looked to be no more than a year apart in age.

Charlie didn't know how their father could let them go off to school each day; he must have needed their help on the farm. He remembered how he'd had to miss school during the corn harvesting, silo-filling days and during the oat-thrashing times—even occasionally when his father was too crippled with arthritis to milk the cows. At least the school hadn't gone to a year round ten weeks on and one week off program like in some places. At least the farmer had his boys' home all summer to put in the hay.

"Have a good day, Isabella. Don't forget to take your lunch pail home, Gregory. Be good," were only a few of the disembarking remarks Charlie uttered to his brood. "Have a good day, Zeb," led to the customary grunt.

"Thanks for coming in for this meeting, everyone. I know it cuts into your day, but the state is always mandating more and more of these school bus safety sessions," Mr. Lincoln exclaimed.

Just like students, the men and women groaned.

After watching an hour-long video, Mr. Lincoln asked for questions.

"Well, this doesn't have anything to do with the movie, but I'd like to ask you a question about the kid at the end of my line," Charlie proclaimed.

"Is there a problem?"

"No, he's not really a problem, but I never see anyone at his house, not even a vehicle, and he locks the door when he leaves."

"Actually, he lives by himself, seeing how he's eighteen. His dad is in the military and goes home when he can."

"Why is he so strange? With no manners?" The others chuckled and nodded as if they all had someone like that on their buses.

"Well now, Charlie, your job is just to get those kids to and from school safely."

"I know. I know."

Now when Charlie sat in the bus waiting for Zeb to saunter toward him in the mornings, he wondered how the young man was managing by himself. Where was his mother? Did he cook for himself? He knew Zeb could get breakfast and lunch at school.

"Good morning, Zeb."

"Uh."

Things on the bus remained the same. The little kids loved Zeb. The only difference that Charlie noticed was that Danielle was passing notes to one of the farm boys as well.

One morning while Charlie performed the laborious maneuver of turning around in a five-point pattern while craning his neck one way and then the other, trying to get a look at the big black car in the driveway, the bus nearly swiped the old dilapidated chicken coop.

But that wasn't the end of it. The bus driver stared at two men approaching him from the house. They walked in exact step; they swung their arms in the same rhythm. Their clothes were neatly pressed, and their shoes shone. The older man flashed Charlie a smile as soon as the door swiveled open.

"Good morning, sir, I'm Zeb's father."

"Nice to meet you," Charlie replied timidly.

"Have a good day, son."

"I will, dad, you too."

"Good morning, Zeb," Charlie announced as usual.

"Good morning, sir," Zeb replied.

Charlie watched the spike-less, jewelry-less, black bootless, blood drip-less lad walk to the back of the bus and sit upright.

Charlie could barely keep his eyes out of the rearview mirror. He was glad he knew the road by memory.

The Lansings started their marathon race down the aisle to Zeb until the first one suddenly halted and made the other four crash like a pileup. They didn't know the stranger in Zeb's seat. Where was their Zeb? They sat in silence.

"Cat got your tongue this morning?"

It was Zeb's voice.

The two girls whispered together, but the boys didn't even dare to do that. They peered from the corners of their eyes. That couldn't be Zeb.

Finnegan and Fallon had the same kind of collision in the center aisle. They looked from the stranger to the Lansing boys. The Lansing boys only shrugged their shoulders and made their eyes say, "We don't know."

Charlie hadn't seen the twins that quiet since their first day of school in kindergarten when they cried into their white handkerchiefs.

"Are you all zombies today?"

Fallon swung around. It sounded like Zeb.

The twins went into a huddle.

Mrs. Oliver's three kids followed suit over *the new boy* on the bus, and Jake, the rich kid, didn't try to bribe anyone to get a seat in the back.

When Danielle stepped up into the bus, she knew something was awry. She searched the children's faces for answers, but no one was talking. It wasn't until her eyes rested on the face of the new boy on the bus that the little innocents saw the effects of a blush. They had never seen Danielle blush. She quickly took her seat.

No one sang out "ooo" for the curve, and Charlie looked at his troupe with disappointment; he never thought he would miss the little quirk.

Would there be a note? They didn't think there would be. After all, "the stranger" didn't know Danielle, and she didn't know him.

"Hey, you little monkey. Pass this up there, would ya?" Zeb said.

Finnegan followed orders, not knowing if he should or not.

Even the farm boys sat staring ahead not saying a word.

Danielle read the note but never sent one in return.

"Say, Charlie," Mr. Lincoln called out as he ran to catch up with the bus driver in the parking lot, "how's Zeb doing on the bus?"

"I hardly knew him this morning! He spoke in a civilized manner, and I got to meet his dad! What a transformation!"

"You gotta feel a little sorry for the kid being shuffled all over the world with so many different schools and then having his mother die about three years ago. I'm glad his father is home now. I wonder how long he'll be on leave."

The following morning, Charlie arrived at the last house before the county line and saw several cars around Zeb's house.

Hmm, I wonder what's going on here.

By the time he jockeyed the bus around, Charlie was met by six or seven little kids still in their pajamas and some young adults, along with Zeb and his father.

"Good morning, sir. I'd like you to meet Zeb's sisters, brother, and all the little munchkins."

"Good morning everyone out there," Charlie replied as he waved.

"Just wanted you to know that Zeb won't be on the bus for two weeks. I'm taking the whole family on a vacation. I've notified the school. See you then, sir."

The bus trips began to mimic the weather. The chill split the air, and the sun stayed hidden behind thick clouds all the day long. Dreary were the mornings and lifeless were the afternoons. The drone of the bus heater was monotonous, and there was no fresh air to relieve any queasiness that seemed to build around the curves and potholes of the mountain road. No one was having fun.

An impending storm was forecast, and the bus drivers clung to their weather reports.

"Well, back to the north forty," Charlie muttered as he started his trek fifteen minutes earlier than the last two weeks. No cars dotted the snowy hilltop, and for a moment, he felt a sadness for Zeb; everyone was gone again. He watched the lad lock the front door and almost forgot about the preppy young man who had accompanied his military dad to the bus. His leather attire, jeans, chains, and spiked hair seemed more natural, and there it was—all of it.

"Good morning, Zeb. Did you have a good vacation?"

"Uh."

Charlie chuckled. *He's back!*

The bus turned into Santa Land for the children and no amount of "you horn swaggerers," or "you hash bucklers," or "you long-necked giraffes," could deter their joy. They only loved it all the more.

Danielle looked to the back of the bus and gave Zeb a little wave.

Charlie maneuvered the bus so slowly along the snowy, icy curve, that the passengers never realized they were making the arc, say nothing of remembering to sing out their "ooo."

The children disembarked with mirth not typical of those going into the school.

The bus drivers were put on high alert to stay in the area in case of a "go home early" weather emergency.

Charlie sat in his kitchen watching the snow mount by the minute. His radio jabbered on and on about the approaching storm; his TV showed pictures of what was happening just north of them, and his beeper went off. That was it; he had to go back to school. The elevated excitement of the students was even higher than the morning's "yay, Zeb is back" excitement.

The children weren't worried; they knew their bus driver would get them home safely. He always did. Charlie was confident; he knew the trip would take longer than usual, but he had been through it before.

One by one, he watched the kids jump and cavort through the snow as they ran to tell whomever was in their house that they were home and weren't they lucky!

The five farm boys sauntered from the bus, probably wondering what their father would have in mind for them today. They didn't seem thrilled as were the others, as thoughts of shoveling manure out of the heifer barn or shoveling silage out of the silo or throwing bales of hay down the shoot for the cows' late afternoon repast came to mind. Charlie knew they wouldn't have a frivolous "snow day."

"OK," Charlie said to himself as he mentally prepared to round the curve of the steep, inclining hill. He grasped the steering wheel with more pressure and sat straighter in his seat. He was ready. He kept the wheels in the ruts of the snow, which were becoming more and more frozen as the elevation increased. He wished he were following a snowplow or a sander; this was going to be a challenge.

The passengers weren't attentive to the conditions. Why should they be? They were carefree kids, not yet in the adult responsibility groove. Zeb was the only one looking directly ahead at the curve and the ruts and the ice.

He saw it coming! Charlie saw it coming! The kids did not. Careening down the hill was one of Lester Fillmore's logging trucks, stacked high with a huge load of tree trunks behind the cab. Zeb started for the front of the bus, not hearing the questions that the kids were flinging at him. Charlie shifted down and veered to the right, knowing there wasn't another inch in reserve between the tires and the embankment. But Charlie's hands left the steering wheel as he grabbed for his chest. Zeb took ahold of the wheel and pushed Charlie's foot off the gas pedal. He pushed down on the brake, but couldn't get to the clutch with Charlie collapsed in the seat. With no gas, the bus came to a stop on its own.

"Everyone! Move to the left side of the bus. Now!" Zeb knew he had to shift the weight away from the plundering bankside; the bus was on a slant.

"Danielle! Call 911 and call the school!"

What's it like when joy leaves children and fear and fright enter them? Zeb didn't have time to think about the terrified faces in parts of the world where his family stayed to be close to his father as was permissible. Usually, they watched the terror only through fences and gates and bombed walls. They knew their patriarch was somewhere on the other side. Zeb had seen little children walking through rubble, crying for their parents, and wounded children sobbing in pain while siblings tried to hurry them along.

Now, in the rearview mirror, he again saw fear and fright.

"Hey, you kiddos, everybody keep looking up into this mirror," he announced as lightheartedly as he could. "We're going to be all right; help is on its way. In fact, you are going to see a lot of people coming to help us out of this bus. Hey, you guys know any songs? I remember my mother always got my sisters and brother and me singing when we were a little nervous. Let's do, 'He's Got the Whole World in His Hands.'"

Some of the children knew the song, and by the time they sang three verses, everyone knew it and sang with the others. Just as it used to comfort Zeb, the children responded well to thinking of more and more things that were "in His hands."

The road quickly became inundated with authority figures. The police set up barricades to stop traffic from going up or down the hill. People were not allowed in the area; parents waited in the field or the woods trying to get as close as possible. The snow and sleet continued. Two huge tow trucks crept up alongside of the bus. Zeb opened his window to talk to one of the men. The tow operator scowled at the spiked haired individual.

"What are you doing up there? Where's the driver?"

"He's slumped right here; I think he's had a heart attack."

"Has an ambulance been called?"

"Yes."

They could hear the siren in the distance.

Zeb listened to the two operators discuss their strategy as he knew he had to give some attention to his passengers also. "Hey, kiddos, who wants to have a picnic?"

They all focused on the face in the rearview mirror. "Yeah," Zeb added, "I mean it! Everyone who has their lunch pail, open it and share with your neighbors while the men out there figure what to do to get our bus straightened out. Deal?"

It was a good deal! Zeb knew that food always made children feel better. It wasn't long before he heard them chatting like they were in the cafeteria.

The tow truck operator banged on the window. "Let's see if you can get those kids out the back door."

"Not until you chain this bus to the trees over there," Zeb answered sternly.

"Don't be ridiculous; we're chaining it to our trucks, not the trees. What do you know anyway, you freak!"

"With that ice-covered road, your trucks will slide right into the bus."

"He's right, TJ. The trees won't go anywhere; they'll hold the bus while the kids get off and the ambulance crew evacuates the driver."

TJ scowled at the spike-haired teenager but began the chain operation.

Zeb could see from the side-view mirror that Mr. Lincoln and the bus mechanic were trudging up the hill with a few falls and spills on the way.

The ambulance crept up the hill with chains on the tires.

"OK, kid, we've got it secured. Unlock the back door."

Zeb flipped the switch and stepped away from Charlie for the first time to be relieved by the medical crew. Mr. Lincoln and Mike extended their hands for the children to jump, but the first ones in line, the Little Lansing girls, wouldn't go to them.

"Let me try," Zeb called out.

There standing in the snow and ice with drops of blood dripping from his jacket's embroidered name, spiked hair that truly became frozen upright, and gold necklaces that swung with each downward placement of a child, Zeb said good-bye to the students and thanked them for being brave.

The next day, the passengers were interviewed for the TV news.

"Weren't you scared?"

"No," said one of the Oliver children, "we sang songs and had a picnic while we waited."

"How did you know to sit on one side of the bus?"

"Zeb told us."

"Who got the bus to stop sliding?"

"Zeb did. He had to help the bus driver because our bus driver got sick."

"Whose idea was it to chain the bus to the trees?"

"Zeb's."

"Danielle, we heard it was you who called 911 and the school. Is that right?"

"Yes, but it was Zeb who told me what to do."

"OK, class, think about that story over the weekend and come back with a written ending, because the author left it right there. It seems to me that it needs some kind of closure. You'll get to vote on which conclusion you like best. Have a good weekend," the high school teacher said as he smiled.

On Monday, Mr. Burrows was anxious for his creative writing students to appear. "Where shall we start?" he asked.

A raised hand by the window started the circular path of "chairs in the round."

As a model railroad circling the Christmas tree, each student read his or her ending.

Mary: "Zeb was presented with an award at the town square with the town dignitaries in attendance."

Brandy: "Zeb didn't want any recognition and begged his father to take him out of the school and let him go with him to his next assignment."

Izzy: "The children gave him a big party at the bowling alley, and Zeb bowled a three hundred game."

Stephen: "Zeb was on all the national television talk shows. He alternated 'his look' each time so people were confused as to who was the hero?"

Clayton: "A movie was made based on the bus story, and Zeb was the director."

Lauren: "It was discovered that the children were all traumatized for months and months after the bus incident, and Zeb's father was sued."

Chan: "Zeb developed cancer and died. The school erected a statue of Zeb on the front lawn."

Gina: "Ten years later, Danielle and Zeb got married, and they had three sets of twins."

Ellen: "All the hills were leveled so that school buses were never in danger again."

"All right! Everyone vote and pass your ballots to me."

"Well, this is interesting," Mr. Burrows said slowly. "We have a three-way tie between Brandy, Stephen, and Loren! Now we'll vote again to break the tie. Will it be the Zeb who wanted no recognition and wanted to go away with his father, Zeb the TV star who camouflaged his looks, or the traumatized children with a lawsuit against Zeb's father?"

"The winner is Brandy with the 'Zeb who wanted no recognition and wanted to go away with his father.' Congratulations, Brandy."

"Where did you get that story anyway, Mr. Burrows? And why didn't it have an ending?" Stephen asked.

"Actually, I wrote it a long time ago and never got around to finishing it."

Now our next project will be with the fourth graders. We will try to do something creative with them and their initials. For example, they can write poems about their names, stories, make up acronyms using the initials, etc. Of course, they are allowed to illustrate their work if they wish to.

"Let's do a few right now. Gina, what are your initials?"

"I have a great one! I'm a GEM!" She answered with great importance.

"You are lucky. What if you had initials like mine," Clayton interjected. The class waited while he sighed and then said, "CAT."

They all laughed. "What are yours, Mr. Burrows?"

"ZEB."

"What's it stand for?"

"Zebadiah Edward Burrows."

Ring, ring, ring!

"There's the bell. See you tomorrow."

It wasn't until the students were in the hallway and Stephen turned around to utter, "Zeb?" did the others stop in their tracks.

The End

"WHAT'S OUT THERE, GRANDMA?"
"OUT WHERE?"
"OUT IN SPACE."
"OH, STARS AND PLANETS AND THE SUN AND MOON. WHY?"
"I JUST HAVE A FEELING THERE IS MORE OUT THERE THAN THAT."
"COULD BE."

Chapter Eleven

CYBERSPACE

A SEQUEL TO "THE FUNDRAISER" FROM BOOK TWO

"You're going to do what?" Elmer questioned as Louey bounded off the bottom step to twirl into the hardware store.

"I'm going to enter this contest!" she professed as she waved a paper in the dimly lit, organic smelling, cacophony of everything-anybody-wanted emporium.

Elmer lifted partially from his display of garden seeds. Louey knew she didn't have to ask her brother any leading questions; she just plunged in with her enthusiasm.

"All I have to do is fill out this form and send it in. If they like what I say, they might pick me!"

"To do what?" Elmer asked.

"To win some sort of award and to be on the Max Maxim Show."

Elmer suddenly had a lot to think about. He scratched his head, which meant he was thinking, and sat on the large pile of dry compost garden fertilizer bags.

"Well?" Louey asked. She didn't have the patience for Elmer's notorious contemplative modes.

Finally, he interrupted his own deliberations with, "Who is Max Maxim?"

Louey clucked her tongue, rolled her eyes, and placed her hands on her hips all at the same time. "He's that gorgeous man on the TV show that I watch every day at four o'clock!"

Elmer immediately lost interest in his sister's "big idea" and went back to replenishing the seed packets.

Add stomping her foot on the old, worn barn boards to her repertoire, and you'll know why Elmer again lifted his head.

"He's the one who announced the contest, and I'm going to write my essay!" Louey said.

"Essay? I haven't heard that word since eighth grade."

"Well, maybe you would have heard it more if you had stayed in school until the twelfth grade, like I did!" Louey proclaimed with an added flare of head lifting, turning herself into some sort of statue that Elmer thought would look nice in someone's flower garden.

Louey didn't wait for her brother to mumble, "I had to work so you could go to school."

"Yes, all I have to do is write about the messages that are going through cyberspace right now."

Down went Elmer to the top bag of compost, which now had enough of a comfortable, hollowed sway to it to make a good thinking spot. Louey looked at her older brother, seeing the once eighth grader who had to be brave enough to tell the teacher that he was leaving school.

"Cyberspace? What messages?"

"Well, I don't know. All those messages that people send on their computers and phones and tweets and stuff."

"How do you know about all that?" Elmer asked.

"Max Maxim!"

"Oh, I see," Elmer added as he scratched his head.

Suddenly, Louey flung around to ascend the stairs to her apartment—the apartment that Elmer had provided for thirty-eight years. He didn't know how she would write anything about what was out in cyberspace; it wasn't until recently that she had finally ventured out of the building, ending her era of being the town's hermit.

He heard Louellen's voice trailing off with, "I've got some good ideas."

Four weeks later, Louey sailed down the backstairs of the hardware store not looking like a pink flamingo but a white egret. Her white-feathered gown with matching slippers and white nylon mesh, which held her hair in several ponytails, might have caused her to be misconstrued as an angel if it weren't for the ponytails.

"Elmer!" The non-angelic voice screeched across the rows of nuts and bolts. The quietness of the store mixed with the elixir of the enamel paint had put her brother into a late afternoon half-trance. But the screech brought down the entire pegboard of "Carpenter's Notions" that he had so meticulously labored to categorize.

"What?" Elmer demanded, blaming his unfortunate mess on his sister.

"Max Maxim just announced that I'm one of the contestants! They've narrowed it down to fifty entries! I'm one of the fifty!" the white egret sang as she twirled between the pyramid of bug spray and the stack of paint-by-number kits for adults and kids.

An influx of messages sailed through cyberspace as Max Maxim waved to his audience. Would people be surprised that they were directly over Lone Moon Creek?

"Did you see the show?"

"I sure did. I can't believe it!"

"How could she write anything about cyberspace? What would she know about messages that are sailing around the world?"

"What does anyone know? I surely couldn't begin to tell others what that quagmire of information is all about."

"At least you got out of your house for the last thirty-eight years."

"Now, don't be too hard on Louey; I think her brother has taken her out in the car once a week since last fall."

"Yeah, she's had a lot of catching up to do."

"Well, tomorrow will probably be the end for her; they are eliminating twenty-five of the contestants."

"I'm still in! I'm still in!" exploded Louey.

"Would you stop flying down here like a mad woman. Now you made me spill a whole bag of birdseed!" Elmer exclaimed.

"Oops. Sorry, brother."

On his hands and knees with a dustpan, Elmer asked, "You're still in what?"

Before she could answer, the door burst open with well-wishers.

"Congratulations, Louey. You must have written a great essay!"

"Gee, I must have," she uttered softly, suddenly seemingly surprised at her own placement in the contest.

"Are you versed in cyberspace?

"Not really. I just wrote what I thought people were talking about all around the world."

"We'll all be watching tomorrow when the seven best will be announced."

This time, Louey perched on the swaybacked pile of compost bags and sighed.

"What's the matter?" Elmer asked as he scooped the last of the seeds back into the bag.

"You know, if I get invited to the Max Maxim Show, you're going to have to drive me to Los Angeles."

Over went the birdseed again.

"Elmer, come upstairs and watch the show with me," Louey called down through the register.

"You know I don't watch no TV," he yelled back in response.

"I know. All you do is work, work, and work. Come on up here; I'm nervous."

"I can't close the store," he insisted.

"Just put a sign on the door saying you'll be back in thirty minutes. Pleeeeeeeease."

"I've never been able to say no to my little sister," he grumbled.

Elmer sat on the lavender couch looking more out of place than would a counter of sparkly jewelry downstairs.

"Here goes," whispered Louey as she tuned in just in time to see Max Maxim run out to his audience.

Elmer looked at Louey in surprise. "I never knew you could whisper," he remarked.

"Shh," she replied. She didn't whisper.

"Isn't this exciting?" the emcee expounded as the audience roared. "Today we'll be down to seven!"

Immediately the crowd chanted, "Seven, seven, seven" as they clapped and stomped their feet. Max let it continue for a considerable amount of time, until with a lowering of his hands he brought his admirers to a hush.

With his beguiling bass voice, Max softly lured his entourage into a bit of history as to how difficult it had become for the judges to eliminate anyone, but it had to be done. He tenderly read the names of those who had to be eliminated. Louey held her breath; Elmer let his eyes plod through the space, wondering why she had what she had in that room.

Suddenly, Elmer jumped when he felt something like vice grips on his arm. He looked down to see Louey's fingers pressing into his flannel shirt. Again, she whispered, which brought about the question of when she had learned to do that once more, but there was no time to ask, as she didn't release her grip but only whispered, "I didn't hear my name, did you?"

"Name? No, I didn't hear your name. Was I supposed to?" It wasn't until the adored TV personality announced the seven contenders did Elmer say, "That's you, Louellen Hardy-Manza. I heard it."

Louey didn't move while Elmer slowly lifted each of her fingers out of his arm.

"I hear someone bangin' on the door down there. I better git."

"I'm coming, I'm coming," Elmer shouted.

Elmer opened the door to a swarm of people.

"Where is she?"

"Who?"

"The star of course!"

"Upstairs, I guess."

"Is she coming down?"

"I have no idea."

"We'd like to talk to her."

Elmer hollered up the register, "Louey, you comin' down?"

"In a minute."

"You people need to buy something while you're waiting?"

They didn't have a chance to look because, with a flourish, Louey appeared. She wasn't wearing one of her feathered outfits, but a suit. Elmer thought it was the one she wore to her high school graduation.

She was peppered with questions. Some she could answer and some she couldn't. Elmer watched, thinking Louey should have a microphone in her hand as she went from person to person. They would all have to wait until the weekend was over to watch the Monday show and the disclosure of the final three.

"Do you think you'll come in first, second, or third?" one exuberant fan asked.

"I don't know if I'll even make it that far, but if I do, it'll probably be third."

"Where ever you end up, just know that we're mighty proud of you."

Elmer was pleased with all the business he had on Saturday. On Sunday, the two Hardys could be seen on their weekly ride, with Louey, arm out the window, taking in all that was out there to be seen and returning each hand wave.

Louey was surprised with the numerous invitations to the homes of several local women who wanted her to watch the show with them. She declined each one, saying she needed to be in her apartment with her brother. Elmer scoffed each time he heard her say that because it would mean another thirty minutes of closing the store.

"Happy Monday," the host said as he saluted his audience. "Have you been waiting for Monday as anxiously as I have?" The cheering revealed the answer! "I guess you have!"

Max Maxim paused for the attention he thought he deserved and then continued. "As you know, the three finalists will be announced today, but let me tell you some of the details first. As almost everyone in the country knows, this contest was open to all who wanted to enter. All they had to do was write an essay on what they thought was circulating around the world in cyberspace. Easy right?"

He waited while the audience either chuckled, cheered, or said, "No way."

"Well, nearly eight thousand people entered!" A wild uproar arose again. "So getting down to the best of the best three descriptions is exciting!" The emcee certainly knew how to engage his audience.

"Now, even though we are going to find out who the three are today, we won't get to meet them until next week."

The crowd turned: a tremendous "boo" sailed through the studio.

"We have to fly them to Los Angeles; they will need time to prepare for the trip, right?"

He had the audience screaming "yeah" again.

"All right, let's get this show on the road! One of our finalists is a physicist. He has his PhD, teaches at a college, and has written several books on cyberspace. Does he sound like he is qualified to explain the mysteries of the subject or what?" The host waited for the thunderous applause to subside.

"Another essay was written by a computer engineer and inventor. He claims he knows exactly what goes on in cyberspace because he has invented a laboratory where anyone can enter and listen for themselves to what is being communicated out there in never, never land. Sound good?" There might have been more applause than for the physicist.

"Well, that's it for me," Louey murmured sadly. "Do you want a cup of tea?"

"Just wait a bit. I want to see who the other contestant is," Elmer said.

"Since when are you interested in TV?"

"Sh."

"And the last finalist has just had the blinders taken off her eyes. She hadn't seen anything for thirty-eight years but now claims she has a pretty good idea of what is swirling through space stemming from the minds of the people. This person is from a little town and is co-owner of a hardware store. Does she sound great, or what?"

The studio audience reacted jubilantly as Elmer turned to Louey and asked, "Co-owner?"

"Well, I had to fill in the blank with something. Wait a minute, is that me?"

"I think it is. Wait for him to say the names."

"So ladies and gentlemen, tune in next Monday to meet Zan Weeb, Olaxiion Smith, and Louellen Hardy-Manza.

Before the country had a chance to meet Louellen Hardy-Manza, Lone Moon Creek wanted to meet Louellen Hardy-Manza. She had engagements every evening and luncheons every day. Breakfasts would have been scheduled as well if Louey hadn't drawn the line at that. Her life had become a whirlwind of activity, and each day brought notifications from the TV network for airline tickets, hotel reservations, taxi vouchers, meal certificates, and more.

Her encounters with the townspeople led them to wonder if she knew anything about cyberspace. When the need to hear her explanation arose in conversation, as it always did, they were left thinking, *She doesn't know any more about cyberspace than I do. What could she have written that swayed the judges?*

Would one of Elmer Hardy's hammers ever break? Would he ever sell a saw that was not sharp? How about the barbed wire fencing? Would the barbs not do their duty? Or would his grass seeds not be true grass? I think not. But would Louey ever convince her brother to fly to Los Angeles with her?

She did. She didn't know how she did it and neither did he, but on Sunday afternoon, they were clinging to their armrests as the huge jetliner ascended the skies.

How do two rural people who have never been out of their little town cope with a situation like this? Saying they managed it as tourists would not be accurate. Tourists are known to look around, to look at everything they see, to jabber with each other, and to constantly point at objects. Louey and Elmer did none of those things. Saying they coped as robots might be more accurate. They appeared as statues. They didn't smile, their heads didn't bob to the left or the right, and they walked stiffly. If their escort hadn't met them at the airport, they still would have been standing there like scarecrows in a cornfield.

The escort wasn't getting paid to converse with the clients, so he didn't care if they spoke to him or not. He didn't care that they ate in silence, walked to their hotel rooms in silence, or didn't respond when he told them he would come for them at 6:00 a.m. the next morning.

"You're wearing that old flannel shirt? Where is your good one?" Louey moaned as she met Elmer outside of his hotel room.

"It hurts my neck, and besides, I'm not going to be in front of the cameras, you are."

"That's true," she muttered.

The escort got them to the studio, in silence.

"What the hell?" Elmer asked no one in particular as he looked at Max Maxim. Max walked over to meet them with rollers in his hair, white cream on his face, and someone running along his side trying to put polish on his nails.

"Welcome, welcome," the charismatic host proclaimed, extending his hand until his manicurist quickly pulled it away. "Someone will get you coffee and donuts while we get set up."

The two Lone Moon Creekians sat stiffly, trying to balance their paper plates and the scalding coffee on their laps.

"They must be the other two," Elmer mumbled as he wondered how he was going to wipe the white powdered sugar from his face.

"The other two what?" Louey asked.

"Your competition."

"Oh," Louey moaned as she wished she could slide out of her chair and run for the door.

The director had the three go through their placements on the stage and practice reading the first two or three sentences of their essays.

"That's all?" Louey questioned.

"That's all. Be back here at noon for makeup."

"What are we going to do for three hours?" Louey asked her brother.

"I guess we can sit on a sidewalk bench and watch the people go by," Elmer replied.

And that's what they did.

Meanwhile, back in Lone Moon Creek, people began preparing and congregating for the show that would feature one of their own.

"Hello, ladies and gentlemen," Max Maxim shouted, peeling his voice above the clapping. "This is it! This is the day we have been waiting for! The winners of the top-three essays on cyberspace are here to read to you. Then you'll hear how our judges have ranked their skills. Are you ready?" Without a doubt, Max Maxim knew how to ask the questions that would arouse his audience.

"Listen closely as Zan Weeb reads his essay."

"Cyberspace is where you enter, except you cannot physically enter, because the realm is not physically there, but it is very definitely there, only not for your physical being.

However, your mind can be in cyberspace, and cyberspace is conducive to the working of the mind because the mind takes with it nothing tangible. Tangibility is not for the domain of cyberspace, but intangible products such as notions, ideas, and thoughts travel easily into cyberspace.

"Can those products be retrieved from the nebulae of cyberspace? Oftentimes they can but on other occasions if we could see or hear or smell or taste or touch those, they would be obvious, but we can't."

"Well! Mr. Weeb sure knows his subject, doesn't he? Come on people, I want to hear your appreciation for his intelligence." The audience weakly applauded.

Elmer looked at Louellen. "What the hell was he talking about?"

Louellen was as white as the sidewalk chalk that her brother had just gotten into the store. "I have no idea," she whispered.

"And now, Olaxiion Smith."

"Cyberspace. What is it? Who is it? Where is it? I'll tell you. Cyberspace is what is bombarding our lives every second of every day and night. Yes, night. While you think you are sleeping soundly, the arrows, the bullets, the spears, the lances of destruction permeate your minds. Where is the war? You may think it's in Iraq or Afghanistan or Ethiopia. How about in your city, on your block, or in your own backyard? Yes, that's where the real war is. It's in every single person. Going through space right now are bombs of terror, not the type that can blow up a building, but the type that that can bomb through your skulls to your very brain.

"For years, you didn't know that the cyberspace garbage that included twisted truths, false reasoning, sugar-coated knowledge, and downright lies had entered your psyche. Even though you were aware that something was wrong, something was robbing your peace and your joy. As hard as you tried, you couldn't recapture the freedom that you once had of being a real person.

"Daily, you saw your children floating further and further into the cyberspace world. Believe me, they are going to get so beyond their purpose in life that you will never get them back. The secrecy that is so alluring to young people will tempt and lure them to such an extent; it will be their destruction, and you will witness it. Yes, they will be ruined!"

Five people stood and clapped.

"Again, such intelligence!" the emcee tried to stimulate the crowd. "Let's hear it for Mr. Smith." A trickling applause pursued.

"Well, that was enough to scare the warts off a hog!" Elmer uttered.

"And now, the third contestant, Ms. Louellen Hardy-Manza from a little town called Lone Moon Creek, will read her essay. Let's give it up for 'Louey,' as she likes to be called."

Louey tried to stand, but she couldn't. Her colorless complexion was now whiter than the snow that had covered the pink flowering crabapple trees one May. She couldn't get any words out of her mouth.

Elmer asked, "Are you gettin' up, or what?"

"Just be patient, folks," the emcee offered, "we have, as they say in show biz, a little technical difficulty here." He ran over to Louey. "Come on; you're on."

Louey clenched the sides of her chair and wrapped her feet around its legs. Elmer remembered her doing that as a little girl when she didn't want to do something. She shook her head back and forth. Elmer knew that was a definite, "No."

Max looked at Elmer in desperation. Elmer just shrugged his shoulders. The signal was made to go to a commercial while Max ran to his director.

Louey turned to her brother and mumbled something.

"Me? I can't read that," Elmer protested.

That brought about a semblance of a word from Louellen: "Pleeeeeeeeeease."

Elmer shook his head over and over until he finally sighed and said, "OK, OK."

Max ran on stage to his silent audience, "The difficulties are over!" Their jubilance returned. "Even though Louellen Hardy-Manza is under the weather, her brother Elmer is here to read her essay! Come on out, Elmer!"

Elmer tucked the flannel shirttails into his blue jeans and patted his hair, thinking that maybe his cowlick was standing up straight.

After he cleared his throat, Elmer stopped and looked at the audience. "I might not do so good. I only got through the eighth grade. I had to drop out and go to work to help support my sister and my mother. Well, anyway, let's see what my sister wrote here.

"Cyberspace. They say messages are going through the air right now. You don't see them; nobody sees them, but I guess they go into machines and they come out as words. Pretty neat, right? I used to listen to the radio and wonder how those sounds came out of the box and television with real pictures! I'm hooked on television, you know. So some kind of signals are going through the air, somehow. I sure can't explain it. But you know, I had blinders on my eyes for thirty-eight years after my new husband died. I guess I died too. I never left my apartment, never went anywhere, never talked to anyone, except my brother who runs the hardware store below my apartment."

Elmer paused to say, "That's me. I'm the brother." The audience chuckled.

"But anyway, the strangest thing happened. A ladies club in town held a photo contest and used our hardware store for the display area. Then their high mucky-muck judges quit and my brother and I had to do the judging, and I got to look at the most beautiful photos taken right from our area. Maybe that was cyberspace. Maybe my dear departed husband and my parents got God to keep sending messages until I finally realized I was missing my life—my world. Through those photographs, I started to see again. I began having an insatiable desire to leave my quarters and go out into our beautiful part of the countryside.

"What a discovery. Some things were the same, and it was like I had never left; there were things I recognized and other things that were altogether different. When we go on our Sunday drives, my brother can tell you how I hang out the window and hoot and holler."

"She does too!" Elmer confided to the audience. They laughed as they focused on his eyes and hung on his every word.

"So what I think cyberspace holds are the caring thoughts between mamas and papas and babies, concerned thoughts emanating from the farmers for their crops and their animals, empathetic thoughts for neighbors not just in one's little rural area but also in the whole world, plus sympathetic concerns for others.

"I think if you could reach out and grab hold of some of the things in cyberspace, there would be many more 'arrows' of goodness and kindness and faith and hope and... as my brother would say, 'That's enough now, Louey.'"

"And she's right," Elmer concluded, as he gave a rough interpretation of a bow.

The silence in the studio was deafening. The people from back home sat paralyzed in their chairs, and Max Maxim was speechless until the roar from the audience became deafening. The people at home danced in their living rooms, and Max Maxim chose to remain silent.

Finally, an announcement was able to go through: "The winners are third, Zen Wood, and second, Olaxiion Smith. That means...

Elmer and Louellen flew over the country that night. Leaning back in her seat, Louey wished she could reach out to the stars and grab some of that cyberspace.

THE END

"YOU WANT TO GO WHERE, MARJORY?
No! YOU CAN VISIT SOFRAN AT HER HOUSE BUT NOT WHERE SHE
WORKS.
JUST BECAUSE."

ᴄ╱ᐤChapter Twelveᐤ╲ᗡ

GIFTS

"**B**rilliant, Sofran! Brilliant!" Trina called out to her secretary as she finished skimming through the activities for the next Dependency Meeting. "You're a doll!" Trina blew a kiss to Sofran as she hurried to her group.

"Yeah, brilliant," Sofran muttered as she returned to her paper work.

In the group meeting, Trina gave herself the liberty of peering over the heads of her charges to see her supervisor nodding approvingly at the state representative. Sofran had constructed a very creative maze that Trina adeptly portrayed on the wall from her PC. Each dead end on the maze contained a neatly printed label, which depicted a source of temptation for the addicted. With grandiosity, Trina marched her pen through the path of the maze, pausing at each and every sidetrack to dispel any thought of entering that tarnished way of life.

This is a stroke of genius, Trina thought to herself as she meticulously kept her pen moving along the narrow corridors. "And this is how life is, ladies and gentlemen; it's a maze. You have to stay on the path and not veer into the dead-end avenues such as you see here."

As she pointed on her screen, she enhanced the drama with clicks from the pen on the words drugs, alcohol, gambling, overeating, pornography, etc. "You get into one of these dead ends and you'll never get out," Trina proclaimed with great authority. "And since you've made good progress, we don't want that to happen, do we?"

The supervisor and the state man didn't see the squirming and downcast looks of the group.

"Now let's see," Trina paused to look into the folder for another gem. "Ah, yes," she uttered with sheer joy that spread across her new sheer makeup; she knew this would be successful. "I have a story here for you. Now as I read it, try to make a mental note of how many people are affected by James, who uses drugs. Does anyone know what the domino effect is?" She stood poised, as Jerry explained the process in articulate detail.

"Very good, Jerry, very good," Trina mumbled, wishing she had had the opportunity to explain it instead of him. She covertly glanced at the two evaluators who stood as statues.

Trina read with great vibrato, much different from the silent skimming she had done before the meeting.

She reflected on Sofran's masterful writing skills as she used her oratorical skills to captivate the audience. She glanced up to see the smiles on her adjudicators.

Her addicts in recovery responded with total recall, regurgitating the names from the story of the people affected by James's drug problem. Trina looked sideways to the back of the room when Charles and Anna named others who would also be affected; those whom Trina had not thought of.

"Very good, excellent. I'd hoped someone would think of them," Trina expounded, covering her ignorance as smoothly as icing over an imperfect cake.

"We'll see you next week," Trina chirped as she looked at the clock.

The group silently departed with no look of relief or hope. Trina departed with pride and success.

"Nice job, Trina," her supervisor called out as Mr. State Man nodded his approval as well.

"Thank you, Mr. Winston," Trina beamed as she used her rigid body to walk to her office with non-addictive superiority.

"Psst, Sofran. That maze was terrific, and the story—the story had them in the palm of my hand!"

"Oh, that's good," Sofran uttered as she looked up from her keyboard.

"I can't wait until next week's session," Trina quipped as she grabbed her coat. "Good night."

"Good night, see you tomorrow."

Sofran pushed her chair back and stared at the screen. *Names, names, names—so many people with problems, so many addictions*, she thought.

"Excuse me," came a little voice from the hallway, "could I speak with Trina?"

"Oh, I'm sorry, she left for the evening. Can I help you?"

"No," the girl replied as the black mascara traveled with her tears.

"Honey, honey," Sofran uttered as she hurried to the doorway. "Come in," were the last words the secretary spoke before the frail girl dissolved into Sofran's compassion. Both women swayed with movement.

Sofran felt the bones and the flesh of perhaps twenty years being crucified against her own body. The deluge of the girl's grief nearly overtook Sofran. The older woman felt her shoulder and neck become saturated with a world of despair and fear and grief.

What could Sofran do? She stood; she stood and held the girl. She stood and held and shushed with gentle sounds and let the girl rid herself of the agonies of a lifetime.

The girl's tears took time to go into remission. *As do all tears since the beginning of mankind,* Sofran deliberated.

"I'm sorry," the little voice stammered. "I can't believe I did that."

"Oh, don't be sorry, honey, you needed that, didn't you?"

"I guess I did, but I hadn't planned on doing it."

"I know. Those things just sort of happen."

"Yeah, I guess."

Sofran could see the makeup-less red face deepen with despair.

"Here, dear, why don't you come in and have a cup of tea with me?"

"No, I just thought maybe I could catch Trina."

"Would you like to make an appointment with her?" Sofran asked.

"Well, maybe. I don't know."

"Let's see what's available," Sofran said gently as she led her to the desk. "Have a seat." The secretary's hands went directly to the keyboard as a hand goes for a stick shift; one does not need to look in any direction other than straight ahead.

"I don't know," the girl interrupted nervously. "Tomorrow will be different; I needed someone tonight."

Sofran didn't take her eyes off the screen but used her left hand to push the Tupperware container of homemade cookies toward the pencil-thin girl.

"Have one."

The slender neck stretched to elevate her sad raspberry-eyes into view with the cookies.

"Valentine cookies?" the girl asked in surprise.

"Sure enough," Sofran replied with eyes only for the screen.

The girl stared into the pink frosting with the red sprinkles. She saw her mother's pretty plate of heart-shaped cookies and glasses of milk around the dining room table for her friends. All the girls were smiling.

"Can you come in tomorrow morning at eleven?" Sofran asked, interrupting the girl's memory of her friend's pink-frosted laughter.

"Oh! Eleven?" The now pink lemonade eyes looked up in surprise at having to leave the childhood party. "Well, no—maybe. I don't know."

Sofran passed the cookies.

"What's your name, honey?"

"Mil."

"Mil?"

"Yeah, it's short for Millicent. I hate it."

"I love it, Millicent! And please have a cookie."

"Did you make these?"

"Yes."

"Why?"

"Well, everybody likes cookies, don't they?"

"Yeah, but why did you make Valentine cookies?" Mil said.

Sofran scrunched her brow, wondering if Mil was asking a legitimate question or was just being negative. When Mil sat waiting for an answer, she finally responded.

"Friday is Valentine's Day."

Sofran watched Millicent's eyes widen like the strawberries that she was going to dip into chocolate on Friday.

The tears had been in remission long enough. Their reenactment brought the still soggy Sofran again to the "crying wall."

Dear God, Sofran thought, *what is troubling this girl?*

"Millicent. Millicent, what is the matter?" Sofran kneeled beside her chair.

Millicent gulped and sobbed vehemently, "I... I... I won't have anyone who loves me on Valentine's Day."

"Oh, Millicent," cooed Sofran as she put her arms around the girl's shoulders and rocked her back and forth. "Do you know that God loves you?"

"God? How dare you say that to me?" Millicent shouted as she jumped to her feet.

"Mil, what's the matter?"

"That's what's the matter!" The girl shouted as she slapped the cookie container off the desk.

Sofran listened to Millicent's running footsteps as she stared at the mutilated cookies, some with their pretty faces down on the yellowed speckled tile.

"Good morning, Cory. Have a seat. Trina should be here soon."

Sofran watched Cory pace the floor as he intermittently placed his hand over his left shirt pocket—the pocket that contained his cigarettes. She watched as he sat and stood and walked, sat and stood and walked.

"How's your little boy, Cory?"

"Oh, he's pretty good. We're having the custody hearing tomorrow."

"Oh."

"You know what Sofran?"

"No, not exactly."

"I think I acted out of revenge."

"What do you mean?"

"I wanted to hurt her. I wanted my son to live with me, not her. But she is his mother and… and… I know I still need more counseling for my addiction."

Sofran watched Cory sit and bury his face in his hands. She went to sit by him. "It's not too late, you know," she said cautiously. "You can convey those thoughts to your lawyer and to hers. It's not too late to set things straight."

"You're right, Sofran. I still can do the right thing, can't I?" Cory lifted his face much like a bucket being hoisted out of the cold water of a well.

They both watched the clock while Sofran typed and Cory paced.

"I can't wait any longer," Cory suddenly severed the silence. "I've got to get to work; I don't want to lose this job."

"I understand, Cory. I'm sorry Trina is late. See you next week?"

"Yeah, sure. Bye."

"Hi, Sofran."

"Courtney! Hi! How are you today?"

"Not good, look at me. This is how good I am."

"Courtney, Courtney, come here and sit down," the secretary invited. "What's the matter?"

"I tried so hard this past week, but I ended up gaining three pounds," Courtney whispered with the breath of one sauntering through a ghost town.

"I'm sorry, Courtney," Sofran sympathized.

"I know you are and so are my mother and my aunts and my friends! Everybody's sorry. What good does that do me? I don't lose weight because everybody is sorry!"

"That's true. I guess I never thought about it in that light."

"Well, how do I lose weight?" she cried. "I can't stop eating! I... I can't. I can't."

"Honey, I wish Trina was here; I don't know where she is," Sofran uttered nervously as she looked at the clock.

"Look how long I have come here—week after week. Where are the answers? Doesn't anyone have an answer?"

"Yes, there must be an answer. There has to be," Sofran uttered as she held Courtney's hand.

The young woman's teary eyes looked up at the clock. "If only I had a reason to give up all that food," Courtney muttered almost inaudibly.

"Mm, Courtney? Do you want to hear what I do?"

"You? You don't have a weight problem."

"Oh, but I do."

As Courtney looked at the familiar figure wondering where the problem was, her lowered eyelids pushed the remaining tears out to the daylight.

"What do you do, Sofran?" Courtney asked with the serenity of a child.

"I give up my desire so someone else can have something?"

"Huh?"

"Well, I know it's hard to understand, but when I want to have seconds or want to eat for no real reason, I tell God that I will give it up if he will take my offering, my sacrifice, and apply it to maybe a woman in North Korea who has been dumped into prostitution or to a woman in Africa who is watching her baby die or to someone in... in America who has lost her child to a demonic cult."

If all the bewilderment in the world could have been deposited upon one face, it was now plastered on Courtney's. After a long beat, she mumbled, "Huh?"

Sofran laughed. "I'm sorry, Courtney. I probably shouldn't have said anything."

"No, no, Sofran, that's OK. I just want you to tell me again what you're talking about. You say it works?"

"Well, it does for me. I can't speak for anyone else."

The two women talked for over an hour about Sofran's "diet" of sacrificing food for the good of others and God's grace.

"Well," Courtney uttered, "this is the damnedest thing I ever heard of, but then again, nothing else works. Maybe I'll try it! I'll be back next week."

Sofran thought of the fallen Valentine cookies. "Please Lord, help her too."

"Trina! What happened? You look terrible."

"I'm sick," Trina mumbled through a thick tongue.

"Why did you come in?"

"I thought I'd better. I missed the last two Wednesdays. It wouldn't look good to miss another Wednesday. Do we have any aspirin here?"

"I have some. Sit down."

"Ooo," Trina moaned as she dashed for the lavatory.

Trina went home for the rest of the day.

"I'm sorry you drove all the way in today, Melinda. I tried to reach you in time," Sofran said apologetically. "Trina went home sick."

"Oh great!" Melinda said disgustedly. "I was frantic trying to get a baby sitter. I had to drive my husband into the city this morning because our other car is in the garage and now this! This stinks!"

"I'm so sorry, Melinda."

"Oh, it's not your fault… Wait!" Melinda looked at her watch and smiled. "I'm going to Pine Acres for a few hours. I'll have a little fun this afternoon!"

"Melinda, no!"

"Yes! Bye."

Sofran shook her head as she envisioned Melinda gambling for the rest of the day and probably into the evening.

"There's some good stuff in here, Sofran. Thanks!" Trina exclaimed as she peered through the folder while hurrying to the Dependency Meeting.

"I hope it helps," Sofran murmured to herself.

"Trina!" Mr. Winston called out, "would you mind if my guests from Ovina County observe your meeting?"

"Oh, not at all," Trina replied gleefully. The group members looked toward the back of the room to see who was going to be in on their private talks and then turned with their shoulders a few centimeters lower.

Trina began with the elaborate puzzle pieces Sofran had designed with quotations on each one. "Let's gather around this large table," Trina beamed, covertly eying her observers.

Back in the office, Sofran worked silently until she heard cellophane paper crinkling at the doorway.

"Millicent!" Sofran expounded.

The crinkling continued as the girl passed something pink and red with curly ribbons from one hand to the other.

"I... I wanted you to have this," Millicent commented, "and I'm sorry for knocking your cookies to the floor."

"Come in, Mil. Come in," Sofran motioned. "I've been worried about you."

"You have?" Mil's look of surprise reminded Sofran of candy kisses on top of peanut butter cookies for some reason. Mil handed the bakery Valentine cookies to Sofran.

"This is very nice of you, Millicent! Thank you."

"Yeah, my mother really did bring me up better than how I acted the other day. I'm sorry."

"Apology accepted. How about that cup of tea?"

"Sure. I bet you're wondering why God gets me so upset, aren't you?"

"Well!" said the surprised Sofran with a laugh, "I am curious."

"It's because I can never find him," Mil responded as serious as silver beads placed around the edge of a wedding cake. "My mother always said he loved me, but where is he?"

Sofran's cookie from the bakery stopped in midair. She looked as though she was posing for a food poster.

"Sofran?"

"I think you just asked me the most interesting question I've heard in a long time." She laughed as the Valentine cookie again became animated.

"Well, Mil," Sofran paused to dunk her cookie before she peered at the young woman, "I'm looking at Him."

Millicent turned to look behind her.

"No!" Sofran laughed. "I'm looking at you, dear girl."

"Me? I don't get it."

"What made you come here to apologize?"

"I don't know; I guess my conscience was bothering me."

"Yes, and your goodness, and goodness is what?"

"God?" Millicent said.

"Yes. So have you lost Him?"

One pair of eyes looked into the pools of the other, and two Valentine cookies posed statuesquely. The incomprehensible mystique of understanding seemed to dissolve, as did the sugar in the confection.

Finally, Mil whispered, "Oh my gosh," as delicately as a wildflower opening to see the Grand Canyon for the first time.

"Brent! Stay with Daddy; don't run ahead like that. Sorry, Sofran."

"Oh, hi, Cory. Hi, Brent."

"I didn't mean to interrupt. I just wanted to tell you how good things are working out."

"That's great, Cory! Would you like to join us for tea and cookies?"

"Oh, no, I don't want to interrupt."

"Oh please join us." Millicent's "goodness" spoke as she handed a cookie to Brent.

It wasn't long before Sofran had Brent occupied with paper, markers, and stickers, and all the supplies she used to create Trina's lesson plans.

"Hey, what's going on in there?" Courtney called through the open door.

"We're having a tea party," little Brent called back never lifting his head from his coloring.

"Yeah, come on in. You didn't go to Trina's meeting either?" Mil asked.

"No, I thought I'd just stop by here," Courtney replied, eyeing Sofran and then the cookies.

"Here, have one," Mil offered.

"Well," Courtney paused to look at Sofran, "I can have one, but the next one is going to a woman I read about; she needs God's help tonight more than I need that cookie."

Millicent put her hand to her chest as if she felt the same God Courtney was talking about.

With paper Valentines in hand, Brent announced, "This is for you and this one is for you and this is for you... And Dad, this heart is for you."

Each recipient was touched by the unconditional love of the child.

"Why weren't you three at my meeting?" came a shattering sound at the door.

The frightened Brent grabbed onto his dad's leg as he partially peered up into the angry face of Trina.

"And I'm getting sick and tired of my clients hanging out in here wasting time with my secretary. If she's not strong enough to tell you to get out, I will. Now clear out of here and stop wasting her time; she has work to do."

"But Trina, they are not wasting my time, I'm... we—"

"Never mind, Sofran. I know you are too sweet to be mean to them, but I'm not. Now scram!"

"Is there a problem in here?" Mr. Winston implored as he paused at the doorway.

"No problem, Mr. Winston, I'm just setting everyone straight about the decorum and rules around here," Trina said with authority.

"Well, decorum and rules are important," he acquiesced as he walked on with his guests.

Sofran watched her demeaned friends file out of the room; tears welled in her eyes. She couldn't look at Trina, so she scrunched herself to the floor and gathered the construction paper and supplies Brent had used to lovingly give others *a little sunshine*.

"I have an idea, Sofran," Trina interjected, thinking she was the creator of good ideas. "I'm going to give you the little office that adjoins my office, and I'll get Bernice out here. No one will want to hang around her; she'll bite their heads off." Trina laughed. "We'll get you moved tomorrow, and aren't you glad you work with a problem solver?"

Sofran never answered; she only listened to the clicking of Trina's expensive high heels striking against the yellowed tiles of the hallway.

Two weeks passed as Sofran worked in silence in her new office except for what she could hear through the adjoining wall and door. Trina had lots of one-on-one sessions. Occasionally, if the door happened to be ajar, a wave or a smile to her would immediately cause Trina to rise and close it sharply.

The secretary had more than enough time to create and devise clever manipulatives and learning tools for Trina's group lectures. Every old paper file was entered into the computer, paper copies shredded, and manila folders saved for project work.

"May I help you out there?" Sofran asked as she heard papers rustling and a constant clearing of the throat.

"I'm just waiting for Trina; I have a two o'clock appointment," the woman mumbled as she shuffled the papers in her hands and cleared her throat.

"OK, I'm here if you need anything."

By two thirty, Sofran walked into the large office with a tray of cookies and hot tea. "I don't mean to intrude, but I thought you might want something soothing for that cough of yours."

The woman with very stringy hair and dark circles under eyes stared at Sofran as would a child who first noticed a strange dog sitting in her living room.

"It's OK," Sofran said quietly. "I'm ready for a *spot of tea*, myself. I'm sorry you have to wait; Trina hasn't returned from lunch yet. I hope nothing has happened. Help yourself. I'll notify Mr. Winston."

"Sorry to interrupt, ladies. I'm sorry to report that Trina has taken ill and won't be able to return to work. I'm sorry, ma'am," Mr. Winston said to the client.

"Well, at least Sofran has been nice to me," spoke the straggly haired woman who was no longer coughing.

"Sofran!" Courtney squealed. "It's you! Where have you been? Why is that mean lady sitting in your old spot?"

"I've missed you, too, Courtney."

"Do you two know each other?" Mr. Winston asked.

"Oh yes. Sofran has been my confidant, and she gave me some wisdom that has been better than a million bucks!"

"When did this all happen?" Mr. Winston asked curiously.

"Whenever Trina didn't show up or when one of her lectures was so boring most of us left."

Sofran looked downward, wondering what Mr. Winston was thinking about Courtney's candid reply. There was no chance to find out, however, as they heard a child's voice in the hallway.

"I found her, Daddy. I can see Sofran in that room!"

"Brent, come back here right now," Cory said to his son.

"Sofran, Sofran, where have you been? I have a booful Valentine for you!"

"Do you know these people, too?" Mr. Winston asked with eyebrows raised.

"She sure does," Cory spoke up. "She saved my marriage. I would have been heading for the cliff if it wasn't for Sofran."

"Wow, Daddy, look in here!" Brent pushed the door open wide so everyone could see the eye-appealing project Sofran had been constructing.

"What's that all about?" the supervisor asked.

"It's something that Trina can use during her lecture to keep the clients interested and involved," Sofran replied.

"Are you the one who makes all those visuals?"

"Yes, sir."

Sofran could hear heavy footsteps above the beat of her heart, *Oh no,* she thought, *here comes Bernice.*

"Here," she bellowed, "you take her. I told her Trina wasn't here, but she's insisting on talking with Sofran." Bernice pushed Millicent into the room.

"I'm sorry, Sofran, but without you to talk with anymore, I'm slipping back to my old ways. I need your insights."

"Yeah, we all do," Cory said emphatically as he looked Mr. Winston squarely in the eye.

The room suddenly went silent. All they could hear was Brent snipping paper in the adjoining room.

Finally Mr. Winston spoke. "I think we have a situation on our hands." He turned and left the room.

"I hope we haven't gotten you into trouble, Sofran," Courtney whispered behind her hand.

"I'm back!" Trina announced as she threw her purse into the file cabinet. "Anything special happening around here?" she questioned her secretary in the small windowless room.

"Well…" Sofran began, just as Mr. Winston came to the door.

"The three of us need to have a meeting. How about at four thirty this afternoon?"

"Fine," they both answered.

"I wonder what that's all about," Trina mumbled as she helped herself to the freshly brewed coffee that Sofran had readied.

"I don't know," Sofran replied half-honestly.

Sofran returned to her desk and wondered if Mr. Winston was going to speak to Trina about her absences, or her lackadaisical involvement with the clients' problems, or her dependence on someone else to produce creative ideas for her classes, or her mismanagement in placing employees in the most positive positions, or her manner of boosting her own ego at the expense of the client's, or…

"Sofran! Come on; it is four thirty."

"Sit, ladies. I sense there is something wrong in our organization. Coffee, anyone? Some of us have degrees in this line of work and some of us don't. Sugar? Some of us never take a day off and some of us do. Cream? Some will stay longer if there is work to be finished and some won't. Napkin? There are those who are very creative and those others—not so much. Spoon?

"I hate to tell you this, Sofran, but I have to let you go," Mr. Winston said.

"Go? As in fired?" She tried to compute the statement.

"What?! You can't let my right-hand woman go! I depend on her!" gasped Trina.

"That's the problem, Trina; you depend on her too much. You're the one making the big bucks, and Sofran is doing most of the work. Plus, she is advising the clients on things she has not been educated in. How does she know what to say to those people? What if she gave them bad advice and they went out and killed somebody or themselves? We would be held responsible."

That dissertation left Trina speechless; all she could do was stare at her supervisor.

All Sofran could do was the same.

The news about Sofran leaving flowed through the facility like hot lava. Mr. Winston refused to handle comments. Trina refused to handle comments. Bernice welcomed comments for the first time ever. Everyone from maintenance to grounds keepers to café workers to secretaries to clients wanted answers, but they weren't getting any.

Sofran had never been without a job. She had worked ever since high school, in fact, even before graduation. Now— now what was she to do?

Sofran went on the volunteer route; she joined everything available. She was busy enough, but why did she think something was missing?

After five years of volunteering with three of those years being at the County Fair, even though it was for only one week out of the year, Sofran finally began to feel comfortable there, and in the current year especially, she looked forward to it. She never knew where she would be placed, but she had worked almost every venue, so it didn't matter.

"Welcome, Sofran. So glad you are joining us again this year," the fair director exclaimed.

"I'm glad to be here," the ex-secretary said truthfully. "What's on the agenda for this year?"

"See what you think of this," Marshall uttered as he unfolded the schematics of the fairgrounds.

Sofran's eyes darted across the entire paper several times. "I hate to admit this, Marshall, but I don't even see my name!"

Marshall laughed along with Sofran. "That's because you're looking too high. Look to the entrance."

"Oh my goodness. You've got me at the main entrance? Selling tickets? I'm not sure I can handle that. You know how busy that place can be with people buying hundreds of tickets at a time!"

Marshall could see the worry cascade across her face. "No, Sofran, not selling the tickets, but working at the back table keeping track of how many tickets are sold."

"Oh," she said weakly, still not convinced that she could even handle that.

"Do you want to give it a try?" Marshall asked.

"Sure, I'll try anything," she responded, which made her a team member who was thought of highly.

Oh the excitement of the County Fair! Sofran didn't know if it emanated more from the children's long anticipated highlight of the summer or from the long winter's work that the needlework contenders put into their creations stich by stitch. Maybe it came from the youngsters who marched their well-manicured animals off the trucks onto the clean, fresh straw or the women who gently pulled jar after jar of preserves and pies out of their toweled baskets. Sofran wondered about the excitement from the people who traveled the countryside setting up and taking down their rides. Maybe she would get to speak with some of them to get a firsthand account of how much excitement that was.

Oh, the flowers! Sofran inhaled and exhaled as she could feel the excitement of the arrangements with the exhilaration of each stem and blossom being prayed over by the gardeners that they would bloom in time for the fair. Maybe she could get over to that building and strike up a conversation with them.

Sofran was glad to hear she was on the one-hour-on, one-hour-off schedule. She could handle that, especially when it gave her time to flit around the fairgrounds.

The bullhorn sounded and the lines of people edged forward through the gate. Sofran's solid hour was fully packed with sorting and calculating; she was stunned when Michaela came in to be her replacement for an hour.

Ah, I love this! Sofran thought, never having had the every-other-hour-schedule to explore the fair before. She was amazed at how she was deep into the crowd even at that hour of the morning. *I guess the kids couldn't wait another minute to get here.* She laughed to herself.

As she munched on warm popcorn, Sofran wandered through the midway, not able to stop looking at the faces of the children. *If only that happiness could last forever.* She thought about the people at the Dependency Clinic. *What happens between childhood and the train wreck?*

"Sofran?" a voice jolted her into reality.

"Cory? Cory!" Sofran reacted with an immediate hug for her old friend.

"What are you doing here?"

"I work here. I mean volunteer here. And what... wait a minute, is this Brent as tall as I am, and who are these two?"

"Yes, this is Brent and my twins, who are now almost four."

"Congratulations, Cory! I am so glad to see you all; I can't tell you how wonderful it is to see you!"

"Have you been OK since you left..." He quickly looked at his children. "Um, left the last job? We missed you so much."

"Aw, I missed you too."

"Daddy, come on," the twins began to whine.

"I better get this caravan moving." Cory laughed. "Can I meet with you sometime? I have lots to tell you."

"Of course. Here's my phone number. Bye kids."

As Sofran turned, she could hear Brent say, "Dad, I feel like I know her."

"Sofran, you still have fifteen more minutes of break time; you don't have to be back yet," Michaela remarked as she looked up from her calculating.

"That's OK. I'll go to the Home Economics building next. That'll take my full hour. Let me help you out."

The two ladies worked in silence, and it wasn't until they heard a woman's voice say, "I don't care what they paid last year, this is what I'm paying this year... and I will take this can of beer in with me, if I want to and you can't tell me..." They started to giggle. They knew that *all kinds* came to the fair.

Security met the woman as she tried to stagger through the gate.

Sofran was not right about needing the full hour to go through the highlights of the quilts, needlework, food, and flower's building. She needed much more than one hour, as she only made it through the quilt section. She had to hurry back to the ticket house.

As she scurried along, she glanced through the wrought iron fence to see the same woman who wanted to pay last year's prices sleeping it off on a bench. Her head was covered with her huge sun hat.

Sofran wished she still had her old job where she could help people—people like that woman.

Within the next two days, Sofran did get back to the buildings that housed or "barned" the prized commodities and animals. It was during her walk past the rows and rows of yeast breads and cakes that she was surprised by Courtney.

"Sofran? It's me, Courtney!"

Sofran looked a few more seconds and then said, "Courtney! Yes! So nice to see you."

A big hug between the two caused crinkly sounds and rattling papers.

"How long has it been?" Courtney didn't wait for an answer; she went into a cacophony of accolades about the food! Sofran recognized the near delirium that Courtney was going into.

"Courtney," she said emphatically, "let's go and sit on the bench out in the shade."

"But, Sofran, I love it here," she whined.

"I know you do, but I... I need to sit in the shade."

"Oh, all right."

Sofran knew she didn't want to leave the delicious aromas and sights of the food. In fact, Courtney immediately pulled out one of the reasons for the crinkling and rattling under her large flowing coat. Sofran watched her voraciously bite into the vanilla cake with the white filling that didn't escape Courtney's quick maneuverings to capture it with her tongue. As they sat, the placating Courtney reached into another inner pocket to expose a wrapped chocolate delicacy.

"So tell me, Courtney, have all the problems of the world been settled since we last were together?"

"Huh?" Courtney replied as she used her tongue to drill into the raspberry reservoir of jelly.

"At one time, you were helping out a lot of strangers around the world by sacrificing certain foods for their welfare."

Courtney's jaw stopped moving. "Oh," she finally spoke, "that."

"Yes, that. Did you give it all up?" Sofran asked.

"You know," she replied thoughtfully, "I did give it up. I could never see any results for the people that I *thought* I was helping. How could I know that they were being helped at all?"

Her rebuttal seemed to give her new strength, and she quickly returned to her treasure trove for a package of gooey-centered candies.

"I have to return to work," Sofran said quietly, "but here is my number if you ever want to call me."

Sofran left knowing she was not one of Courtney's favorite people anymore.

As she hustled through her work, Sofran looked quickly at the outside bench. *Good, she's not sleeping out there today.*

"You look flushed, Sofran. Are you all right?" Michaela asked.

"Oh yes," she responded with uncustomary sadness. "I met someone I once knew."

"Well, you never know who you're going to meet at the fair!"

"That's for sure."

Sofran couldn't refrain from thinking about Courtney leering at the cakes and strudels and...

Oh no, that woman is back, she said to herself.

"I am entitled to a senior citizen price; I am eight-eight years old! Oops, a little spill here, oh well. More beer for you and less for me. I'm a pro at spilling things," the woman said with a giggle.

As soon as Sofran heard the woman say, "I'm a pro..." she dropped the handful of tickets and spun her revolving chair to face the customer. Yes! It was Trina!" She quickly rotated the chair so Trina couldn't look back and see her. Sofran sat almost paralyzed while she listened to the arguing going back and forth with the ticket seller. Again, security was summoned, and Trina was escorted out of the fairgrounds.

Oh my, I can't believe it. Trina really did have a problem, but I didn't know she would ever let it get this bad. How awful for her; she must have been disgraced when she had to leave her position. I wonder who took over for her.

"Sofran, Sofran! Are you all right?"

"Oh, yes, I was just deep in thought."

"Your shift is over for the day; you can go home now."

Thank goodness there are only two more days of the fair; that fair is starting to get creepy, Sofran thought as she turned off the light.

"Sofran, aren't you going to walk over to see the animals?" Michaela questioned.

"Um, I think I'll stay right here and help you."

"Don't be silly. Get out and walk for a bit. It'll make you feel much better."

I guess she's right, I'll be safe with the calves, chickens, and pigs.

Ah, she was right. What beautiful animals and so well groomed. Hello, little calf. You don't have any problems, do you, little one?

Sofran drank in the calmness of the building and breathed in the sweet smell of hay as she slowly walked through. Then suddenly... *wompf!*... she was on the ground.

"Oh, I'm sorry. I'm sorry. I didn't see you," the young woman apologized. As she pulled Sofran to her feet, she suddenly said, "Wait a minute! Aren't you Sofran from the clinic?"

In all her discombobulation, Sofran finally said, "I used to be. Why?"

"Weren't you Trina's secretary?"

"Yes, but how come I don't remember you?"

"I only saw you once. Then you were gone."

"Is Trina still there?" Sofran asked curiously.

"Her? Hell no. She was fired a couple of months after you left."

"Do you know why?" Sofran asked.

"I heard all sorts of things; I don't know what was true, but... Oh God, here he comes. Hide me; he's after me!"

"Who's after you? What's the matter?"

"Just keep turning as I turn so he won't see my face. Talk about the animals," Melinda pleaded desperately.

For some reason, Sofran did just as she was told. She could see the man leave the building and go into the horse barn.

"What's going on?"

"Well, if you don't remember, I have a gambling problem, and I'm trying to elude my husband so I can sneak out to the casino."

"Oh yes, Melinda," Sofran shook her head, suddenly remembering her from the clinic.

"Thanks, and wish me luck," Melinda called back as she ran out a different door.

Wish her luck? What did you think of that little episode, you sweet little calf? Don't ever grow up.

"How was the animal barn?"

"Very strange."

"Well, we're bringing it to a close, Sofran! Are you going to sign up for next year?" Marshall asked.

"Um, I'll have to think about that," Sofran answered, knowing she was going to decline.

"This is your last break, Sofran. Make it a good one!" Michaela cheered her on.

"I'm not going too far, only over to the hot dog stand and back to our bench."

Sofran ate her overflowing, accoutrement-ed hot dog as she watched the people pass by. *Who are they? What kind of lives do they have? Have they had an easy life? A hard life?* Thoughts and more thoughts came to her mind.

"Hey, can I have a bite of that hot dog? Move over, honey."

"Trina!" Sofran shouted as she jumped from fright.

"I'm not, Trina, I'm... Loretta Young!" She laughed uproariously as she gulped her beer and threw the empty can at the fair sign. "No, not Loretta Young. I'm Betty Davis. Do you want to see my eyes?"

"Trina, stop it," Sofran implored.

"Do you know me?"

"Yes, I know you. I'm Sofran."

"Sofran from work?"

"Yes."

"Do you know they fired me?"

"They fired me too."

"Whaaaaaat? I didn't know you were a drunk!"

Finally, Sofran had something to smile about.

"I'm glad you're happy," Trina mumbled as she suddenly began crying.

"Oh, Trina, I'm going to go right over there and get you a hot dog and some coffee. Then when my work is done, you are going to go to my house. Would you like that?

"Yes," she replied softly, as she wiped her tears away.

THE END

"Agnes, do you know why Mark Lehman's horse farm used to
be called Bushel Basket Lane?"
"Migrant workers used to harvest the crops and send the
produce out by rail."
"Mm, that's interesting," Marian uttered.
"In-teres-ting, in-teres-ting, isn't that in-teres-ting,"
Marjory sang from the next room.
"Marjory, stop that," her grandmother directed.

Chapter Thirteen

Bushel Basket Lane

"And don't you be runnin' down Bushel
Basket Lane again. You know I'll find out
about it."

"Yes, ma'am."

"I know where you are every second; so don't try to
pull the wool over my eyes. I know everything."

"Yes, ma'am. I hear ya."

"You better be hearin' me, cuz I mean it. I know where
you are every minute of every day. You can't fool me, ya
know."

"I know, I can't fool you."

"That's right and don't you forget it."

"Yes, ma'am."

"Now, run along and go play."

Willie walked backward as he continued to wave to his ma. He waved and waved to the woman on the porch until he walked far enough beyond the junk cars and pickup trucks where he could duck and run through the woods to Bushel Basket Lane.

"Where ya been, Willie, we been waitin' for ya?" asked Simple Simon, the pie man.

"Had to git my lecture," Willie replied as he looked up at the huge stack of bushel baskets.

"What's a lecture?" little Reenie asked as she pushed dry dirt with her bare toes.

"It's like a what-ta-do," Willie answered with great superiority.

"What-ta-do, what-ta-do," little Reenie immediately began singing as her leg kept time with the beat.

"Didn't ya learn last time? Ya can't tell her a dang thing. She just sings it out over and over. Apt to drive us all crazy," Simple Simon commented, feeling exasperated with Willie's forgetfulness about Reenie's idiosyncrasy.

"Yeah, I forgot. Sorry."

"Just remember fer next time."

"I will. Whatta we gunna do today, Simon?"

"Gotta fill up these bushel baskets with apples. Ya wanna help?"

"Sure."

"Where's the rest of the kids?"

"They's already in the or-chid. Come on, run."

Simple Simon, the pie man, grabbed half the pile of baskets and held them over his head as he ran. Willie followed suit and galloped after his friend as Reenie let out a wail.

They knew. Each boy stopped, took one basket off their pile, and dropped it on the ground for Reenie. She imitated the boys and tagged along singing, "Pickin', pickin', pickin' apples."

"Bout time ya got here," seven of the eight boys chanted together as they bobbed up and down putting apples in the baskets.

"Couldn't be hepped," the pie man retorted. "Willie had to git his lecture, and Reenie, ya know, it's always one dang thing or a'tother with her.

"Yeah, we know," Cucumber Joe answered without stopping his work.

Reenie sauntered onto the scene just in time to get her next lyrics. "Yeah, we know, yeah we know, yeah we know," she sang robustly for a tiny-framed girl.

The girl pickers laughed; they loved their little Reenie.

The young migrant workers, plus Willie, picked the ground clean. Each heavy basket was carried by two children who felt the wire handles dig into the palms of their hands while wondering if one day one arm would be longer than the other.

The biggest of the boys started to itch and twitch, not hardly being able to wait until they could scale the apple trees and be the superheroes, as they shook the branches releasing the remaining apples.

Those children on the ground scurried backward knowing they didn't want to be caught under the rain shower of apples. Jennalee grabbed little Reenie, who didn't appear to grasp the situation but innocently stood looking upward. "Reenie run! Iss gunna be rainin' apples!"

As Jennalee hustled Reenie to safety, the others were entertained by the girl singing, "Rainin' apples, rainin' apples, rainin' apples." Followed immediately by a thunderous applause of hard apples hitting the softer ground.

"Hey, Willie, catch!" a boy from across the way yelled. Willie had just enough time to look up and catch the apple. "Good catch," Simple Simon called out.

Willie grinned; he knew the fun they were going to have!

"Play ball!" Cucumber Joe hollered. Each apple sailed across the lot to be caught and placed into someone else's basket. The heavy burden of work had been lifted.

"Me do, me do, me do," sang out Reenie as the older girls took it upon themselves to gently toss apples to the youngest worker.

The game ceased as quickly as a summer shower might end when the whistle sounded beyond the grove of apple trees. It didn't matter whose mother was sounding the sweet repose, or from whose front porch shanty it hailed from, it meant come, rest, and eat. Everyone ran to the sound, accompanied by the sweet little voice singing, "Let's go eat."

Willie looked ahead at Bushel Basket Lane to see every front door open and the women scurrying across the dirt road to the shade of the huge trees. It was there that the migrant workers would have their picnic lunch. The men came across from the potato fields and stopped to wash up in the large wooden barrel of rain water.

Willie knew better than to grab a piece of chicken; he had learned last time about waiting for the blessing. Everyone sat quietly and waited for the oldest man to speak words of gratitude that they had food to eat. Willie didn't quite understand the reasoning behind all of that, seeing how they always went from town to town to get food. He couldn't imagine them never having any food, but he accepted their ways.

With the last "amen," the women's morning work of preparation soon disappeared into the outdoor laborers. That in turn caused a ritualistic display of calmness and satisfaction. The children knew they could rest or play; the men knew they could rest; the women knew they could bed down their infants and start peeling the battered apples for the evening's pies.

"Hey, Willie, want to go fishin'?"

"Yeah! Do we have time?"

Simple Simon pointed behind his hand at the old man who said the blessing. He was sound asleep on the grass. That meant no one had to go back to work until he awoke.

"He'll sleep for about half hour," the pie man whispered.

"Come on, Cucumber Joe."

"OK, put your belly right on the edge of the creek bank here," Simon directed as he and Joe did the same thing while leaning over the bubbling waters.

"And don't puke into the water again like last year," Joe commanded.

"Don't worry. I won't," Willie retorted with high hopes.

The three of them dangled with hands outstretched to grab the first fish that went by.

"They're under the shady bank that we're lying' on right now."

"How do you know? Willie asked.

"Old Grandfather Clem said they like the coolness under the creek banks when the sun is hot on the water," Simple Simon whispered.

Willie could feel the thickness of the grass push into his stomach. He tried to take a deeper breath but couldn't get much air while fighting to balance his body on the edge.

Cucumber Joe picked up a stone. "Ready?"

"Ready," Simon responded as his fingers tensed.

Cucumber let the stone fly under the creek bank. That did it! Six fish darted out of their refuge! "Get 'em. Get 'em!" the pie man yelled and not with the melodious tones that Reenie would have used.

Willie felt a vigorous movement between his hands; he clutched it tighter. He felt the hardness of the fish mightily flailing against his own strength. He thought he was about to slip headfirst into the water, but he didn't let go.

"Grab his ankles!" he heard the master fisherman yell to Cucumber Joe.

"Hang on; hang on to that fish!" the boys commanded.

"Pull me back," Willie cried in desperation, thinking he was either going to vomit or faint.

The battle ended with Willie lying flat out, panting in the thickness of the grass while the fish flopped on the strangeness of dry soil.

"Ya did it!" both boys applauded, even after they had given up their chance of catching anything in order to help him.

Willie looked like a king parading through the ranks of people as the fish lay flat across his outstretched hands. The onlookers clapped for him as he marched by. One woman came forward to receive the offering. "Thank you," she uttered, "this will be supper for the elders tonight. They thank you too."

"Grab the bushel baskets," commanded the veteran worker.

Along with the men, the children marched to the carrot field with the same lightness as what they carried, knowing later everything would be heavy.

"So where were ya all day?" Willie's mother asked as she sat with her legs dangling off the edge of the porch.

"Just with my friends."

"That's good. Ya didn't git into any trouble did ya?"

"No, ma'am."

"Good thing, ya know, cuz I know where you are every second, and don't think you can git away with anything."

"Yes, ma'am."

"Hope you ain't too hungry, cuz we ain't got much here tonight."

"That's OK," Willie replied as he thought about the picnic lunch, the fish, and the apple pies.

"Hey, man, where you been all week?"

"At school. How come you guys don't go to school?"

"We do sometimes, but mostly, we don't stay in one place long enough to make it worthwhile. My ma teaches us."

"Your mother knows how to teach stuff?" Willie asked.

"Oh yeah. She's really smart; she went to college."

"Jeepers," Willie said softly.

"Grab some baskets. We're going to the vineyard."

"What do they grow there?"

Simple Simon looked at Willie in disbelief. "They grow grapes."

"Oh, I never knew that." *I wonder why my mother thinks the Bushel Basket people are stupid,* Willie wondered.

The men used long clippers to cut the blue bunches and then swing the clippings to a child who would place them into a basket. The baskets filled quickly, and the youngsters had to hustle to dump the contents into the carts in order to run back for more. Willie wished that they could toss the grapes like they did the apples and make a game out of it.

Just as he thought that, something hit him in the back of the head. He turned to see one of the girls giggling. *Did she throw a grape at me?*

It wasn't long before it happened again. *Why is she doing that?*

"Stop that," he said directly to her.

"It wasn't her," Cucumber Joe said seriously.

"Then who was it?"

The man with the clippers pointed unobtrusively at a boy across the way. The man laughed and whispered, "Fire back when he's not looking."

Willie waited for his moment and fired. He hit his mark, but the boy questioned someone else. Finally, Willie realized that it was a game! The time passed quickly and it was a challenge to discover who was throwing the ammunition.

Willie was surprised when he heard the lunch whistle; maybe he had eaten too many grapes. No one else seemed to be surprised, and at the rate of their pace, it was obvious that they were hungry. He knew he would be too by the time he got there.

He didn't know why the women hustled out of their shanties carrying the food with such enthusiasm and joy. They must think they were doing something great. *Wait a minute*, he thought, *they were doing something great.* He wondered why his mother never seemed to be exhilarated by feeding him.

Reenie was asked to say the blessing with the old man because it was her birthday. Willie wondered why there had been no mention of it before. As Renee snuggled close to the old man, Willie noticed every child's lips curl into a smile as well as those of the women. He didn't know why, but he should have. The old man prayed.

"Thank you Lord that we have food to eat and can gather food from your earth for others."

"For others, for others, for others," Renee sang.

"Thank you for your bounty and let us not forget that it all comes from you," the old man continued.

"From you, from you, from you," Renee continued.

"You who brings us such happiness. Amen."

"Amen, amen, amen, I say to you," Renee concluded.

Everyone clapped as her mother brought out the surprise birthday cake.

"Ah," could be heard escaping from the mouths of the laborers as their rest period began. The old man was already nestled into his grassy spot.

"Do you want to go fishin' today, Willie?"

Willie felt the girth of his stomach and replied, "Not today. How about something quiet?"

"What's quieter than fishing?" Simon reacted.

"That's true, but you guys can do the angling over the bank to catch the fish."

"Let's go!"

Willie stretched out on his back as the other two tended to their mission. He watched the clouds, thinking of what they were piling themselves into. It wasn't long before a long low rumble escaped the fast-moving canvas. Simon, the pie man and Cucumber Joe jolted to their feet.

"Did you get a fish?" Willie asked excitedly not registering the fact that there was no fish in sight.

The two boys took off like a shot, much in comparison to the bolt of lightning that pierced through Willie's clouds.

"Where ya goin?" Willie shouted as he, too, ran.

When they reached the shade of the huge trees, the women were not in their houses washing the pots and pans, but scurrying with their skirts flying along with the others to the vineyard. Every bushel basket had been taken so the boys ran empty handed.

The thunder became more in command of its world and the lightning strove for dominance with its threatening sharpness in trying to reach the earth.

Willie ran with the full baskets as fast as the others were. He felt the first drops of rain hit the top of his head. The women were on the carts uncovering and covering as fast as the baskets were dumped. The men's speed doubled or quadrupled or whatever those words were that Willie's teacher tried to teach him. He never thought he would need those words.

As he reached a cart just as Simon did, Willie yelled, "Rain doesn't hurt grapes, does it?"

"No, but if we don't get these ready for shipment by tonight, we won't get paid."

The rain-soaked workers plodded back to their houses; they had accomplished their mission. Willie thought about the day as he slowly walked home.

"Look at you!" his mother screeched. "Don't ya have any more brains than to come in out of the rain?"

"I guess not," the boy said unemotionally.

"Who were you playing with that didn't have any more brains than you?"

"Just some kids."

"Well, there is no supper for you, just go to bed."

Willie was glad for sleep.

"No school today?"

"Nope. Christopher Columbus weekend," Willie said.

"Good, you can help us in the pumpkin field."

"Pumpkin field, pumpkin field, be my little pumpkin field," sang Reenie as she paid no attention to anyone else.

"Doesn't look like anyone will be throwin' any of these pumpkins," Willie said as he laughed. "How did they git so big?"

"I don't know," answered Simon, the pie man, "but our backs are gunna hurt tonight."

"What's that thing?"

"It's a scale to weigh the pumpkins."

"What fer?"

"So when these git to the market, the poundage will be known, plus we get half a cent per pound."

"Huh?"

"That's why my mother is walking across the field; this is going to be the arithmetic lesson for some of the kids."

"Is it going to be your lesson?"

"No, mine will be with the potatoes when we dig them out of the ground."

Willie thought about his math lessons in school where they never had anything real to figure with.

"Cucumber Joe, we need you on this one and bring Tunin' Fork Freddie with ya; this one is a beast!"

"We'll make almost a nickel on this one," Freddie exclaimed as he laughed.

Willie didn't know if he was serious or fooling, and he sure didn't want to disclose his lack of computing skills.

By the time the lunch whistle sounded, the men and the children were sure they couldn't lift another pumpkin. Five large wagons were filled to capacity.

"All right, children, pick one that's still lyin' in the field for your jack-o'-lantern."

"Yay!" they all yelled as they ran and scattered with a newfound energy.

"Can this really be for me?" Willie asked as he sat in the shade with his pumpkin next to his leg.

"Yeah, you bet, and after lunch, we all git to carve our own."

"Wow." Willie sighed as he lifted his prize onto his lap and patted the orange orb as if it was a baby's head.

The men and the women stayed after lunch to help with the carving. The old man was the only one who drifted off to sleep. Willie thought his was a masterpiece and others did also. What an assortment! They all walked *the pumpkin gallery* to see the greatest artwork ever!

The jack-o'-lanterns sat quietly as they watched their creators return to the field.

"Where'd you git that thing?" Willie's mother torpedoed the question as he walked toward her on the crumbling sidewalk.

"I made it."

"You did not."

"Honest."

"What kids around here have their pumpkins already?"

"Um."

"See, you're lyin'. I can tell when you're lyin'. Give me that thing."

"No," Willie screamed, as he turned and jumped from the porch. He held his creation like a football and no one was going to take it from him. His mother relented on the chase when her high heels fought against the crumbling cement.

"What are you doin' here?" Simon asked in surprise.

"Can my jack-o'-lantern stay here with you?"

"Sure."

"Thanks. I've got to hurry home."

"So where is it?" his mother asked as soon as she heard the door open.

"I threw it into the creek," Willie replied.

"Good. We don't need that creepy thing around here. Now git to your homework, or you'll end up like those dumb bunnies who come and go over on Bushel Basket Lane."

Willie felt tears stream along his cheeks as he went to his room.

He flipped open his math book. *Ugh, I'll never be able to figure these out*, he said to himself.

Tommy weighed the pumpkin. It weighed twenty pounds. His father said he would give him a nickel for every pound that the pumpkin weighed. How much money could Tommy earn?

Earn? Willie thought. *That kid wasn't doing any work. Why would his father give him money for doing nothing?* Willie drew twenty circles for pumpkins and then wrote five under each one. He knew how to count by fives. Even Reenie could do that as she skipped along.

"What?" he said aloud, "this can't be right." He counted again. It was right. Willie let his head rest in his hand as he thought about how hard his friends had to work to get a half a cent. He wondered what a half cent was.

The sun was coming over the horizon as Willie left his house and ran to Bushel Basket Lane. "Yay, Saturday, yay, Saturday, yay, Saturday!" he sang and laughed.

"What are ya doin' here so early?" Simon called out as he looked up to see Willie.

"Can't wait ta git to work and checkin' on Jack, too."

"Jack?"

Without answering, Willie ran to the wooden table that housed everyone's jack-o'-lanterns. "There you are!" he squealed as he spotted his creation.

"Too bad you can't come here the night when we light all the candles," Simon, the pie man, proclaimed. "It'll make your eyes pop out of your head!"

A plate of flapjacks passed under Willie's nose as the woman asked if he'd had any breakfast.

"What fields did you work on this week?" Willie asked as he and Simon watched the rationed two drops of real maple syrup curl on the top pancake.

"We did carrots, cauliflower, and turnips."

"What's on for today?"

Before he could answer, they heard, "*Potatoes, potatoes. Who's got the potatoes.*"

It was potatoes all right! The men unearthed thousands and thousands of the brown oddities, still covered with dirt, as the children stayed bent over the nuggets to fill the baskets. The bigger boys carried the heavy baskets to be dumped into the wagons.

Gee, this could bring up some good math problems, Willie thought to himself. He laughed when he looked over at a group of children with Simon's mother. *That's exactly what they are doing,* he thought resentfully as he recalled how he was being taught.

"Can my pumpkin sit by me when we eat?" Willie asked.

"I suppose," Simon responded with a dumbfounded look.

Willie and Reenie were the only ones who sat with their pumpkins.

The peaceful lunch was suddenly unearthed not by the men's shovels but by the screeching of Willie's mother.

"So there you are! I knew I'd find you! You think you're smarter than your mother? Well, you're not. And you've been lying to me—and look at you sittin' there like a fool with a pumpkin." She continued the tirade as everyone stared at her with mouths agape. "Give me that damn thing," she commanded. She didn't wait for her son to pass it to her, but crouched low to snatch it away. "Here's what I think of your disobedience," she scowled as she stepped to the large rock.

Willie's life changed that day—the day the orange pulp splattered high into the sky and settled downward upon his friends, young and old. On his own legs lay part of the toothy mouth and the stem. He could see a chunk of orange rind next to the old man. Reenie cried as she pulled a wet piece of inner pulp from her hair.

"And I don't care what you do anymore." His mother ranted her grand finale. "See who you wanna see; do what you wanna do. You're never gunna amount to anything anyway."

Oh no, thought Reenie's mother as her eyes darted to her daughter. *Please, Lord, don't let her sing that.*"

The group sat quietly as they watched the exiting, theatrical march. No one spoke; no one made a sound, not even Reenie. Finally, the old man said, "No rest time today. We better get back to work; there's a big storm coming this afternoon."

Willie thought the storm had just left.

Perhaps after the potatoes were all above ground, and the migrant workers traveled to the next farm, Willie went with them.

Nobody really knew. Nobody tried to find him.

THE END

"JACOB WON'T COME HERE AND VISIT ANYMORE IF YOU KEEP
PESTERING HIM TO TELL YOU THAT STORY. HOW MANY TIMES DO
YOU HAVE TO HEAR IT?
I KNOW IT'S YOUR FAVORITE STORY BUT DON'T WHINE IF HE DOESN'T
WANT TO TELL IT TODAY."

THE UNABRIDGED VERSION OF MARJORY'S FAVORITE STORY.

Chapter Fourteen
THE TRAIN

Worn smooth were the boards with no visible grain with foot-worn centers a half an inch lower than the unused peripheries and no dust in the corners—stairs.

Nan peeked out of her door to look on the majestic empty staircase.

Where are they? She wheeled her chair around and went back to the front window.

"Lace be gone!" she murmured to the white curtain as she dramatically pulled back the curtain on her center stage.

"Act one," she announced with much inflection just as Gemma would do.

"Ah," she professed, as the actors paraded back and forth on her stage. "Could it be Mrs. O'Malley returning home to her twelve children with a fish: one fish for them all with the bones to be eaten by the little sinners who were naughty that day? And there is Mr. Sullivan pulling his empty ice wagon, much lighter than the morning when his back bent low, making him look like a crippled man. Drip, drip, drip.

That was all he could show his children when he returned home for supper. That and some damp straw that lay on the bottom of his wagon."

What does your father do for a living, son?

Well, sir, he goes off early in the morning with an empty wagon and comes home with a...

With a what, boy? Speak up!

With an empty wagon, sir.

Your father isn't much good. Is he, boy? Answer me!

Yes, he is good!

Whack. Don't ever talk back to me. Do you hear me?

Yes, sir.

Nan wiped away a tear. "What a sad play this has started out to be," she sighed as she tucked her little embroidered handkerchief back into her pocket.

"Oh no!" she gasped. "There are those bad boys." She watched as they sauntered down the street with their hats either cocked back on their heads or off to the side. She had begun to notice that the position of a man's hat told what kind of character he was trying to portray. She had never realized that fact when she was little. Nan straightened her back as she thought of herself as being a bit more intelligent nowadays.

They were bad characters, all right!

"Look out, Tommy," she called out, pressing her forehead to the windowpane. "Run, Tommy."

Tommy didn't start running in time; the bad boys had his hat; the bad boys had his coat. They tossed both around and around as Tommy screeched like a banshee rooster trying to grab for his belongings. The biggest one shoved Tommy's hat into the sleeve and put a stone into one of the pockets. He slung it with all his might. It whirled and sailed, landing on top of the awning of Angolini's Bakery.

Tommy screamed, cried, and threw dirt at the bad boys while they laughed and sauntered away.

Where's your coat and hat, boy?

I don't know, father.

You don't know? What the Sam Hill's the matter with you? Get back out there and find them, and don't come back until you do!

Nan let the lace curtain unfold. *That's enough of the play for now,* she thought somewhat wearily, knowing it had only just begun. She questioned her own endurance when she realized she could only watch such tiny portions at a time. She sat worrying about the sinning children who would have to eat the fish bones and about the ice man's son trying to think of his father's worth and now Tommy.

She wheeled her chair around and sat staring at the inner wall of family portraits—all family her mother had told her about over and over. Her eyes wove from photo to photo looking at them for the millionth time—looking at them for the first time. Expressions, no expressions. Intimacy, no intimacy. Caring, not caring. Who were they?

Why did the older ones look so stern? Her mother told her they were supposed to pose like that. She hoped so. Who would want mothers and fathers who looked like that all the time?

Sometimes Nan would turn her relatives into story characters. She wished she could reach up on the wall and rearrange the portraits. Sometimes she wanted Great Grandmother Nina or Cousin Lewis to stand by Abigale. Or have the darling baby with the long curls, who was actually great, great grandfather, to be by great Aunt Lorraine or sometimes by the six brothers. But since the day Mother hung the pictures on the wall, they never, ever have been in any other order than what they are today.

When Nan was little, she would use her hands as blockades to those not in the story. What she could see through her fingers were those characters in the story. As she became older, she used pieces of paper for the same purpose. Now Nan had elaborate fans with peek holes that framed the characters that she designed using her mother's embroidery scissors. On each fan, she elaborately printed the name of the story. Of course, new fans were constantly in the making. Each day, Nan went through her fan box and selected stories that she would recite to herself. With five or six characters or, however many were in the story, it magically eliminated the cascade of others who occupied the wall.

Nan had been very considerate in ensuring that everyone was included in at least one story. For a long time, she didn't want to include Great Uncle Nester because he looked like a mean, wild man. And for a long time, Nester was not in any of her fan stories until she became a little older and realized that she could have characters of great disdain. Nester is now very popular, being in stories of everything from pirates to bank robbers.

Nan knew just where to sit and just how to hold the fan to align the openings with the correct pictures. It was almost impossible for her mother to do it until Nan gave her exact instructions as to whom she should focus upon in the left-hand corner. That was the secret—the left-hand corner.

Where are they? Nan wondered again as she wheeled herself to the door and looked out at the stairway? She didn't know why she looked; she hadn't heard them; all had been quiet in the hallway. Sometimes she thought if she looked at the stairs long enough, she could create the people who used them. It never happened, but she thought maybe it could.

Her eyes followed the beautiful carvings that patterned themselves every twelve or sixteen inches; she didn't exactly know which. The banister had an ever so graceful curve as it escalated higher and higher to the second floor. The staircase had once been theirs, along with the whole house. That was a long time ago, however, and Nan didn't really remember, even though her mother told her about it sometimes.

Nan thought maybe that's why all the family portraits were in one huge grouping; she thought her mother ran through the entire house grabbing all the frames from the various rooms and rehung them just in one place—one place to watch over her daughter and herself. Nan wasn't really sure. Her mother didn't talk much about it.

Nan looked from the top of the stairs to the bottom and from the bottom to the top counting the beautifully carved posts. It didn't surprise her when she came to a different total most times. Her eyes would play tricks on her because she had to count from a low level at an angle. The curve, too, played havoc with her counting. She pulled her tally sheet from the utility bag that had been strung to the side of her chair and entered the total. She noticed that seventeen times she had calculated the same number. She remained in that position looking for similarities in totals. Her paper was almost full. In another week or so, she would have to use the back. *No*, she thought as if pulling herself up short, *not on the back*. She knew the laborious work it would be to constantly flip the paper from back to front to check numbers. She felt proud of herself that she had thought of that near calamity before it happened.

Nan felt a draft and looked in the opposite direction of the stairs to the front doors. There were two huge doors, but only one was used. They closed in the middle so if they were opened, it would make a very wide doorway. Her mother had told her that she remembered when the big doors were opened quite often. When Mother was younger, there would be much company and parties in the house, and when people entered, they first saw the impressive staircase. Nan noticed that the tiny panes of etched glass were permitting only the slightest of daylight to enter. It wasn't that the glass was dirty; it was that there was only a bit of daylight remaining to enter.

Nan wheeled backward and closed the inner door to keep the draft away from her. Then she returned to her window.

Her spirits lifted when she saw that four lights were now burning on the upper end of the street. She leaned forward and to the right until she could feel the cold windowpane touch her head. Now five, six...

"He's almost here!" she exalted. Nan knew that if she were in the window, Mr. Halston would wave to her. Sure enough, just as he made the lamplight glow, he gave a wave and a smile that lit up the night!

Nan watched him as he proceeded down the street with all of his paraphernalia.

She liked Mr. Halston. She did hope, however, that he would never get his handlebar mustache too close to the flame. Mother always said, "Nan, don't worry. He knows what he's doing."

She listened to the old clock ticking; it was a "here" and "gone" sound. Nan didn't know why or where the little sounds went. She knew she could easily hear them when she focused on the clock. However, during the other minutes or hours, it never even dawned on her to hear the clock. She was almost positive that the same sound came out all the time. How could she just not hear it when she wasn't thinking about it? It was during this contemplation that Nan heard noises in the hallway.

The little knock, the same one that she heard each evening, made her laugh out loud and call, "Come in. Come in!"

"We're sorry we're late, honey child." Gemma's voluptuous voice filled the entire tick-tocky room. "Land knows, when you want to get out on time there's another whole stack of dishes to do. Lucius too. They had him down in the cellar trying to find a crate that would be good for the little boy's puppet show. Nothing can ever wait till the morrow. How are you today, honey child?" she asked, giving Nan a hug and fixing her collar at the same time.

"I'm fine, Gemma. I missed you."

"I missed you too, baby. All right, Lucius, scoop up this pretty damsel and up the grand staircase we will go!"

In what didn't seem like any effort at all, Lucius bent over Nan and used his strong arms to lift her out of the chair. She almost looked like a porcelain doll with her long skirt and her tiny leather shoes.

The three of them ascended the staircase, just as they had every evening when Nan's mother was at work.

Lucius placed Nan in her "upstairs" chair, while Gemma grabbed an apron off the hook. "Are you hungry, sweet pea?"

"I sure am." Nan laughed as she did every time Gemma asked that question.

"Well, we'll see to that right now." Gemma chuckled as she grabbed the mixing bowl with one hand and opened the flour bin with the other.

Nan loved being in Gemma and Lucius's upstairs apartment. They talked and laughed, kidded and cooked, sang and whistled, and told stories and made sock puppets or paper dolls, or whatever Nan wanted to make!

While Gemma and Lucius prepared the meal, Nan was royally entertained to the point that she didn't even see what was being served until it was time to eat. She would often say, "Gemma, when did you make this?"

After dinner, Lucius would lift Nan out of the chair and place her on the sofa with the full goose-feathered pillows behind her back. It was on that sofa that Nan heard stories that her two friends wove masterfully, was read to, or watched their big old hands crafting something just for her.

Sometimes Nan would drift off to sleep, but only for a short time. She never wanted to miss anything. Then, late at night, Lucius would carefully carry Nan down the curved staircase with a statuesque frame of a much younger man who was walking downward to greet his guests.

Nan's mother would then get her daughter and herself ready for bed. Nan loved her mother's beautiful bedroom with the four-poster bed and the canopy overhead. She loved the big round mirror over the vanity and Mother's music boxes. Mother used to have more, but now she says she needs to get rid of a few things that they only collect dust. Nan didn't understand that statement because Gemma and Lucius and Mother were always dusting and cleaning.

Nan's bedroom was attached to the master bedroom. She liked it there; her mother always left the door open between the two rooms. Nan counted, sorted, and made up little plays about the roses on her wallpaper as she listened to her mother saying prayers in the next room.

Mornings were nice for Nan. She and her mother had quiet mornings together. Not the laughing, whistling, and rambunctious times that she had upstairs, but good times. Nan knew her mother was a quiet woman; Nan didn't mind quiet. Her fastidious mother liked everything clean and in its place. Her teacups were in precise rows with all handles slanted identically, the family portraits never slanted, and the sewing box was tidy. Nan knew all of this, and she liked her mother's ways. Besides, she always had Gemma and Lucius to add fun to her life.

That morning, after all the housecleaning chores were accomplished, Mother walked from the old clock to the green glass vase to the set of silverware in the wooden box. Nan knew that one of those "dust collectors" would soon go away. She didn't know exactly where such items went to but Mother would leave with it, maybe today, and that was it! It would be gone. Before she and the object left the house, Mother would always say, "Dear, you really don't care if we keep this or not, do you?"

Only once had Nan objected and that was to the clock, which kept her company when she was alone in the house. When Nan stated her wishes, Mother immediately put it back on the mantle and never approached the subject again. Nan always thought her mother was a little sad about the things that collected dust. Sometimes she would see her mother touch the item in such a loving way.

Nan was right. "Dear, you really don't mind if we keep this or not, do you?" It was the glass vase. Nan sometimes used that vase to let the sunshine dance on it by lowering and raising her head. But Mother always knew best, so she said, no. Mother wrapped it in newspaper and set it on the little table by the door.

Mother settled in her favorite tapestry chair and reached for her notepad and pencil. This, Nan knew, was a quiet time; Mother was writing numbers. She said they were numbers about the house and numbers about the cost of things. She worked almost every day on her numbers. Nan watched the pencil point descend a long row of numbers, and then her mother would write a number and the pencil would go up a long row of numbers and so on. Nan would imitate that process sometimes in the late afternoons when she was doing her self-entertaining. She knew it was something of importance.

After that, Mother would read the paper. Nan always waited quietly because she knew sooner or later Mother would read out loud something of great importance or something that made her laugh. That was the best part: when Mother laughed. Nan didn't like the readings that made her mother shake her head, and she definitely did not like the words stock market. Nan didn't know what kind of market it could be, but it bothered her mother so it bothered her too.

Nan thought Father was working at the stock market from what she heard mother and Gemma talking about sometimes, but she didn't know what was taking him so long; he had been gone for such a long while now. She missed her father.

"Are you ready to get some fresh air, Nan?" her mother asked.

"Oh yes," Nan replied with sudden exuberance.

"Then we shall go!"

Nan loved this part of the day. Mother packed a picnic lunch and soon Nan could feel the warm sunshine on her arms. Slowly, they went along the sidewalk, with Mother stopping every so often to talk with the shopkeepers, or to buy a piece of fruit, or to look at the wares. Everyone knew Nan and Isabelle. Isabelle had lived in the same house since she was married. Nan was born in that house, except upstairs where their upstairs used to be.

"Sounds like you need a little oil on those wheels, Nan," hollered out Mr. Shapski. "Here, I'll fix it up for you right now."

"Thank you, Mr. Shapski," Isabelle said politely.

"Thank you, Mr. Shapski," Nan imitated her mother.

"This was getting pretty hard for you to push, wasn't it Isabelle?" the big man asked as he got off his knees.

"I thought the wheels weren't turning as well as usual, but then again, I'm not as young as I used to be either." She sort of laughed.

"Mother, can we go into the church today?"

"No, Nan, not today," she tried to whisper to her daughter so Mr. Shapski wouldn't hear.

Nan began to whine.

"Nan, stop that right now!"

Isabelle was crimson with color.

Mr. Shapski leaned in close to Isabelle and whispered, "I can help you get Nan and the chair up the steps to the church if you wish."

"No, thank you, we don't have time today," muttered Isabelle and then hurriedly pushed the chair away.

As they passed St. Bernard's, Nan looked up and up and up to see all of its height. She and mother hadn't been inside the church for so long. She missed it. They used to stop each and every day for a little visit. Nan loved the immensity of it all, and Mother would let her wheel around at will to look at the statues.

Now it was just the quick whisk of going by that always made Nan turn her head farther and farther until Isabelle would say, "Nan, turn around and face forward. Do you want to fall out of the chair?"

Nan liked the park, however, and as soon as they went through the huge iron-gate, she forgot about the church. It was there, too, that they visited with the regulars. It seemed as if certain people did the same thing every day, just as she did. Nan liked that.

As mother ate her lunch, she would pause every once in a while to read a verse of poetry to Nan. Nan didn't really get the meaning of the verses because they weren't like Gemma's stories that had a beginning and an ending. Nan thought that maybe Mother read just parts of the story and forgot to read the rest aloud. She didn't know for sure.

Nan was content eating and watching the ducks on the pond. She always saved food for those who waddled up to see her. They seemed to know her.

Mother would sometimes look up and comment, "You should eat more of that food yourself; you're so skinny." But she never bothered about it, just went back to her reading.

Again, on the way home, Nan looked at the church but that was all; they never visited the church on their way home.

Isabelle got ready for work. Nan sat and listened to the clock. *I shouldn't listen to it now,* she thought. *I'll have plenty of time for that later.* She knew if she put her mind on something else, the tick of the clock would go away. But for some reason on that day, her mind would not let go of the sound. She thought of her fans, the window, the portraits, her utility bag full of supplies, Gemma, and Lucius, but nothing worked. Her mind kept saying, "Clock, clock, clock." And the ticking didn't stopped until she heard her mother scream.

Nan jolted upright. She pressed her palms down on the wheels to start them turning. "Mother? Mother?"

Her mother sat sobbing on the edge of the bed with a broken music box in her hands.

"Don't cry, Mother." Nan began crying too.

"This was my favorite music box," she sobbed.

"I know. Father, gave it to you on your wedding day," Nan said, trying to give Isabelle her handkerchief.

"What are we going to do, Nan? What are we going to do?"

"I don't know, Mother."

In that question, Nan didn't realize that her mother was presenting an accumulation of all their problems, not just the music box.

"Well," Isabelle finally uttered with a last sob that shook her shoulders, "I've got to go to work."

Isabelle dictated to her daughter all the same precautions that she did every day before leaving Nan alone to wait for Gemma and Lucius.

"I will, Mother," Nan replied. "I love you too. See you tonight."

Nan wheeled to the window. She needed to see her mother as she walked.

She remained at the window long after her mother disappeared out of sight. Many people walked back and forth; some went into the shops and out of the shops—all going somewhere. Nan didn't felt like directing them in a play. Maybe later. She had no thoughts right then.

She turned to look at the photos on the wall. There was Father, laughing and holding little Nan in his arms. What was that stock market that kept him away from her and Mother for so long? Mother would be laughing and happy again if he were there. She scowled at the thought of that awful market, whatever it was.

She wheeled herself in to look at the broken music box. It lay on the dresser very much in distress. Maybe she could fix it. She brightened!

"No," she realized as she shook her head, but maybe Lucius could!

That thought brought hope to Nan! Away she went to the window to put on a play using the characters on the street.

Mrs. Angolini was hanging out of her upstairs window trying to reach Tommy's coat with a long stick. Tommy and his father were standing in the middle of the street yelling directives to Mrs. Angolini. Several people gathered to watch. Victory! She raised the stick like a flagpole while the people applauded.

"Oh no!" Nan gasped. Mrs. Angolini flung the pole with the coat up into the air. It came down like a spear, almost piercing Tommy's father. Everyone laughed while the embarrassed man scooped up the coat and grabbed his son by the arm to march him home. Nan hoped that Tommy wasn't in store for a spanking. She remembered once that her father had given her a spanking; she hadn't known what a spanking was, and she hadn't liked it one iota.

There goes Mrs. O'Malley with her fish for supper again. Nan tried to imagine what it would be like to have eleven brothers and sisters. She held up her fingers and propped a pencil between her knees. There were the eleven children and herself; she named them all, except herself, of course. She liked her new family, especially the biggest sisters and the little ones. The siblings in between didn't seem to impress her very much. Nan laughed when she put all her fingertips together and made them "dance." She wished she had all those sisters and brothers; it would be fun.

Mr. Shapski rolled the awning closed and then started sweeping his boardwalk. He suddenly stopped and straightened his huge body; his knuckles jutted out as his fingers wound tightly around the broom handle. Nan could see why he posed in that position. The gang of bad boys was heading down the sidewalk. Before they got to Mr. Shapski, they crossed over and walked on the opposite sidewalk.

"Good for you, Mr. Shapski," Nan called out behind the windowpane. The valiant man inspired a surge of excitement in Nan; she wheeled around and quickly rifled through her box to find just the right fan. Nester was definitely to be one of the characters in the upcoming exciting episode! Great Uncle Edward would save the baby!

"Oh what fun," Nan giggled as she brought her episode to a dramatic ending and went back to her window show for more ideas.

Nan tilted her head in order to see something wriggly coming down the boarded walkway. She thought it was a huge bird. It had lots of feathers and long black legs. No, there were six legs and those were women wearing colorful dresses with wraps of feathers wound around them. Nan had never seen such beautiful women with tall feathery hats, shoes with long skinny heels, and jewelry all wound around their necks. They were walking arm in arm and laughing and talking. *Where are they going?* wondered Nan. She watched their dresses sway to the right and to the left until they were out of sight. She would ask Gemma about them.

She wondered why her mother didn't have any of those feathery shawls. Suddenly, Nan felt like wearing something pretty. She went into her mother's room and opened the closet. She looked at the dresses; there was nothing there like what she saw on the women. Wait a minute. *What are these?*

"Oh, how beautiful," swooned Nan as she touched the fabrics ever so gently: a periwinkle blue satin, a startling red silk with beads of silver sewn on, something gold that was so shiny, fancy blacks, and a beaded white dress. Nan's eyes darted from one to the next back and forth, back and forth. She pulled each one out as far as it would come, exposing more glitter, shine, and gorgeous intricacies! Why hadn't she known of these before? She tried to picture Mother wearing them but she couldn't.

Her affection rested with the periwinkle blue satin. To Nan, it was the most beautiful dress in the whole world. She pulled and turned the bottom flounce so it lay somewhat exposed beyond the others. Nan backed her chair away from it so she could gaze upon the sea of blue at a wider angle.

For a long time, Nan merely sat and looked at the garment, which made her feel as if she could transpose herself into a different person.

Slowly, she wheeled forward. She needed to take the blue beauty off the wooden hanger.

She clutched the dress in her hand and shook it, and tried to pull up at the same time. She shook it with both hands. She tried to think if there was a stick in their apartment that she could use. She thought of Mrs. Angolini's stick and wished she had it there. Nan went to the kitchen and came back with a wooden spoon. No, she couldn't reach the hanger.

Slowly, she planted her feet flat on the floor and used the garments on either side of her prize to pull herself up. She was doing it! She was rising, until her legs gave way and she fell forward to the floor. Her hands didn't come in front of her face to spare her.

Nan pounded hard on the boards. She lay without a sound until she cried out with pain and continued to cry unceasingly. Her world was now nothing but listening to herself using an awful voice with an awful sound. At one point, she thought that perhaps the sound was not coming from her own mouth, but she knew it was. The pain in her chin was the most intense, but she could feel tributaries of pain slowly creeping into her cheekbones and into her forehead as well. She pulled her hand to her mouth and felt something wet. She remembered watching the bad boys fighting in the street and seeing blood ooze from boys' lips and then blood covering hands and faces and shirts. She had never seen blood from her mouth. Nan couldn't look at her hand; she quickly shoved it under something that had fallen onto the floor. It was a petticoat, she thought.

She stopped screaming and now only sobbed. She pulled the white petticoat up to her mouth and let it lay on her lips. At first, it was cool and silky soft. It almost brought her comfort. Then it became wet, warm, and heavy, and as many times as Nan tried to turn it to a clean spot, it became saturated all over again. She tried to rise up on her hands, but realized she had hammered them onto the floor too.

Nan slowly let her crying ebb to nothing. The sounds of her own voice had scared her. She didn't want to hear them anymore, no matter how much she hurt. She laid perfectly still, half in and half out of reality. She thought of Gemma and Lucius; they would come soon; they would help her.

In her thoughts, Nan could see the handlebar mustache close to the flame and fish bones wrapped in brown paper for the children. Someone was running fast with Mr. Sullivan's ice wagon, and then they tried to get it through the doors of the church.

"Glory be to sweet Jesus!" Gemma screamed in horror.

"Lord Jesus," Lucius moaned.

Ever so tenderly, the old couple picked up their honey child and carried her up the staircase. Gemma was wailing to the Lord, and Lucius was crying tears onto the bundle in his arms.

"Lucius, lay her on our bed and you run for Doc Harper—and I mean run!" Gemma accented her command.

The old man carried out her orders, and Gemma regretted her words when she heard his fast footsteps on the steps. "Be careful on the stairs." She prayed as she ran for water and towels.

Nan's face had already discolored and was growing huge. Gemma started a litany of prayers as she began lying cold cloths on the battered face. Memories began exploding through her head of seventeen years ago when the darling little girl fell the entire length of the staircase. The bubbly, precocious, beautiful child of four years ran to greet her father and tripped on the top step. Gemma had been in the kitchen preparing supper when she heard the thumping and screaming from Mr. McFinney.

Gemma stared at Nan's mouth. She wasn't sure if her honey child was breathing.

"Please hurry, Lucius, please hurry," cried Gemma as she worked like an Angel of Mercy.

"I'll take over, Gemma." Doc Harper rushed through the door with his black bag. "Lucius, you better go and get Isabelle."

Again Gemma listened to her husband's footsteps descend the damnable staircase.

In between examining Nan and applying bandages, Doc Harper used his professionalism to calm Gemma as well. He knew the memories that were going through her head; he had the same ones.

One of his saddest cases was telling the McFinney's that their daughter would never walk again and that her mind would always be that of a child. That was after all the specialists had told the parents the same thing. They had taken Nan to four hospitals and were preparing to take her to Europe when Doc Harper finally made them understand.

That's when Gemma and Lucius came to live in the house on a full time basis. Mr. McFinney gave them the upstairs. They knew he was so distraught over the staircase that he no longer wanted it to be part of his living quarters. In fact, he had a wall constructed so that when the door to the lower quarters was closed, he did not have to look at it.

Twelve years after the accident, Mr. McFinney took his own life after the collapse of the stock market. Everyone kept it from Nan. Nan was only a child.

Now, at twenty-one, Nan was still a child—a child suffering with pain.

Gemma and the doctor worked on Nan with loving hands. Smelling salts were used, and Nan came back to this world. The blood was cleaned away and cold cloths were applied. Dr. Harper concluded that there were no broken bones.

"Gemma," Nan suddenly uttered, "I'm sorry."

"Oh, my honey child, don't you be sorry for nothing. You're going to be OK. You're all right, my little darling."

Nan seemed to take comfort in that and closed her eyes. In an instant, however, they were open again when she mumbled, "Gemma, I want to show you a beautiful blue dress."

"Maybe later, sweetheart. You just rest now."

Gemma couldn't imagine what blue dress Nan was talking about until she pieced the puzzle together of Nan being found in Isabelle's closet.

Gemma had just changed the water in the washbowl again when she heard footsteps on the stairs. Her heart went out to Isabelle not knowing what to expect and having to rush up the stairs under such circumstances.

Isabelle was absolutely white when she rushed into the room. Gemma and Doc Harper immediately rushed to her and supported her on either side.

"Nan," she called out. "Nan!"

With little slits of eyes and puffiness that made her look like she now weighed a hundred pounds more than she did, Nan said, "I like your blue dress, Mother."

"She's going to be all right, Isabelle," the doctor told her. "She's just bruised up pretty bad. Here, come and sit down."

Isabelle sank into one chair while Lucius had already occupied the other trying to catch his breath.

"You all right over there, Lucius?" Doc Harper asked.

"I will be in a minute, Doc," he panted as Gemma went to him.

The next two weeks were devoted just to Nan. Isabelle and Gemma did not go to their jobs, and Gemma moved downstairs to help with the caring.

Gemma became aware that Isabelle was getting more and more distraught over money matters and watched her devote several hours each day either to going through papers or meeting with the man from the bank.

One day, Isabelle asked Gemma if she and Lucius would move downstairs so that the upstairs could be rented out. She also asked Gemma to work fewer hours at the restaurant and stay with Nan when she couldn't be there. Isabelle had a chance to work extra hours if someone would be in the house with Nan.

So Isabelle started to go to work earlier and slept later in the mornings. Lucius and Gemma moved their personal belongings downstairs and left the furniture for the new tenants.

After two weeks, Nan was still endowed with coloration on her face and hands, but her spirit bounded back to normal.

"Can we go outside today, Gemma, please?" she begged.

"You know, honey child, I think that is just what the doctor would order."

"I don't want to see the doctor again, Gemma," Nan began to whine.

"No, no, we're not going to see the doctor today." Gemma laughed. "That was just a funny way of saying yes we're going outdoors."

"Oh," replied Nan with great perplexity peeking through her colors of yellow, green, and blue.

Nan certainly was the center of attention as Gemma wheeled her along the street. All the shopkeepers and customers stopped to chat and ask about her recovery. Some handed her small packages of sweets and delicacies. Gemma was pleased to help Nan answer all of the questions.

"Gemma, there's my church!" Nan pointed excitedly. "Can we go in, Gemma? Can we?"

"Well, I don't know, Nan. Are we supposed to go in?"

"Oh yes. God is always there waiting for us! We can go in at any time to visit with him!"

Gemma looked at the large stone building, not knowing quite what to do.

"Mother and I used to stop here every day, Gemma. It's all right."

"Well, I guess we can," Gemma uttered slowly.

"We'll only need to wait a few minutes, and someone will come by to help you get me in there," Nan said in a very promising way.

Nan was absolutely right! Within minutes, two men came out of the church and helped them in.

When Gemma turned the chair around and faced the sanctuary, she gasped.

It startled Nan and she blurted out, "Gemma, what's the matter?"

"I never seen a church this big."

"Isn't this your church?" Nan asked.

"No, child. Lucius and I go to a tiny church on the edge of the city."

"Oh, I didn't know that."

"Can we go all the way up the aisle to the big cross?"

"Sure, Gemma. Let's go."

Gemma wheeled Nan down the aisle with all the solemnity of a father taking his daughter to her bridegroom. Her slow pace gave her time to take in the magnificence of the ceiling and the scrollwork on the columns. Her eyes drifted to the stained glass window depicting Pentecost. Never had she seen thousands of colors illuminated by the sunlight all at one time.

"Gemma, I can wheel myself now. Mother always lets me go around the church by myself."

Without a word, Gemma's hands released, and she continued to release her eyes to the beauty and magnificence of the church. She walked from window to window and statue to statue. She noticed the finery of the altar clothes and the fresh flowers. She took in the exquisiteness of the communion rail with its polished wood and kneeling pads of red velvet.

Gemma stood in front of the huge marble altar with its brass candleholders and elegantly embroidered cloth, and she let her eyes rise and rise and rise. There was her Jesus! There He was on the cross. Gemma sank to her knees and cried. With sobs of tears that could be heard throughout the church, Gemma wept.

"Gemma, Gemma," Nan screamed from far away. "Gemma, I'm coming. I'm coming. Gemma, what's the matter?" the girl asked with a voice that could have penetrated all of eternity.

Nan pulled and yanked on Gemma's shoulder until Gemma looked at her.

"I'm all right, honey child," she said compassionately after seeing the fear in Nan's eyes. "Something just came over me that absolutely set me to crying."

"Oh, that's all right, Gemma," Nan uttered as she learned forward to hug her friend. "Mother used to cry in church too."

"Well," Gemma said with a sigh as she wiped her eyes with one of Lucius's handkerchiefs, "this is some church."

"Isn't it though, Gemma? I love it here! Can you walk around with me now?"

"Sure, honey child."

Gemma used the communion rail to pull herself up, and she and Nan slowly walked down the middle aisle of St. Bernard's.

On their way home, Nan turned as far as she could toward Gemma and asked, "Can we go there again tomorrow? And to the park, too?"

"We'll see; we'll see."

Nan was optimistic that that meant, "Yes."

"Put on a play with me, Gemma," Nan said during the time of day when she was usually alone. "Here, sit by the window with me."

The two "directors" sat with keen alertness as they watched for interesting "characters" to walk by.

"Oh no," laughed Nan, "there's Mrs. Angolini leaning out of her window again with the pole." Sure enough, there was an article of clothing on her awning. Nan hoped it wasn't something of Tommy's again; his father would be mad.

Gemma and Nan applauded as Mrs. Angolini retrieved the jacket. This time she didn't cascade it down to earth; she took it inside with her.

Beep, beep, beep. There was Mr. Monroe with one of the few automobiles in the city. Everyone dashed off the dusty road and stood on the sidewalks staring at the auto and sharing exclamations. Nan wished Mr. Monroe would turn around and come back, but she knew he was a busy man and had more important things to do than to parade through Main Street again.

"There they are, Gemma. That's who I was telling you about. Look."

"Oh good Lord of mercy," Gemma said disgustedly.

"Aren't they the most beautiful women you've ever seen?"

"Get your eyes off those women," Gemma said.

"Why?"

"They're not for you to be lookin' at," Gemma said sternly.

"But someday I'm going to be one of them. When I get big," Nan said assertively.

"You come away from that window, young lady. We're going to work in your new scrapbook."

Gemma wheeled her away so quickly, Nan didn't have time to complain.

"Now here's a box of old Christmas cards; you paste them in the scrapbook."

"Oh, all right, but tonight I want to look at Mother's pretty dresses again.'

"Yes, you may do that; those are honorable dresses."

Gemma liked working in Isabelle's beautiful kitchen: it had everything that anyone would ever need to cook with. Oftentimes, she would let Nan help with the meal preparations. By the time Lucius got home from work, everything would be ready. It was a treat for him not to have to wait for supper.

Lucius told his "family" all about his day's work, and the two women told him of theirs. On more than one occasion, Lucius looked at his wife as if to say, "You'll have to explain that to me later."

Nan wanted a story after supper. As she lay on the sofa to rest her back against the soft pillows, she asked to hear the "Railroad Story."

"The Railroad Story again?"

"Yes, please, please, please," she begged.

"Land sakes, child, you're going to turn into a railroad," Lucius joked.

"I know I will." Nan laughed.

"Well," Lucius began as he settled back in one of Isabelle's big overstuffed chairs, "a long time ago, my daddy told us about leaving the South, if we could get on the Salvation Train. So my daddy talked to a lot of people about the train and how we could go to the North to live."

"But it wasn't going to be easy to catch that train, right, Lucius?" Nan interjected, already caught up in the story.

"That's right, Nan. My daddy heard that some people got killed if the bad men caught them going on that *train*."

"And your father wanted to take your family away from the bad men, didn't he, Lucius?"

"That's right, honey child. He wanted his children and his wife to have a better life. So he planned and planned just how to do it, and we talked every night about how we were going to escape. He told all us little ones how we were going to have to be quiet and do just what we were told."

"It wasn't a real train like we have at the railroad station, was it, Lucius?" Nan asked.

"No, but it was like a train movin' on to the North; sometimes we were on a raft; sometimes we were in the back of a wagon; sometimes we were stuck for days in someone's barn." Lucius stopped and seemed to be staring into the flowers of the carpet.

"Is the story over all ready?" Gemma chirped as she came in from the kitchen and sat on the end of the sofa.

"No," Nan said quietly. She was used to long pauses in the train story.

"But we progressed on," Lucius said hurriedly, knowing he had lapsed into the past, "until we were finally led by lantern right down into the cellar of this very house!"

That was the part that Nan liked best, and she clapped and clapped as she did each time Lucius told it.

"And my grandfather and grandmother helped your family, didn't they, Lucius?"

"They sure did, honey child. And Gemma's family came to the North the same way we did."

I'm glad." Nan beamed. "Because when you and Gemma grew up, you got married and came back to this house!"

"We sure did." Gemma laughed as she rubbed Nan's feet, which were now in her lap.

"Who wants to play dominoes?" Lucius called out.

"Me!" yelled Nan.

"Me!" yelled Gemma.

Nan went to sleep that night dreaming of all the happy families who came into her house from the Underground Railroad. She dreamed she was in the cellar giving everyone cookies.

Lucius had dreams that night of running and beatings and fear. He did not dream of a nice cellar but of being caught and watching his father being hanged.

Gemma was too restless to dream. She tossed and turned wondering why Isabelle hadn't come home yet.

At six o'clock in the morning, Gemma heard Isabelle go into her bedroom.

"Yes, honey child, I think today would be a good day to eat lunch in the park. I'm sure your mother will sleep better with peace and quiet in the house."

Gemma didn't show Nan her worried expression; after all, Nan was just a child.

Nan received much attention on the street and Gemma, too, felt like she was fitting into the neighborhood with so many compliments on her good care giving.

Once they were past the shops, not only did Nan's head turn toward St. Bernard's but also Gemma's. Nan didn't need to whine or beg or cry.

"Of course we'll go in," Gemma said.

This time Gemma sat in the last pew as Nan started her course of religious adventure.

Gemma could just barely remember going to church with her grandmother when they were still in the South. There must have been fifty or sixty people all crowded into a tiny wooden building that they called their church. There were benches with no backs; there was no organ or piano, just wooden planks over a dirt floor and a Bible sitting on a handmade podium. The preacher came in every Sunday from the next town over. He surely could preach. Gemma chuckled to herself as she remembered hiding under her grandma's arm when he got to hollering about the devil coming after you if you didn't follow God's ways.

"Lord of mercy," her grandpa would say. "He could scare the whiskers off of a catfish."

What Gemma liked best was the singing. Everybody sang like there'd be no tomorrow. Of course, the truth was they didn't know if there would be.

Sometimes people cried when they sang or clapped or stood right up on the bench and hollered to God. Gemma knew God had heard them; her mother said the people way down to the big house could tell when they were having church.

"Are you praying, Gemma?" Nan came up behind Gemma so quietly that it made the old woman jump.

"Well, I wasn't exactly praying," she answered with a little bit of embarrassment when she realized she hadn't been keeping her eye on Nan, "but I was thinking about God."

"Do you pray in your church, Gemma?"

"Of course I do, honey child."

"Could I go to see your church someday, Gemma?"

"Of course you can, dear."

"Yippee," Nan shouted. The sound reverberated throughout the church, giving the alabaster castings of St. Anthony and St. Francis a bit of a start.

"Gemma, come and see the beautiful statue of St. Augustine. My grandfather gave it to the church long ago."

"It's very nice, Nan. Your grandfather was a good man."

"I know. And my father was a good man too! I wish he'd come home soon; I miss him. I'm going right up to the crucifix and say a special prayer for him right now. Do you want to go with me?" Nan asked excitedly.

"No, not today, honey child. I'll wait here for you."

Gemma watched as the little daughter with the skinny arms wheeled herself up the center aisle to pray for her father's return. Tears welled in Gemma's eyes to the point that she had to wipe them away with the back of her hand.

Nan prayed with all her might just as her mother had taught her to do.

One afternoon when Nan was occupied with her fan stories, Gemma looked up from her mending and asked, "Isabelle, do you really have to work both jobs? Isn't there something we could do to lessen the burden for you? You look exhausted all the time, and you're getting so skinny."

"This is what I have to do, Gemma. Maybe after the new tenants upstairs have been here for a few months I can start to save a little money."

"I don't know," Gemma uttered as she trimmed off a thread. "I guess times aren't easy for anybody right now. But you know I can take in ironing, too."

"Now there's an idea. Let me think about that. Oh, look at the time. I've got to go. Bye, precious angel."

"Bye, Mother, see you tomorrow," Nan said.

Isabelle rushed out with her satchel. The sleeve of the beautiful blue dress could be seen hanging out of the unclosed top.

What on earth? thought Gemma.

With the passing days, Nan and Gemma saw less and less of Isabelle. She slept until it was time for work and then hurried out with her bag.

Gemma confided in Lucius about the declining health of Isabelle and told him they needed to do more for her.

Lucius never saw Isabelle anymore, but it was Lucius who detected the smell of cigarette smoke on the fancy dresses in Isabelle's closet. It was Lucius who heard rumors about Isabelle's "job," and it was he who suspected that the reason for Isabelle's bloodshot eyes was alcohol.

"Oh, no, no, no," Gemma muttered as she held her head in her hands.

"I'm afraid it's true, Gemma. You've got to help her; we owe it to the McFinney's who so generously took us in when our families fled from the South."

What could she do? What could she do?

Each day Gemma cleaned more, cooked more, took care of the concerns of the tenants, and started an ironing business to add money to the household account.

Things got worse. Some mornings Isabelle didn't come home at all.

Nan became irritable and depressed. The only time she seemed happy was when Gemma took her out into the world.

On their walks, Nan knew she never had to ask about visiting the church; they went in every day.

One day as they entered St. Bernard's, Nan looked up at Gemma and said, "I need to pray for Mother, don't I?"

"Yes you do, honey child. Yes you do."

"Let's go up front, Gemma."

The two worried souls went forth, preparing to pray like they had been taught: Gemma by her grandmother and Nan by her mother.

When they finished, Nan turned to Gemma and asked, "Gemma, can we go to your church and pray too?"

"Sure we can, honey, but why do you want to go there?"

"When you prayed that the train would bring you to safety, it did. I want to go and get that prayer for Mother."

"Oh, baby," Gemma cried as she wrapped her arms around Nan.

The park was very peaceful that day; the soft air gave the two women relief for their souls—relief that they couldn't get at home anymore. The trees swayed in a mesmerizing fashion, oftentimes emitting little whisperings of hope. Nan was in no hurry to go home, nor was Gemma. Home had become a troubled place for the two women; the walls held an air of restlessness and dismay.

Long after their usual departure, they began the slow trek toward home. From the iron gate of the park, Nan could see a woman walking up the front steps of the church.

"Gemma!" Nan screamed, "Mother just went into the church."

"No, honey child. Your mother is at work.'

"No, Gemma, I saw her!"

"No, Nan, it couldn't have been your mother."

Nan began having a tantrum, yelling and pointing. People stopped to look at her.

"Nan McFinney, you stop this nonsense right now," Gemma said in a low, stern voice.

"I will not stop. I'm going to go see my mother!"

Gemma could see people whispering behind their hands.

Nan was pushing the wheels of her chair as hard as she could.

"I know she's in there. I saw her," she cried. "Mr. Shapski, you'll help me get into the church won't you!" Nan hollered out to the man.

Mr. Shapski looked at Gemma and looked back again at the terror in Nan's eyes.

"Gemma?" he respectfully waited for her approval.

"Yes, we need to get this thing settled."

From the big doors, they saw no one in the church. In the darkened interior, they only saw the flickering candles.

"I know I saw her, Gemma," Nan whispered over her shoulder.

"It's OK, baby, sometimes our eyes—"

"Gemma, listen."

Way in the distance, they could hear crying; someone was crying.

"It is Mother!" Nan's voice sparkled.

Before Gemma could even get her hands back on the handlebars, Nan started down the aisle.

"Mother. Mother," she called out.

The entire church echoed with jubilant sounds of God answering Nan's prayer.

Isabelle turned and ran to her daughter. "Oh, Nan, can you ever forgive Mommy? I'm so sorry." Isabelle sunk to her knees and laid her head in Nan's lap.

Nan leaned forward and kissed her mother's hair.

"Gemma, please forgive me too," Isabelle cried as she took hold of Gemma's hand.

"Mother, we're not mad. Gemma, Mother's train is here, isn't it?"

THE END

ᴄᴧᴏChapter Fifteenᴄᴎᴏ

THE COUNTDOWN

WITH CHARACTERS FROM "COUNTRY ARMS," "THE
HIGHWAY," AND "THE RAP SHEET" FROM BOOK ONE
A PRESSING SITUATION" FROM BOOK THREE, AND
"WAITING" FROM BOOK FOUR

"So you see, Marjory, you'll be just fine!"

"Yes, I'll be just fine."

"I'll be in the hospital for five days and then I'll be home!" Agnes said as cheerfully as she could.

"Yes, five days, you already told me that."

"I know." Agnes laughed. "I just want to be sure you heard me."

"I hear good, Grandma," Marjory said.

"I know you do. Now tell me, who is going to stay with you the first day and the first night?"

"Betty."

"Right! And what are you and Betty going to do that will be fun?"

"We're going to her house and then we're going next door to the farm, and we're going to pick mulberries and bake a real pie!"

"Exactly! And who is going to stay with you the next day and night?"

"Mae."

"Yes! And what are you going to do to help her?"

"The sprinkling! And Mae is going to do the ironing!"

"Right!

"Grandma, are you going to keep asking me stuff?"

"I am. OK, the third day and night?"

"I'll be with our cousin Lorraine from over on the big highway who works in a money booth, but she has the day off so it will be us who are going to stop and pay money!"

"You sure know your stuff, kiddo!" Agnes said.

"And then Katie who just moved into an apartment and doesn't have that big house anymore. We're going to go to a city and see a big aquarium. I love fish."

"I know you do, baby." Agnes sighed, feeling like she was going into a maudlin state of mind. "And how about the last day?"

"Liz! Liz! Liz!" Marjory's excitement escalated.

"What's making you so excited about Liz?"

"I have some new clues for her about my mother and father!"

"What are you talking about?"

"I'm only telling Liz," Marjory announced firmly as she crossed her arms.

Agnes knew better than to try to get an answer out of her granddaughter when she crossed her arms.

Agnes had never been away from Marjory—that is, not for a whole day and night. Ever since her daughter and son-in-law (Marjory's mother and father) disappeared forty-three years ago, Agnes has been on duty. Now Agnes has to have surgery.

But Agnes has prepared for all this. She has coached Marjory forward and backward; she has mapped out everything for her friends who have most graciously consented to stay with Marjory.

"So this is the day; this is day one," Agnes said.

"Where's Betty?"

"She'll be here any minute. Do you have any questions before I go?"

"Nope. Have a good time," Marjory said.

Agnes was relieved that Marjory was calm; she didn't know what her reaction would be to being away from her.

"Here's Betty and I see Jacob parking his car."

"Is Jacob coming to tell me my favorite story?" Marjory asked.

"No, dear. He's going to drive me to the hospital."

"What are you going there for? Why won't Jacob come in? Why is Betty here?"

"Marjory, stop, pause, big breath, think."

"Oh yeah, I remember."

"Now you and Betty stand on the porch and wave."

"OK."

"We're going to have a big day, aren't we sweetheart?"

"We sure are, Betty." Marjory smiled as she gave her friend a hug. "I love you, Betty."

"I love you, too, Marjory."

"Here we are, way out in the country!" Betty beamed. "Do you want to play with my new dog, Donovan II?"

"Yes, yes, yes, I love dogs!"

"How about we put the leash on Donnie II and we'll walk to the farm?"

"Welcome!" Mildred called out as she strode down the hill from the haymow. "I've been expecting you. How are you, Marjory?"

"This is Donovan II. He's a dog!"

"Well, by golly, I guess he is." Mildred laughed as she scratched the dog behind the ear. "Do you know that he is going to stay with me tonight while Betty stays with you?"

"Where's my grandmother? Is she going to stay with the dog too?" Marjory asked.

"Marjory, stop, pause, big breath, think," Betty instructed.

"Oh, I remember."

"Would you like to see the chickens and the cows?"

"And the cats?"

"And the cats."

Betty and Marjory had lunch with Mildred on the back steps of the old farmhouse while two of the cats rubbed against their legs and lay in the sun. The women picked the luscious purple mulberries until the buckets were full and their stained fingers matched the juice.

"Well, my dear, we'd better get home and make the pie. What do you think of that?"

"I think yummy! Bye, Mildred. Bye, Donnie Boy."

"Did you have a fun day, Marjory?"

"I sure did, Betty, and we are going to have a piece of pie with vanilla ice cream after supper, right?"

"Yes."

"Will Grandma be back to have some pie? Where is your dog?"

"What if we think about your pretty glass collection? Would you like to bring it downstairs?" Betty asked.

The two ladies wiled away the evening with colored glass, mulberry pie, and board games.

"Who's sleepy besides me?" Betty teased.

"Me!" Marjory shouted as she raised her hand. "Can you listen to my prayers like Grandma does?"

"Of course," Betty said.

Betty could hear the nighttime peace settle upon the house. She hoped Agnes's surgery went well and that Donnie II wasn't giving Mildred any trouble. She had had a nice day with Marjory and felt comforted that she was able to help a friend in need.

Mae would come in the morning.

"Where is she? Where is she?" Marjory screamed as she ran in and out of her grandmother's room. Betty jolted upright as she was wrangled out of a sound sleep.

"Marjory. Marjory, it's OK. I'm here."

"Where is she? Who took her?"

"Honey, she's in the hospital, remember?"

"No, she would never leave me. Who took her away from me?"

Betty listened to Marjory's voice become more and more frantic as she tried to console her.

"We've got to find her; we've got to help her. She needs me. Get in the car. We'll find her," Marjory shouted as she ran downstairs to the door.

Betty was afraid that her charge was going to run out of the house. "Marjory, wait. I'm coming."

"Hurry, Betty, we've got to go!"

"Grandma's going to be mad if we don't put a coat over our pajamas," Betty said. The ploy slowed Marjory and kept her from running out of the house.

What am I going to do? Betty thought to herself as she drove up and down the dark streets.

The longer she drove, the more agitated Marjory became. What was she going to do?

Betty got onto the big highway and headed for the hospital.

"We're sorry, ma'am, but do you think we could just peek in on one of your patients?"

Marjory began running up and down the hall screaming, "Grandma!"

Betty quickly explained the situation to the nurse.

"I'll see what I can do."

"We're going to look through the glass window at your grandma, and we're going to be very, very quiet so we don't wake her. She's sound asleep and having wonderful dreams of you! Isn't that nice?" Betty said.

Marjory pressed her forehead against the glass and waved to Agnes; she smiled as she watched her grandma sleep.

"OK, Betty, we can go home now," Marjory whispered.

Betty squeezed the nurse's hand. "Thank you."

"Good morning, Mae."

"Good morning to you. You don't look very rested."

Betty quickly told Mae about the night's escapade before Marjory came downstairs.

"My goodness, I hope there won't be any more of that!" Mae exclaimed.

"Any more of what?" Marjory asked as she entered the kitchen.

"A... a... more people who don't want their clothes ironed and run around wrinkled," Mae replied.

"Yucky," agreed Marjory.

"Well, I've got to run along," Betty said with a yawn. "I need to pick up Donovan from Mildred's farm."

"Tell him hi," Marjory said as she reached for the cereal.

While Marjory was getting milk out of the refrigerator, Betty whispered, "If you need any help, call me."

"We'll be fine."

"How about we get all your morning chores done, and then we can walk to my house and have lunch. Then you can what?"

"Sprinkle!" Marjory said.

"You know what you can do after you sprinkle all the clothes?"

"What?"

"You can go outdoors and water all my plants!"

"Yeah!"

What is it about Marjory and water? Mae wondered as she ironed. *I think she would be happy all day if she had some sort of water project.* Mae watched out the window as Marjory went back and forth from the water spigot to the garden. She was having a wonderful time.

"Hello? Oh, hi, Betty. Yes, she's fine; she's outside watering all my plants. That'll tire her out, right? How did your dog fare at the neighbor's house? Sure, I'll call you tomorrow."

"Marjory," Mae called out, "why don't you come in for a while? I don't want you to get a sunburn. We can have some lemonade and cookies on the shady porch."

Mae got everything ready. "Marjory! Are you coming? Marjory?"

Mae checked the iron; it was off. She went out back; she walked around to the side of the house. She checked the front lawn and then the entire lawn. Where was she?

"Marjory! Marjory! Where are you? Oh my Lord, where is she?" Mae asked aloud as she darted to the front sidewalk to look up the street and down.

She ran next door and called to Mrs. Hannihan who was sitting on her porch.

"Did you see anyone leave my house and walk up the street?"

"Went that way," Mrs. Hannihan said.

Mae began running.

"Oh my dear Lord. Oh no. Oh no. Oh no." Her mantra coincided with her footsteps. Mae could feel the sweat running down from her temples; her heartbeat pounded out panic. There!

"Marjory! Marjory, stop... Stop!"

"Hurry up, Mae. Grandma is waiting for us."

"Wait... wait... for... me. Stop!" Mae panted. "Let's... go back... and get... the... car."

"Good idea, Mae."

"Excuse me, is there a way we could see one of your patients?" Mae asked.

"She's my grandmother, and I was here last night and I know where she is," Marjory announced, ready to make a beeline to Agnes.

"Ah yes, there was a note left by the night nurse. Can you be very quiet and just look through the glass? I just checked in on her and she is sound asleep."

"Yes, I can be quiet," Marjory said.

There she was, the love of Marjory's life. Marjory smiled and waved and blew kisses.

"OK, Mae, we can go home now."

Marjory slept through the night, but Mae remained on alert and checked her several times.

"Good morning, sunshine," Lorraine sang as she entered the kitchen and gave Marjory a hug. "Mae, you don't look like little Miss Sunshine!"

"Marjory, dear, could you go upstairs and get my sweater? I left it on the chair," Mae said.

When Marjory left the room, Mae told Lorraine about losing Marjory and the trip to the hospital and about Betty's nighttime dash to the hospital.

"My goodness. What excitement!" Lorraine exclaimed.

"What's exciting?" Marjory asked.

"When Christmas comes and you get those nice presents."

"Yeah, I like that."

"And what are we going to do today?" teased Lorraine.

"You know!" Marjory said. "We are going to get in the car, and we are going to stop at your money booth. We're going to give the lady money!"

"What! Give the lady money? Do you have any money?"

"Yes! It's under my bed! Do you want me to get it?"

"Naw, let's let the dust bunnies have it!" Lorraine said.

"Dust bunnies? You're so funny! Let's go!"

"Not yet, Missy, we have chores to do."

"Boo, hiss."

"OK now, after we go through the toll booth, what are we going to do for the rest of the day?"

"Just keep driving."

"Oh, you are funny! How about we go out for lunch and then we'll go to a movie?"

"Yes, I love movies!"

"Which one would you like to see?"

"Let me close my eyes and I'll point to a poster."

"You're on."

"What did I choose?"

"*Grandma's Secret Eye.*"

"That sounds funny. Let's go in."

Of all the dull, boring movies, Lorraine thought as she stretched her legs. The music droned on and on, the dialog was senseless, and the characters were ugly and crude.

"Marjory, do you want to leave?"

"No, I like this."

Lorraine closed her eyes and slouched in the seat. "Oh well, if she likes it, I can endure."

"Lorraine, Lorraine," Marjory said loudly as she shook Lorraine's arm.

"What's the matter?" She jerked herself upright, feeling guilty that she had dozed off.

"I know where Grandma's secret eye is!"

"Huh?"

"Let's go. I gotta see my grandmother. Come on. Come on."

"Shut up over there; we're trying to hear the movie."

"What are you going to do when you get to the hospital?" Lorraine asked, still confused by what Marjory was trying to tell her.

"I know where her secret eye is and I'll show you."

"Marjory, wait, you can't just run to her room," Lorraine said.

"Yes, Agnes is awake and sitting in the solarium. She can have visitors," the nurse said.

"Oh my, look who's here! Marjory, what are doing here?"

"I'm sorry, Agnes. She just had to see you."

"It's OK, Lorraine. I was missing her," Agnes said.

"Marjory, what are you doing? Stop touching the back of my head. What are you doing?"

"I'm looking for your secret eye. You always say you have eyes in the back of your head. Where are they? I saw a movie and they were there."

"Well, my dear, I hate to disappoint you, but that is just a saying. There are no eyes back there."

"Let's go, Lorraine," Marjory said disgruntled.

"Agnes, how are you feeling? You're looking great."

"I'm feeling great, and I'll be home after two days. Sorry Marjory took you on a wild-goose chase."

"Good thing we have lots of money; we have to go through the toll booth again," Lorrain said.

"Again?"

"Good morning, ladies!" Katie announced as she reported for duty.

"Hi, Kate. Hi, Katie."

"How's everything working out over here?"

"Great!" Marjory answered.

"That's good! I saw Betty and Mae in the market. They said things have been… eventful."

"What's eventful?" Marjory asked in between spoonsful of cereal.

"Never a dull moment."

"Yeah, never a dull moment," she reiterated.

"Lorraine, was your time *eventful* too?" Katie asked.

"Ah, to be sure—to be sure! I'll give you a call tomorrow. Bye you two."

"Did you move, Katie?" Marjory asked.

"Yes I did; now I live in an apartment! And later we're going to walk there to see it. Would you like that?"

"Am I going to move?"

"Oh, no, no, you and Grandma are going to stay right here."

"Good."

"I love this grocery shopping, Katie!"

"That's good. We need to have food in the house when Grandma comes home from the hospital, right?" Katie said.

"Right!"

"OK! Everything is put away. Do you want to see my apartment?"

"And then can we drive to the aquarium?"

"Yes."

"What are these boxes?" Marjory asked.

"Just things I have to unpack."

"Can I see?"

"We don't want to look through all of these boxes, Marjory! But there is one that you would love! It's my colored glass collection. Now if we could just find it. Hmm, where could it be? It's labeled, so it shouldn't be too hard to find. Just be careful around here Marjory. Some of these piles are way too high. I told my helpers not to pile them so... *Crash!*

"Marjory! Oh Lord help us! Marjory!" Katie frantically dialed 911. "Yes, we need an ambulance. Hurry!"

"I don't think anything is broken but we need to take her in for observation," the EMT told Katie.

"Katie, I'm sorry," Marjory cried as she lay on the floor. "I tried to get the box that was on top."

"Don't worry about that, Marjory. I'm just glad that you are OK."

"I hope I didn't break any of the colored glass."

"Grandma! I'm in the hospital too!" Marjory announced proudly as the nurse wheeled her into the solarium.

"Why are you in that wheelchair?"

"She's fine, just had a little tumble," the nurse reassured Agnes.

"Yes," Katie broke in, "I'm so sorry, Agnes. We were in the midst of my boxes and Marjory tried to get the tippy-top one down by herself."

"But, Grandma, it was the colored glass collection!"

"Oh, well, that would be the reason, for sure," Agnes said.

"Ladies, Agnes is going to have her lunch here in the solarium. Would you like to join her?" the nurse asked.

"Yes, I'm starving!" Marjory laughed.

"What can we do now, Katie?" Marjory asked as they drove back into Lone Moon Creek.

"The nurse said you should rest this afternoon, so how about I stop at my apartment and get the box of little glass animals. Would you like to look through them this afternoon?"

"Oh yes. They'll be quiet and rest with me."

Katie was so glad she had wrapped them with extra padding.

"Well, well, well, how's the hospital girl?"

"Liz!" Marjory cried.

"Hi, Kate! Hi, Marjory! Heard you had some excitement yesterday!" Liz laughed.

"We did!" Kate replied.

"Yeah, I'm exciting!" Marjory interjected, looking from one woman to the other.

"I shall bid you adieu and return to my unpacking," Katie said.

"Bye, Kate."

"Liz," Marjory whispered into her ear, "I have clues."

"You have clues?" Liz whispered in return. "What kind of clues?"

"Clues to help you find my mother and father," Marjory said.

"Oh, I see. Do you want to tell me what they are?"

"You already know that they went to a paint store, right?"

"Right."

"But did you know that they were also going to get their little baby—me—some colored glass to hang in the sunny windows?"

"No, I didn't know. How do you know that?"

"I just know; I know things."

"Well, that certainly is a clue, which I am going to write in my notebook," the retired policewoman said. "Anything else?"

"Yes, cereal."

"Cereal?"

"They were also on their way to the market to buy their sweet little baby—me—cereal."

"Oh, that's an important clue also," Liz said.

"Well?"

"Well what?"

"Where's your notebook?" Marjory asked.

"It's out in the car. I'll go get it."

When Liz returned she asked, "Is there anything else?"

"No, that's all for now. And, Liz, Katie couldn't take me to the aquarium yesterday. Can you take me today?"

"That's a great idea."

"Oh, Marjory, look how beautiful!"

But Liz didn't have to tell Marjory to look. Marjory was mesmerized by the flow of the fish and the colors and the light. The light—how could the light get under the water? Marjory wondered.

Marjory didn't move from the large aquarium, even though Liz tried to coax her to look at the smaller tanks also. "No, Liz, I need to stay here."

Marjory watched a little green fish swim with two larger ones. They stayed together all afternoon until the two larger fish suddenly disappeared. Marjory couldn't spot them anywhere. She ran back and forth trying to find them.

"What's the matter?" Liz asked as Marjory's hands were all over the glass and she was knocking into people as she sidestepped in one direction and then the opposite.

"They're gone! The two big green fish are gone! They left their baby! We've got to find them!"

An attendant rushed over. "They're not gone, ma'am; we raised the back wall because it's feeding time. They are in there having their supper."

All of the panic drained from Marjory as she held onto Liz's arm. "Can we go home now, Liz?"

"Of course." Turning to the attendant Liz whispered, "Thank you for being alert to the concerns of your patrons."

"It's my job. Come again."

"Your grandma will be home tomorrow. Are you excited?"

"I think I have another clue for you, Liz," Marjory replied.

"Oh really? What is it?"

"I think my mother and father might be under the water, but they have light. Don't worry, they have light."

THE END

"When can we go down into Howard's Hollow to see
Brownie?"
"Maybe in the spring."

Chapter Sixteen

Howard's Hollow

"Got the chains ready?"

"In the box on the porch."

"Got the shovels out of the shed?"

"Got 'em."

"How much sand in the barrel?"

"Barrel's full. How about those blankets?"

"Piled right there by the door."

"Stew smells good."

"I'm keeping it warm."

"Is the wood box full?"

"Filled it this afternoon."

"What's the matter, boy?"

Brownie had lifted his head off the wooden floor and
stared toward the window.

"I know, boy, there's going to be some action tonight.
Go back to sleep. You might not get a minute's peace later
on."

Brownie lowered his chin to the floor but he didn't
sleep.

For three generations, the warnings continued:

Don't take the road down into Howard's Hollow.

Don't be foolish. Go around.

You know what happened to your uncle. Don't go that way.

Your grandmother thought she would die down in Howard's Hollow.

It doesn't matter if it takes longer to go around, at least you'll be safe.

You can use the car only if you promise not to go the way of Howard's Hollow. It's not safe.

Gr-r-r.

"Settle down, boy," Irma commanded as the shadows from the roaring fire danced eerily across the meager parlor.

"Did ya stock up on more coffee?"

Irma nodded. "More coffee."

Irma, Brownie, and Heyward sat silently; they were entertained only by the crackle of the dried wood while watching the snow and sleet compete for the best seats on the window ledge.

"Here comes one," Heyward exclaimed as he sat with his big gnarled hands clutching both arms of the wooden rocker.

Irma drew her sweater closer to her chest as Brownie went to her knee for a stroking. They watched the headlights snake down the hill into their hollow, pass their house, and start up the other side. Heyward's old head turned in perfect sync with Irma's, neither one consciously breathing, just staring at the red taillights.

It wasn't until the lights were out of sight that the old couple relaxed their grip on the worn rockers. Even Brownie knew that the travelers had made it safely out of the hollow. He lumbered to the rag rug in front of the fireplace and sighed as he lay still.

Ticking and clicking became the symphony of the night. The clock on the shelf and the sleet on the window vied for the old couple's attention. Little did the ticks and clicks know that their sound was not appreciated. Irma tilted her head to let it rest against the wood and rocked back and forth thinking of the funeral flower arrangements that people had placed along the road. Oh, how she hated those reminders.

"You are not getting serious about that boy down in Howard's Hollow are you?"

Why that remark from her mother never left Irma's memory, she didn't know. There it was again. Why tonight?

She looked over at "that boy from down in Howard's Hollow" just as he turned to her and asked, "Whatcha thinkin'?"

"How do you always know when I'm thinking about you?" Irma asked.

Heyward didn't answer. He cocked his left ear toward the road just as Brownie emitted a low growl.

"Oh no, don't tell me," Irma whispered.

Sure enough, headlights pulsated through the pummeling storm carrying passengers or maybe a single driver who thought he could beat the odds; who thought he could outfox the warnings of the warn-ers, and who thought he was not going to waste time by going around.

Heyward watched from the window to the right of the front door, Irma from the left, while Brownie paced between the two.

"He's slidin' sideways."

"Oh Lord have mercy."

"Straighten it out! Give it some gas," the old man hollered as if the driver could hear him, "or you'll never get over the hill. That's it!"

"Oh no, he's spinning, the car is slowing," Irma added.

"Just a little farther. Keep your foot on the gas; you can make it," Heyward called through the frozen windowpane, which was now touching his forehead. Brownie, too, was barking his orders.

"All right, you two, calm down now. He made it."

"How do you know it wasn't a she?" Heyward asked.

"I'm in no mood to be arguing driving skills with you tonight." Irma set the old man straight. "Want some tea?"

Heyward looked into the fire recalling the winter's night when Irma defied her mother's warning about going to see her beau in Howard's Hollow. It took him, his father, and his brothers two hours to pull her out of a snowbank. His Pa drove her car up and out of the hollow for her. As she drove on home, making up a story to tell her mother, Mr. Howard walked back to the house, grumbling that it was no night for man nor beast to be out in that weather.

It wasn't always that easy to rescue the rebels. As a boy, Heyward remembered waking to screams and crying—just a terrible commotion downstairs. His mother was in her robe trying to corral the children, and his father was carrying people through the biting sleet into the house. His mother ordered Heyward back to his room, but he sat at the top of the stairs and listened to what was to be his nightmare for years to come. Three people died that night.

"Here's your tea, old man," Irma said.

"Ah, you do love me."

"Maybe I do and maybe I don't."

The world stabilized after a while. The clicks of the sleet stopped as the ticks of the clock continued. *A good sign,* Irma thought. "Come on, we're headin' for bed. Pray for all travelers tonight, dear."

"I already have, my love."

"Good glory be!" Irma jolted upright as she heard Brownie barking furiously downstairs. "Heyward, wake up. Come on!"

"Put on the porch light!"

The reflection of the ice world almost blinded the two old people. The prior sleet storm had given in to the demands of the falling temperatures and coagulated into an even coating of thick ice. It covered everything. But Brownie would not have been barking at an ice coating.

"Heyward, quick!" Irma shouted, as she was the first to spot people walking toward the porch. A woman was trying to walk and hold onto a child with each hand. The children were slipping with every other step. When she tried to pick up one, she slipped and fell. The children were crying while she unsuccessfully tried to console them. She kept looking back and calling out to others.

Heyward swung open the door. "Come! Come in."

Irma grabbed the blankets and wrapped each one. "Sit here. I'll build up the fire. Are there more people out there?"

"Yes, two more. My husband and my son. They are trying to ease the car off to the side of the road without letting it slide over the embankment in case another car comes down."

"I'll get my boots on and go out," Heyward volunteered.

That's why I love him, Irma thought to herself.

The Perkins family spent the night with the Howards. Irma hustled around bedding down the two little ones right on the couch where they could see their mother. Later their dad would carry them upstairs to be placed in the little bed next to their parents. Irma's three daughters once occupied that room. The older boy got to have their son's room. He was awake for hours looking through Tom's memorabilia and reading his comic books. Morning came with pancakes and real maple syrup, eggs, bacon, and apple fritters.

"I love it here," the little girl exclaimed as she wiped a drop of syrup from her chin.

Heyward was the first one to hear the sand truck lumbering down the hill. "Guess you'll be able to get out of the hollow pretty soon now, the troops are coming in." He laughed.

"How's it going in there?" Lou called out as he banged on the door.

"Come in, Louie. Want some coffee or breakfast?"

"Can't, Heyward. Got miles and miles of roads to sand this morning. Saw the car up on the hill. Glad it was over to the side so I could get my truck through. Are you the company?"

"Yes," blushed the mister. "I feel pretty embarrassed thinking I could make it in and out of this hollow on an icy night."

"Never mind," murmured Irma, "everything turned out just fine."

"Might not have if it weren't for good folks like the Howards," Lou felt a need to inform the adventurers. "For a long time now, they have helped a lot of folks. Gotta go."

Irma and Heyward bid their guests a less eventful trip and watched the vehicle scale the hill to leave the hollow.

"Well, they were nice."

"Yup."

"I'm going upstairs to make up everything fresh."

"You're not expecting more company are you?" Heyward asked.

"You never know."

Irma stopped at the top of the stairs to look out upon the earth below. There they were: eleven gravestones. Today, the tops glistened because of the sunshine on the ice, but some days they wore their snowcaps, and some mornings birds perched to chatter about the agenda for the day. Heyward's grandparents started the family gravesite when their first child died. Out in the country it was customary for there to be a family cemetery in a peaceful area by the homestead. Her in-laws were out there, Ma and Pa Howard, a daughter, an aunt and baby who both died in childbirth, a cousin who just came to this country, three people who died on the night of the terrible snowstorm were buried there because the police could not find any relatives and they had no money for a burial, and Tom.

"God rest their souls," murmured Irma as she always did.

Ah, her three girls. *What fun and what fights they used to have in this room,* Irma reminisced as she changed the sheets. Now they were so far away with their own families, and they had no hollow or gravesite in their backyards. They visited once every summer; they never came in the winter. They claimed that their home was a nightmare in the bad weather. They even claimed the other kids teased them about living in Dead Man's Hollow. They often tried to convince their father to move across the country to where they lived, on flat land, but no, he couldn't leave his homestead. Irma thought she could, if he really wanted to, but she was confident that he never would. Anyhow, she couldn't leave Tom.

"Heyward, Heyward!" she yelled, "Come here! Quick!"

"Good glory be. What is it?"

"Look!"

"Look at what?" Heyward asked.

"That's just it," Irma panicked. "Tom's things are gone!"

Heyward made a circular motion with his old body to detect that the baseball relics were gone, the comic books and the football trophies too.

"Do you think...?"

"Yes, I think that boy took them," Irma replied.

Heyward left Tom's room with not another word as Irma sat on the edge of the bed and cried.

"Got the fire roarin'; you comin' on down?" Heyward asked.

The Howards stared into the blaze, somehow letting it use its beguiling ways to draw their compatibility back into balance.

"I'm sorry he took Tom's things," Heyward said softly.

"I know you are. So am I."

"Maybe we'd been keeping his room exactly how he left it for too long."

"You might be right."

The same questions that they couldn't answer for a million times prior to that day ascended into their minds.

Why didn't we insist he couldn't go out that night? Would he really have been benched if he missed the basketball game? Why didn't the school call off the game? He could have walked to the top of the hollow and waited for the school bus, couldn't he? Would his friends really have thought he wasn't cool if he didn't drive to the game? Would Jenny have broken up with him if he couldn't pick her up?

Irma and Heyward had waited that night with stress almost dripping out of their pores. The snow and sleet beat upon their little house as if it could bury it before anyone could say "Jack Robinson." They'd wondered if that night would be the night that the hollow completely filled with snow and they would never be heard of again. No, but it was the night that Tom lost his life driving home—driving down into the hollow.

It was Brownie who managed to pull Heyward out of his trance. "OK, boy. OK let's go out."

Irma made a comforting dinner for her husband; he needed a comforting dinner. She watched him and Brownie walk through the graveyard.

"Oooee, it's freezing out there!" Heyward came in clapping his gloved hands together. Brownie went straight to the fireplace. "It's already ten below."

"Ah, you did yourself proud, dear," Heyward smiled as he patted his stomach.

"I think we both needed something tasty."

"We are going to have a restful night tonight, my dear."

"How do you know that?" Irma asked.

"Weather report said there will be nothing falling from the sky, just a freezing cold night."

"I'll take it."

The full moon looked down upon the sleeping rural countryside, probably admiring the vastness of the frozen vista. Nothing moved except an occasional fox or perhaps an owl. The trees stood at attention. Wait! Something quite long and black was slowly maneuvering along the country roads. The moon itself was bewildered.

"Brownie, stop. What's the matter?"

"Someone's walking up the steps, Heyward."

The old man peered from the upstairs window. "What on earth?" The full moon made the black vehicle shine like a rare onyx. "Irma! There's a limousine down there."

"Limousine? Out here in the sticks?"

"Sorry to bother you, sir, ma'am. I think we have something that belongs to you."

The driver stepped to the side and there stood the boy, the thief, holding a box.

Irma gasped. Brownie growled.

"At this time of night?" Heyward questioned. "I mean, come in, please."

The boy sheepishly walked behind the uniformed driver.

"May I ask why you would be out here in Lone Moon Creek in the middle of the night?"

"It wasn't planned that way, sir, we, uh, we…"

"We were lost," the young thief blurted. He felt relieved that he wasn't the only one who'd done something wrong.

"I'm afraid a lot of the roads out here in the country aren't on my GPS, and the boy's father really didn't give me good directions. He kept saying something about going down into Howard's Hollow."

"Well you found it!" Irma announced as she finally decided to be hospitable. "Here, sit at the table. Are you hungry?"

"I'm starving," the boy quickly proclaimed unashamedly.

"I don't think your grandfather would want you to have anything until you apologize to these nice people," the limo driver stated emphatically.

"This stuff ain't nothing good. It's just a box of junk. Who would want it?" the boy said.

Irma quickly removed the apple pie from in front of the boy as the driver glared daggers at him.

"How much gas do you have in that buggy of yours?" Heyward asked.

"Buggy," the youth reiterated as he snickered, validating his notion that these were truly country bumpkins.

Irma couldn't imagine what her husband had in mind, but she knew it was going to be profound.

"What were you thinking?" the employee of the boy's grandfather asked.

"We've never been in a limousine before. I thought maybe you could take us for a little ride."

Irma looked curiously at her husband without saying a word.

"We'll get dressed and be right back."

"Well, isn't this something," Heyward mumbled as he and Irma stepped into the back of the limo. "Here, son, you sit right across from us."

Did the full moon yet know what was happening? It had never seen the Howards embark on a journey quite like this. The long, black, shiny onyx climbed out of the hollow with the grace of an antelope. While the frozen air paralyzed every living thing in the terrain, the vehicle was as toasty warm as Irma's cranberry muffins.

"Pick any road you want to, driver, I know them all; I can always get us back," Heyward said.

The four of them looked across the fields. They could see smoke streaming straight as pokers from the chimneys of the locals, with nary a breeze to draw the smoke left or right; they could see the ice along the banks of the creek with the ripples tumbling through the center. Heyward pointed out deer and rabbits, a coyote, and a bobcat. Irma spotted a flock of geese. They drove past Tom's school and their church, the little movie theater, and the grocery store. The flag, well lit by a spotlight, was frozen too. Heyward pointed out the campsite where Tom and the other scouts had learned how to survive the elements and the old swimming hole where he learned how to swim. The goalposts were still up, and the row of outdoor basketball hoops stood waiting for the first ball to sail through.

"I know where we are now," the boy called out. "This is where we went down the hill sideways, and we had to spend the night at your house. Right?"

"Right and you stayed in Tom's room and stole his things."

"Well, where is this Tom anyway?" the boy sassed.

"I'll show you. We won't even need a flashlight with the bright moon out there. Pull right into the driveway, sir."

The old man and the boy walked to the gravesite. Irma could see Heyward put his arm around the shoulders of the young lad. He talked for quite some time. Irma knew her husband was wiping his tears away. She hoped that they wouldn't freeze to his face.

Afterward, the four of them sat at the table passing around the sandwiches and pie as Tom's things also circulated. Heyward explained the significance of each one.

"I'm sorry I took Tom's things; I didn't know they meant anything to anybody."

"I know you didn't, son."

"Next time think!" the driver interjected. "Say, we'd better get your grandfather's limo back. Are you ready to go?"

"How about the two of you coming back some day to visit? I'd kinda like to take another ride in that buggy!" Heyward said.

"You're on!"

When the driver reported back to his employer, he referred to Howard's Hollow as: Howard's Hollowed Hollow.

THE END

"Grandma, do we have to live here forever?"
"Would you rather live someplace else?"
"How about on the moon? Wouldn't it be fun to be up there? Then we can look down on everybody and see what they're doing!"
"Marjory Lane! Are you telling me you want to be an eavesdropper?"
"No, just a moon walker."
"Ai, yi, yi."

Chapter Seventeen

The Barn Owl

Gabe held his breath as Miss Ochali returned the literary essays. He thought his was pretty good; he hoped she thought so too.

He listened to her comments as she went from student to student.

Here she comes, he said to himself as he stopped breathing.

Gabe's eyes darted downward as something red flashed in front of them. In big letters the words "SEE ME" seemed to be drowning in red ink. His eyes lifted to look at her. Miss Ochali was scowling somewhat like the barn owl back home at his family farm.

His father and his uncles all concurred that their barn owl was the original one—the one that they remembered their grandfather telling them about. No one knew how that could be, but they went along with it, just as they went along with all the stories that they heard and told and retold. Not one of the brothers had ever left the farm. To them, it was their heritage, their legacy, and their reason *for being the way they were.* And what was that way? Arrogant, unchanging, and demeaning. The consensus among the brothers was that to leave the farm would be asking for a curse.

Needless to say, one small house could not possibly accommodate five families. Therefore, as people drove by, they slowed their vehicles to a crawl in order to see what addition was being added next. Some equated it to a kid's rendition of a cereal box, shoe box, or Cracker Jack box house taped together to make room for everyone. Every year, it grew and spread as it sprawled across the lawn and then down the slope to the garden and over into one of the horse pastures.

Maybe when Grandpa Sullivan had the five boys he became rather arrogant as he walked through town with the five pillars of muscle while people stepped aside to let them pass. The school board knew that when the plowing and planting had to be accomplished there would be no Sullivan's in school on those days. Of course, the school schedule was designed with the farmers in mind. There was no school in the summer, as the boys and girls sweat through the hot blistering haying days of the season. Even when school resumed in the fall, there were no Sullivan boys there when the corn and the oats had to be harvested.

One by one, the brothers each quit school, seeing no real need to be away from the work on the farm, and as nature takes its way, each one married and brought his bride home. More and more cracker boxes were built and attached to the hub of the house as scores of babies came into the world. The brides were big on sending their children to school and earnestly wanted their kin to achieve good grades, but was it possible that the influence of the fathers could easily daunt the best intentions of the women? Yes, and it did. Somehow, the Sullivan influence in the school was intimidating not only to the school board but also to the principal and its teachers. The thirty or so kids soon learned that their daddies could get them out of any type of altercation or scrape.

So it was as Gabe sauntered into Miss Ochali's room to find out what the "SEE ME" note was all about.

"Yeah, you wanted to see me?"

"Yes, Gabe, please sit down," she directed as she covertly hid her anxiety. "I read your essay," she said slowly as she looked at Gabe.

"It was pretty good wasn't it?"

"Gabe, it was excellent—a beautiful piece of literature."

"I thought you'd like it," the young man uttered arrogantly.

"I really did... but you didn't write it!"

"What do you mean I didn't write it?"

"I know how you write, and unless you had some sort of miracle, there was no way you could have written that!" the teacher replied.

"How do you know? Maybe I put a lot of time and effort into that paper."

"Whoever wrote it had advanced skills in writing. I don't think you are at that level yet."

"I guess I'll have to get my father in here, and he'll tell you I wrote it."

"That might be a good idea. I'll schedule a time."

Gabe strode out of the classroom with all the swagger he had inherited from his male lineage.

Three days later, Miss Ochali looked up from her grading tasks to see a mountain of a man pave his way between the rows of desks as if he were a combine sailing through the oats.

"Do we got a problem here?" the mountain asked as he looked down on the tiny sparrow.

The teacher arose, looked him squarely in the eye, and said, "We just might."

"All right, spill it; I've got a load of work I gotta be doin' at home."

Gabe peered around the arm of his father, knowing he was safe.

"Gabe claims he wrote this essay," Miss Ochali said.

"And you say he didn't. Is that correct?" Mr. Sullivan quickly commented, having no time to waste conversing.

"Yes, sir," Miss Ochali spoke definitively, not wavering from her conviction.

"Well, how're we gunna prove this one way or a tother?"

"Sit down and I'll read it to you. Here, you take my chair," she said graciously, knowing he would never fit comfortably in a student's desk chair.

The Morning Sun

Braced against the cold, crisp morning, Champ and I began our daily trek to the awaiting cows in the barn. Had they had a good night? Do they wait as people wait knowing they would be fed? I turned to look at my relatively straight footprints in the snow—a new pristine covering upon the ground. I laughed to see the paw prints that Champ had already made helter-skelter, hundreds more than mine. He was a free soul when he was released into the morning air.

I checked the horizon. Something was alive just over the ridge. It wouldn't be long before the majestic sphere would show its first rays. Light. Everything responds to light.

"What's that, Hooty?" I stopped in my tracks as I did every morning to hear the barn owl's dissertation on light. He had our rapt attention as he spoke his peace.

"I think you're right," I called back in owl language as Champ gave one bark to solidify our solidarity.

Ah, there they are! Those strong beams of light. How far do they reach? The white snow covering soon glistened with diamonds. Champ circled and twirled, scampered and dug his nose into the jewel field at the bedazzlement.

"You'll never catch one, you silly dog." I laughed as we continued on to the barn, me with my straight footprints and Champ with his joyous entitlement prints. I could hear the cows mooing; they knew we were coming. I could hear the backdoor of the house slam; I knew my love was also on her way to do the morning chores. Would she see the dazzling jewels on the fresh snow or stop to listen to the barn owl hail his knowledge upon the world or lift her face to let the rays bring a bit of warmth to the frozen morning?

Yes, he knew she would.

"You wrote that?" Mr. Sullivan bulleted his question directly at his son.

"Um," Gabe mumbled, thinking about the consequences he would face if he lied to his father. "In a way I did." Gabe was on a crusade to save himself.

"And in what way is that?" his father asked as he looked up at the school clock just as he once did as a kid.

"Well, since our whole family is connected and our lines go way back through the generations, one could say I wrote it through my lineage."

Mr. Sullivan tilted his head while staring at his son. Finally, he said, "What the hell are you talking about?"

Miss Ochali wondered the same thing but not necessarily in those words.

"Well, you know how our family is in the old part of the house, the original rooms?"

"Yeah."

"One day, I wondered why one of my floorboards in my room had such a sway to it every time I stepped on it, so I pried it up, and there were boxes and papers under there."

"Are you telling me the truth?"

"Yes, sir. There were stories, poems, essays, and all sorts of writings neatly placed in boxes and albums."

"Where did they come from?" his father asked.

"They were all signed by your grandfather, my great grandfather, Gabrielle M. Sullivan."

Miss Ochali couldn't contain her excitement any longer. "Gabe, do you know what you have there? You have come upon a treasure!"

"Now don't get his hopes up. It's not money treasure, son; those words aren't worth anything."

"That's where you and I would disagree, Mr. Sullivan. I think words are a treasure," the petite Miss Ochali replied sternly.

"Let's get back to the point. Why are we here?"

"I wanted to find out who wrote this composition and now I know. But, Gabe, you can't pass off your great grandfather's work as your own!"

"I know," Gabe mumbled as he lowered his eyes, "but his was so much better than anything I could have written."

"I would love to read more of Gabrielle M. Sullivan's work; would you mind sharing it with me?" the teacher asked.

Gabe looked at his father for permission. The tower of a man rose and nodded as he warned, "My son better get a good mark in this class."

Did Gabe's grades get better? Did he begin to write more maturely? Surprisingly, yes!

Miss Ochali became the overseer of Gabrielle M. Sullivan's written words for the entire semester. She often shared with her classes the opulence of the man, whom none of them knew, except Gabe, who slowly became the proud recipient of his line of lineage. He watched his classmates as they sat transfixed on his great grandfather's words; he listened to the discussions after the readings, which surprisingly brought critiques even from those who wanted nothing more than to quit school. When Gabe first saw some of the girls wipe away their tears after hearing one of his great grandfather's stories, it astonished him. But for Gabe, the crème de la crème was hearing about the history of the times. How did that man and his young bride ever start with nothing but a plot of earth and develop so much? The more he heard of that laborious life, the more Gabe was astounded with how his great grandfather could balance the farm work with the art of writing. What the man saw and did during the day came out on paper during the evening hours, not in hopelessness but in joy, beauty, and aliveness! Everything from picking rocks out of the fields for the building of the stone wall property lines to building the barn to digging the cellar for the house came out as words of love and hope for the future and a good life.

Gabe began to walk across his family's land with new eyes. He looked at the old apple orchard and the chicken coop that still maintained its original location. The cold spring water still spewed from the same place as it had for his ancestors, and the hollyhocks—his great grandmother's favorite flower, which were started just for her by her new husband—were there!

"Your stories are coming to life, Gabe! Good job!" Miss Ochali wrote on Gabe's latest essay with her red pen.

"There!" Mr. Sullivan grinned as he slammed the report card to the old wooden table, "I knew I'd scare some sense into that little pip-squeak of a teacher."

"Dad, it was me who got the B, not you," Gabe said boldly.

Mr. Sullivan's eyebrows raised as Gabe's mother stopped cold by the kitchen sink.

"You know, if I'd ever talked to my father like you're mouthin' off to me, I'd have landed out west somewhere!"

Gabe walked silently to his room and to his writing journal. *Maybe this is my solace, too, great grandfather*, Gabe thought as he felt his nerves calm as soon as he touched the pen.

Oh, no, another "see me" message.

"Thanks for coming in, Gabe. Don't worry, you're not in trouble." Miss Ochali laughed. "It has taken me all semester, but I finished reading through your granddad's manuscripts and papers. Truthfully, I am so taken aback by his work that I want to ask your family's permission to share them with my brother, who is a publisher."

"What's that mean?"

"I can see a book or a movie coming out of all of this."

"You're kidding."

"No, I'm not kidding, but my brother would know better than I of the possibilities. Can you give this invitation to your father so we can talk about this?"

Gabe sighed as he took the note; having his father in school was not a burning desire of his.

"Now what?" Mr. Sullivan steamed as he read the note. "Oh great, that little pip-squeak is lookin' for trouble again?"

"She is not looking for trouble!" Gabe rebutted harshly. "She just might have some good news for this family."

"That would be the day that this family had any good news," he hollered at the back of his son who was proceeding upward toward his writing domain.

Mrs. Sullivan was left to listen to her husband grumble about the fate of their lives.

"Five families on this farm and what do we have? Debt, debt, and more debt. We work our fingers to the bone to bring some life out of this place, and what is it? It's a desert; it's a doomed place with no joy, no happiness, only seven days a week of milkin' cows and plowin' fields and maybe watchin' the corn shrivel on the stalk or the hay mold with the rain.

"I remember bringing in a wagon load of loose hay and pitchforkin' it up into the mow and tyin' up the shocks of oats and placin' them out in the field like Injun teepees. There was no barn cleaner; we tossed it out with shovels. Now we got those great big monster machines that go through the fields like robots, but guess who the robots are? Are you listening to me? We are. We are the robots. Do we ever have any fun? We used to have fun on this place when we were kids. My grandfather and my father made it fun. What has happened?"

Mrs. Sullivan knew not to answer. She listened as he mumbled off to bed.

"Thank you for coming in, Mr. Sullivan," the petite Miss Ochali said as she stood.

"What has he done now?"

"Didn't Gabe tell you about the good news?"

"He don't tell me nothin'," he remarked as he scowled at his son.

"Well, the crux of the matter is I would like your permission to send your grandfather's literary work to my brother who is a publisher."

"What for?"

"If it's publishable, your family might reap the rewards of a book deal or maybe even a movie."

Mr. Sullivan sat with a blank expression on his face until suddenly dollar signs marched across his mind's line of vision.

"You mean, those words of his could make us rich? We could afford to get off that farm and have a real life?"

"Well, Mr. Sullivan, don't get ahead of yourself; there are no guarantees of anything. His work might not be anything they want. Who knows? But would you like to test the waters?"

"Hell, yes, we'll test those waters. Did you hear that Gabe? Your great grandfather wrote like we was livin' in some sort of enchanted land—a place that had magic and look-ee here... It just might be magic!"

"He wrote what was true," Gabe said in defense of his idol. "To him, it wasn't magic or a dreamland; it was real and he loved it. He saw the farm as his paradise; he praised every aspect of it and was thankful. You and your brothers have desecrated it with your minds; you think it's no good and that your lives are no good. Well, you are making it that way!"

Miss Ochali could see the sweat run down her student's hairline as he clenched his hands so tightly that they looked white compared to his tanned arms.

"You've got big talk for a schoolboy; maybe you ought to quit and really learn what work is," retaliated Mr. Sullivan.

"All right, gentlemen, let's get back to why we're here," Miss Ochali interjected, feeling like she was settling a dispute between two of her students. "The decision?"

"Yeah, send it to whoever does that stuff and hope to God it'll make us rich!"

The teacher and Gabe stared at the mountain of a man as he stalked from the room.

The news flew through the Sullivans' house like wildfire. Buzz Saw told his brother Crowbar who told Mallet Man who told Whetstone who told Pickax. The five of them huddled around the old antique kitchen table like bees on clover.

Immediately, their minds erupted out of the muck and mire of their lives to see sunshine, vacations, and new houses! They called their wives and children into the old kitchen and jubilated until the original wooden cupboards and the old woodstove shook with the vibrations of excitement.

As Gabe walked from the barn, he couldn't help but look up at Hooty who was alarmingly calling out to the world about some kind of tale.

"What's the matter, old boy?" Gabe called to him. A few hoots and squawks made the hair on the back of Gabe's neck lift.

Did Hooty know what was transpiring inside the house with the five brothers and their families? Gabe didn't know. Even after he heard the regaling halfway to the house, he didn't know it could be about that!

Just inside the kitchen door, Gabe stood a long while sorting through the remarks before he could put them all together. His Uncle Pickax was swinging his wife around the floor as they sang about Hawaii. Uncle Crowbar's family was definitely moving to Hollywood where the movie was undoubtedly going to be made. Whetstone's wife was standing on a chair trying to get an audience to tell them what their new house by the ocean would look like, while Uncle Mallet Man passed beer cans to his sons to salute their new lives at the drag races with the cars they were going to own. His own father sat with his hands behind his head, smiling at his family—smiling because it was he who had delivered the good news that finally brought some mirth and cheer into the household.

Oh, no, thought Gabe, *none of this is for certain; there might not be any book or movie! This has to be stopped!*

"Dad, stop them! Why did you tell them? This is not a certainty. My teacher is going to send the manuscripts to her brother. That's all we know!"

"Don't be such a pessa... pess... whatever the word is! Look at this happy family. I haven't seen them like this in years, and you're not going to ruin it for them!"

Gabe turned and ran outside. Hooty was still on a tear.

"You knew, didn't you?" he shouted in the direction of the haymow.

With the windfall coming, it was only natural that the family members should spend their savings! After all, it could be replaced when their royalty checks came in!

Uncle Whetstone's wife was the first to react. On the very next day, she drove into town to visit with the people at the realty company. She gave them the specifications of the house she wanted by the ocean.

"Does that mean you are going to sell your part of the house out there on the farm or will you rent it out?" asked the chief realtor.

"I don't know! I never thought of that!" She giggled when she thought about even more money coming their way.

When she returned, she ran into the barn looking for her husband. "Whetstone, listen to this: we've got more money coming in!"

Uncle Pickax and his wife followed when the realtor in town was recommended by his brother.

"Oh sure, my wife and I go there at least once a year; I could tell you from here about several places that are for sale. Will you be keeping your place here?"

"I don't really know. I haven't thought about it," Pickax replied.

"Just to give you a clue," the realtor said as he leaned in, "you're going to need all the money you can get to have a house in Hawaii."

Gabe's drag-car-lovin' cousins and their father drove the farm's pickup truck to the races, which were three hundred miles away. Missing three school days was nothing to them; they were going to use the "educational trip" excuse when they returned. They scouted the cars and the drivers. They had enough money to buy one car and curiously met up with a loan shark who gladly loaned them enough for another, with interest of course.

"No problem," was Uncle Mallet Man's response.

Aunt Susie was already wearing her diamond-studded sunglasses and forcing Uncle Crowbar to tuck in his shirt and wear a white belt. She ordered eight more movie magazines, which would definitely make the mailman wonder why anyone on earth would need fifteen movie magazines a month.

The hubbub of selling or renting their addition to the house was running rampant from one brother to the next. All but Buzz Saw was on board with that idea; they wanted the extra money for their new lifestyle, but he had no plans of moving anywhere. Gabe was glad about that.

"Dad, you've got to stop them! It's getting out of control! They don't know if there is going to be any money!"

"Son, look at them! Have you ever seen them this happy? Your aunts are over the moon, and the kids are actually tolerable! Why ruin that?"

Gabe knew he was up against a brick wall; arguing with his father was useless. Finally, he asked, "And what are we going to do? What about us?"

Buzz Saw pulled himself up straighter in the wooden kitchen chair and said, "We're not going anywhere; we're staying here to work the farm. You will be my main farmhand!"

"Dad, I'm going off to college in six months." Gabe released the information knowing he should have divulged it sooner.

"You're what?"

"Yes, I've been accepted at two different colleges."

Out of the corner of his eye, Gabe could see the relatives slowing creep out of the kitchen, leaving him to face his father with Mrs. Sullivan silently standing by the stove stirring the blackberry puree.

Which lasted longer? The silence or the mother's constant swirling of the wooden spoon in the thick sweet prospective jam? If the barn owl had perched himself on the cupola of the barn, he would know, as he could stare downward into the side kitchen window.

"What brought this about?" Buzz Saw's voice sounded as irritated as a buzz saw.

"Miss Ochali said I have *potential* and that I am *gifted*, just like my namesake, Gabrielle M. Sullivan."

"You're gifted, all right! Gifted to work on this farm that he started all by himself with my grandmother. You are to stay here and be his dutiful great grandson!"

Buzz Saw sauntered to the door. Gabe and his mother knew the matter was closed. "Besides," he added as he swung toward his son, "I never would give you all of my hard earned money to throw away on college!"

Hooty studied the figure walking slowly to the barn and proceeded to imitate the lowered head and the slouched shoulders. He even kicked at the air as the man kicked at a loose stone.

The wooden spoon ceased to rotate as his mother asked, "What are you going to do about money?"

"I haven't told you about this before because I wanted to see what Dad would do. But since he isn't going to do anything to help me financially, I need to tell you something."

Annette Sullivan lifted the heavy pot from the fire and set it in the pantry to cool before she would ladle it into the jam jars for the winter's consumption. She sat at the table. "I'm listening."

"When Miss Ochali went through great grandpa's papers, she found something. In a little box was a coin with a folded letter and the letter said that the coin was to be for my college tuition."

Mrs. Sullivan didn't utter a word; she just stared at her son.

"Mom, did you hear me?"

"I did hear you, but I'm not understanding it."

"I know! To me it's like a miracle, but Dad is going to..."

Uncle Whetstone and Aunt Lila bought their dream house on the ocean's front. Uncle Crowbar and his wife moved to Hawaii. Uncle Mallet Man and his family went to race their drag cars and move with the action. Uncle Pickax, Susie, and the kids moved to Hollywood, California.

Buzz Saw and Annette remained on the farm with renters coming and going. There had been artists and reporters, retirees and shoe salesmen, and computer geeks and pastors. There was no renter who wanted to work on the farm. Mr. Sullivan had to hire farmhands through his ad in the paper. His number-one farmhand was at college and not welcomed in his home.

But who did return home? Uncle Crowbar was the first to return from Hawaii. ("That foreign *country* was not for him.") Truth be told, he had run out of money. Then came Uncle Mallet Man. ("All that racing dust made me cough.") Actually, he couldn't afford to fix his smashed race cars. Aunt Lila and Uncle Whetstone left their ocean home after discovering "they couldn't bear the sound of the crashing waves day and night." In reality, they couldn't stand the crashing mortgage. Uncle Pickax and Susie held out the longest, but their house also went into foreclosure and they returned.

The barn owl couldn't help but notice that along with their baggage came their gloom and dismay as before; their hopes for a more glamorous life had been dashed.

The only one not home was Gabe, and Buzz Saw was never going to forgive him for leaving the farm.

As the years passed, no one in the family mentioned the book or the movie anymore. They knew it was never going to come to fruition, just as their glamorous dreams were never going to develop. So the work went on and more additions were added to the sprawling complex as the older children married and had children of their own. The doom never left, and the joy that Gabrielle M. Sullivan wrote about was not even a memory.

"What's the matter with that crazy old bird?" Buzz Saw growled as he looked up at Hooty flapping his wings and screeching. For seven days, each Sullivan uttered a similar phrase. The children began to imitate the owl as they flapped their arms and hooted back and forth to each other.

"I never saw him act so looney," Pickax commented.

"Something must be in the air," Crowbar agreed.

Something was in the air all right! Buzz Saw read the letter to Annette:

Coming home, like it or not. I have a surprise for you!

"What does he mean he has a surprise for us?" Annette asked her husband.

"How do I know?"

"Dad, Mom, there's going to be a documentary made here on the farm!" Gabe relayed the news excitedly.

"What's that?"

"It'll be a movie for TV telling about the life of my great grandfather and how he started this farm all by himself with his wife. It'll be factual and bring in the history of the day and the adversities Gabrielle and other farmers had to deal with."

Neither Buzz Saw nor Annette said a word, so Gabe went on. "But the best part will be how it will include his writings depicting the beauty of nature and the joy of his life just to be alive on this marvelous piece of land!"

Still not a word from his audience. "All with beautiful music in the background," Gabe insisted, trying to drive the point home.

Finally, his father spoke, "Will we get any money for this?"

"Dad, no, this is not about money. It's about history and education."

"You came home to tell me that?"

"Yes, and to tell you that the movie crew will be here tomorrow with cameras and the whole nine yards!"

"What? You did this without my permission?"

"That's another thing, Dad." Gabe said softly as he carefully removed a folder from his briefcase. "This says that Gabrielle M. Sullivan left the farm to me when I turn thirty, and Dad, I'm thirty now."

Buzz Saw looked at his wife. "Yes, he is," she said.

"What the hell is going on here?" Buzz Saw questioned as he immediately looked up at the top of the barn. "You knew, didn't you?" He yelled as he pointed his finger at Hooty.

A wild fire could not have spread quicker. "The house" went into a state of lunacy with all the news. The diamond-studded sunglasses came out of the drawer; the women dug through their purses looking for lost makeup; the men toasted with cans of beer; the brochures of faraway places were found, and the drag racing channel was brought into focus.

Gabe stood in the driveway and shook his head.

However, with all immense projects, no one had time to stand around to shake his head. The day the trucks rolled into the driveway brought more excitement than the Sullivan's had seen in a long while. Gabe was the liaison between the crew and the farm. Even though the others were obviously in plain sight, the crew only dealt with Gabe. The ladies were donned in pretty dresses, and the children wore their best school clothes. The men combed their hair each day and worked exuberantly at their chores, often looking to see where the camera people were.

Fortunately, the crew was accustomed to gawkers, and even though they had to remind members of the family to be still or to move back, they didn't become irritated. Gabe didn't know how they were going to accomplish their goal of recreating the farm as it looked eighty years ago, but they were the professionals, and it soon became evident. The cameras panned the horizon, bubbling creek, woods, and an original stonewall. There were close ups of wildflowers in the fields, apples dangling in the orchard, nighttime stars, and rough bark on the trees. The cupola on the barn became a favorite shot, especially when Hooty was there to call out his orders. The script was written with the aid of Gabrielle M. Sullivan's journals, poems, essays, and stories. The background music would be composed after the music director studied finished tapes.

For two years, the production was created through every season, every hour of nighttime and daytime, storms of wind, rain, snow, and sleet. A three-week drought was a blessing to the director. He wanted to show it all. To depict how the elder Sullivan coped with the adversities while keeping his extraordinary joy for life was the director's highest ambition. The music was arranged and rearranged as more and more tapes were sent to the musicians' studio.

The family no longer gave heed to the crew; they regressed into their normal apathetic nature, knowing there was nothing in it for them.

"When are they gunna be done here?" Buzz Saw questioned his son. "We can hardly get our work done with them hangin' around. I'm gettin' sick and tired of them bein' here!"

"Well, wear your best shirt next week, because they are going to start interviewing you and the family," Gabe said.

"Really?" his father shouted as he jumped up from the chair. "What are they gunna ask?"

"I don't really know. I think it will be casual conversation."

Out came the ironing boards and the presoaking stain detergents. New sneakers were purchased, and the barber in town clipped for all he was worth. Their day was coming; after all those years, their day was coming!

Gabe spent his evenings reading the selections that had been chosen to best depict his great grandfather's talent and joy of his farm:

Halfway into the autumn, when the wind knew to blow a little stronger and the leaves gave all their power into creating the colors, the little lamb decided to be born. Had we ever heard or known of an autumn lamb? No, but we were novices to the ways of nature, and Linann and I knew that anything was possible

It was Hooty, our resident barn owl, who alerted us to the arrival in the dead of night. Out to the barn we ran with blankets over our heads and an old copy of a veterinarian's medical book wedged between our locked arms.

I remember Linann, hardly old enough to be a bride, studying the medical book by the light from the lantern. She became the teacher, and I was the student. We waited as we listened to the rain pelt against the barn. Linann stroked the ewe to comfort her and even sang to her. I looked on with such pride at the teacher and now the nurse. The baby was born in quite a flurry—at least my heart was in a flurry—and when Linann wrapped the baby in a blanket and placed it in my arms, I knew the world was at peace; the world was good.

Gabe smiled as he closed the folder. He knew there once was great love on the farm.

"No," laughed Buzz Saw, "we didn't always have these names. I was christened Redford, Pickax was Rupert, Whetstone is really Ronald, Crowbar is Reginald, and Mallet Man's real name is Rosie. Can you tell my mother wanted a girl?"

The interviewer laughed.

"Yep, all my life, never even left when the others went out to find their pots of gold. I'm the stable one; I'm the rock," Buzz Saw bragged flamboyantly.

"He is my son," Buzz Saw looked momentarily at Gabe. "He's a somewhat confused young man, but I guess that is the way the world is goin'. He went off to college and has lots of hair-brain notions on how the world ought to be full of love and ballet dancers and wispy, crispy leaves falling from the trees!"

Buzz Saw waited for the interviewer to immediately join in a camaraderie union with him and laugh while he slapped his knee and agreed about the young kids of today. But that didn't happen while Gabe stared as his father in disbelief.

"Oh no, don't be calling me Rupert. I prefer Pickax. Sure, we got the whole clan livin' here. Ain't people gunna be surprised when they turn on their TV's and see all us?" He laughed and waited for an answer.

"Yeah, I had a real dream once when Gabe here told us we were going to be rich, and I took all my savings and headed out to Hollywood to let the money roll in. But did it? No. Me and Susie and all the kids had to return to this no account place where there is no glamour."

The interviewer looked at Gabe to see him shaking his head in dismay.

"No, this land is no beach front." Whetstone laughed as he edged closer to the interviewer, ready to divulge anything that he was asked. "We got that stupid little creek that runs through our land and a couple of ponds. One's for fisin' and the other for swimmin', and oh yeah, out of the side of that mountain gurgles the coldest ice water you'd ever want to stick your feet in on a hot day. But they ain't no ocean like me and Lila had once outside our front door. So we're back here with a babble and a gurgle and a splash."

"Ronald, would those be words your grandfather would have used in his writings?"

"I hope not!" Whetstone cupped his hands to whisper to the interviewer. "Course, Gabe would probably think they were just dandy."

The interviewer looked at Gabe, who was chuckling. "I would think they were just *dandy!*"

"Reginald! Tell me, which name did you use in school?"

"I told the teachers to call me Crowbar, but did they? No. I finally quit anyway; they weren't teaching me anything."

"Tell me what you think of this selection that your grandfather wrote. We might use it in the documentary:

"I let the dirt fall slowly through my open fingers. It fell mostly downward to the plowed field, but a scattering of it sailed eastward with the slight movement of a breeze. Where would that finally settle? No one probably knows; it was of no consequence. The big consequence lay across five acres of my farm. The ground was ready for the corn seeds; the horse neighed his readiness to pull the wagon, which held the burlap bags of kernels, but it was the planter who was not ready.

"I stood motionless as the sun went higher and higher into the sky. Why couldn't I move? This was to be an all-day chore. What was holding me back? Was it the thoughts that suddenly entered my head? Thoughts of... What if the corn doesn't grow, what if we have a drought, and what if there comes into this valley a blight like that that killed the hops? And just then I could see her long skirt flying as she darted along the rows of soil with a glass jar of water for me. There came my hope and my joy. We would farm this land together, and through good and bad we would do the best we could."

"Crowbar! Are you asleep!" the interviewer asked.

Crowbar shook himself. "By golly, I was prit near asleep," he laughed. "That's what those teachers used to do to me; they'd read some sappy thing, and try as I might, I couldn't keep my eyes open."

"So you don't know if we should use that selection or not?"

"No, don't ask me. Ask the big-shot college boy over there," Gabe's Uncle Crowbar announced as he pointed to him.

"I liked it," Gabe answered.

"Me, too," added the interviewer.

"Last but not least. I think I'll start right out by calling you Mallet Man," the interviewer announced.

"I think you had better!" Warned Rosie aka Mallet Man.

"So, Mallet Man, tell me, what do you think of that barn owl up there?"

"Him? He's crazier than a loon."

"Why do you say that?"

"He knows more than all of us put together."

"Mm, interesting," replied the interviewer as he wrote that in his notes. "What do you see when you look around this land?"

"It sure ain't no Hawaii!" Mallet Man chortled as he looked at Gabe.

"How so?"

"Do you see them tall hollyhocks over there? Picture them as a bed of tropical Hawaiian plants, now them was beautiful. What my grandmother saw in these, I'll never know. And birds! What do we got here? Sparrows and chickadees, robins and hummin' birds. No big deal. And trees! Do you see any palm trees around here with coconuts hangin' from them? Of course not. We just have these ordinary ones, nothing spectacular."

"Hmm, I wonder why your grandfather thought they were spectacular."

"Well, he never was anywhere other than right here; he never took any vacations."

"Let me check my notes. Wasn't he born in Portugal?

"Portugal? Where's that?"

"And didn't he emigrate from his native land and come to America only to go back to Europe during the First World War?"

"I think I heard something about that."

"Thank you, Mallet Man; you've been a big help."

344

The sisters-in-law huddled in the shade of the sprawling old maple tree as they giggled and twittered, constantly touching their hair and blotting their lips.

"Here he comes! Here he comes!"

"Good afternoon, ladies. Can you tell me where Annette is?"

"Oh, she didn't want to be out here; she's in her kitchen cuttin' some corn off the cob or some crazy thing. But we're here!"

"And how nice you all look, but right now I need to speak to Annette."

Red glossed lips turned downward and sighs of disappointment whispered through the air as the interviewer and Gabe walked to the old kitchen.

"Hi, Mom, can we come in for a few minutes?"

She didn't say anything, just shrugged her shoulders as if to say, "If you want."

"You have a very fine son here, Mrs. Sullivan," the interviewer contributed.

Immediately, Annette looked at Gabe and smiled the most beautiful smile—one that Gabrielle M. Sullivan would have appreciated and written an entire discourse on.

"Can you see the beauty that your grandfather-in-law saw in this farm, Annette?"

"I did see it through his eyes," she uttered nostalgically as she stopped her work and sat in the wooden chair. "I saw it the night Gabe was born and there was no doctor to come to my aid. It was grandma who helped me the best she could. It was the two of them who knelt by my bed in thanksgiving when at last I had my baby boy and the three of us dedicated the child to God to use as He pleased. Gabrielle M. Sullivan saw in this boy the promise of eternity and saw the beauty and promise of everything he had on this farm."

The interviewer knew that this segment was definitely going to be included in the documentary.

"Do you see it still, Annette?"

"Only in the eyes of my son," she said quietly. "The others have lost the love and the delight of this place. It's a sad place now," she murmured as she let her voice trail off. She returned to her work.

"How about us? How about our children?" The women bombarded the interviewer with questions. "The children have waited all day and actually stayed clean for this."

"I'm sorry, ladies, but by the time I drive to the city, I'll have just enough time to catch my plane," the interviewer wisely said as he ran to his rental car.

As he drove off waving through the open window, he could hear one of the women say to the children, "Oh, go on. Get yourself filthy if you want to. We missed our chance."

"Well, I suppose we better watch this," Buzz Saw said to his brothers.

"Yeah, I said some pretty interesting things to that guy. I'm sure my part will be in there," Pickax muttered.

The words *A Tribute to Gabrielle M. Sullivan* narrated by Gabrielle R. Sullivan came across the screen as an orchestra of strings sailed into people's living rooms like a soft breeze.

"Annette, did you know Gabe was going to be in the show?"

"Yes."

They could hear Gabe's voice in the background saying, "This is what Gabrielle M. Sullivan saw when he first laid sight of his new land." On the word "saw," panoramic views of the hills and dales, including the white cumulus clouds surrounded by the bluest of skies, drifted across the screen. The tumbling of the water in the creek followed by the placidness of the lone duck swimming effortlessly on the still pond to the dancing, gurgling water that exploded out of the side hill made Whetstone ask, "Where is this place?"

The voice of Gabe continued, "Would he be pleased? Would it be enough to make him stay?"

The artistic eye of the photographer brought the audience into the minute intricacies of nature with slow motion shots of wildflowers opening, baby birds using their wings for their first flights, a silhouetted owl hooting at a full moon, and chipmunks marching across a fallen tree trunk while pausing to look backward, seemingly surprised by seeing their own footprints in the snow.

"I don't think this is even our farm," Pickax snarled.

Buzz Saw gasped when a close up of his grandfather and grandmother appeared on the screen. Gabrielle, attired in a suit, and Linann, adorned in a long flowing wedding dress with a crown of wildflowers on her head and a bouquet in her hands, caused even the most critical of the teenaged girls to whisper, "Oh, how beautiful!"

"She entered my life on the wings of a pure white dove. She brought with her the sunshine, the rainbows, and the soft mist that rises above the creek on a summer's morn. She was my mind, my heart, my soul. I became invincible because of her," wrote Gabrielle.

"You never wrote anything nice like that about me, have you?" Lila grumbled into Whetstone's ear.

"And 'invincible' he seemed to be," Gabe continued, "but so too were all the farmers up and down their valley. Progress was being made on every plot of land for miles around. The land was being tamed; America was being built. Would their backs be broken or their spirits decimated before it could be finished? Would the retaliation of nature be enough to chase the farmer's away?"

On the screen rolled the retaliation of nature shots with the entire woods being pelted and whipped by the wind, trees almost doubled over by the force of nature, skies shooting forth lightening and releasing sleet on the tormented hay fields, snowstorms that took away anything visible beyond one's face, and floods that stole away rich top soil and droughts that pushed the water table so low that it couldn't be raised in the well.

"God spare us! We prayed as we gathered the chickens into the coop and rushed the cows into the barn. We could see it coming up the valley—that tunnel of whirling wind that we had only heard about. The dog and the birds and all the wild animals seemed to know to hide—to protect themselves. We rushed to pull the two sheep and the lambs into the barn. That sound—the haunting sound that might ring in my memory forever—traveled through our land as Linann and I buried ourselves under a pile of cornstalks. I held her so tightly, I wondered later if she could even breathe.

348

"When the quietness came, we pulled ourselves out from under the pile, probably looking like woodchucks popping out of the ground in the spring. And there stood the house, the barn, and the outbuildings, but on the south forty lay a path of downed trees, upturned soil, and a creek whose path would forever be changed."

"The torments of nature did not discourage Gabrielle and Linann; they were made stronger because of them and more and more, as the years went by, they could be found in quiet thanksgiving for all that they had," Gabe continued as the music swelled with the haunting melody created by the cellos and violins.

"Along came their first child, a girl—a girl for Linann," Gabe said as a photograph appeared.

"Aw," swooned the women and the girls as a little round face looked out from under her handmade bonnet and long white dress.

"Soon to follow were two more girls and then a son—a son for Gabrielle." More family photographs were shown with the three girls and the boy.

"Gabrielle Sullivan wrote this about his son," Gabe said:

"What would I do without my little shadow; the one who sways when I sway, and the one who jumps when I jump! As my big fingers go into the calf's mouth to get her used to drinking milk from a pail, his little fingers follow the same path as he squats to look the calf in the face, and say, 'Eat, calfie, eat!'

"What could be more fun than watching him find the eggs in the haymow and the strawberries on the side hill?

"The full moon wouldn't hold its mystery or the peepers tell their stories or the barn owl call out to the stars with important information without my little shadow. He brings everything to life."

"America was going through big changes. From the farm, they could hear the distant whistle of the train; three farms up the road, they could hear the motor of a tractor. Linann might be in the house teaching the girls how to use the new treadle sewing machine, while the two Sullivan males went to town to listen to the politics of the day. Things were changing; there was unrest in the government."

"Nothing different than today!" Crowbar howled as he slurped his beer.

"When are they going to show us?" the kids whined. "When is this going to be over?"

"Shh!" warned Annette.

There were the hollyhocks and the clothes hanging outside on the line, the gooseberry bushes and the elderberries clinging to the barn's stone wall, wild morning glories twirling around the post of the mailbox, and stones in the ruts of the driveway after the spring rains ran through.

"That stuff looks familiar," Lila commented. "But I never knew it would have been the same as years ago. Hmm, interesting," she commented.

"Gabrielle M. Sullivan continued writing, continued to draw pictures with his words. He didn't do anything with his essays and journals, just kept them in boxes and albums. Those were his memories. He never had any aspirations of having them go out into the world. His life with Linann and the children was his joy, his precious joy.

"As all things change, his daughters announced one by one that they were to marry and leave the farm. Gabrielle and Linann knew that was natural, but he worried about his wife, who felt the sorrow of losing her daughters. Ronald stayed on the farm and brought his wife to live there. They had five sons."

"Here we are. Here we are. They're getting to us now!" Mallet Man roared.

The kids snickered with laughter as they saw the photograph of the five boys sitting by the creek with their feet dangling in the water. The women thought it was adorable. The men sort of shuffled in their seats.

"Gabrielle M. Sullivan's entries became less and less as the time went by. Maybe his age was catching up to him; maybe too many changes of modernization were happening on his farm; maybe his sons were edging him out of his glorious domain. But for some reason, we don't hear as much of the joy and peace that he wrote about when he was younger, not until the birth of his first grandson who was named after him. Redford and Annette were to have the first grandchild and Gabrielle wrote:

"Another little shadow waiting to be born! How the years have passed! I hope he'll see the beauty that is still here on the farm. Some are acting like this is just a drudgery or a concentration camp. If only they'd open their eyes like Hooty. Hooty has seen everything. He knows when the pond is completely frozen over, and he knows when it's safe to go ice skating. He knows when the first autumn leaf changes color, and he knows when the pumpkins are ready to be carved into jack-o'-lanterns. He knows exactly how many barn cats there are and will call out in the night when the next calf is due to be born. My kin could get involved with all that Hooty does, but I guess they don't care to. But the new little one will learn

to appreciate all that is here, I just know it. And for that, I am most grateful."

"The grandfather almost lost his little shadow that night along with the child's mother. Somehow they pulled through, but Gabe was never to have any siblings."

Buzz Saw looked at Annette as she wiped away her tears.

The music came up as the camera panned across a willowy meadow, stopping at the family resting place. There was Linann's gravestone engraved with "Love Life" and on Gabrielle's was penned "Live Life."

Annette listened with pride to her son's closing statement.

"Thank you for being a part of Gabrielle M. Sullivan's life and history, and remember to 'love and live' your life to the fullest. Good night."

THE END

"ARE WE GOING TO CARRIE'S BIRTHDAY PARTY?"
"OF COURSE."
"I HOPE A TRAIN GOES OVER."
"I DON'T."

ᶜ✒Chapter Eighteen✑ᷓ

UNDER THE BRIDGE

Even Carrie didn't know why her house was under the bridge, and she was the one who lived in that house; in fact, she had lived there for one hundred years as of that day. Her bridge was not the water kind but the train kind. Everyone had always called it a bridge, "the Railroad Bridge," so of course, she did too. Carrie had been born in that house and her father claimed that a train rumbled overtop just as she was being born, so he didn't hear the labor screams. He said he was glad for that. The eight other children's births had not coincided with a train, and their screams were heard clear over to Louisa's porch. Henceforth, Louisa always went a running to be the midwife.

One day after the birth, all of Lone Moon Creek talked about another baby living under the bridge. Louisa was in a snit, however, because she was the last to know.

"Never heard one scream," she grumbled. "How was I supposed to know?"

Carrie's father couldn't answer his children or his neighbors as to why the house was under the train bridge. All he knew was that his father refused to move so that the railroad company could demolish the house in order to lay the tracks through that gulley. After a big brouhaha, they said

353

"fine" and built the bridge right over the house. His wife was fit to be tied, but Carrie's grandfather took it as a victory.

For the past forty years, the town had adopted Carrie. Some even called her granny. Not a day went by that someone wasn't at her house with meals or the newspaper, or toting in their own vacuum cleaner or food processor. They saw to it that her walkway was shoveled in the wintertime, the garden tended to in the summertime, and the woodchucks trapped whenever one popped its little head out of a hole.

Why did almost everyone take Carrie under his or her wing? If the truth were known, and it was, Carrie was a treasure trove of information. She knew everything about the town and way too much about the people! The things she could spew from her memory were not always things that should be common gossip and, undoubtedly, many of her visitors were there only for that reason.

She had been well advised about her one hundredth birthday celebration and was told to be prepared for, well, anything!

On her special day, she stood on her porch holding tightly to a white pillar as a group of well-wishers sang "Happy Birthday" a cappella. She watched four men carry a tower of a cake from a truck to the umbrella table on her front lawn. She'd wondered why that table had appeared the night before. The cake cutter and the ice cream scooper person arrived along with droves of people. For hours, people stepped onto the porch, wished her a happy birthday, left a card, picked up a dish of ice cream with cake, talked with the locals, and waved to Carrie.

Not one adult, but several children whined, "I wanted to see a train go over the house!"

They were countered with, "Be glad you didn't. Would you want grit in your ice cream?" or "No one would have been able to talk or hear."

The normal contemplative answer for the children was, "So."

There was some curiosity about the entire afternoon passing without a train going over the house. Some wondered if the railroad company had been asked to hold the trains back because of a special celebration. No, they don't accommodate birthday parties. It was just the way it was: some days saw very few trains and other days there were many.

Sixty miles away, a novice news reporter had finally gotten an assignment that would make the *Nightly News*. It was going to be big. She smiled as she left the city, anticipating a human interest story that the public would love. Her GPS had been programed, and she tooled along the state highway exhilarated that she was finally making it into the "big time" of news reporting.

Somehow, the one-hour-and-ten-minute trip turned into four hours. She thought she had followed the narrator of her GPS to a T. Why had it taken her way up onto some mountain with dirt roads and sheep that languished on the grass in between the two ruts meant for tires? Maybe she shouldn't have stopped to ask how to get back to the state highway; maybe she should have believed the talking "know-it-all" and stuck with it. In the end, she was right back at that sheep place, which led down the mountain into Lone Moon Creek. Laurel called her news station to report that she had made it to her destination.

"You better step on it! We need your story with pictures in one hour and thirty-nine minutes."

"Right, boss. I'll get it." *No problem,* Laurel said to herself. *She's an old lady who's one hundred. It'll take about ten minutes.*

Laurel stopped to ask where Carrie lived. The first person she approached knew.

"I'm on a roll now," she complimented herself.

"Well. That's the strangest setup I've ever seen," she muttered as she craned her neck to look at the top of the railroad bridge. Trestle, I guess I should say. Why on earth would that house be under the trestle?"

"Come in," Carrie called out.

"Hello, I'm Laurel. I'm here to do a story about you."

"I was told you were going to be here around two o'clock when all my well-wishers were here to help me celebrate. I guess you are late."

"I guess I am." Laurel laughed at the spunk of the old woman.

"That's all right. We can talk anyway. What would you like to know?"

"To begin with, I was astounded to see that your house was under a railroad trestle!"

"*Is* under—it still is," Carrie corrected her.

"Yes, absolutely. Now what would make the best story: You living one hundred years or you living one hundred years under the train tracks?"

"Are you asking me?" Carrie looked up from a birthday card she was scrutinizing.

"Sorry, I guess I was talking to myself."

"You're kind of young for that, aren't you?"

"Let's start with you telling me what you can remember about the area and any changes you've seen."

Carrie stared at the young girl in disbelief.

"I mean if you can remember things," Laurel added, not knowing she was digging herself deeper into a hole.

"I can start back a hundred and fifty years with accuracy, beyond that might just be hearsay."

"Can you give me just key words such as telegraphs, electricity, and so forth?"

"Are you in a hurry?"

"Actually, I am. I have to have my report submitted in one hour and nine minutes."

Carrie tipped her head back to rest it on the chair and closed her eyes. She took a deep breath and started her litany of changes over the last century and a half. Laurel pushed the button on her recorder. After only hearing about five of the innovations, Laurel heard a sound that roared up the valley and careened over her head. She screamed and put her arms on top of her head as her body lowered into a ball. At the same time, the little granny continued her list, never flinching and never slowing, only progressing onward, like history.

When Laurel heard the decrescendo of the noise, she slowly lifted her body out of its cocoon to hear Carrie bring her list to a close.

"Is that what it's like when a train goes over top?" The uncurled reporter's voice quivered.

"It always has been. I don't foresee any big alternatives now. So did you get my list of changes?"

"Oh! I forgot... Yes. Listen." Laurel pushed the button.

"All I hear is the train," Carrie said.

"They can take out all that background noise. You're on there, Carrie. Now, how about you tell the viewing audience a couple stories of some of the more 'colorful characters' in this town."

"Colorful characters? Ah, yes. Once there was a fellow who was a real lady's man, if you know what I mean. Anyway, that man got the shock of his life when..."

Laurel ducked again as another train seemed to want to come down through the roof to scalp them. Carrie, on the other hand, continued with her story and was in fact almost to the end as the reporter lifted her head and felt her hair.

"How many of those stories do you want?" Carrie asked.

"Maybe a few more. Let me just check the sound," Laurel said.

"But that's the train again."

"They'll get rid of it, don't you worry."

"The bank was robbed once just as the preacher walked in the door. One teller had fainted and the other was—"

"Oh no!" Laurel yelled. "This is ridiculous. How can anyone think straight around here?"

Carrie apparently never heard Laurel. She went on reciting her story of a colorful character.

"Why are there so many trains? Is this normal?"

"Some days it is, some days, not so much."

"Have any famous people come out of Lone Moon Creek, and could I ask you to talk fast before we're blasted again?"

"Sure, this is the hometown of the first crabapple-grape tree and the birthplace of the two-room schoolhouse and the first..."

Laurel literally held her hands over her ears and ran out to her car. Carrie went on and on about the phenomenal people and inventions. She leaned forward to push the "off" button on the machine and waited for the flyaway interviewer to return.

"I have no more time left. I have to send this in right now," Laurel stammered as she plugged the machine into her computer. "Thank you for your time and be sure to watch yourself on the *Nightly News*."

"Good-bye, dear," Carrie called out as she watched the young girl run like she was being chased by bird shot. She didn't have the heart to tell Laurel she had no television set. However, lots of other residents did, and she knew many would be tuned into the *Nightly News* as they were each evening.

Over eight dozen people asked Carrie at her party if she would come to their home to watch the show. Curiously, she thanked them but refused each person.

"No, you tell me about it some other day."

Keith called out, "Dorothy, come quick, Carrie is on the news."

"And this, ladies and gentlemen, is our centenarian of the week. Because of technical difficulties, however, it won't be until next week that we present the whole program about the history of Lone Moon Creek and the woman who lives under a train bridge."

The following week, Carrie's segment aired.

"Now, ladies and gentlemen, on her first big assignment, here is Laurel."

"Good evening everyone. As I launched out on my first big assignment, trying to find a little town called Lone Moon Creek, I thought maybe I was 'up the creek' when I was sure my GPS had led me astray. But low and behold, after four hours of searching, I found it. Unfortunately, I had missed the birthday party, but our one-hundred-year-young Carrie was most gracious in taking the time to talk with me.

"On your screen, you'll see the dear, Carrie. She has lived in the same house for one hundred years. Her eight brothers and sisters were born in that house also. There had been some sort of dispute between her grandfather relinquishing the house to the railroad company and the building of the trestle over the top of the house. In Lone Moon Creek, they call it 'the house under the bridge.'

"When asked what changes Carrie had seen over the years, she had a long list including the wringer washing machine. Interesting characters included the pastor who went in to rob the bank and notorious inventions included the crabapple-grape tree, which grew inside the two-room schoolhouse.

"So if you travel through Lone Moon Creek, be sure to drive past the little house with the train that travels over top. Good night."

The townspeople scratched their heads:

"That wasn't the Carrie we know. Our Carrie could talk about the town for hours. She barely said anything on the news."

"And some of the things that she reportedly said weren't even true."

The producer shook his head. "That was terrible, Laurel. What kind of reporting was that? You barely said anything. You had a unique opportunity to put together a fantastic human interest story, and look what you did."

"But, sir," Laurel whined, "the trains kept going over the top of the house, and the noise was overwhelming; I couldn't hear her. I thought we had equipment that would take out background noise. I tried to operate it, but I still couldn't hear Carrie."

"So you are the one who broke our expensive equipment! I've been blaming Steve. You're fired, Laurel."

History did march on, just as Carrie always said it would. She passed away when she was one hundred and two; the railroad company rebuilt the old trestle after the state had the house torn down, and the link to the past was forgotten.

Almost.

Laurel never forgot the interview with Carrie as the trains torpedoed over the top of the house. Thirty years later, her movie, *The House under the Bridge*, was a must see, and this time, enough of the train noise was removed so one could distinctly hear the old granny.

THE END

ᑌᔪ⌒Chapter Nineteen⌒ᕫᓬ
The Obit Box

"**M**arjory, time to get up. Come on now, rise and shine." Agnes didn't expect any rapid response, so she turned her attention to the newspaper.

"Oh my word!" Agnes murmured through the morning kitchen air. "What?" she questioned the print of the newspaper as she leaned in further.

Agnes's eyeballs darted back and forth, descending just enough to get to the next line.

"Whoever knew this?" Again, the daily reader of the *Harold* spoke to the effects of the typeset as if it was going to answer. She had completely forgotten about the vow to keep her white bathrobe sleeves off the smudgy newspaper; too often, she had to presoak the embarrassing black *Harold* remains.

Now it seemed as if the pall from the paper was coagulating with her thoughts as she read John O'Shannesy's obituary.

That old coot did all this? Agnes thought. *I can't believe it! He came out of the service as a major? That was his business in the city?* The place she had gone so many times to do her Christmas shopping. *Twin baby girls who died? Five children? Two of whom were doctors?*

How on earth did I not know any of this? Agnes questioned herself as she reached for the coffee mug handle. Her eyes jolted to the right, surprised to see that her fingers were at least five inches from their target.

John O'Shannesy from Lone Moon Creek—a complete stranger, Agnes reasoned as she rose to get the scissors. Raising her arm to the tool shelf exposed the telltale sign of her dragging the recently bleached cuff across the black words of the even blacker obituary.

"Marjory, please get up right now. Do you want to sleep your life away?" Agnes hollered.

You never really know a person, Agnes reflected as she snipped around the perimeters of John O'Shannesy's life.

"Oh! You scared me half to death!" Agnes gasped as the younger woman walked into the kitchen.

"What are you cutting from the paper?"

"It's old John O'Shannesy; he died. Do you remember him?"

"I don't think so," Marjory replied as she bopped the o's in her bowl trying to make them sink into the milk.

"Yes you do; he walked around town like an old beggar man."

"Nope."

"Remember when we used to go Christmas shopping at that big store in the city? That was his."

Marjory almost tipped over the chair as she ran out of the room.

"What on earth? Where are you going?"

Agnes was carefully filing Mr. O'Shannesy into the obituary box under "O" when Marjory returned holding her favorite music box.

"Now I remember him!"

"Oh? How?"

"He gave me this."

"No he didn't, honey. I think Sister Agatha or maybe Aunty Anna sent that to you."

"It was Mr. O. He came right here to the front door and handed it to me when I was little," Marjory said.

"Where was I?" Agnes furrowed her brow, not believing there was so much she was unaware of that morning.

"Doing the wash," Marjory said with absolute recollection.

"You never cease to amaze me, Marjory. You remember the darndest things."

Marjory giggled as she hugged the music box. "I really do, Grandma. I really do!"

Agnes sat with the obituary box, leafing aimlessly through the alphabet of people. Periodically, she would pause to read one or another.

"Lord of mercy, all these people," she said with a sigh. Keeping this record, this record of surprises and unknown facts, brought Agnes to question what she knew or ever knew about anyone—about Lone Moon Creek. For forty-three years, for as long as her little Marjory had come to live with her, she had kept this record of people of whom she thought she knew. With her life turned upside down, Agnes found the pursuit of clipping and filing as a fun distraction, a dalliance, since she had limited time for spending on personal hobbies.

"Are my mother and father going to be in that box someday?" Marjory asked.

Not only did Marjory's voice startle Agnes, but the question also brought nerve endings to the forefront much as would the sudden screeching of a train's wheels.

"We don't know, dear. We just don't know."

"Where did they go? Why don't we know?"

Agnes caressed the sides of the obituary box as she listened to Marjory stomping up the stairs to her room. All those years and not one fact did Agnes know about her daughter and son-in-law.

It would be an obituary that Agnes couldn't write, but someone, somewhere, had the facts. Will she open the paper one morning and read about the forty-three years that she had missed?

THE END

"CAN WE GO TO SEE PROMISE SING AGAIN THIS YEAR?"
"OF COURSE, HE'S A HOMETOWN BOY, ISN'T HE?"
"AM I A HOMETOWN GIRL, GRANDMA?"
"YOU SURE ARE!"

Chapter Twenty

A PROMISE NOT KEPT

Don't cry, little cowboy, don't cry.

Be brave. Your mama can't help you.

Look to the farthest star

And keep the tears from your eyes.

Don't cry, little cowboy, don't cry.

P romise Warren strummed the last chord while the audience cheered and applauded the country western star.

"Great show tonight, Promise," his manager yelled across the quickly darkening stage as the star unconsciously allowed his boots to clomp against the creaky boards.

"Yeah, right," Promise exhaled as he left the outdoor arena of the state fair.

Landin knew the singing idol always deescalated this way after the show when he was close to his hometown, Lone Moon Creek.

Promise's pickup truck felt the freedom as it left the streams of headlights and ascended into the rural countryside. Promise, too, felt the heat of the night flee his tense body as he lowered the window to let real air enter his lungs. Copious planted trees were replaced by sporadic trees; neighboring houses ended their march of being in formation with unrelated houses; huge barns replaced tiny garages, and shiny, wild eyes reflected back at the driver.

No road signs alerted Promise; he didn't need manmade signs. His guitar-hardened hands gripped the steering wheel with strength and determination, until he turned onto "his" road.

It was the turn that stole any confidence he might have had; it was the turn that brought forth sweat, fear, anger, hatred, and un-forgiveness. Why after all those years could he not release the heinous bond that held him by the throat?

I can't save you, little cowboy, don't cry.

I know you're riding your horse through hell.

Just know I love you, and

We'll meet up there, by and by.

Don't cry, little cowboy, don't cry.

Why did he ever write that song? Promise quickly pummeled the radio knob with his fist to hear a cohort also singing a heart rendering song. *Are we all a bunch of pathetic whiners?* he thought to himself as he jerked the tuner knob to find something cheerful. He couldn't.

Through the silent black night, Promise new the creek was on his left; he knew the grove of fir trees where he used to hide was also on his left. He saw the neighbor's woodshed aglow through the branches of the apple trees to the right. He supposed old Josiah was there stacking wood. Old Josiah used to let him hide, while he used his ways to calm his grandfather. Where did his mother hide? How come he never knew where his mother hid?

Promise slammed on the brakes. Maybe he should just turn around. He didn't have to go to the house. Why should he?

The deadened truck must have been an invitation for a doe and her young one to run across the road. They trusted him; why couldn't he trust his grandfather?

Promise reached for the worn paper in his shirt pocket; he didn't have to read it; he knew what it said.

"Take care of your grandfather, son. I'll be back soon. Love, Dad."

I tried to care. I wanted to care.

But my heart hardened, it turned to stone.

Only straight ahead could I stare.

I would not cry. I would not moan.

The words and haunting melody of his latest song wove its way through Promise's mind. *What's the matter with me? I'm not a kid anymore.* He slammed the gear stick into first and pulled into the driveway. He could see one light on in the house; he knew that was the lamp by his grandfather's chair.

"Enter. Who is it?"

"It's Promise."

"Wipe your feet."

Promise did as he was told; he always did. He stood before his grandfather.

"Well, if it ain't the big-shot singing boy. What's the matter? Cat got your tongue?"

Promise bore his guitar fingers into his own calloused hands and clenched his teeth.

"Ya stayin' more than ten minutes this time?"

"I guess not," the tall cowboy replied as he turned on his heel and ran from the house. Promise sat in his truck with his hands covering his face. Why couldn't he stand up to that man?

The pickup peeled out of the driveway, and Promise drove like there was never to be another tomorrow. At that moment, he didn't care if another concert or music award or adoring fan was to be in his future.

Where were you last night?" Landin asked with concern.

"Just driving around," Promise responded with a hangdog look as he entered the trailer.

Landin knew better than to pressure Promise with questions when he was in his old stomping grounds.

"Well, you better get some fast sleep; we'll rehearse before tonight's concert."

Promise collapsed across the bed and fell into a sleep riddled with back sheds and stage lights, snow forts and clapping people, shirts tangled in barbed wire, and a guitar smashed.

"Great. Super! Bring up the lights!"

For two hours, Promise was not the scared boy being browbeaten by his grandfather. He was confident and in control. Even though his songs could pull the very guts out of a lumberjack, he never wavered from his command of the stage. He watched people cry—some overtly and some hiding behind handkerchiefs; he watched how joyful songs could inspire some to grab hold of their neighbors to twirl and laugh; he noticed the snuggling during the love songs.

As always, the show would end, and his grandfather loomed large against the remaining lights of the midway.

"Going out again tonight?" Landin asked.

"Yeah, got a little business to tend to."

Landin exhaled slowly as his thoughts quickly calculated the days left at that gig. He hated watching what it did to Promise each year.

When did this all start? Promise rehashed the problem as he always did when he drove the backroads of Lone Moon Creek.

His dad was grandpa's superhero, and he was his grandfather's best little pal. What happened?

Was it when dad was first deployed to the war zone? No, he was still OK then. Mom was upset, but grandpa took it bravely; he was the one who coached them on never giving into fear and certainly never losing hope, ever.

He and Grandpa became best buddies, especially when his mom seemed to slip into days of depression. They'd do all sorts of things together in the woods and the workshop. Grandpa let him get a dog, and they'd fish in the creek and stop to visit with old Josiah.

Promise was glad that his father wanted them to live with grandpa instead of the house they had been in. He surely would have been lonely with just Mom, with her being so sad all the time.

There was school, and that was a happy time, but not as happy as when he saw his grandpa waiting for the school bus! That was the best. He got lots of help with his homework, and he soon became a top student!

Then came the letter. The MIA letter.

Promise suddenly erupted with moans and groans, repulsive sounds—not the melodious notes he had created for his audience only an hour before.

"No, no, no," he screamed to the high heavens.

I have to see my grandfather, right now!

Promise swung the wheel fiercely to the left to jettison onto the shortcut, the seasonal road. Still only dirt, the ruts were deeper than he ever remembered, but narrower too. Two vehicles would be hard pressed to squeak past each other. Vicious curves and occasional tree limbs called for brake stomping.

Ah, macadam would let him return to his thoughts.

Why didn't my grandfather tell me about the MIA letter at first? He must have told my mother; she stayed in her room more than ever. The army said that dad was "missing in action." Why didn't he explain that to me? I was old enough to understand. Instead...

"I knew you'd be back, just like a bad penny," the old man hollered to his grandson. "What do you want to do, come in here and sing me a song?"

Immediately, Promise slipped into his boyhood; his head lowered to his chest, and his eyes filled with the same salty tears that he well remembered.

"Yep, there you go; you can't be a man like your father was. He was strong and brave—a real soldier. I tried to make you the same, but the harder I tried, the wimpier you got. And your mother didn't help, always taking your side and lettin' you play that damn guitar!"

"Don't you dare bring my mother into this. She was kind and good. Do you think she liked living here with a tyrant like you? She wanted her husband, and I wanted my father!"

"Now see here, if I didn't let you two live here, where would you have been? Out on the street?"

"It would have been better than this place!" Promise yelled as he blindingly ran for the door.

"That's it, run away! I bet your father wished he could run, but he was a captive. They held him and tortured him for years and years. Do you think you could take that? I tried to toughen you up, but to no avail. Just go. You are free; you're not a captive like your father."

Promise ran to his truck.

You don't want to hear me sing? How about this? Promise's brain screamed as he slammed one of his CD's into the truck's player. He turned the volume on high as he lowered the window.

What's in a man's heart? Only God knows.

It's all caged in, some as stone, some as fire.

Why won't you let it out? Only God knows.

Does it not burden you? Do you of it not tire?

What's in your heart? Only God knows.

Promise yanked the CD out and sailed it to the floor as he made the dirt driveway rise in a dust storm. He wiped away tears with the back of his hand.

It's impossible trying to talk to him. He used to be my best friend. Maybe he could see that I needed to toughen up, but I was just a boy. I didn't know he thought Dad was being tortured. I thought missing in action was just...just that you were missing. He thought dad was being tortured?

"What the hell is that?" Promise said aloud as he peered at something ahead on the dark road. He slammed on the brakes. "Josiah? What are doing out here?"

"Gul-dern, billy goat got away from me," he panted.

"Here, I'll help you get him." The tall cowboy half-laughed as he vaulted from the truck.

Sure enough, it wasn't long before Promise had corralled the goat, and Josiah offered a little more sweet hay to the bad boy for the night.

"So how you been?" Josiah asked as he motioned to one of the four mismatched kitchen chairs for his visitor to sit.

"Good, real good, until I came home. You know what I go through every year."

"Yeah, it sure is a sad situation," Josiah drawled as he poured the coffee from an old percolator. "You two used to be such buddies. I loved watching the pair of ya."

Promise leaned in toward the old man. "Josiah, did you know that grandpa thought dad was being tortured?"

Josiah took a while to answer as he stirred in the milk. "I know that's what he thought. He used to talk to me about it.

I told him he didn't know that; none of us knew that. But I couldn't dissuade him. He was positive about it. In fact, he used to make up pictures in his head of what kind of torture they were using on him. I'd say, 'Wendel, you don't know that. Maybe he escaped and was in a different country.' But he always came back to the whippings and beatings, and burning and starvation tactics, and... You know what he always added?"

"No, I have no idea," Promise answered weakly.

"He'd say, 'Good thing I brought him up strong; he'd never give up information about our country.' I'd say, 'Wendel, the first thing is, you are makin' all this up in your head, and the second thing is, you were never tough on your son.' He and your dad had the same nice relationship that you and your grandpa had—once."

"Yeah, once," the singing star moaned.

"Little by little, I could see what was happening, and I tried to talk to him. I thought he was listening, then it wouldn't be long before I'd see you hiding in the woods or down by the creek."

"It wasn't fun," Promise mumbled.

"Can't imagine it was, but he never wanted you to go through the torture your dad did."

"That was all in his head; there might not have been any torture!" Promise exclaimed.

"I know," Josiah said with a sigh.

"Been out driving again?" Landin asked the weary traveler.

"Yeah, stopped in to visit with an old friend."

"And?"

"Yeah, stopped there too, but only for a few minutes."

"Things not any better?" Landin said.

"Naw, but I did learn something."

"What's that?"

"He had a purpose for his meanness."

"One more concert and then we're out of here until next year."

"Good."

Promise threw himself into his work like never before. He had a new CD that zoomed to the top of the charts. He was performing in bigger and bigger clubs.

"How does it feel to be on top?"

"Well, Landin, it feels good, but look where I'm getting my songs."

"What do you mean?"

"My best songs are coming from grief and depression and hard times."

"What's wrong with that? That's apparently what the people want. They can relate, I guess."

"Yeah, maybe, and you know what else? I wonder what kind of songs I would be writing if I had an ideal life with no problems."

"Then your songs wouldn't have any soul, I suppose."

Why do you drag it along? It's weighing you down.

Release your grip; take my hand.

I'll give you relief all round.

I once carried one; it was my demand.

I know about the cross.

"Wendel, you in there?" Josiah hollered through the screen door.

"Yeah, Josiah, come on it. Good to see you. Here, sit a spell. Let me get the coffee going. So what brings you around?"

"Just missing you, neighbor. Used to see you once in a while," Josiah said.

"Yeah, I don't get around like I used to; the knees are screaming most of the time."

"I know what you mean. I guess we turned into two old codgers, not like we were once."

It was as if the two men transcended into a state of reminiscence as Wendel poured the black coffee.

Josiah started to chuckle. "Remember that day when you and Promise were running up and down the side hill trying to catch that jackrabbit that the little guy wanted?"

Wendel laughed. "What a time we had! But we got him! That rabbit took up residence over here; Promise sure loved that animal."

There was a long pause. "How about that time the three of us were down by the creek and Promise was catching fish one after another and the two of us caught nothing!"

They both laughed and sighed at the same time. "How about Smooches? What a great dog he was."

"Ah, yes, another great friend for Promise. I wanted him to be happy because his dad was away in the army," Wendel said.

"And you did a terrific job, Wendel. Promise was happy, and he was coping nicely with the situation because of you." After a long pause, Josiah continued, "But what happened? Everything started to break down over the years."

"It went all to hell," the whiskered grandfather said slowly. "You know I got that letter about my son being MIA."

"Yeah."

"It started working on me and working on me until I was about going crazy. I kept visualizing all sorts of things that the enemy was doing to my son—how they were torturing him."

"But you didn't know that," Josiah said pleadingly as if his reply would make some difference now.

"I can't explain it. I just knew I was right. Then I would look at my little dear Promise and wonder how on earth he would ever survive if he was the captive. He would crumble, Josiah. He couldn't face that situation. I had to toughen him up."

Josiah could see Wendel's hands begin to shake.

"I think I can understand your position, but he was still a young boy at that time. What? Maybe eleven or twelve?"

377

Wendel silently affirmed with a nod of his head. After another long pause, Wendel thought aloud, "Maybe if I had told him about my plans, he would have understood."

"Just in natural ways, boys become men. I don't think you have to make a program out of it," old Josiah commented nonjudgmentally as he scratched his beard.

"Is that what I was doing? Making it a program?" Wendel asked.

"Yeah, I guess, something like the military."

"And he hated it, didn't he?"

"Well, I would say that in the first place, he didn't know why you had changed your attitude toward him. You were like a sergeant or a general, or whatever those bosses are."

Josiah listened to the clock tick from somewhere in the next room. He didn't know how Wendel was going to react to the conversation; he was prepared if he was ordered to leave.

Wendel did react with slamming his coffee mug to the table hard enough to make it slop over the brim. "But I still loved him! He was the one who started hating me!"

Josiah remained silent as he watched Wendel limp to the sink for the dishrag.

"He didn't know your motives, friend. I didn't either. I used to hide Promise when he asked. Too bad we didn't bring all this out in the open."

"He'd run out of the house with that damn guitar and stay out in the barn for hours just a wailing away and singing. Used to make me so damn mad. Then his mother would go out and sit with him. She wasn't trying to make a man out of him."

Josiah could see Wendel's temples pulsating behind his gray hair. Wendel exhaled a long breath of air.

"Wasn't easy for any of you, was it?" Josiah asked.

"Never got another letter from the army. I tried and tried to get some information. They didn't know anything. I just got more and more bitter, and I took it out on... Promise."

Josiah witnessed the confession and remorse of a broken soul.

"No, I'm not going out there anymore," Promise said resolutely when Landin asked.

"That might be for the best," the manager replied softly, knowing that the altercation had to end somehow. Promise was miserable every time he was close to home.

But he did know how to rise to the occasion. Was that something his grandfather had taught him? His debut at the state fair was extraordinary; he drew in a larger crowd than ever. His new songs were precious; his old songs were golden. Everyone in his entourage was jubilant over his performance.

"You nailed it, buddy!" Landin exalted. "Say, some of us are headed for some food, want to go?"

"Um, no, I need to drive through Lone Moon Creek for a while. I like to drive past the school, the downtown, and such."

Landin could feel his brow furrow. "Why don't you make it quick and then join us?"

"Will do. See you later."

How did the truck know where to go?

Promise felt like he wasn't steering; he wasn't directing; he just went all around town wherever the truck chose. With that accomplished, the truck began taking the county roads up into the hills. Promise merely sat and took in the sights: over there was where he and his grandfather always went to pick the best apples; there was his friend's house where the two boys would play while the men sat and talked; there was the farm where each autumn the family sculpted a cornfield maze and had pumpkin games for the kids—grandpa liked that place.

Suddenly, Promise took control of his daydreaming and slammed on the brake just before the truck turned into his driveway.

"No!" he yelled. "I'm not going there." He jockeyed the truck around and headed back.

"Hey! Glad you made it. Here, try some of this pizza. Did you have a good ride?"

"It was OK."

"You didn't make any stops?"

"No, no stops."

"It's for the best," Landin said.

"Yeah, maybe."

"Oh, here. Some old guy left you this note."

"Three more concerts, everybody. Make it another super night!" Landin announced just before the lights went up.

The crowd roared when the first three notes were played.

Everything is gone. I can't go home.

The love that was is no more.

Stripped of everything, I'm all alone.

In the world with not even a front door.

Everything is gone. I can't go home.

"Steaks tonight! You going to join us?"

"Maybe later. I've got to see a friend," Promise replied.

"Josiah! It's so good to see you!"

"Same here. Come on in!"

"I got your note, Josiah. Is something wrong?"

"Wrong?" the old man repeated. "I think something is finally right!"

"What's going on?"

"I had a little talk with your grandfather the other day."

"Oh no," Promise groaned as he slid down on the chair.

"Somebody next door is feeling mighty bad about how things turned out with the two of you," Josiah said.

"Yeah, right."

"I'm serious, Promise. He's hurting."

"But look what he did to me!"

"I know this sounds crazy, but he thought he was helping you."

"How could he even think that?"

"Let's look at you now. *Now* is where I can see he did help you."

"I don't understand one word you're saying," Promise moaned.

"In your career, aren't you persistent, diligent, self-disciplined, punctual, dependable, supportive—?"

"Whoa, whoa, whoa," wailed the country singer. "What do you know about my career?"

"Did you think I haven't been following your reviews? I know every move you make across the country and back—always back. Why do you think you are so driven? So successful? And so—"

"Don't say *talented*. He didn't give me that; my mother did!"

"Granted, your mother can be thanked for that blessing."

"I remember when he smashed my guitar into a million pieces!" Promise exclaimed.

"I remember too. That's when you came to my place and locked yourself in the woodshed for three hours," Josiah said softly. "But you never skipped out on your chores again, did you? And you worked hard to earn enough money to buy another one."

"Yeah," Promise uttered quietly. "He didn't baby me."

The two men sat for a long time in silence. Finally, Promise passed Josiah a tattered note, the same note that he carried always: *Take care of your grandfather. Be back soon. Love Dad.*

"Um, this looks familiar," Josiah mumbled. "Just saw one over at Wendel's house, only his said 'Take care of my boy. Be back soon. Love you.'"

"So none of us kept our promise," the tall cowboy said slowly after a long period of reflection. "My father never came back; my grandfather didn't take care of me, and I didn't take care of him. What are we? The promise breakers?"

Josiah quickly scribbled something across the front of his fishing magazine as Promise wrote something on the back of his dad's note. At the same time, they handed each other the words: the Promise Breakers.

"Make a song out of it," Josiah commanded.

"Don't worry. The memo I just wrote is a reminder to do just that!"

"So what are you going to do, Promise?"

"I only have two more concerts. I won't be back until next year. I'll go see him tomorrow after the show."

"I think you'll be glad you did!"

Was there a new excitement about that performance? Did Landin hear something he had never heard before? Did the music lift itself to the high heavens of God? Was Promise singing from the depths of his soul?

Whatever it was, it took the crowd to inner depths of almost being traumatized, of being connected to something beyond themselves, of a new spirit of understanding.

It wasn't until Promise told Landin that he was going to the countryside to see his grandfather that his manager knew the reason for the magnetic concert.

This time there was no deviating around the hills of Lone Moon Creek; the truck drove directly to his homestead. Promise was a composite of nerves, sweat, and fear. He couldn't swallow for some reason, and the moisture from his hands wouldn't dissipate, even though he wiped them over and over on the legs of his jeans. He looked for the one light that would be glowing from the lamp by his grandfather's chair. He suddenly swallowed and choked on the ultra-surplus of the buildup. The drama of getting through the choking spell as he parked the truck made the no-light clue inconsequential.

Grandpa, are you in there? was the only thought on his mind.

He waited.

His cowboy boots shuffled back and forth.

"Oh no," he said aloud as thoughts of his grandfather lying dead on the floor took over his consciousness.

He pushed open the door and ran through the house, calling out in every room, searching for the man to whom he was going to come to reconciliation with. Why was he so late? Why hadn't he done this years ago? God was punishing him. God had given him plenty of time to make this right, but he had been too stubborn to use the time.

"Grandpa. Grandpa, I'm sorry, where are you? Where are you?"

Promise ran to the barn, the sheds, and into the fields. He ran as far as Josiah's place.

"Lord have mercy, what's the matter?" Josiah asked as he saw the speechless, panting pillar of a man leaning against his door.

"I can't... find him." Promise stumbled over the words with barely enough breath to push the syllables from his mouth.

"Promise," Josiah said softly, "it's the second Wednesday of the month."

When there was no reaction form Promise, Josiah continued, "Every month he goes to the government department in the city to try to find new information on your dad. If it's too late to make the journey home, he'll pull off the road somewhere and get a room."

Promise turned into a heap of—what? Slushy snow? Compost for the garden? Silage from the silo? Whatever it was, it took him right down to his knees on the porch.

"Hey, are you all right?" Josiah asked as he grabbed at the cowboy's arm.

"What a scare," Promise mumbled. "I thought he was... I can't even say it."

"That's why we have to get things in order while we can; there isn't that much time left for any of us."

Promise had a restless sleep that night. He imagined his grandfather did too, after not getting any news about his son for all those years.

"What's going on up on the stage?" Promise asked the next morning as he watched the commotion.

"We're in for a hell of a storm tonight. They're tying everything down; we don't want a reoccurrence of what happened in Janesforth," Landin replied.

Promise was disappointed: disappointed with the storm coming, disappointed with not connecting with his grandfather the night before, and disappointed in himself. But as always, the words that bounded from the lips of the man he thought he hated came to the foreground: *when the going gets tough, the tough get going.*

Promise looked out at the crowd. Thousands of people who had ignored the warnings about the storm, probably thinking it would hold off until later, were present, anticipating a voracious finale. Promise and his troupe didn't disappoint them. The star wouldn't allow his own feelings to deter the expectancies of others.

Within twenty minutes, the raindrops started as the umbrellas went up. No one left the grounds, not even those who didn't have umbrellas. However, when the thunder and lightning came upon them with a vengeance, people scattered like little chicks. The performance continued as the metal roof became just another percussion instrument that seemed to have the drummer in a state of euphoria. The wind couldn't confiscate any of the equipment and the performers held strong.

Even the bold streaks of lightning that pierced the sky couldn't compel Promise to give a less than superior performance. Was this what his grandfather was trying to instill in him? To never give up and stand his ground? Stand his ground he did as he sang to a handful of people. Promise looked from one to another. Why? Why would they stand there in the torrential rain?

Grandfather? Promise knew he missed a note or two as he looked into the familiar face. There stood the man with two canes and a huge cowboy hat that kept the rain off his face. He wore a long slicker and stared straight into Promise's eyes.

He came! He's here! He came to one of my concerts! He wants to get our lives back as much as I do. Thank you, God.

After the final chord, Promise literally leaped from the stage and ran to the man.

"Grandpa, I'm so glad you came and I'm sorry for—"

"Promise," the man spoke as he dropped the canes and grabbed hold of the cowboy's arms. "Promise, I'm your father. I'm home. I kept my promise."

THE END

"Do you remember how we got up to that sheep farm,
Marjory?"
"I think it was up a hill and around some curves and past
some trees."
"Oh, yes. That's got to be it!"

Chapter Twenty-One

Know the Teacher

"I'm afraid we're going to lose him."

"I am, too, Dan."

"Why won't he cooperate?"

"He absolutely hates this place, and he hates us."

"But why?"

"We've got to do something." And so went the
conversation in the teachers' room as it had for the past two
months.

Jeffrey, why? Miss Ericson silently asked as she
watched him sleeping at his desk. *Well, at least he isn't
causing a ruckus today*, she consoled herself. She couldn't
help but do a double take at the sight of the boy's peaceful,
angelic face.

Dan Lonbocco counted fifty-nine clicks of Jeffrey's
pen as the class took their history test in *silence*. He refused to

march to Jeffrey's desk and take the pen away as he did the last time. Mr. Lonbocco knew the lad was baiting him.

"Oh no! Not a throat-clearing day!" Mrs. Rathbone sighed. She knew what that was like. After twenty minutes of listening to the raspy throat explosions, Jane Rathbone suggested that the *patient* go to the nurse's office.

"Can't! She told me never to come back!" Jeffrey replied.

The class roared with laughter. Instead of sending him to the office like before, the teacher asked, "Would you like a throat lozenge?"

"Mrs. Rathbone, I'm surprised at you. How do you know I'm not deathly allergic to what's in that lozenge?"

"Um, you're right, Jeffrey, that's an excellent point. Do you carry some of your own, seeing how this is quite a problem for you?"

"I'm not allowed to anymore. I don't know why."

"Because you were throwing them at the back of the girls' heads in tech class," someone from the side of the room volunteered.

Again, the class broke out in laughter as Jeffrey vehemently pushed his desk, tipping it over in the aisle. "Who said that?" he roared as he bounded to the direction of the voice. The room went silent.

Mrs. R might be short, pudgy, and old, but she was at Jeffrey's side before he lifted his clenched fist. She touched his arm and very gently and softly made that age-old sound: "Shh, Jeffrey."

What got through to the boy? What diffused the bomb? She lifted her eyes to give a silent "thank you."

The other kids were confused about their love/hate relationship with Jeffrey. On the one hand, he had the nerve that they didn't possess, and on the other hand, they were getting annoyed with his constant interruptions and need for attention.

"Yes, Jane, that definitely is one of his characteristics," Dan agreed concerning Jeffrey's neediness. "What can we do about it?" he asked as he finished his brown-bag lunch.

Again, the conversation at lunchtime had focused on Jeffrey.

"He slept in my class yesterday and oh how peaceful it was," Melanie Ericson added. "In fact, the other students did nothing to wake him. I think they enjoyed having a *normal* session for a change."

"I can well imagine!" Ron Rollings interjected as he tipped back his chair and tapped out a rhythm on the table.

Jane couldn't help think, *I bet Mr. Rollings was a cutup when he was in school too!*

Ron continued, "The chorus was all in place on the risers. We had started practicing our first song, and I saw Jeffrey standing and singing with the sopranos. It wasn't long before he popped up with the tenors and then the basses. It wasn't really causing a consternation until he got in with the altos and all hell broke out. You know Bertha? Well she doesn't put up with any nonsense, and she pushed Jeffrey right off the back of the riser. He was OK, and I suggested that he go out and get a drink of water, which he did, except he didn't come back. But later, someone said he was sitting behind the stage curtain because she could see his feet."

Heavy sighs could be heard around the table. What to do? What to do?

"All right, class, we need three people at the chalkboard and the rest of us will use our computers. Raise your hand if you want to be at the board," Mr. Lampier announced. "Here is your math problem."

Todd Lampier was surprised that Jeffery wanted to participate at the board. Everyone delved into the problem and the only sounds heard were the clicking of the chalk against the slate: the old-fashioned sound that Todd opted to retain in his classroom. He scanned the class and was pleased to see how everyone was working diligently, especially Jeffery. The chalk dust was almost flying as Todd watched the student's arm zoom in and out.

"All right class, most of you are finished. Let's check out the answers at the board first."

All eyes looked forward and all eyes nearly fell out of their sockets when they looked at Jeffrey's work. Not only had Jeffery presented the math problem and solution in the center but also around the periphery he had drawn an ornate, symmetrical, Gothic-style border.

"Well, Jeffrey, that is quite phenomenal!" the teacher remarked.

"Thanks, Mr. L."

Todd couldn't wait until tomorrow's lunch break; everyone needed to hear something positive about Jeffery. As he was erasing the board after class, he noticed curse words written minutely in the ornate border.

Oh, Jeffrey. Why are you so filled with hatred?

"Are we going to have a good game today, Jeff?"

"Sure, Coach Brown."

"This is your last chance. Don't blow it."

Jeffrey took his position at first base. He knew he had to have gym class in order to graduate. The game sailed along with no errors and no problems until Big Stan Naclowski crashed into Jeffery, knocking him flat with the ball rolling off. Stan stood smugly on base, unaware that someone was soon to jump on his back and put his hands around his throat. Coach Brown and the pitcher had to pry Jeffrey's hands off Big Stan.

Jeffrey walked slowly to the locker room.

It was a rare occasion when the gym teacher could spend any time in the teacher's lounge during lunch hour; he was always on guard between the playing fields and the gymnasium. But today the assistant superintendent took his place so Henry Brown could meet with the others on the "Jeffrey Situation."

"Thanks everyone for meeting today, especially you Henry. We're going to do some brainstorming about what we can do for our troubled student. I think underneath it all, he's a good kid, but if we don't act now, I think he is going to quit school."

"How about the school getting a tutor for him and letting him have all his classes in the study room?"

"How about if he only comes to school two days a week? Maybe he'd appreciate school more."

"Maybe he should transfer to a different school; he isn't happy here."

"He goes to the school psychologist now, but I understand he won't utter a word."

"What are his strengths?"

"He likes music; he's a good artist, and he's good at sports."

"He does average work, but his need for attention is above the norm."

"He has a volatile temper."

"The other kids sort of like him, but he doesn't let them in. He doesn't want to get close to anyone."

"Not even us. Haven't we all tried to ignore a lot of his antics and to treat him kindly even though we'd like to strangle him sometimes?"

"He doesn't know you."

"What was that, Henry?"

"None of the students really know us," he continued, "they come to school with blind trust that we're going to like them and treat them with respect, and when they push our buttons to the limit and we push back, they think we hate them. You know what we should do?" Henry waited for an answer.

"No, Henry," Dan replied, "we don't know what we should do!"

"We should all take Jeffery to our homes on a Saturday or a Sunday and let him spend the day with us and our families so he can get to know us. I know a little about some of you like Jane. You have that nice sheep farm, right? And Dan, if Jeffrey could be with you and your family for a day, he'd see what it takes to run an organic vegetable business plus teach school. Melanie, do your handicapped parents still live with you? It's a wonder it's not you sleeping at your desk instead of Jeffrey sleeping at his. He has no idea the effort you people put in to tend to your families plus teach. Maybe it would do him some good. Listen, I've got to get back. Let me know what you decide."

"Take him to our homes? That would be crazy, wouldn't it?"

"I don't know? Would it even be legal?"

"We've got to get his mother's permission."

"Maybe she would come with him. You know, we don't know a thing about his family, do we?"

"I've been talking with the guidance counselor, and he says Jeffrey lives with his mother, who works three jobs. The father has taken off—they don't know where. He used to knock the kid around quite a bit, according to the mother. There are no other family members in this area."

"Oh, there's the bell."

"What do you usually do on a Saturday, Jeffrey?" Coach Brown asked him.

"Nothing much, just do the chores around the house for my mother then hang around."

"Do you want to go with me to the Boys and Girls Center?"

"For what?"

"To help the kids with their sports, games, and swimming."

"What for?"

"Well, a lot of those kids have no one at home because the parents are working. So they depend on the club to give them a safe place to be, and they have fun."

"Do they have bowling?" Jeffrey asked.

"Yes, they do."

"OK, I'll go."

"See you Saturday at seven."

"Seven?"

"Mr. B.. Mr. B.!" the children yelled as Henry Brown walked in. They encircled him while the little ones hung onto his legs.

"Hi, kids. This is Jeffrey. He's going to help us today."

At least half of the children left the security of Mr. B.'s legs to show affection to Jeffery. In total blind faith, they trusted him to be a nice person. Jeffrey stood very still, not knowing how to accept the show of faith and affection.

"Who wants to begin as a calisthenics leader?" Coach Brown asked.

Jeffrey watched as Joey led the group and then chose Annie who chose Jeffery. Mr. B. was surprised to see how shy the brazen, arrogant lad was in front of the children.

Jeffery's movements were so stiff that Robbie called out, "Look, we're robots."

"Yeah, cool!" Mr. B. yelled out as a form of encouragement. "Jeff, have them be crocodiles."

Without missing a beat, Jeff was prone on the floor with his head lifted, using his forearms as the huge mouth.

"Little kittens crawling across the ceiling," Jeff yelled as he flipped on his back and crawled with all fours in the air. "And I'll choose you."

"Thanks, Jeff, nobody ever picks me." Aaron smiled from ear to ear.

"Good job, my man," Mr. Brown congratulated Jeff. "Who's ready to go bowling? Oh, I was afraid of this; can you try to console Annie, she's crying."

Jeff looked like he had been asked to deliver the Gettysburg Address at the White House.

His "What's the matter with you?" first line would not have won him any medals in a child-rearing class, but to Annie, they were words of love. She pulled his arm to have him sit, and then she scampered onto his lap faster than a cat.

"Oh, Jeffrey, I'm not any good at bowling; I always get the butter balls."

"You mean gutter balls?"

"Yes, those things." She cried even harder as she threw her arms around his neck.

"Um, well, do you want me to help you?" Jeffrey asked.

Mr. B. watched as Jeff helped Annie pick out a ball that was appropriate for her size, tied her shoes, got her in the lane that was using the gutter guards, and knelt beside her as he coached her on how to roll the ball with both hands.

He looked like a proud papa when she exclaimed, "I love this game!"

"Mr. Lampier, what are you doing here?" Jeffrey asked.

"I stop by almost every Saturday."

"Is it time for volleyball yet?" Joey asked.

The kids picked teams. Jeffrey was on one side, Mr. Lampier on the other, and Mr. B. was the scorekeeper. Jeffrey watched how his math teacher set up the ball for the "little guys," giving them a perfect position to hit the ball and then be available to tip it over the net with his long arms. The two teachers didn't know how their customary show-off, attention-seeking student was going to react. He did make a few flamboyant plays that made the kids say, "Wow," but he quickly followed the lead of Mr. L.

"That was fun," Jeffrey exclaimed along with most of the children.

Lunchtime, a free swim, a movie and a scavenger hunt ended the day with everyone tired but happy, even Annie.

"Thanks for all you did today, Jeffrey," Mr. Lampier said as he shook the lad's hand. "See you in school."

Henry could see Jeffrey's mood plummet the closer they got to his house.

"Thanks for helping me out today, Jeffrey. Did you have a good time?"

"Maybe."

"And I hope you all had a nice weekend," Mr. Lampier stated as the class settled into their math class. He looked at Jeffrey. Jeffrey averted his eyes.

"Raise your hand if you would like to work at the board."

Everyone delved into the math problem. It wasn't long before Isaac, at the board, was trespassing into Devin's writing space. It wasn't evident that it was intentional, but it happened.

"Get out of my space," Devin snarled as he pushed Isaac just hard enough to make him lose his balance.

"Hey, you creep, don't you push me," retaliated Isaac as he jumped to his feet ready to pounce on Devin.

This was so out of character for Mr. Lampier's class that no one moved, not even the teacher. No one except Jeffrey. He was in between the two boys before Mr. L. started loping up the aisle.

"All right, boys, settle down. Settle down; this is no place for a fight."

Was it the shock of having Jeffrey as the mediator instead of the troublemaker, or the reason for the problem? Mr. L. knew he couldn't take the credit.

After class, Jeffrey was approached by classmates who complimented him. He had never been complimented by his peers. Was this how Aaron felt at The Center when Jeffrey chose him?

"You are kidding me!" Miss Ericson squealed, which caused her to choke on her apple.

It wasn't until the apple incident was over that the conversation returned to the story of the weekend and the referee in the math class. Coach Brown even popped his head in to be sure everyone heard about the great Saturday with Jeffrey.

"Could this crazy plan actually have credence?"

"I'm telling you, that kid is bone dry—dehydrated of quality attention."

"Well, I'm in on this," Melanie Ericson proclaimed. "When Jeffrey comes in for Spanish class, I'll ask him if he'd like to ride my horses. Plus, my parents would be thrilled to have some company for a change."

"I'm game too. You know, with the long weekend, I could arrange for him to help with the harvesting and selling at the farm stand. My kids would appreciate an extra pair of hands." Dan Lonbocco laughed.

"Don't forget to get the mother's permission."

"But face it, I'm never going to use this stupid Spanish stuff," Jeffery retaliated when Miss Ericson tried to explain to the class how important homework was.

For a few minutes, she resigned to never invite him to her place. But because teachers are normally forgiving people, by the end of class, she called him over.

"Jeffrey, would you like to help me with my horses on Thursday?"

"Why?"

"Just thought you might like something to do over the long weekend?"'

"Oh, yeah, the long weekend," he mumbled dismally. "Well, maybe."

"I'll call your mother to see if it's all right."

"Yeah, whatever," he commented while walking away.

"Hey, Jeffrey, hold up a minute," Mr. Lonbocco called when he saw him in the hallway. "Do you have any plans for the long weekend?"

Suddenly, Jeffrey felt important knowing that he actually did have plans. "Sure, I'll be riding horses on Thursday," he announced proudly.

Mr. Lonbocco knew that Melanie had joined the "rejuvenation" program.

"My family and I will be harvesting the autumn gardens and going to market with the produce. Do you want to help?"

"You'll be doing what?" Jeffrey asked.

"It's time to pick the pumpkins, the gourds, and the apples. It's a big job for my little kids. How about it? Saturday?"

"Um, I might be busy Saturday. What about Friday?"

"Perfect. I'll call your mother. And Jeffrey? Don't bring any pens that click." The history teacher watched Jeffrey's face turn red. "Just joking, pal. See you later."

"Wait up, first baseman."

Jeff swung around to see Big Stan Naclowski striding quickly toward him. Jeffrey tightened every muscle in his body in case the mountain man planned on barreling into him.

Naclowski projected his hand forward. "Sorry about the other day. Shake?"

Jeffrey offered his hand.

"Good for you," Mr. Lampier uttered as he witnessed the non-altercation during his hall duty stint.

"Well, this is where I live, Jeffrey."

"Way out here?"

"Yes, it's quite a drive into school every day, but we need lots of space for the horses. Come in first to meet my parents; they are anxious to meet you."

"Mama, Papa, this is Jeffrey."

"Ooo, Jeffrey, how do," they responded as they wheeled their chairs closer to the visitor. The mother and the father extended their hands in welcome. Miss Ericson could see a lot of unanswered questions on Jeffrey's face. Melanie then spoke to them in Spanish, while they smiled and nodded. They, of course, understood their daughter; it was Jeffrey who was lacking in the skills.

"Would you mind helping my dad down the ramp while I take my mom? They're going to watch us bring the horses out of the barn."

Melanie chuckled to herself as she watched how carefully her student was in maneuvering the wheelchair. She could hear her dad trying to converse with Jeff, except Jeff wasn't responding. Again, he spoke in Spanish.

They sat in the shade while Miss Ericson and Jeffrey walked to the barn. "They know we're coming; can you hear them neighing?" Melanie asked.

"How many are there?"

"We have twelve right now, but there have been as many as twenty. Remember, calmness is key. Speak softly. They'll go to the watering troughs first. I filled them before I picked you up. Always check that the corral gates are closed before you do anything. We don't want to spend all day tracking runaway horses. Step back or they'll run you over."

"I didn't know horses were so big." Jeffrey spoke as if he was a little boy.

Probably underneath it all, that's all he is, the Spanish teacher thought to herself.

"When can we ride?" Jeffrey asked.

"As soon as they're fed, and we muck out the stalls."

"We have to do that?" Jeffrey said in utter amazement.

"Do you think my parents are going to come over here and do it?"

Before Jeffrey could contradict her statement, she called out to her folks in Spanish and told them that they were expected to come over to clean the stalls. They had an uproariously good time laughing over that.

Finally, the two were riding.

"Miss Ericson, how do you do all this plus teach school?" Jeffrey asked.

"It's my life, Jeffrey. During the week, I have help come in to take care of my parents and others to tend to the horses. I'm not superwoman, you know."

Jeffrey lifted his eyebrows.

Mr. Lonbocco knocked on the door as Jeffrey ran down the stairs.

"How was the horseback riding?"

"Fantastic!"

"Hope you're ready to do some work today. Kids, this is Jeffrey."

Jeffrey looked into dark Asian eyes, Peruvian eyes, light Irish eyes, dark African eyes, and medium he-didn't-know-what eyes. They were all different to be sure. Dan Lonbocco could see the confusion on his student's face.

"Yep, they all belong to my wife and me. Aren't they quite a crew?"

"They sure are." Jeffrey smiled, and just as he did so, the nationalities converged on the American to give him hugs. It reminded him of the kids at the center who welcomed Coach Brown the same way. It made him feel important. He didn't remember feeling important like that before."

"OK, kids, we're home. Grab the baskets, and we'll meet you in the apple orchard. Start picking up just the good apples that are on the ground. We'll be there shortly."

"Come in, Jeff. I want you to meet the Mrs. and the rest of the kids."

"How nice to meet you, Jeffrey. I've heard so much about you. This is Ange, and this is Benito. And the baby here is Dakota."

"Hon, we'll be back when it's lunchtime. Love ya."

"Love you too."

"I didn't know you had all those kids, Mr. Lonbocco."

"You see why I love and teach history?"

"Um, not really," Jeffery said.

"You will someday." Dan laughed as he handed his student a bushel basket.

"OK, kids, Jeffrey and I are going up into the trees to give them a good shake. Don't stand underneath!"

"Good job! Now everybody run to the pumpkin patch. Choose one for yourselves and the rest are going to market. Ike, get three for the little guys, would you? Heave-ho, Jeffrey. These big ones are monsters."

"We'll get the gourds after lunch. Come on! The race is on!"

Mr. Lonbocco said to the kids, "Sell, sell, sell!" Then he followed it with, "Our economic system was built just like this." Jeffrey stopped in his tracks. That boring unit on economics was starting to have some meaning. Those children were from all over the world. Their countries depended on their economy too.

"Everyone on the risers. We'll start with "Let It Be." Raven, do you want bass guitar today? Sid, how about percussion? OK, folks, your long weekend is over, back to business," Mr. Rollings commanded. "A little more melody, sopranos. Basses, not so powerful."

The conducting stopped when the school secretary handed him a note.

"OK, group, listen. I have to leave. The band director will be here in ten minutes to fill in. In the meantime, I'm choosing Jeffrey to conduct the chorus."

Jeffrey froze; he couldn't do it. All heads turned to him. He couldn't move. Would Mr. Lonbocco say, "No, I will not adopt a child." Would he ever hear Coach Brown say, "No, that kid will never get a second chance." Would Miss Ericson say, "I don't have time for my parents; they can't live with me?" Would Mr. Lampier ever be unfair to one of the kids?

Jeffrey stepped off the risers and perched himself on Mr. Rolling's platform. Everyone clapped; were they hoping he would go into one of his crazy antics and give them a free for all for ten minutes? He nodded to Raven and Sid, who played the intro, and he lifted his hands. The chorus responded, but they also waited for Jeffrey to do something devilish spontaneously. The band teacher sat in the back of the room listening. Jeffrey brought the song to a close just like Mr. Rolling would do.

"Good job, everybody," the band teacher praised the group as he shook hands with the conductor.

"Here's a bag of squash from the garden. Help yourselves."

"Tell us about Jeffrey working on the farm with all your kids."

"It was great. He pitched right in and worked well with the children. I couldn't tell, however, if he made any connection with the nationalities of the kids and history. But I think he did start to think about economics in a practical way," Ron said.

"Same here," Melanie interjected. "Not with economics, but he worked right along with me. He loved the horses, but I know he felt foolish when he couldn't understand what my parents were saying in Spanish. Maybe now he won't think of it as a waste of time."

"He certainly is getting more professional as he works with the children at the center. He is developing by leaps and bounds," Coach Brown added.

"Well, you people have convinced me. I'm going to ask him to come out to my sheep farm," Mrs. Rathbone remarked confidently.

"I'm surprised that you teachers have a life out of school," Jeffrey remarked seriously as they drove along the county lane. Jane Rathbone almost went off the shoulder of the road as she tried to contain her voluptuous laughter.

"Well, of course we do." She continued to laugh as she pulled onto her property. "Come and meet my husband."

"Hello, Jeffrey. How's your throat?"

"My throat? Oh, yeah, it's better," he mumbled.

"Good. Let's go out to the barn. We had three new babies born today, and there might be as many as eight more coming right along."

"Jane, quick, over here."

"This isn't going to freak you out, is it Jeffrey?" his English teacher asked.

"Um, I don't know. I've never seen anything like this."

She couldn't tell in the grayish lighting of the barn whether he was ashen or not.

Bruce knelt by the ewe uttering words of comfort as Mrs. Rathbone began stroking the trembling body while softly saying, "Shh."

Suddenly, Jeffrey lifted his head to look at his teacher just as she looked at him; that was the same procedure she used to quiet him in class.

"OK, folks, we're on," Bruce announced.

Jeffrey didn't know if he was even breathing. Maybe he had become a pillar of salt. After several minutes of what seemed like no oxygen, he only knew that he was still alive when Jane placed the blanketed little bundle into his arms. Then he didn't know who he was or where he had gone. Who was this person feeling tears trickle off his chin and drop onto the blanket? Certainly, it was not him!

"Come on midwives. You're needed over here," Bruce called.

Five more lambs were born that day, with one occurrence bringing a set of twins. But it was to the mother whose baby died that Jane and Bruce gave the most attention. Mrs. Rathbone sat with her for a long time, stroking and "shhing."

When they left the barn, the sunshine was blinding, but Jeffrey said, "I think I see now."

"What kind of English is that?" Bruce laughed.

"Sorry, I didn't finish. I think I see now what you teachers are bringing into the school," Jeffrey said.

"Like what? Lambs, pumpkins, horses, and apples?" Bruce teased again.

"Yeah right. You know, we did have those things when we were in elementary, but now we don't have the visuals, but we have our teachers."

"Somebody is getting deep over here!"

"Bruce, cut it out. Go on Jeffrey."

"I guess I could say that you guys are bringing in a lot of life experiences, or something like that. I think I used to hate you because I didn't know you."

Mrs. Rathbone wiped the tears from her cheeks.

"What's up with the chief?"

"Have no idea. I got the word too."

"It's just what I need—a meeting at 3:20."

"Thanks for coming in folks. I know it was short notice. Jeffrey's mother stopped in today."

The teachers held their breaths, maybe feeling something like Jeffrey did in the sheep barn. But those teachers knew the feeling of being delighted with a new bundle; they waited for the good news—the accolades.

"Jeffrey's father showed up, and the boy left with him. I'm sorry, but Jeffrey is out of our school system. They're going to Nevada. I'll need your transfer records as soon as you can get them together, except I'm not sure if he will enter into another school."

THE END

"How is your music writing coming along, Marjory?"
"I have three new songs! When is Erin coming back from her vacation?"
"I don't know. The people over there at her church are pretty upset that they don't have an organist anymore."

Chapter Twenty-Two

The Last Chord

A Sequel to "Gravy Money" from Book Two

"Oh, I don't think so, Erin. I wouldn't fit in with your fancy lifestyle. You know how I am. I like the *plain-Jane* type of life."

"But, Mom, I really would like you to come here. I haven't seen you in almost two years."

"I know. I've been missing you so much, but I know you have to get on with your life. I don't think you were very happy here, so if you have found your niche, I'm glad. I just don't think it would be for me."

"It's not what you think, Mom. That's what I am so excited about; I really want you to come and see how I live now."

"You mean you're not in a high-class condo overlooking the ocean and going out to eat in fancy restaurants?"

"Not really, Mom."

"And your closets are not bulging with high-style fashions?"

"No."

After a long pause, Erin pleaded, "Please, Mom, please come to see me."

"I'll need to go into my savings, but I'll do it," she answered slowly.

"Thank you. I don't think you'll be sorry."

Sigrid leaned back into her overstuffed chair—the chair that had become her favorite after her husband passed away and left her to raise Erin, their only child. She thought about her pretty Erin: the girl who wanted everything, and the girl to whom she gave everything.

Why did she do that? Why couldn't she say no to her? She knew better; she knew she had to stop, but she couldn't. Erin would only have to pout or cry or tell her she was a… a… loser, and she would crumble.

Now it was still happening. Erin wanted her mother to visit after the girl had abandoned her home, her job, and her organ playing at the church? Everyone and everything. Sigrid had a bad feeling about giving in to her self-centered daughter. She did not want to be on an exotic island where wealth dripped from the palm trees and her Erin stood underneath catching every drop. The thought gave her a cold shiver. She drew the afghan around her body and scrunched deeper into her husband's chair.

She thought about the little church that still had no organist. The pastor had stopped calling and asking if Erin had returned or was going to return. It embarrassed Sigrid to tell him she didn't know what her daughter had in mind for the future. It was almost unbearable to hear him drone on and on about the lack of attendance and how it would never pick up without some music.

She felt like retorting, "Don't the people know that God is enough?" But she didn't. She kept quiet just like she had learned to do with Erin.

The director of the music department at the college stopped calling too when Sigrid had no definitive answer about Erin's return.

And now she wants me to go there! She knows I have limited funds; there is no extra money for luxurious trips with expensive restaurants and fancy hotels!

Sigrid wriggled into a different position, hoping to change her thoughts. It didn't help.

Maybe she's rich now; maybe she has found a great job. Maybe she met someone and is married, and he's rich. "Oh," Sigrid groaned aloud. "What is Erin going to say when I step off the plane wearing one of my familiar dresses, with the same shoes and the same pocketbook?" Will she say to her new husband, "And here is our new maid, whom I flew in from the States."

I know she wants to show me how "real people" live; all her life, she has tried to convince me that living poorly was ridiculous, and someday she *"was going to escape that travesty."* Sigrid could hear her daughter shouting as she stomped up the stairs to her bedroom.

One praise-worthy asset of Erin's was saving money. Sigrid was glad her husband had taught her that. Unfortunately, he'd taught her too well. He never taught her to spend it on others. She wouldn't help a neighbor or a charity if her life depended on it. Every penny was hers.

Sigrid lifted her old suitcase out of the closet. She remembered first using it when she took the train to her girlfriend's wedding. What a wonderful trip that was. She felt so grown up with her own money. Mm, maybe she too was guilty of developing Erin's adulation of money. She thought of her daughter's beautiful matching set of luggage, knowing what Erin's reaction to her pauper's pack would be.

She tried to explain the trip to her friends, but each one knew immediately the anguish Sigrid was feeling. For years, they had watched Erin's drama permeate her mother's heart.

Perhaps she should have asked Erin to forward her the trip money, but she couldn't; she just couldn't. Why hadn't Erin thought of that on her own? Why should her own mother have to pay when she and her husband were probably languishing on their beach estate?

Sigrid continued to grumble throughout the meager packing process and the clicking of the shine-less suitcase locks.

The cab driver offered a grunt of disapproval as he assessed the address on the notepaper, comparing it to the woman's attire; he knew there would be no big tip. Anyone going to the Refuge would not have money to waste on gratuities.

As they sailed past some of the most beautiful homes Sigrid had ever seen, she tried to envision which one was Erin's.

That must be it! she thought as she slid to the edge of the seat. Oh, it was beautiful with tropical plants blooming from the road's edge to the huge front door. She could see the blue ocean in the background and knew that the inhabitants must sit on the veranda and watch the waves every day. Would she be there watching the waves also?

The driver drove past.

Finally, he slowed the cab to allow Sigrid to see another majestic villa. The tall palm trees each bent away from the ocean breeze, while the vivid flowers encircled a fountain spraying the swans' backs with delicate droplets of water—a reprieve from the sun. Sigrid's eyes darted to a motion: a little child in a white dress was frolicking on the grass with her mother.

Was that Erin? Does she have a child? Is that why she wants me here?

Sigrid's arms were outstretched on top of the driver's seat while she asked, "Here? Here?"

The driver laughed uproariously as they departed farther and farther away from the mother and child.

Sigrid returned to leaning against the back seat as she watched the large island homes dissolve into small modest homes and then into hovels. She wondered if the cabbie was taking her the long way in order to maximize the bill. Suddenly, he stopped and called out, "You're here."

"You must be mistaken, sir; my Erin would never live here."

"This you, yes, you." And before she could offer another rebuttal, she and her old suitcase were standing alone on the sidewalk as the cab left, leaving the road's dust on Sigrid.

Now, what am I going to do? The novice traveler worried as she looked up and down the road.

"Mama!" Erin called out as she flung wide the door and ran to her mother.

"Erin?"

"Yes." She laughed. "It's me."

"What are you doing here?" Sigrid asked as she assessed the low stucco house with the pink trim and tile roof.

"I live here, Mother."

Just then, Sister Philomena raised a window and hollered, "Erin, quick. We need you!"

Erin grabbed her mother's luggage with one hand, and her arm with the other. "Follow me, Ma. We're going into the palace. Run!"

"Erin, stop. I can't see!" Sigrid protested.

"Don't worry, Ma. Your eyes will adjust. I've got you. Just follow me."

Could Sigrid be dreaming? Those were the same words she'd told her little daughter when they left the black movie theater and the same words she'd said when they had to weave themselves through the darkened parking lot. They came out of the woods with those reassuring words. Now it was the big girl using them on her mother.

"In here, Erin. She's hemorrhaging badly," Sister Philomena whispered as she grabbed another stack of towels. "Here, apply pressure like this while I run for Sister Carmelita. Julian is on his way to town to find the doctor. Ma'am, would you soak those towels in warm water?"

"Of course," Sigrid answered. Erin knew she would; her mother always pitched in to help others.

Sigrid watched over her left shoulder as Erin not only performed her medical duty but also spoke words of comfort to the woman. She listened to words that she hadn't heard uttered since Erin was a little girl caring for her dolls.

She was such a good little mommy. Sigrid didn't know what had happened to her kind nature as she grew older.

The two ladies in white whisked into the room with Julian directing the doctor in also.

"Thanks, people, we'll take it from here," Sister Philomena said sincerely.

"Sorry you had to be welcomed like that, Mom. Oh, and this is Julian. Julian, meet my mother."

"You have a very special daughter here," Julian remarked as he put his arm across Erin's shoulders.

"Erin? Is there some place we can go? I'd like you to tell me what is going on?"

"Of course, Mom. I'll show you to our room."

"This looks like my bedroom at home!"

"That's what I said when I first saw it, and Mom, I'm ashamed that I hated it."

"Why would you hate it?" Sigrid asked.

"Because it was plain and ordinary and simple, like—"

"Like me?"

"Erin, we need help out here!"

Julian and Erin held the wrenching man as he relieved his stomach of his cheap wine and tequila—not a good combination in the early afternoon.

"Mom, grab that other bucket. Good job. You got it there just in time!"

Sigrid watched her daughter wipe down the man's face, hands, and feet as Julian passed her warm washcloth after warm washcloth. The two of them walked the groaning man to a room and sat with him while they waited for the next onslaught. Surely, there would be another.

Sigrid sat on the edge of her bed wondering where her narcissistic daughter had gone.

Two years ago, back in the States, Erin was intolerable and haughty and...

"Mother, come quickly!" The blasting of the horn from the roadway was a definite signal that "drop-offs" were going to be in need of attention.

The truck screeched away and soon the dust settled enough so that the group of vagabonds, transients, or convicts could be seen.

"Oh," Sister Gabrielle sighed as she saw the condition of the family. Sigrid walked straight to the mother and the baby. Without a word, her outstretch hands and kind eyes reassured the battered mother that her baby would be safe. As soon as the baby was repositioned, the mother collapsed to the sidewalk. Julian and Erin ran to the sobbing woman, as the siblings dove to their mother, as all species of kindred spirits would do. The white-frocked sisters then fluttered to the children. Would the seagull going across the blue sky wonder what the to-do was all about down on the enigmatic world?

The clothes bins were opened, the showers were running, Sister Gabby was fine-tuning the activities in the kitchen, and prayers, songs, and tender love were slathered on the broken family. Tears were wiped, wounds were bandaged, shoes were fitted, and clean hair was brushed. The five year old even got her long hair braided by Sister Angelique.

Every child had their own personal friend at the table until their mother, at last, entered the dining room. Unfortunately, the seagull couldn't see the encircling ring around the mother, but Erin and the others could. Their mother, all clean and beautiful, in a pretty dress and sandals, and a smile on her face, brought tears to the eyes of the onlookers. Erin bawled into her own mother's outstretched arms.

The last towel had been washed; and the last dish placed on the shelf. The children were sound asleep, the floors were mopped, the last thank you prayer to God had been uttered when Erin and her mother retired to their room.

Sister Angelique's whisper, "Your mother is a good person," resounded in Erin's head.

"Whew," Sigrid sighed. "I never dreamed I would be having such an eventful day!"

"What do you think of my new life, Mom?" Erin asked humbly.

Sigrid looked at her daughter for a long time before she spoke. "Erin," she began and then halted for quite some time. "Erin, I am... shocked! For years, I agonized over the path your life had taken. I prayed and agonized, prayed and agonized. I blamed myself. I thought I had ruined you. I couldn't change you and knew I never could. I'd pray, 'God, you've got to step in; you've got to step in to change her. Please, do something.' And it looks like He did!"

Then it was Erin who couldn't speak. Finally, she uttered, "You thought all of that was your fault? What on earth made you think that?"

"A mother always blames herself for everything, I guess."

The two generations clasped hands, bridging a ravine that hadn't been passable for years. Then...

"Erin, come quickly. We need you!"

The days and nights passed quickly. No one knew what was in the future. It wasn't until Sigrid asked Erin if she was ready to go home did the future come into focus.

"Home? Why would I go there?" Erin asked.

The question seemed to startle Sigrid. Was this the "old" Erin surfacing? Did she not have one fond memory of her home, her town, her friends, or her job?

Erin realized that her quick answer had somehow hurt her mother. "Mom, let me explain further," Erin said in appeasement. "I don't like that person who was once me. I like the new me, and I don't ever want to fall back into the haughty idiot that I was."

The mother/daughter team cleaned the dining room after they had fed seventeen people that morning. Sigrid mulled over her thoughts of "those people" having no home, and those people having no family, and those people having no job, but Erin did, back in the States.

419

Couldn't she bring her new nice ways back to the States and fit them into her daily life? She would ask her again after the sisters and Erin returned from begging for money out on the streets.

"Julian, wait until you hear this," Erin announced as she dashed into the Refuge. "Some lady has donated a piano to us. We can sell it and probably get a couple hundred dollars!"

"Good deal." He beamed as he looked fondly at Erin. "Can she keep it there for a while?"

"I'm afraid she wants it out; she has a new one coming this week."

What a twitter arose from the nuns as they oohed and aahed over the piano. One or two pressed down a few keys, but it only led to more giggling and commenting.

"Years ago I could play a few songs, but not anymore." Sister Stephanie sighed.

"I was a terrible failure." Sister Veronica laughed. "The teacher told my father that either I would have to go or she would!"

"Erin, for goodness' sake, sit down and play something," her mother interjected. "She plays beautifully!"

Erin's face drained of color, her hands began to shake, and she grabbed for Julian's arm to keep herself upright. No piano music filled the air. Erin was helped to bed and fell asleep with a cold washcloth on her forehead.

Sigrid watched her daughter sleep, just as she had when Erin was a baby. She wondered why her talented virtuoso would become upset with her request.

It must be true. Erin did not want to go back into the past.

Sigrid went to the door when she heard a slight rapping.

"Is Erin still asleep?" Sister Lucia whispered.

"Yes, she's in a deep sleep. What's wrong? Why are you shaking?"

"It's Julian. He's been hit by a car; he's in the hospital."

"I'll go. Let me go," Sigrid pleaded.

"Thank you, Sigrid. I'll have a cab pick you up."

Sigrid stayed by Julian's bedside the entire night. She looked at his face, wondering what kind of life he had experienced. Where was his home? Why was he making it his mission to help others? Why were he and her daughter so much alike—sacrificing their entire lives for the welfare of others? Had he once been like Erin: selfish, self-centered, and materialistic? She did not know.

Just before dawn, Julian roused and reached for Sigrid's hand.

"Tell Erin I love her," he whispered and smiled.

"Oh, I will, Julian. And Julian…"

The good sisters encircled the gravesite as Julian was buried that Friday. Erin didn't tend to the needy anymore. Erin stayed in her room. Her mother and the sisters tended to her. Erin forgot how to be a person; instead, she was an object with no past, no present, and no future. She knew she breathed because she counted those breaths incessantly. She knew nothing more.

Outside of her bedroom walls, people came and went day and night: some near starvation, some covered with sores, some filthy with nothing of their own, some with children in tow, some lice infested, some addicted to drugs, and some brokenhearted like Erin, but always someone.

Sigrid worked with the sisters, knowing there was a void with both Julian and Erin gone from the workforce. They all tended to Erin, hoping that she would come out of the *place* where she was.

Little by little, Erin began to respond to the kind coaxing. Sometimes she would go to the dining room to sit at one of the long tables with the other non-communicative people. She would watch them and forget to eat. It was most often her mother who would lift the fork with her daughter's hand wrapped around it until the routine became methodical again. Somehow, unbeknownst to the others, Erin would place herself into the person she was most transfixed on. She became the person and vicariously knew what that individual was experiencing.

It was during one of those fixations that her mind jolted when she heard a C, E, and G on the piano. A little girl with long brunette ringlets used her pointer finger to skip, skip, and skip on three of the white keys. The girl's mother called her back to the table and slapped her hand for touching someone else's property. The little girl cried.

Erin left the table and played the same C, E, and G. She looked back at the girl. The girl wiped her tears and made eye contact with the woman at the piano. Erin played another short succession of notes and motioned for the girl to come forward. The child looked at her mother, who looked at Erin. The pleading eyes of her youngster, whom the mother knew had nothing materialistic in this world, led to giving the girl permission to return to the piano.

"You," Erin said to the girl and motioned to the keyboard. The little finger played some different notes. Erin imitated those notes. The child giggled. The succession continued, with Erin imitating exactly what the child played.

Erin lifted the little girl onto her lap. This led to her using both hands. The competition was on! Would Erin be able to keep up with her? The music brought several nuns swirling into the dining room. Sigrid lowered the water pitchers into the sink and covered her mouth with a dishtowel; the guests looked up from their rice and beans.

Giggling ensued from the musicians. The levity was as uncommon in the shelter as would be a seven-layer chocolate cherry birthday cake with frothy white seven-minute frosting.

The little one suddenly leaned back on Erin, yawned, and plopped her thumb in her mouth with her other hand twirling one of her ringlets. That's when the real music poured out of Erin's soul like lava from a volcano. Sigrid wept into the dishtowel upon finally hearing the music that she knew was inherent to her girl. No one moved. None of the guests brought one more spoonful of food to their lips.

When the last chord sounded, the reverberations resounded until the final one brought the child's mother forward to retrieve her sleepy child; it made the sister's unlock their arms to return to their assignments and Sigrid to envelope her newly *awakened* daughter.

Erin came out of her dark place because of the piano. The sisters vowed that they would never sell it after they saw its healing effects not only on Erin but also on the people who came to the shelter. Because of Erin's talent, the souls of the marginalized were fed and nourished. When ready, they could leave feeling more like *whole people*. Some didn't know why, other than that they had food in their bellies, the filth of the streets had been washed away, and they had been protected from the wiles of the world so they could rest peacefully for a while. However, the sisters knew that when Erin played her music, the stirrings of the soul were as real as any of the tangible commodities.

Sigrid traveled back to her home only to put the house on the market and to gather a few belongings. Then she returned to Erin's *palace by the sea.*

THE END

About the Author

Teresa's first published book, Stories from Lone Moon Creek was released in 2015, followed by Stories from Lone Moon Creek: Ripples and Stories from Lone Moon Creek: Reflections.

Receiving much acclaim in the market and being compared to the works of Laura Ingalls Wilder in her Little

House Series, her books have firmly established Teresa as a recognized professional novelist in the literary world.

Stories from Lone Moon Creek: Splashes, is the next installment in her Lone Moon Creek Series, providing more of the heartfelt stories demanded by her readers.

Teresa was born in Cooperstown, NY and lives in Worcester, NY. She attended the K-12 Central School in Worcester and graduated with eighteen others in her Senior Class.

Continuing her education, she received her degree in Elementary Education from SUNY at Oneonta, New York.

Teresa taught Kindergarten and First Grade at Worcester CS for twenty-five years developing the love of reading and writing.

She has always had a fondness for the arts and has delved into painting, piano education, creativity, garden sculpting, quilting, and writing.

She says rural life has a kindness and goodness with a touch of mystique which she tries to describe in her stories.

Teresa has three children and nine grandchildren.

CPSIA information can be obtained
at www.ICGtesting.com
Printed in the USA
BVOW08s0216020917
493667BV00001B/2/P